The Biloxi Connection

A NOVEL

DAVID J MATHER

PCW
A Peace Corps Writers Book

Also By David J Mather

One For The Road

A young Peace Corps volunteer finds adventure and heartbreaking romance in the lawless foothills of the Andes. Set in beautiful Chile in the late 1960s, this coming-of-age novel paints a vivid picture of a forgotten way of life.

When The Whistling Stopped

In this sequel to One For The Road, murder and intrigue follow a young couple's quest to expose an amoral mill owner responsible for the death of thousands of black-necked swans. The twists and turns of this eco-thriller make it hard to put down.

The Crescent Beach Series

Crescent Beach (book 1) State Trooper Rusty McMillan goes undercover to bust marijuana smugglers on Florida's Gulf Coast. He gets the evidence he needs, but before any arrests can be made, the area is slammed by a lethal storm and Rusty is forced to join the community in a life-and-death struggle.

Raw Dawgin' (book 2) In this sequel to *Crescent Beach*, Rusty nostalgically returns to the fishing village, only to find it in turmoil. Violence erupts between the commercial and sports fishermen, a Colombian cartel seeks revenge for one of their own, a convicted felon comes after his ex-wife. Add Rusty's attraction to his best friend's wife, and his peaceful little town is anything but.

The Biloxi Connection (book 3)

Gator Bait (book 4) Tammy's life turns into a nightmare out west where she is held prisoner and horribly abused by her ex-husband. Norm leaves Crescent Beach to bring her back; but the ex follows them, thirsting for brutal revenge. Meanwhile in Crescent Beach, a game warden is murdered by a gator poacher and Rusty goes undercover to find the culprit. When the poacher learns Rusty's true identity, the hunter becomes the hunted.

The Biloxi Connection

A Peace Corps Writers Book – An imprint of Peace Corps Worldwide

Printed in the United States of America
by Peace Corps Writers of Oakland, California.

For more information, contact
peacecorpsworldwide@gmail.com.
Peace Corps Writers and the Peace Corps Writers colphon are trademarks of PeaceCorpsWorldwide.org.

ISBN-13: 978-1-950444-00-7
Library of Congress Control Number: 2019939622

First Peace Corps Writers Edition, June 2019

B & J

OVER 60 YEARS OF FRIENDSHIP,
AND COUNTING

Author's Note & Acknowledgements

THE BILOXI CONNECTION is the third novel of the Crescent Beach Series. All of the novels take place in and around the fictitious town of Crescent Beach in Florida's Big Bend Area. It has nothing to do with the town of Crescent Beach on Florida's east coast – I picked the name because it is ubiquitous in Florida. All narrative, names, characters, and events are products of my imagination. Any resemblance to actual persons, living or dead, is purely coincidental.

* * *

Once again the internet proved invaluable for my research, whether providing mere tidbits or copious amounts of information. The article from americanaddictioncenters.org, "Understanding Oxycontin Withdrawal," was very helpful.

I'd like to thank several people. The first is Big Bend resident George Blake who provided both technical information and amusing stories from his years of clamming. I'd also like to thank Rich May, an ex Peace Corps buddy and a good friend of many years, for reading my manuscript and providing his always valuable insight and opinions. A huge thank you goes to "Eagle-Eye" Jill Andrews who discovered well over two hundred errors in my manuscript. Another big thank you goes to Mary Benoit, artist extraordinaire, who, aptly assisted by my wife Lindy, provided the artwork for the cover. Finally, as with all my other novels, I'd like to thank Lindy without whose help and infinite patience this book would not have seen the light of day.

The Biloxi Connection

Prologue

The four-man Coast Guard crew, dressed in bright orange flight suits, had run the obligatory preflight check of the Sikorsky Jayhawk helicopter over two hours ago. They had the nightshift and wouldn't be off until six the next morning. They were killing time, drinking coffee, thumbing through magazines, playing solitaire when suddenly the warning horn went off. They bolted up out of their chairs, grabbed flight helmets, and hightailed it out of the ready room. In charge was the pilot, a lieutenant commander, who made a beeline to the info center for instructions. The others fast-walked to the helicopter sitting on a helipad next to a canal leading out to the Gulf of Mexico. Besides the lieutenant commander, the crew was made up of the lieutenant jg co-pilot, the flight mechanic, and the aviation survival technician. They took their stations and waited for the lieutenant commander.

The Jayhawk had the typical Coast Guard paint job of mostly white with orange nose, orange diagonal stripe midway, and orange tail. It was a twin engine, medium range search-and-rescue helicopter sixty-five feet long with a four hundred mile range. The distinctive bulbous nose contained sophisticated search and weather radar. Included in the instrument panel's myriad of gauges, screens, switches, and dials were the newest and most sophisticated Navstar systems and a Collins RCVR-3A radio.

The lieutenant commander quickly climbed into the craft and immediately began flipping switches. The instrument panel lit up, creating a greenish hue in the cockpit.

"What's up, Commander?" the flight mechanic asked.

"Small craft missing. Fishing guide and his client headed north out of Crescent Beach this morning and never returned. Let's do the run up."

The crew professionally and quickly ran through all the checks. The rotor slowly began to turn. The co-pilot received clearance for lift-off. The flight mechanic shut the side door and the chopper filled with noise as it slowly climbed up to two hundred feet before turning due west for the coast. Clearwater lay below them, and the lights from Tampa and St. Petersburg twinkled off to the south. Although the ballgame was over, they could still see the lights from the Devil Rays' Tropicana Field as well as the lights strung along the Sunshine Skyway crossing Tampa Bay. The lieutenant commander turned north and began following the coast, climbing to five hundred feet and cruising at a hundred and sixty miles per hour. It wouldn't take long to get to the search area a hundred and fifty miles north of Clearwater.

The lieutenant commander spoke into the little microphone attached to his helmet. "You in touch with base?" he asked his co-pilot.

"Roger that. They have our heading. Nothing new as far as the missing boat."

"What are the tides and water temperature?" the lieutenant commander asked the aviation survival technician.

"Low was at eight-thirty, which means high tide will be in about a half hour. Gulf's just over eighty degrees."

The co-pilot looked over to the lieutenant commander. "Why were we contacted so late? You'd think if they hadn't returned by sundown, we would have been contacted then."

"Tides. It's real shallow around Crescent Beach, and no one goes in or out during low tide except airboats. Wife of the fishing guide—guide's name is Jimmy Talbot—figured he was

running late and had to wait for more water to get back in. But when she eventually tried to radio him and got no answer, she began to worry and finally contacted us. And now the heat's on big time because it seems that his client is an important federal judge out of Atlanta."

The aviation survival technician was excited. He was the junior member of the crew and this was his first time out. In Coast Guard jargon, he was referred to as a rescue swimmer because his job was to be lowered down to the water in emergency situations. He was fresh out of school, having gone through the twenty-four week Coast Guard course in Elizabeth City, North Carolina, where he learned how to maintain and operate all survival equipment, and then the three-week Coast Guard EMT course in California. He didn't wish ill of whoever was out on the water, but he hoped that he'd get wet and have a chance to test his mettle.

When they passed the lights of Crescent Beach and approached the search area, the lieutenant commander ordered everyone to put on night vision goggles. With the goggles they could see the Gulf clearly. Whatever had happened to the two men certainly wasn't because of weather. The winds had been calm all day. The moon was half-full. It shone beautifully on the waves that were less than a foot. The lieutenant commander told his co-pilot to lay out a grid pattern. The flight mechanic opened the side door to better look out. The lieutenant commander turned west and started the search.

It didn't take more than twenty minutes before the flight mechanic spotted something. "There," he said, pointing. "About three o'clock."

The lieutenant commander swerved to his right and dropped to a couple hundred feet. "That's got to be it, alright." He dropped another fifty feet. "Doesn't look good."

They could see the light-colored hull of a boat upside down. They did not see any movement or evidence of its passengers. The lieutenant commander turned to the swimmer, saying through the headset, "Son, looks like you're going in."

"Yes, sir." The swimmer shed his night goggles and flight suit, and began to put on a shorty wet suit. The flight mechanic stood and began operating the controls of the winch with a two hundred foot cable and safety harness. The swimmer's belly was suddenly tight with anticipation: he hoped like hell that he wouldn't have an emergency bowel movement. He reached for his neoprene booties, mask, snorkel, flippers, and fluorescent inflatable life vest. Once he was all set, he nodded to the commander who further lowered the chopper until it hovered at a hundred feet. The backwash of the chopper's blades created a spider web pattern on the water. The swimmer, with a powerful waterproof flashlight in hand, climbed into the harness. He gave the flight mechanic the thumbs up. The flight mechanic swung him out a little from the craft, and began to slowly lower him to the water.

The swimmer released himself from the harness. Once he was free and clear he gave the okay sign and the chopper immediately pulled up higher. The water around the boat calmed almost instantly. The swimmer switched on the powerful flashlight. He shined it in all directions as he swam around the boat. Nothing. He took a breath and went under. Seconds later he gasped, taking in a mouthful of water. Choking, he surfaced immediately. Spitting out his snorkel and spitting up water, he forced himself to calm down. He took several deep breaths before reinserting the snorkel. He went back down for another look.

Wrapped in a tangle of nylon line was a dead man. The swimmer shined the light over the body. Cause of death was ob-

vious: multiple gunshot wounds in the upper torso. The swimmer surfaced, took another couple of breaths, and went back under. He played the light over the face of the corpse. The eyes were open and looked surprised. Short, balding, a little overweight, dressed in high-end sports fishing clothes and boat shoes, the swimmer guessed that this was the judge. But where was the fishing guide? He swept the light around. A couple of life preservers were trapped underneath the hull, and several upside down fishing rods were still wedged in their holders. The cause of the boat's sinking was obvious: a jagged line of bullet holes on one side at the waterline. The holes were not in a straight line; rather, they were concentrated in a couple areas with so much material blown out that there were good-sized holes. There must have been over a hundred rounds fired.

He surfaced again. One more look to see if he had missed anything. He went back under. Other than the corpse and bullet holes, it was just a normal looking sports fishing boat. He made sure he didn't move a thing. Whatever happened here obviously had been no accident and would have to be investigated. He came up for air, swam a little ways from the boat, and signaled the chopper. The co-pilot and flight manager were watching with binoculars and immediately informed the lieutenant commander who brought the chopper back down. The swimmer harnessed himself, and the flight manager winched him up. Once safely back into the chopper, the swimmer reached for his helmet; all eyes were on him. He quickly spoke into the microphone.

"There's a man's body trapped under the hull, Sir. Dead with a whole lot of bullet holes in him. Judging by his clothes and stature, my guess is that it's the judge. But only one body. And looks like the boat sunk because there are a zillion bullet holes in one side at the waterline."

The lieutenant commander wasted no time. He asked the co-pilot if he had the exact co-ordinates of the boat's location.

"Yes, sir."

"Then contact Yankeetown. Give them the co-ordinates and have them trailer up a boat that..." He turned to the swimmer who had begun putting on his flight suit. "How long is that boat, do you figure?"

"Twenty, twenty-two feet."

The lieutenant commander turned back to the co-pilot.

"Tell them to trailer up a boat and a couple bladder bags that can float a twenty-two foot sports fishing boat. Tell them an apparent homicide has been committed and that they should contact Captain Smathers of the State Police in Cross City and the sheriff in Perry. I imagine they'll want to be in that boat. But tell them that one man's still missing, and we think it's Talbot. They might also want to trailer up a smaller boat that doesn't draw much water to look for him near shore. And tell them to check tides and currents over the last twelve hours. Might help find the missing man. With the temperature of the water as high as it is, he'll be floating before too long." The lieutenant commander shook his head slightly. "Not like when I was stationed in Lake Superior. In that frigid water when some-one goes down, he stays down."

"Yes sir," the co-pilot said, and got on the radio.

"They probably won't get here until daylight, but that's not that far off," the lieutenant commander said. "There's nothing more we can do now, so we'll go back. Good job, son," he said, to the swimmer before turning south.

Two and a half hours later, two Coast Guard boats were launched at a small campground about a half hour ride from Talbot's boat. Underwater photographs were taken before the body was removed and Talbot's boat was floated and towed back to the campground. Captain Smathers and the Perry sheriff transferred to the smaller Coast Guard boat to search for Talbot close in shore. Word had gotten around Crescent Beach, and a regular flotilla showed up to assist in the search. But, at sunset, they gave up and returned. Mid-morning the next day, Talbot was found face down and riddled with bullets on an oyster bar. Captain Smathers and the Perry sheriff were the first to disembark from the Coast Guard's shallow draft boat. They carefully crunched their way over the oysters to the corpse. The sheriff kneeled down and gently turned Talbot's head.

"Talbot, alright. God, what a mess. Looks like crabs or fish or something already done nibbled some."

"You knew him?"

"Yeah. Heluva good guy. Knew these waters like nobody else." The captain nodded. He had never met Jimmy Talbot, but knew plenty about him from Talbot's marijuana smuggling days. Jimmy Talbot had outfoxed the state troopers more than once. "He was a real straight shooter, church goin', family man. Got a knockout for a wife." The sheriff stood up. "Ain't lookin' forward to telling Crystal, tell ya that."

"Crystal?"

"His wife."

"Guess she's his widow now."

Chapter One

Rusty looked over at Crystal in the gray, pre-dawn light. She was breathing deeply, sound asleep. Her long brown hair spilled onto the light wool blanket she had pulled up to her chin. God, she's lovely, he thought. He loved everything about her. He eyed her contour from head to toe, and resisted the temptation to draw her to him. He looked at the bedside clock—almost six. The sun wouldn't be up until seven. He put his hands behind his head. How long had they been an item now? he wondered. It was at Tiny's and T's wedding a little over two years ago when it began. He smiled, thinking how their friends had picked up on the vibes right away. They had started saying stuff like, 'we're having a get-together on Friday, Rusty. Why don't you and Crystal come on over;' or, 'we're going scalloping tomorrow. Do you and Crystal want to come along?' The town had them a couple way before they ever slept together. But that may have helped to consummate the deal, he thought—maybe with everybody thinking they had done the deed, he and Crystal had thought 'what the heck.' But it was still months after the wedding when they finally consummated their relationship.

That first time, at his place after dinner. Somehow they both had known it was going to happen that night. They were nervous with each other, not their usual selves. Hardly any conversation at the table. Puppy dog looks on his part. He kept fumbling with the silverware. He had said that he'd make dinner. The day before he had caught some trout. He put them and some asparagus on the grill. Had a salad all made. Bought a good bottle of white wine—most expensive in the Winn-Dixie. Kendall Jackson, if he remembered correctly. He had even lit candles on the table. After dinner, he wouldn't let her do the dishes; told her to relax and enjoy her wine. He topped off her glass before turning to the dishes. He could feel her eyes on him. It made him self-conscious and he dropped a plate. That damn plate! No, it was a wonderful plate, he thought. That plate started the ball rolling. She jumped up to help clean it up and he had put his arms on hers to stop her. 'I made the mess,' he had said, 'I'll clean it up.' But he didn't take his arms off hers. They looked at each other. Those liquid blue-grey eyes of hers ate him up. Suddenly they were all over each other and couldn't get to the bedroom quick enough. He didn't clean up that plate until the next morning.

But the guilt! He had woken up thinking that Jimmy's ashes had been scattered only five months earlier, and there he was, in bed with her. It was like he had violated Jimmy's friendship. Even though Jimmy was dead, it seemed way too soon. It just wasn't right! Crystal said that Jimmy would be happy that they were together. 'Didn't Jimmy ask you to take care of me if something happened to him?' she had asked. 'Yeah,' he had answered, 'but I don't think he meant this!' He said maybe they shouldn't see each other until he could get his head on straight. She tried to talk him out of it, but reluctantly agreed when he wouldn't budge. Turned out that he couldn't stay away; didn't make it a full week. He ached for her. That was over two years ago and they'd been an item ever since. But he still felt the guilt. Jimmy's killer was on the loose. The FBI thought they knew who did it—some hit-man for a Colombian cartel—but the guy had come up with an ironclad alibi. Before he had been shot, both Jimmy and Rusty had known that Jimmy's life was in danger. Rusty shook his head, thinking, me, a retired state trooper and MP with thirty years of law enforcement experience, and I didn't do a damn thing to prevent it. I wonder if it was because of Crystal? Maybe, deep down, I didn't do anything because if Jimmy were gone I could make a play for her. But that's bullshit! Still, I let Jimmy down.

Rusty climbed out of bed and walked into Crystal's living room. The first thing he saw was Jimmy's trophy for the CB 250, the annual Crescent Beach two-hundred-and-fifty lap stock car race. There had been no race these last two years, and he'd bet that there'd never be another. It had been Jimmy's enthusiasm and energy that had sparked the event and kept it going year after year. Rusty picked up the trophy. At least Jimmy had finally won, and it was somehow fitting that it was the very last one. He put the trophy down and turned on a lamp. He walked around the room. Crystal hadn't changed a thing; nor should she, he thought. Pictures everywhere showed Jimmy with clients proudly displaying strings of all kinds of fish: speckled sea trout, grouper, redfish, cobia, kingfish, tripletail.

The sky was beginning to show red. Rusty walked out to the deck and looked out over the calm Gulf. A beautiful November morning. A lone blue heron flew by, on its way to some secluded estuary. Judging from the oyster bars, it was about mid-tide and rising. He looked at Jimmy's boat, his now, tied to the dock across the street. He had bought it from Crystal, but kept it here because it had deeper channel access to the Gulf than his place. He shook his head. Here I am, in Jimmy's house, sleeping with his wife, and fishing in his old boat! Rusty looked to the east. The sun was just peeking over the tree line several miles away where the salt marsh met land. The trees gave the vivid orange sun perspective as it slowly climbed the sky.

The screen door shut softly behind him. He didn't turn around. He soon felt Crystal's arms around his waist and her cheek against his back. He put a hand over hers. Neither said anything for a long moment. Finally, Crystal said, "Feeling guilty again?" He nodded. Silence. They stood there for a long while before Crystal continued. "Don't," she said. "How many times do I have to tell you, Rusty? There's nothing you could have done. You know how cautious Jimmy was before it happened—paranoid, really—and yet he was taken totally by surprise. To get the jump on Jimmy like that, the guy must have been a real pro. There's nothing you could have done and you got to stop beating yourself up about it." She paused before continuing. "And as for us, Jimmy knew all along how you felt about me, although he also knew he never had to worry about it. He also sensed my attraction to you. And I believe that's exactly why he asked you to take care of me. He knew that there was a very good chance that we would get together if something happened to him. Well, something did happen to him, and we did get together. What we are doing is not something bad and I believe with all my heart that Jimmy would approve."

"It eats me up that the killer is out there somewhere scot-free. And if it's the hit-man like the FBI thinks, then he's the lowest of the low—no passion or anger or anything, just cold-blooded murder for money."

"Let it go; there's nothing you can do about it."

Rusty turned to her.

"I can't, Crystal; I've tried. I can't shake it...I've decided to set up another meeting with Captain Smathers, see if there's anything new. There must be something I can do."

"Something the State Police and the F.B.I. can't? You'll only be shoveling smoke."

"Probably, but I got to try."

They heard an outboard motor and looked as one towards the point where a large, custom-made pontoon boat was edging around the corner. In town it was known as the ‘aircraft carrier.’ Rusty laughed. “No mistaking that boat. Sammy’s getting an early start today.”

Other than for the controls, the boat was like a barge, twenty-six feet of all flat deck, no railing, and supported by two gigantic, rectangular pontoons. It was powered by a big Mercury in the stern. The barge had very little freeboard because it was freighted with rolled up bags of clams. Besides the clams, there was a four horsepower Honda oil-less compressor, two three-hundred foot hoses, several plastic milk crates containing clothes, towels, a mask and wetsuit, and other diving gear. There was barely enough room for a cooler and the two plastic chairs where the men sat. Sammy’s chair was behind the controls. He looked like a bear at the helm: his black hair was long and in disarray, his gut prodigious, his arms hairy, and his beard bushy although his upper cheeks and below his nose were clean-shaven these days. He was wearing a greasy, white tee-shirt, jeans, and flip-flops. A few feet away sat a smaller, wiry man, bronzed and weathered from the sun. Like Sammy, he was dressed in jeans, and flip-flops, but had a light jacket over his tee-shirt. He had a red bandana tied tightly around his head. He looked like a pirate.

“Looks like Sammy’s got some help today,” Crystal said.

“I guess you can call Charley, help. And you can bet your britches that the cooler between them is full of beer,” Rusty added, smiling. “Speaking of britches, I better get dressed.”

“You’re not coming back to bed?” Rusty shook his head. Crystal cocked a hip. “Might be worth your while, Handsome…”

“That a fact?”

“Yep.” Crystal held out her hand.

“In that case,” Rusty said, and took her hand.

Charley saw them enter the house. He turned to Sammy. "Looks like Rusty's visitin' agin. Was on Crystal's deck in only his skivvies."

"Now ain't you a reg'lar peepin' Tom," Sammy said.

"Rusty's a lucky guy."

"Crystal, too. She's had herself two good men in her life. Me, I can't even find one good woman!"

"Amen, brother," Charley said.

"You heard anything from Minnie?"

"Not a peep, but don't expect none. Word is that she and that loo-tenant at the prison are hot and heavy. Been that way fer some time."

"Thought she always said she and the loo-tenant was cross-threaded?"

"Guess they got themselfs retooled."

"Women! Ain't none of them worth a hoot. Can't trust them none a'tall."

"That so? How 'bout Rebecca? She can't do nuthin' wrong in yur eyes."

Sammy frowned. He was worried about his niece. "She's done changed, Charley. Can' figger her out none a'tall these days," Sammy said, shaking his head. "Ever since she sprouted hooters and pimples and started high school, she's been dif'rent. Acts like I bore her to death. Rolls her eyes sometimes while I'm tryin' to talk to her. Don' want nuthin' to do with her parents, don' want nuthin' to do with me, and don' want nuthin' to do with clammin'. Don' want to come out here no more, or help in the nursery none neithers."

"She's a teenager, Sammy. Got growin' pains is all. She'll grow out of it."

"I dunno. She's been actin' mighty peculiar if'n you ask me," Sammy said, as he pushed down on the throttle when they entered the main channel leading to the Gulf. Loaded like they were, he had to make sure that the boat didn't dive under the water as he brought her up to speed. It was calm enough for three-quarters throttle. Sammy and Charley were silent as they plowed through the water. Sammy's clam lease was several miles to the south.

Like his father before him, Sammy had been a mullet fisherman most of his adult life, but the combo of the '93 storm and the soon-to-follow ban-the-net law passed by the Florida legislature put the kibosh on that and he was forced to change occupations. He became a regular Mr. Fix-it for the wealthier citizens of Crescent Beach; but, he hated it. He sorely missed working out on the Gulf. The life of a fisherman suited him just fine with Mother Nature being his only boss. After the ban-the-net law, the State of Florida initiated retraining programs for the net fishermen. One of the programs was clamming. The cooperative extension service, working in conjunction with the University of Florida, set up the Cedar Key Aquaculture Association where would-be clammers could take courses. Five-acre leases in the Atlantic and two-and-a-half acre leases in the Gulf were handed out by the state. The leases in the Gulf were smaller because there were more estuaries which meant more algae which meant more food which meant the clams grew faster.

At first, a lot of fisherman participated in the program, but they thinned out when they discovered how difficult the clamming business was. By the time Sammy decided to jump in, he had missed out on the free leases. But he eventually bought a lease cheap from a discouraged fisherman and took the Cedar Key course. He built a nursery for raising baby clams behind his trailer. He built the pontoon barge with help from Tiny, the local shrimper, and Charley. The first year he started with a hundred thousand baby clams. This year he had increased his crop threefold. Next year he hoped to jump to a million. Sammy was not afraid of hard work.

Sammy pulled back on the throttle as he approached the PVC pipes stuck in the mud that marked his claim. When he had the barge where he wanted, he said, "Stick in the spud, Charley."

Charley got out of his chair and carefully made his way forward. Through a large vertical galvanized pipe attached to the bow, Charley jammed a smaller diameter pipe into the mud. It held the barge firmly in place. Sammy turned off the motor. He sat back and folded his hands across his impressive gut. The sun was warm and the water gently lapped the barge. A brown pelican thinking them crabbers and suspecting there might be some scraps soon, landed nearby. After awhile, Sammy smiled and turned to Charley. "Jest don' get any better than this. Shor beats banging nails on a roof or tearin' apart an ol' water heater to replace the element, don' it, Charley?"

Charley was facing the sun with his eyes closed. He nodded, then said, " 'Cept fer one thing."

"What's that?"

"I'm starved. Whacha got fer vittles?"

"You kin reach the cooler. See fer yurself."

Charley bent over to open the large red cooler. He pulled out a plastic bag sitting on top of the ice. The bag contained two small cartons of Tropicana orange juice, four Ring Dings, four Hostess Twinkies, and a pile of Lance peanut butter crackers. Charley took an orange juice and Ring Ding. "What's yur pleasure?" he asked Sammy.

"Twinkie for starters."

Charley handed him the snack cake and the other orange juice. As he put the bag back in the cooler, he said, "You know you don' gotta keep this stuff cold. You kin leave 'em out fer a hundrid years and it won't bother them none." Sammy, mouth full with creamy filling on his chin, was too busy eating to answer. He devoured the Twinkie. Charley brushed some of the ice away that was covering a case of beer. He was indignant. He slammed the cooler shut. "Busch Lite! Thought you said you was bringin' beer, Sammy?"

Sammy patted his belly. "Tryin' to slim down."

"Then give up them Twinkies and Ring Dings. Lord a'mighty, Busch Lite!"

"Thought you said you ain't met a beer you don' like? Hand me a Ring Ding, wouldya?" Charley, shaking his head, reopened the cooler.

After a mammoth bite, Sammy asked, "You goin' to Town Meeting tonight?"

"Hadn' planned on it."

"Could use yur support."

Charley turned to look at Sammy. "What's up?"

"Condo people wanna take our ballfield away. Gonna petition the town to put in a couple o' tennis courts." Sammy was a member of a loosely organized softball team that played at the local field on Sunday afternoons. Their season paralleled the big leagues: they started up in the spring and played through the fall. It was just for fun and oftentimes coed. "The head honcho of the condo association is behind it. He's got most of the condo people and a bunch from Rich Man's Row to sign a petition. Wants to put the courts smack dab in the middle of left field."

"Don' like that guy, much," Charley said. "Anybody who wants hisself called William, instead of Bill or Billy, is trouble fer the town, I say. Far's I kin tell, he's tryin' to make this town like where he come from." Charley shook his head. "I jest don't understan' why people does that. I mean, why come here in the first place if you don' like the way it is?...Yeah, I'll go. Imagine it might get interestin', what with Craig now a councilman and all."

When they finished breakfast, Sammy stripped down to his underwear and began putting on a wetsuit. "Hardest part of the whole damn job, this," he said, tugging at the suit. When he finally had it zipped up and his weight belt fastened, he turned to Charley who was still in the plastic lawn chair, digesting the two Twinkies. "Crank up the hookah, wouldya?" Charley got up and started the Honda compressor that caught on the second pull. Charley attached one of the three hundred foot hoses to the compressor while Sammy put on his hood. Charley looked at Sammy, all suited up and holding his mask.

"You're scary-looking, know that Sammy? And funny-looking, too, with that mustache shaved off."

"Had to 'cuz my mask leaks if I don'," Sammy said, as he fiddled with the regulator and mouthpiece at the end of the hose. When everything was all set, he put his mask on and climbed down the ladder into the water. "Whoa! Water's done chilled some. Swear it's dropped ten degrees this week!" He pulled the mask down and took a look under water. Even though it was only six feet deep, he couldn't see the bottom. There was four feet of visibility at best, which was pretty good: in the summer months it was murkier and he often couldn't see his hand in front of his face, making it necessary to do everything by feel. Sammy went down and located the line of clam seed bags where he had left off a couple of days earlier. The barge was perfectly situated. He went around to the bow. "Might as well git started. Hand me one of them rolls."

Charley lowered one of the forty-pound rolls containing five separate mesh nylon bags tied together, with each bag holding about a thousand thumbnail size hard clams. The bags would be harvested with a winch after a year when the clams were cherrystones at one and one-quarter inches thick. All the clams grown in this area of the Gulf were hard clams, their names only differed with size. Little necks, for example, were the same kind of clam as a cherrystone, but they were only one inch thick. But cherrystones were what Sammy was shooting for because they were the most popular and fetched the highest price. It was tricky, though; lots of things could go wrong between seeding and harvest. In a storm the bags could get torn up from the bottom and lost. Rolling moss could pile up against the bags or slip in underneath, acting as a wall the current could push against until the bags freed up and scattered. Black or red drums could eat thousands in one sitting, as well as blue crabs that could burrow under the bags, grabbing the clams from below. When Sammy had lashed the five bags to the others already on the bottom, he returned to the barge for another roll. It would take him hours to set and stake all the new bags with leaded lines. After twenty bags, Sammy's stomach was already screaming for food. He decided to take a break and climbed up onto the barge.

"About time fer a snack," he said, popping a beer and tearing at a package of peanut butter crackers with his teeth. Charley joined him. The beers went down fast, and each grabbed another.

"I'll be danged, that beer was alright! Must be the crackers," Charley said.

Chapter Two

Charley and Sammy, half-buzzed from the day's beers, finished rinsing the salt off the barge and hoofed it over to City Hall. They could hear the Pledge of Allegiance when they arrived, but they didn't go in, not because they were unpatriotic—far from it—but because the Pledge of Allegiance reminded them of school which they both had hated. They waited near the front door. Pickups outnumbered the cars two to one in the parking area. There were also a few golf carts, a couple of bicycles, and Craig's shiny Harley. Sammy walked around the motorcycle.

"Nice bike," Sammy said.

"You kin have it," Charley said.

"What's wrong with it?"

"Nuthin', jest the driver. Craig's crazy. Took me fer a ride the first week after he bought it. Was after poker. Never shoulda. I got on that bike drunk and got off it sober! Scared the livin' daylights outta me, he did!"

Sammy and Charley entered the building and sat down in the rear row of folding chairs. The town clerk was standing at the podium, reading the minutes of the last meeting. The mayor, the four councilmen, and the town's lawyer sat at a long, shiny red cedar desk that spanned the front of the room. The turnout was excellent. The different social groups of the town were easy to pick out. The church people with the women in long dresses and the men clean-shaven and tidy, sat together in one section. The fishermen, wearing white rubber boots, and their wives sat in another. The condo people and most of the people from Rich Man's Row sat together close to the front. Others were scattered about. Norm, the town's doctor, and Tammy, who owned and ran the local bar and restaurant, also lived on Rich Man's Row, but they sat in the front row.

Twelve years ago there had been no such thing as Rich Man's Row. In fact, there had been no street at all, only beach-front. The natives and longtime residents had built their homes mostly at ground level, or at best a couple of cinderblocks up off the ground, and away from the beach because of tidal surges. But then a dribble of wealthier people began to move into town. There was no zoning. The prices of the lots were a bargain compared to other waterfront property in Florida and they quickly snapped them up. Soon a road was built and large substantial houses on stilts began to sprout along the crescent-shaped beach. Compared to the fishermen's trailers, doublewides, and small, modest homes, these new houses were mansions. Consequently, the street was dubbed Rich Man's Row.

Next to Tammy sat Virginia, the mayor's wife of close to sixty years. She suffered from Alzheimer's and looked around vacantly. Ralph, the local realtor, was holding her hand. He was dark-haired handsome and a model citizen. For the last several years, Crescent Beach real estate had been going bonkers with many people flipping properties. People would buy a canal lot, and after a few months sell it for a tidy profit. Then the person who bought it would do the same. Being the only realtor in town, Ralph was profiting nicely. Privately, though, he bemoaned the fact that the town was quickly changing from a tight-knit community to one of impermanence.

Ralph was also the town's biggest anomaly because he was gay. There is an adage that the farther north you go in Florida, the farther south you are. Crescent Beach was in the conservative Bible belt and in the land of sweet tea and y'alls. Considering his sexual persuasion, it was nothing short of courageous for him to move here after graduating from the University of Florida twenty years ago. He didn't advertise the fact he was gay, but neither did he hide it. When the town first found out, it was blown away, and oddly it was the church people who were the first to shun him. He was extremely sensitive and it hurt, but he stuck it out. Little by little he won the town over. On his own he began to tend the town's flower gardens, buying poinsettias out of his own pocket and putting them around City Hall during the Christmas holidays. Lilies during Easter. He helped with communal suppers, cut real estate commissions for needy families, and was the first to help neighbors clean up after tidal surges.

Craig, the owner of the Harley and the councilman sitting to the mayor's left, was Ralph's partner. Other than maybe the Storm of the Century, Craig's coming out was the biggest surprise in town over the last ten years. Maybe ever. Craig had been closet-gay. He had posed as a stud, *the man.* He would bring buxom blondes over from Gainesville to parade around town. He was macho, talked tough, was physically a big guy, outgoing with lots of bravado. He had also been homophobic and had given Ralph serious grief for years. One big reason for that was the guilt Craig felt about his own sexuality. He would disappear for a week, saying he was going camping; but, instead, he would make a beeline to some gay bars he knew of in Atlanta. One night at Tammy's bar, he had gotten very drunk because he lost to Ralph in an arm-wrestling match in front of half the town: a huge loss of face for someone with his image. He wrecked his airboat when he left the bar and was seriously injured. The only person who offered to take care of him was Ralph. During his convalescence they fell in love. But, Craig still tells himself and Ralph that he is bisexual, that he's not a hundred percent gay. Ralph never says anything, only smiles. When the '93 storm destroyed Craig's family camp on Snowy Key, he moved in with Ralph. That was seven years ago. He had been there ever since.

Beau saw Virginia looking at him. Sighing inwardly, he smiled encouragingly at his wife before he picked up his gavel and banged it three times. He thanked the town clerk for reading the minutes, then turned towards the crowded room, saying, "New business. First up is the request to construct two tennis courts at the municipal sports field. I have in front of me a list of," Beau glanced at a piece of paper, "thirty-nine signatures, twenty-two of which are from legal residents of Crescent Beach. This is a substantial number. The council and I have discussed the proposal. I personally feel that it might be a good idea because it would give people who do not fish, something else to do. It might also attract new citizens and part-timers which would mean more revenue for the town. However, there are two major problems. First, the town has no room in its budget for such a project. Secondly, Councilman Craig, to my left here, plays on the local softball team. He has brought it to my attention that the courts would be built smack dab in left field." Beau looked around the room. When he located the president of the condo association near the front, he said, "William, I believe you are the author of this petition. Would you like to address these concerns?"

William stood. He was six feet tall with thinning fair hair and looked in pretty good shape. Like the other condo people, he was better dressed than most, wearing clean, pressed slacks, a light blue oxford shirt, and tasseled loafers—quite a contrast to Sammy and Charley who had come straight from work. "Yes, Mr. Mayor, I would. As to the first problem, I believe it can be easily remedied. There are plenty of grants out there for building public sports facilities in the state of Florida. Obviously it would take some time with the red tape, but it could be done. It shouldn't cost the town a cent. With the facilities we have here, or rather don't have here, this town should qualify easily for a full grant."

Beau interrupted him. "Unfortunately I, along with the council members, have more than a full slate. Time is precious. Would you be willing to pursue one of these grants?"

"Absolutely."

"How about the ball field?"

"Mr. Mayor, I have a good view of the softball field from my condo. Frankly, those so-called games are about as ragtag as it gets. The quality of play is ridiculous. Our group here," he said, nodding towards his contingent, "could play better with one arm tied behind our backs. They also do not participate in the Big Bend softball league, no games against Cedar Key, Steinhatchee, and the like. If they did, they would be a laughing stock. Half the time they don't field enough players to play amongst themselves and, consequently, they have to change the rules. They cut out either right or left field, where if someone hits it to the wrong field, they're automatically out. So, what's the big deal putting in the tennis courts if, more often than not, they cut out one of the fields anyway? We chose left field because it's better oriented and the sun doesn't blind you."

Incredulous, Craig exclaimed, "You're telling us that you want to leave us two-thirds of a field! That's bullshit!"

Beau slammed his gavel down. "Easy, Craig. Let William speak his piece. You'll get your turn."

William ignored Craig. "And alcohol is consumed there in prodigious quantities. They set a bad example for the young people of this town. Sports are supposed to be a healthy endeavor, not getting drunk on a Sunday afternoon!"

Sammy, who played third base on the team, had heard enough. He yelled out, "Billy Boy, why doncha leave things be! We don't need no girlie sports in this town. Yur always tryin' to change things aroun' here. If'n you don' like the way it is, why doncha go back to where you come from!"

"Attaboy, Sammy," Charley whispered.

Beau banged his gavel again. "You're out of line, Sammy."

William's face was bright red. He angrily turned to Sammy. "At least where I come from, we don't have sex perverts on our teams!"

There was a collective gasp. There was no mistaking what William meant: both Craig and Ralph played on Sundays. Craig bolted up from his chair. William knew instantly that he had gone too far. Ralph looked worriedly at Craig who had an extremely short fuse and was quickly making his way around the desk. Everyone was talking loudly. Craig wasn't the most popular guy in town, but Ralph was. Most of the long-term residents were furious. Insults flew back and forth across the room. Beau was banging the gavel, calling for order. Virginia looked confused and scared. Charley had his arms around Sammy, holding him back. Norm wondered if he'd have to sew anybody up. The town's lawyer was shaking his head. Craig came around the desk, heading for William. Ralph quickly put Virginia's hand in Tammy's lap, and jumped up to restrain Craig.

No punches were thrown, although most of the men were out of their chairs. The condo and Rich Man's Row crowd looked nervous, as well they should. Slowly, the room took note of Beau's insistent gaveling and quieted down. Ralph was still holding Craig back. Although several inches shorter than the burly Craig, Ralph was easily the most fit in the room. Beau looked around. Several small groups were still talking animatedly together. Most of the church people had fled. William had quickly disappeared when he saw Craig coming around the desk. Beau didn't see any way to continue. He banged his gavel and, in a stentorian voice, announced, "One week from today we will reconvene this meeting at the usual time; THAT IS, if all parties can control themselves and conduct town business in a CIVILIZED manner! This has been disgraceful! Meeting adjourned!" Beau banged the gavel twice, then rushed to Virginia.

Most everyone quickly left the building. The lone stragglers were a solicitous Beau with his arm around Virginia, and the trio of Norm, Tammy, and Ralph. As they slowly made their way to the door, they heard the throaty growl of Craig's Harley. As he roared off, Ralph said, "He's gone to clear his head. I just hope he doesn't kill himself on that thing; he drives way too fast when he's like this." Beau locked the door behind them when they exited the building. Ralph bid them goodnight, saying, "Guess I'll head on home so Craig's got someone to rant and rave at before bed." Ralph set off for his house across from the cattle gap where the highway entered town.

"I've had enough ranting and raving, thank you," Beau said. "That was a disaster! Like schoolyard children."

"Pretty low blow from William," Norm added.

"Wasn't it, now. C'mon, dear; enough excitement for one night, don't you think? Time to go home and let Skillet out." With her husband's soothing arm around her, Virginia visibly relaxed. She smiled sweetly at him. "Up you go," Beau said, as he helped her into their golf cart. "Night all," Beau said, and scooted off.

Tammy and Norm followed Beau and Virginia towards Rich Man's Row. Norm's house, like all the others on the street, was on stilts. They passed Beau and Virginia's; Beau was leading Virginia up the stairs. When Tammy and Norm arrived at their own stairs, the phone started ringing. Tammy reacted first. "Probably the restaurant. I'll get it," she said, and ran up. When Norm entered the house, Tammy had laid the phone down, and her mouth was tight as she faced him. "It's for you," she said, and huffed her way towards their bedroom. Norm knew immediately who it was. He went over and picked up the phone.

"Hello?" He was right: Bev, his ex-wife. "No, I don't think so…What! When?…I don't know. We had plans to go to Biloxi with friends then…Yes, I know…Yes, Bev…" Tammy had been listening from the bedroom. She came around the corner and pulled out a kitchen stool across the room from Norm. They looked at each other while Norm talked. "Alright, I'll talk to Tammy about it. Yes, Bev, I know he's my son…Yes, Bev. I'll get back to you in a day or two…Goodbye." Norm hung up the phone. Hands in his pockets, he slowly walked over to Tammy. He pulled out another stool from under the counter. Tammy waited expectantly.

"David seriously hurt his back snowmobiling in the Alaskan bush. He's been flat on it since, although he's getting around some with a walker now. He's moved into town and several doctors have examined him. They all concur that he needs an operation to fuse some discs. He called his brother who adamantly recommended a specialist at Sarasota Memorial. John says that he's the best and is used by many of the major league baseball teams during spring training. John pulled some strings and the specialist fit him into his schedule. It's a hell of a long trip, but worth it if the doctor is really that good. But the first time he can see David is right after Christmas; and if he recommends surgery, he would perform it right away. David is flying to Sarasota the day after Christmas, and Bev wants me to come down not only to support David, but also so we can celebrate New Years together as a family again."

Tammy's mouth was still tight. "Convenient," she said.

"What do you mean?"

"She breaks up with her tennis pro boyfriend, and now she wants to spend New Years as a family just like the good ol' days. Pretty transparent, if you ask me."

"Tammy, my boy has been hurt and needs to be operated on! I should be there."

"What about our New Years trip to Biloxi with Rusty and Crystal? Do we just cancel all that? Lose our deposits? The first dang time I've been able to get away from the business in years, even if it's only for the better part of a week, and now it's kaput because of that woman who's been bleeding you for years with major alimony you can't afford!"

Norm shrugged his shoulders. "Honey, what can I do?"

Tammy stood up abruptly. "I don't know! But I do know that that woman pisses me off. You mark my words, she wants you back!"

"Doesn't matter if she does, or doesn't. Point is, I don't. I'm more than happy with my Miss Tammy, thank you very much." He reached out for her hand. "I think you should go to Biloxi, Honey. You'd still be able to get away from the business. And you'd have a blast with Rusty and Crystal. But I really should be with David. Any back operation, no matter what, can be tricky. It's serious business." Norm gave her hand a little tug. She didn't resist and allowed Norm to pull her in and hold her close. "When you get back, you can tell me all about it." After a pause, he added, "Just don't wiggle that saucy butt of yours too much so some hunk comes panting after you."

Tammy couldn't help smiling into Norm's shoulder. Her voice muffled, she said, " I don't think you have to worry about that."

Chapter Three

There wasn't much to work with, but Rebecca's mother Katharine had made their rust bucket of a trailer as homey as she could. It was spotless inside. Fourteen feet wide by fifty-six feet long, it had a bathroom and utility area that separated the master bedroom in the rear of the trailer from a smaller bedroom. Towards the front was the open combination dining and living area. An eating counter partitioned the kitchen off from the dining/living. Pressboard cabinets on the thin kitchen walls were painted lime green. Prints of bright flowers in cheap frames adorned the living area. The two easy chairs and multi-pillowed couch were swathed in floral print and all three faced a large old TV with rabbit ears. A vase of plastic flowers and a TV Guide were on the coffee table in front of the sofa. The wall-to-wall carpet was worn and threadbare. The ceiling was low and a tall man could hit his head on the domed overhead lights. Sammy had to be careful whenever he came over.

The trailer was on a ragged interior lot with grass that needed mowing and cabbage palms that needed booting. Katharine's husband Clem was working six days a week at the marina, and the last thing he wanted to do on his day off was to cut grass. Katharine felt it wasn't her job, and Rebecca wouldn't be caught dead pushing that old lawnmower. The lot next door belonged to Katharine's brother Sammy who also lived in an old trailer and rarely tended to mowing what barely passed for a lawn. About the only difference between the two lots was the color and length of the trailers and the new limestone driveway leading to the clam nursery Sammy had built out back.

Katharine put a bowl of oatmeal down on the eating counter next to a glass of orange juice. She rapped again on the bathroom door. She was a dark-haired, stout woman, not fat really, but heavy boned and solid like her brother. The trailer swayed a little as she walked. "Rebecca, oatmeal's on the counter and the bus'll be by soon. Git a move-on!" There was no reply, but Katharine didn't expect one. She returned to the kitchen. A couple of minutes later, Rebecca emerged. She was a pretty fourteen-year-old whose body was budding and there was a good chance that she would bloom into quite a beauty. She was fair and slight like her father. Her light blond hair was pulled back into a ponytail and a tad of make up covered some pimples in the chin area. Her sharp, young breasts, although mostly covered by an unbuttoned man's oxford style shirt, looked pointy in the tee shirt tucked into her skin-tight jeans.

Rebecca sat down at the counter and began to toy with her oatmeal. Eventually she took a bite, then quickly made a face. She reached for the orange juice to wash it down. What slop, she thought. Pig swill! She took another small spoonful, made another face and reached for the OJ again. She stuck the spoon in the oatmeal and pushed it away. These days Katharine had given up trying to make her eat. Rebecca's a big girl, she told her husband, if she wants to starve herself, that's her business. Katharine went into the living room and sat down to thumb through the TV Guide. Rebecca's stool had a swivel seat and she slowly spun around, taking in the trailer as she finished her juice. What a dump, she thought. And this town, too. Nothing to do except fish. Boring! Boring! Not like Tallahassee!

Rebecca's best friend was from Tallahassee, the daughter of a man who had accidently clipped Rebecca with his boat trailer a couple of years ago and knocked her off her bike into the canal. She had been badly hurt and initially taken to the Perry hospital. But when raging infection set in, she had been transferred to a hospital in Tallahassee. She had almost died. During her recovery, she was visited in the hospital non-stop by the man and his family; that family included a girl the same age as Rebecca. While Rebecca healed, the two began to spend a lot of time together and they soon became inseparable. Rebecca visited her often in Tallahassee, sleeping in one of the twin beds in the girl's room that was bigger than both her trailer's bedrooms and bathroom combined. There was a cool, kidney-shaped pool to swim in at the house. When the girl and her family spent weekends in Crescent Beach, they would bring their golf cart. Rebecca and her friend would take turns driving it all over town. Her friend's dad had a sporting goods store and he had presented Rebecca with a new bike when she had healed. Then he had given her another to use when she visited in Tallahassee. She and her friend would bike to the movies. Or to the mall. Or to the big community pool where all the other kids hung out in the summer. Tallahassee was so cool! Not like here!

Rebecca heard the bus. She saw it pass, heading to the point where it would turn around and come back to pick her and the other kids up in front of the real estate office. Because Perry was so far away and because there were so few children in both the country and in Crescent Beach, the one bus transported both high school and middle school students. Rebecca was the only high school student in town who took the bus…not because there weren't others her age, but because they all belonged to the church group and were being homeschooled. The bus drove all over limestone back roads to pick up kids. What was normally a twenty-five minute drive to Perry took over an hour and a half.

Rebecca got off her stool and picked up her small backpack full of books by the front door. She had left it there when she had returned from school yesterday afternoon. If she had any homework, it was ignored. Like the oatmeal, Katharine had given up fighting with her about studying. As Rebecca opened the door, Katharine said, "Have a good day at school, dear."

"Right," Rebecca said, shutting the door behind her.

Katharine sighed. She just didn't know what to say to her daughter any more. She stood and walked into the kitchen to pick up Rebecca's bowl and glass. She dumped the oatmeal into the garbage and as she began to wash the bowl, made her plans for the day.

Once in Perry, the bus turned right at the Chamber of Commerce building where it went down West Lafayette Street to the Taylor County Middle School. After dropping off the younger students, it continued past the Pine View Memorial Gardens on North Peacock Avenue and soon arrived at the high school. Backpack slung over a shoulder, Rebecca headed to her homeroom. She walked alone. Although a blue-collar pulp and sawmill town, the people of Perry referred to Crescent Beach as the Redneck Riviera. This didn't help Rebecca make friends. So far, the girls treated her like an unsophisticated rube and most of the boys were only mildly interested. But Rebecca pretended that she didn't care; they were all stupid, anyway. That is, everyone but Billy Streeter. He was cool. He was a junior, had his own truck, and Rebecca thought he was the cutest guy going.

Billy's family was, for Perry, quite wealthy. His father was one of the muckety-mucks at the Buckeye Pulp Mill and they lived in one of the nicest houses in town. His mother was very busy with all the right clubs and organizations, and had meetings and events all the time. His father, too, was hardly around. He worked long hours at the mill, and when he was home he would shut himself in his study and didn't want to be disturbed. On his sixteenth birthday, they gave Billy a brand new 4X4 Ford F-150 because they didn't want to have to drive Billy to visit friends or to the various school activities. Consequently, Billy had free rein to come and go at all hours. He started hanging out with the wrong people and got into drugs. Drugs cost money. His father only gave him a minimal gas allowance, saying that when he was young, he had to work for everything he got. If Billy needed money, then he should get a job. But most all the jobs were menial and entailed physical work. Billy avoided anything resembling hard work as much as possible, and doing something not too taxing, like flipping burgers at McDonalds or Burger King, he felt was beneath him. But he needed money to pay for the drugs. He became a thief.

He started his fledgling career by going through his mother's old purses in the closet. Occasionally he found some wadded up bills or loose coins. He progressed to her wallet, carefully taking only small amounts that she wouldn't miss. He never touched his father's wallet because his father was such a penny pincher that he would notice immediately. Billy's truck gave him mobility and, as his habit deepened, he expanded his repertoire to stealing from unlocked cars, garages, and carports. He worked his way up to houses of the better neighborhoods of Perry and Cross City, even as far away as Chiefland. He always wore plastic gloves and never broke a lock or a window; usually he always found some door or window open. The first thing he'd do was to check out the medicine cabinets. It was unbelievable how much pain medication was doled out by the doctors, almost every house had painkillers of some sort: Vicodin, Lortab, Oxycontin. Oxycontin by far and away was his favorite: he lusted after Oxycontin. It was a time-release medication meant to act over a twelve-hour period; but snort it or smoke it, and hoowee, what a high! Almost instantaneous! But he also stole money, jewelry, knives, guns, a chainsaw and other assorted tools: all small stuff easily moved and hidden. He sold the booty to a fence located in the Old Town Hammock. His fence in turn sold to pawnshops all over central Florida. Everything was a cash deal with no paperwork.

Rebecca was sitting alone in the high school cafeteria when Billy sauntered over with a tray full of food.

"Mind if I join you, pretty lady?"

Rebecca was floored! Billy Streeter wanted to sit with her! He knew that she existed! She tried to act cool, but her blush gave her away. She casually motioned to the empty chairs all around. "Plenty of room, Billy."

Billy sat next to her. "Looks like you've got me at a disadvantage."

"What do you mean?"

"You know my name, but I don't know yours."

She smiled. "Rebecca."

Billy returned her smile. "Pretty name. Biblical, too." He took a bite of sandwich, Rebecca a sip of milk. "Are you from Perry? Haven't seen you around."

"Nope, Crescent Beach."

"Redneck Riviera."

"Ha, ha."

"No offense," he added quickly.

Rebecca shrugged. One side of the untucked shirt slid over. Billy noticed her pointed breast pushing at the tee-shirt. Rebecca noticed Billy notice. It made her feel good, but she brought the shirt back into position. Billy returned to eating his sandwich.

"That's a pretty good commute. Your parents bring you in?" Rebecca thought, right, in that rusty old Honda with over two-hundred-thousand miles on it.

"Nope, the bus. Takes forever. Big waste of time."

The school bell rang. Billy wolfed down the rest of his sandwich and Rebecca organized her tray. "Time for class," she said, needlessly. She wished she could stay talking with him.

"Yeah. I've got Math. What about you?"

"English. Sentence structure. Boring."

He smiled and high fived her. "I'm with you."

Standing, she said, "It was nice talking to you, Billy."

Billy stood and picked up his tray. "Likewise." Rebecca turned to go. Billy hesitated, then said, "Hey, how about I give you a ride home today."

Rebecca turned back immediately. "Gosh, that would be super! Would you really?" Then she thought of him dropping her off in front of the rusty trailer. She backpedaled. "I better not. My parents would give me all sorts of grief, you know, without their permission and all."

"They don't have to know. I can drop you off at the cattle gap and you can walk to your place."

Rebecca thought about it. She didn't think long. "Deal!" They smiled and high fived again.

"I'll meet you at the bus after the last bell. *Ciao,"* Billy said, before walking away. Rebecca felt like skipping to class. Three hours later, she met Billy. Together they walked over to his pickup. She climbed into the cab.

"Nice truck," she said, truly impressed. Her Uncle Sammy had a 1981 two wheel drive F-150 so rusty that you could poke your finger through the fenders.

"It'll do," he said, starting the vehicle. Brand new truck; must be rich, Rebecca thought. Billy pulled out of the parking lot and headed to Highway U.S. 19. At the traffic light, he checked his watch before turning south. "Have to swing by the sawmill for a second before we head out. Got an errand to do." Even though it was broad daylight, lights were on everywhere around the mill and the strong scent of pine was in the air. Billy pulled into a parking area full of pickups. "Be right back." He left the cab and walked to a shiny black Chevy Malibu at the far end of the lot. Rebecca saw a black man get out. Billy pulled out a wad of cash and peeled off several bills. The black man passed him a small brown paper bag. Billy returned. He tossed the bag onto the seat between them and hopped up behind the wheel. He smiled at Rebecca. "Alrighty then. Crescent Beach, here we come!"

Rebecca wasn't sure if she should scooch over a little closer to Billy or not. She remained close to the window. They passed the entry road to the Buckeye Pulp Mill. "That's where my dad works. He's a big shot in the office." That explains the new truck, she thought. She wondered what Billy would think if he knew she lived in a rusty old trailer. "What's your dad do?" Billy asked.

"Works at the marina. Mostly operating the boat lift," Rebecca answered softly. Billy nodded. They turned onto the Crescent Beach Road where the houses quickly disappeared and pine plantations began. A couple of miles later, Billy suddenly turned onto a limestone road between two plantations.

"Where are you going, Billy?" Rebecca asked, nervously.

Billy laughed. "Relax. Just out of sight from the highway. For a little toke."

"Toke?"

Billy laughed again. "I forgot, you're just a freshman, aren't you?" He pulled into a log truck entrance to one of the plantations and turned off the motor.

"Barely," she answered

"What does that mean?" he asked, as he picked up the brown bag. She didn't answer. She watched him pull out a large, clear baggie full of what looked like chopped up green tea."

"What's that?"

"Grass," he said, looking over. Seeing her confusion, he added, "As in marijuana. Open the glove, would you, and hand me the butane lighter and pipe." She did as he said, and watched him fill and pack the pipe. He lit the pipe and took a big drag, holding the smoke in several seconds. When he exhaled, he said, "Aah…Good stuff." He turned to her. "That, my dear, is what's called taking a toke." He held the pipe out. "Want one?" Rebecca's eyes were big. She shook her head. He laughed again, and took another toke. He thumbed out the pipe and asked her to put everything back in the glove. "That's more like it," he said, starting the truck again and turning around. When he turned on to the highway, he said, "You were saying about 'barely' being a freshman…"

She noticed that his eyes had become glassy. "Yeah," she began. "I had a real bad accident a while back and missed a bunch of school in the fall. We weren't sure if I might have to stay back a year. But, I didn't."

"What happened?"

She told him all about being knocked off her bike, breaking an arm and a leg, and all the infection.

"Whoa," he said. "That must have been a big hurt."

"It was. My body, especially my arm, ached like the dickens for the longest time."

"You're okay now, though, right? You sure look pretty darn good."

Rebecca blushed. "I'm fine, but I sure hope I never go through something like that again."

He nodded. They drove along in silence. "So you had a lot of pain, huh?"

"Yup. Lots."

"Did the doctors give you anything for it?"

"Sure, bunch of stuff."

"Like what?"

"Mainly Oxy-something."

"Oxycontin, maybe?"

"Yeah, that's it; but the stuff made me feel funny so I stopped taking it. Still got gobs of it."

Billy turned towards her. "Is that a fact? 'Gobs?'" She nodded. Billy was poker faced as he turned back to the wheel.

Chapter Four

Rusty pulled into the Cross City state police barracks. He looked at his watch. A couple of minutes early. Good, Captain Smathers was a punctual kind of guy. He got out of his pickup and walked towards the front door. Surrounded by live oak trees, the one-story rectangular building had a pale brick façade that went up eight feet or so where it met a faux board-and-batten section that was part of the flat roof system cantilevered out over a walkway. It was cubism at its worst and Rusty thought that if its grimy walls were brightly painted it could have doubled as a Dairy Queen. Rusty noticed two cruisers in the rear parking lot. Both were pointed out towards the highway. He entered through a thick glass door and looked at the clock above the desk that was manned by a corporal. Eleven sharp. The corporal looked up.

"Can I help you, sir?"

"Captain Smathers is expecting me."

The corporal stood immediately. "Who should I tell him?"

"Rusty McMillan."

The corporal nodded and went down the hallway. He returned less than a minute later. "Last door on the right," he said, pointing. Rusty knew that. He knew where Smathers' office was—same place it was seven years ago when Rusty was working undercover in Crescent Beach, trying to get the goods on Jimmy and other marijuana smugglers. Rusty walked down the hall. Captain Smathers was waiting for him at the door.

"Sergeant McMillan, good to see you again," the captain said, extending his hand and smiling. The captain's uniform was sharply creased and spotless, his tie snugged up tight. Rusty, in jeans and a sweatshirt, couldn't help feeling out of uniform.

"Plain old Rusty now, Sir," Rusty said, shaking the captain's hand.

They entered the office. Smathers motioned Rusty to sit in one of the two chairs in front of his desk. When they were both seated, he said, "I've always wondered why you retired so early, Rusty."

Rusty was sitting ramrod straight in the chair, an old habit from meetings with his superiors when he was a trooper. "Burned out from highway duty, Sir; got tired of cleaning up all the messes and seeing lives ruined. Just didn't want to do it any longer. I figured with my three tours of MP service in Vietnam and all the years as a trooper that I'd have a large enough pension to support me. So, I decided to opt out…What about you, Sir? I know it's none of my business, but you've been in a long time, much longer than me. Don't you ever think about retiring?"

Smathers briefly massaged his eyes. "Yeah, I guess forty-two years is a long time, but I'm thinking that I'd like to make it an even fifty. That is, if they don't kick me out first for being too long in the tooth. And frankly, Rusty, I've been doing this so long, I don't know what else I'd do. I don't have the patience for fishing, don't like hunting, and have no real hobbies. My wife passed four years ago and this is my whole life, these barracks are my home. I'd probably go nuts without it…What are you doing now? Fishing?"

"Among other things. I'm also working part time as a mechanic at the local marina, sort of their troubleshooter for any engine problems. In the summer when it's bonkers, it's full time, plus some. Although I don't really need the income, it comes in handy, and truth is, I love to tinker on engines."

The captain nodded, then his expression changed. Rusty could see that he was done with the chitchat. "So you're here to see if there's been any more progress on Talbot and the judge?"

"Yes, sir."

"Sorry to say, none. Dead end. Because of the federal judge, the FBI is still poking around, but word is they're not getting anywhere and toning it down."

"What about the blond guy you showed me a picture of. I thought he was a prime suspect."

"Ironclad alibi. He was staying at a fish camp on the Manatee River in Tampa when Talbot was killed. The owner vouched for him; said the blond guy rented a small outboard and was in sight the whole time he fished. The blond guy did go to a couple of Devil Rays' games while he was there, but was able to produce the ticket stubs. He's a real fan and has a collection of every ticket stub he's ever bought at the Trop. The only discrepancy was that the Feds checked videos of the crowd in attendance and the second day the guy's seat was empty the whole game."

"What did he say to that?"

"He laughed and asked the investigator if he had ever been to one of the Devil Rays' games. Said they were the least supported team in both leagues and there were tons of empty seats. Said he just shifted around and sat wherever he wanted whenever he wanted."

"Convenient."

The captain shrugged. "But likely; better seats for free. Even if he didn't go to the game, there was not enough time to go up north and do Talbot if he was putting in all those hours fishing.... And the guy was only a suspect because he's been seen associating with members of the Colombian cartel that you think was responsible for the hit. No one really knows what his connection is, only theories. So who knows, maybe we were totally off base."

"Maybe, but I still believe Jimmy's death is connected to the cartel." Rusty paused, then added, "And I find that empty seat interesting." The captain shrugged again. "I assume the FBI checked around Perry—motels, restaurants, gas stations, grocery stores—to see if anyone could ID this guy from around the time of Jimmy's death?"

"Ad nauseam. *Nada.*"

"How about the camping area where they pulled Jimmy's boat out. That's gotta be where the killer launched from. Any regulars that go there who might have seen something?"

"Nope. Was midweek, mid fall. Hardly anyone goes there then. The feds didn't come up with anybody."

Rusty didn't say anything.

"You became close with Talbot, didn't you?"

Rusty nodded. "Yeah, by the time I left Crescent Beach I considered him my best friend…And, yeah," he looked Smathers in the eye, "I know he was involved with the square grouper trade, but the bottom line was he was a hell of a good man. I did get the evidence you wanted back in ninety-three, but I chose not to present it." Smathers eyes flicked. This was news. "It would have destroyed a fine family. I couldn't do it."

"Turned out okay. He got rid of Espantoso."

"Yeah, and when we revealed Espantoso's identity and it came out that Espantoso had been shot dead center in the hand as well as in the head, I believe the Colombians figured out pretty quickly who was responsible. I convinced Jimmy to give you that info, and that's what I believe killed him."

"So you're feeling guilty."

"I'm feeling like I should have done something, anything, to have avoided the hit. But, I didn't."

"And you want to do something now." Rusty nodded. "So what do you want to do?"

"Start at the beginning."

"Meaning?"

"I'm going to retrace the FBI's steps and start asking questions all over again." The captain opened his mouth, but Rusty cut him off. "I know, I know. It's more than a long shot, but I gotta try. Do you have any of those big glossy pictures of the blond guy you showed me before? I'd like a couple to show around." The captain stood and walked to a file cabinet. He pulled a folder out of a lower drawer and laid it open on his desk. The blond guy, a regular Robert Redford, was staring at Rusty. Rusty picked up the picture, looking at it closely. Finally, he asked, "This guy got a name?"

The captain pulled a sheet out from the file. "Joe Slater."

* * *

Seven hours by highway to the south, Joe Slater was shooting trap at the Gulf Coast Clays between Naples and Everglades City. He was the best the shooting instructor had ever seen, and he had seen a lot of shooters over the years at competitions around the country. Besides the instructor, Slater had drawn a small crowd of spectators as he shot standing behind the third of the five different trap shooting stations. Each station was sixteen yards back from the single trap house that launched the clay pigeons away from the shooter at a different angle each time—straight away, to the left, and to the right—and five shots were taken at each station making twenty-five in a total round. But Slater wasn't standing at the customary station. Rather, he was shooting *Handicap* which meant that he was standing further back, the rules stating anywhere from seventeen to twenty-seven yards. Slater was twenty-five yards back from the station. He was also shooting *Doubles* which meant that the trap house was sending out two clay pigeons each time instead of one.

When Slater finished his round of fifty shots, he had missed two targets. Taking off his hearing protectors, he smiled at the small band of spectators when they applauded him. Slater was indeed Robert Redford handsome with his razor cut, longish blond hair and winning, pearly-white smile. Tall and lean, well-dressed in casual-but-expensive L.L. Bean outdoor attire, he walked over to the clubhouse where he had left his hand-tooled, hard-leather shotgun case. The instructor accompanied him.

"Not bad, Joe," the instructor said, smiling.

"Thanks, but with this baby, it's hard to miss," Slater said, patting his Perazzi DHO side-by-side twelve gauge shotgun. It was one of the only side-by-side models Perazzi had ever made. It was a beauty, and it was rare.

"May I?" the instructor asked, holding out a hand. Slater passed it over. French walnut burl stock and forearm, and finely engraved side plating scenes of woodcocks and forest. "Twenty-seven and a half inch barrels?" Slater nodded. The instructor brought it to his shoulder. "Sweet. Get it at Cole's?" he asked, handing the gun back.

"Nope, went to the factory in Bresica. Custom made for me."

"Sweet," the man said again. They arrived at the clubhouse. Slater put the gun in the case and slung the strap around his shoulder. "Ever consider competing?" the instructor asked.

"Nope. I live on a boat. Don't have room for trophies."

Cocky, the instructor thought; but then he had a right to be. "See you next week?" Slater nodded, and the two men shook hands.

Slater walked over to his burgundy Porsche. He carefully laid the case in the back, and smoothly shifted through the gears out to the Tamiami Trail. He headed north, and a half hour later pulled into the Hamilton Harbor Yacht Club where he owned a wetslip for his fifty-six foot cabin cruiser. Like his car, the boat was an eye-catcher with its sleek fourteen-foot beam, immaculate brightwork, and especially its perfect 'fighting lady yellow' paintjob. Slater was fluent in Spanish, and had named the boat *Pituca*, a Spanish idiom meaning fancy or well-dressed lady.

Slater grabbed the shotgun case and boarded. Going below to the main stateroom, he took out the gun and laid it on a teak table before opening the rosewood doors of a large cabinet. With gun oil, a couple folded squares of soft cloth, and a cleaning rod in hand, he sat in an easy chair and began to clean the barrels while reminiscing about his trip, a Christmas present to himself, to the Perazzi factory in Italy two years earlier. The master craftsmen had taken all kinds of measurements and made up a test gun to determine the best fit for him. Slater chose the blank and grade of wood for the stock and forearm, elected the barrel length and bore, and selected the woodcock engraving. From the factory viewing area, he watched as the gun began to be assembled. By the time he had finished a lunch of homemade pasta and wine at the nearby Perazzi family restaurant two days later, his gun was ready. It wasn't cheap—$50,000—but he could afford it.

He glanced up at the open cabinet where there was a world map with different colored pins stuck in it. Each pin represented an assassination he had done, most for the Colombian cartel out of Miami. In the States, most of the pins were clustered around cities like Chicago, New York, Los Angeles, Miami, and Tampa. He had been very busy over the last ten years. About an inch north of Tampa was a sole pin. It was that job that had paid for the gun. Slater frowned. But there had been collateral damage. He was supposed to take out a fishing guide who used to run marijuana for the Colombian cartel—the fishing guide had iced one of theirs and it was payback. Slater figured that his best bet was to shoot the guide out on the water, miles from anyone else; but it turned out that day the guide had a client with him. So, it was a no-brainer; he did them both. He was careful and there was no connection between him and the men: just a random killing of an ex-smuggler and some schmuck tourist fisherman. The authorities would kick tires for awhile, he figured, then let it drop. But it turned out to be a big deal because the other guy was a federal judge out of Atlanta. The FBI was brought in and pressured to look hard. And they did: they linked the fishing guide to the cartel. The cartel didn't like the attention and the *Don* let Slater know it. Somehow the Feds got wind of Slater, and came sniffing around. He needed an alibi quick. He contacted the owner of the fishing camp east of Tampa who had provided the boat he had used when he iced the guide and judge. The guy also happened to do a fair amount of drug trade with the cartel, and Slater was the middleman. With that leverage plus a couple of grand, Slater got the guy to give him an alibi, and the Feds soon left him alone.

It was a scare, though, and Slater decided not to accept any more hit jobs from anyone for awhile. He talked with the Colombians about other possibilities of employment: he had been involved with them since dealing pot way back in his University of Miami days. He was one of their *locksmiths*, a man who could be trusted, and they didn't let him down. After things quieted, they set him up to run bricks of cocaine in the *Pituca* to a casino owner in Biloxi, Mississippi, who was a distributor for the entire Midwest including Chicago. Last year Slater had made four deliveries. This year another four were planned. It was extremely risky, of course, but the payout was astronomical: his accounts in the Cayman Islands were more than fat. In a couple more years, he could live like a king anywhere in the world. He could have a boat twice the size of the *Pituca.*

Slater finished oiling the gun and put it away in his gun safe. He returned the oil and cleaning supplies to the cabinet. Looking at the sole pin again, he thought, funny how things work out: wasting that judge may have been the best thing that could have happened. He thought about the next trip to Biloxi. Between Christmas and New Years. Perfect time with everybody partying, including the Coast Guard. Who'd suspect the *Pituca?* Just a rich fat cat coming in on his yacht to gamble and celebrate the new year in style. And once the coke was taken care of, there would be his fully-comped R&R at the casino for a week. Then a little skiing trip to Aspen to follow. Let the good times roll! Slater's stomach churned deliciously just thinking about it. Smiling, he closed the rosewood doors and headed aft to his cabin for a shower.

Chapter Five

Sammy was a much better clammer than poker player. It was a good thing the clamming was going well because if he depended on his winnings at the poker table, he'd be in the poor house. Six months ago he had become part of the regular Thursday night poker group that met at the Crescent Beach Club. The group included Beau, Norm, Charley, Louie who ran the marina, Craig, Ralph, Rusty, and Tiny. Beau's elderly Lab Skillet was under the table as was his pal, Bad Dog, an ugly little white dog with a pit bull head. He belonged to Louie.

Sammy couldn't figure out why he lost more often than anyone else. He didn't realize that his face was an open book and his mannerisms gave him away at every turn. When he had a good hand, he could hardly contain himself. He'd look at his cards again and again as if he couldn't believe his luck. He'd rub his chin every few seconds, and he was too quick to throw in quarters when it was his turn to bet. When he was bluffing, he scowled as if he dared anyone not to believe he hadn't been dealt something terrific, and he never looked at his cards, just kept them hidden in one of his big mitts.

Charley said, "I pass."

Sammy stopped rubbing his chin. He quickly threw in three quarters. "Seventy-five cents to stay in, Mayor."

"Too rich for me," Beau said, and threw in his cards. The others all followed suit.

"Dang nab it! 'Bout every time I git somethin' good, you boys chicken out!" Sammy exclaimed, as he raked in all the antes. Another bad habit was Sammy's always showing off his good hands after people folded which, of course, continually reaffirmed his mannerisms. "Lookee here! Full house, kings and tens! Dang!" But Sammy really didn't mind losing. The camaraderie and the pile of beer he'd put away at each session made it worth it. He used to drink with his brother-in-law Clem, but since Rebecca's accident, Clem had given up all alcohol. Cards were more fun anyway than listening to Clem. It was Sammy's deal. The others leaned back and sipped their drinks and beers while Sammy shuffled. "Seven card stud, deuces wild," he said. Everyone anteed up and looked at their hands. Overall, Louie and Charley won more than anyone else. Charley was lucky and cagey: a good combination for poker. Louie, on the other hand, was a number cruncher and systematically counted cards and figured the odds. Charley and Louie were good friends, but were extremely competitive: whenever one beat the other at anything, it made his day.

Craig won the hand with a straight flush. As he pulled in the substantial pot with both hands, he asked, "Beau, what about the ball field?"

Beau drained his scotch before answering. "The tennis courts aren't a bad idea. It's just a shame there isn't room for both."

"So what happens if that son-of-a-bitch does get a grant?"

Ralph reached out and put a hand on Craig's forearm. "Easy, Craig."

Beau shrugged. "Then it'll probably have to be voted on by the town."

"Ain't there a law or somethin' says you poleeticians ain't supposed to talk business outside o' town meetin'?" Charley asked.

"Dumb law," Louie said.

"I agree," Beau said. He turned to Charley. "That law is archaic. How are you supposed to work things out by limiting all discussion to town meetings alone? It's absurd."

Charley raised his hands in defense. "Don't make no sense to me, neithers. Jest pointin' it out is all."

Sammy looked up from making neat little piles of his quarters. "If'n there's a town vote on it, Craig, we're gonna lose. There are more o' them than us now."

"Maybe a state grant could include funds for land purchase, too," Norm put in. "There's that land beyond the ball field that can't be built on because of all the EPA and wetland restrictions. I don't think the regs apply for something like a tennis court, and it doesn't matter if tennis courts get wet now and then with a surge, as long as they're not clay."

"Most of that land is owned by family members spread all over the place," Beau said. "Something like ten siblings have title to it. To get them all on board would be tough."

"Nothing ventured, nothing gained. I think it should at least be mentioned to William. While looking into grants, he could find out if they might include land purchase. And if so, and the family members could agree, it probably could be bought for a song. There's nothing else they can do with it." Norm said. Glancing around the table, he saw that glasses and beer bottles were empty. He turned to get Tammy's attention. When she saw him, he circled the table with a finger. She nodded.

A few minutes later Tammy arrived with drinks: beers all around except for Beau's scotch and Norm's Jack Daniel's. When she set a bottle of Bud in front of Rusty, she asked him, "Has Norm told you that he's not going to Biloxi?"

"No." Rusty looked at Norm. "What's up?"

Tammy answered for him. "He's spending New Years with his ex in Sarasota."

Norm frowned. “Because one of my sons is having a serious back operation. He’s flying to Sarasota from Alaska, and will be operated on right after Christmas. I feel that I should be there.”

“Understandable,” Rusty said.

“But unfortunately,” Tammy said, “our reservations are not refundable, being New Year’s holiday and all. So I’d like to tag along with you and Crystal, Rusty, if that’s alright.”

“Of course, Tammy” Rusty answered, immediately.

“Maybe I can pick up somebody to celebrate with,” she said, looking pointedly at Norm.

“Not funny,” Norm muttered.

There was an awkward silence until Charley asked, “You two still havin’ yur party?” For the last several years, a week or so before Christmas, Norm and Tammy hosted an open house Christmas party that usually went until the wee hours. It was quite the event and most everyone in town looked forward to it.

“Why wouldn’t we, Charley?” Norm asked.

Charley looked from Norm, to Tammy, and back to Norm. He shrugged. “Jest wonderin’ is all.”

“Beau, do you think Virginia can come? I mean, do you think she could handle it?” Tammy asked.

Beau shrugged. “We’ll see.”

Ralph asked, “How’s she doing?”

“Not so good. There are fewer and fewer good days. And seems like each good spell is shorter than the last. But when she’s back, it’s like the sun coming out on a cloudy day.” Beau paused and looked around the table. “Last week Skillet and I…” Suddenly there was a solid thump against the underside of the table and the glasses and bottles rattled. Everyone laughed. “No, no, Skillet,” Beau said, smiling and reaching under the table. “You lie down now.” When Skillet was settled, Beau continued. "Anyway, we were taking a walk past the ball field out to the woods. It had been warm and humid the day before and had rained that night, but when we were walking the weather was clearing with a brisk, cool wind. Big white fluffy clouds were flying across the sky. Occasionally I could see different parts of the path in front of me lit up briefly as the clouds pulled away from the sun. A small patch of the trail would suddenly be illuminated in a crystal clear light. But it was fleeting; after a second or two, the clouds would pass in front of the sun and everything was in shade again. That's sort of what it's like with Virginia these days."

No one said anything. Finally, Tiny broke the silence. "'Cept when T and Boda visits," Tiny said. T was married to Tiny, and Boda was their two-year-old daughter.

Beau smiled. "Yes, Tiny, that is an exception."

Tiny looked proudly around the table. "Y'all should see Miss Virginia light up when she sees Boda. And Boda, too. She gets so wiggly that T has to put her down. She runs right over to Miss Virginia jest a gigglin' and a smilin' and all. T tells me that Miss Virginia and Boda play non-stop. And Boda don' like to leave none, neithers; T has to drag her away. That is, if'n she's still awake." Tiny looked at his watch. "Speakin' of, Beau, we should be moseying pretty soon."

Beau looked at his watch. "Right you are. Guess we're calling it a night, Gents." Tiny and Beau finished their drinks and stood. Skillet crawled stiffly out from under the table. Bad Dog followed and went to Louie, looking for a pat. Louie scratched his ears. "Tammy I'd like to settle up, and please put Tiny's tab on mine."

"Now that ain't necessary…" Tiny said, waving one of his big paws at Beau. Beau cut him off.

"Tiny, if it weren't for you, T, and Boda, I'd have to give up poker nights. It's the least I can do. Besides, I've won enough poker money off you the last several years to buy you beers until I go to my grave."

"If that be the case, Mayor," Sammy said, "you kin buy me beers anytime you want, seeing's how yur winnin' my money now." Everyone laughed.

Beau smiled. "Tammy, put a beer on my tab for Sammy, too. But not because of the poker, mind you, Sammy. It's just a partial payback on all those clams you've been bringing me and Virginia."

"Aw, you don' gotta do that. All them clams had the uglies: markets won't take 'em."

Louie was mystified. "The 'uglies?'"

"Yeah," Sammy said. "They had spats all over 'em."

Louie was doubly mystified. "Spats?"

Charley rolled his eyes. "Louie, you don' know what spats is?"

"Past tense of spits?" Louie offered.

"They's baby oysters that kin stick onto the clam's shells," Sammy said. "People who eat clams don' like 'em lookin' like that. Don' affect the taste none; but it's cuz they jest don' look purty."

"I swar, you don' know nuthin', Louie," Charley said, "except maybe computers and numbers."

"Louie's numbers work for me," Norm said. "He's been making a tidy profit over at the marina. Beau and I are mighty pleased." Beau and Norm were the principal owners of the marina. There were also a couple other silent partners, doctors from Gainesville who were friends of Norm.

Louie smiled and saluted Norm with his bottle. But Charley was just getting started. "What's floaters, Louie?"

"Bubbles that sometimes float around in your vision?"

"Like I say, you don' know nuthin'! Everybody knows it's a new-growed stone crab claw that ain't packed full with meat yet so it's holler-like."

Beau turned to Tiny. "Good time to leave, Tiny. This could go on all night. C'mon, the girls are waiting." The pair thanked Tammy and left. Down on the street, Beau lowered the mini-stairway Charley had built for Skillet and the Lab stiffly climbed up into the rear seat of Beau's golf cart. Once both dog and driver were settled, with Skillet's chin on Beau's shoulder, they followed Tiny's pickup across Humpback Bridge to Rich Man's Row.

T was in Beau's living room looking at one of Virginia's bridge trophies when she heard Tiny's truck approach. She put the trophy down and quickly scanned the little brass plates of the others. They were from all over the southeast: Highlands, North Carolina, St. Simons Island, Charleston, Savannah, and St. Augustine among others. T shook her head sadly. It must be awful for Virginia to see these everyday, knowing that she'll never be able to play again. She looked over to Virginia and her daughter who were sound asleep on the leather couch. Boda's head was in Virginia's lap. Teacups and saucers and a teapot were spread around the coffee table. T heard her husband and Beau coming up the stairs. She opened the door for them.

"Now ain't that a purty sight, huh Beau?" Tiny asked, looking at Virginia and Boda. Beau only smiled. Skillet, the last up the stairs, trotted over to the couch. Once he had ascertained Boda's identity with his cold, wet nose, he decided to call it a night. He trotted over to his beanbag, circled it a couple of times, and plopped down. Tiny went over and carefully extricated Boda. When he brought her to his chest, Boda, even though sound asleep, automatically put her arms around his monstrous neck. T walked up to her husband and put an arm around his waist. She was of Latin blood and quite short: she didn't come up to his shoulders. With his two girls up close and personal, Tiny beamed.

"Looks like there's been a tea party going on," Beau said.

"For hours. Virginia must have sampled every imaginary tea there could possibly be," T said.

"I'm sure she loved it."

T smiled. "She did."

"C'mon, T, it's late. Night, Beau. Gotta put my girls to bed."

Beau walked them to the door, thanking T profusely. When he shut the door behind them, he leaned against it, looking at Virginia. She looked so peaceful. There was none of the anxiety, or fears, or frustration that played across her face most days. He hated to rouse her, but she had to wake up next to him in bed or she'd panic. He sighed as he pushed himself from the door and walked to her. He gently woke her. At first startled, she smiled when she recognized him.

"Hello, Dear," she said. She looked around, surprised to find herself in the living room. She stared curiously at the teacups. Beau watched as the confusion slowly cleared. "That's right, we were playing tea." She looked at Beau. "I was playing tea with that sweet little girl."

"Yes, dear. You had quite a good time. Now, come on, time to get into a proper bed. Virginia slowly got up. Beau put an arm around her as he led her to their bedroom.

"Do you know the little girl's name, Beau?"

"Yes, Dear. It's Boda."

"Boda…That's an unusual name. Boda means wedding in Spanish, did you know that, Beau?"

Beau nodded. “That’s how she got her name. She was born at her parents’ wedding.”

Virginia giggled. “That was cutting it rather close, I must say! I imagine that it must have been quite the exciting wedding!”

“Yes, dear, it was.” he said, as they entered the bedroom. In his mind he said to Virginia, You were there, Dear, don’t you remember? You were the maid of honor.

Chapter Six

It was on the third ride to the cattle gap with Billy that Rebecca took her first toke. She coughed, got a little dizzy, but succeeded in getting high. Since then, she had become a pro, constantly smoking pot with Billy. They started meeting behind the gym during free hour for a toke or two. In class afterwards Rebecca found it hard to concentrate on what the teacher was saying. Instead, she'd become fixated on the smallest things, like the spot on Professor Collins' tie or the fly buzzing against the window trying to get out. Even though she continually ignored homework, Rebecca had eked out decent enough grades by paying attention in class. After all, what else was there to do? Now, when she smoked pot and Billy asked her how her class was afterwards, she'd just shrug. Boring, she'd say, but she really didn't have a clue.

She was gaga over Billy. When they weren't together, she'd daydream about him. He was so cute and cool and confident. And Billy was popular; everyone seemed to know and like Billy. Once they started hanging out heavy, the various cliques in school began to open up to her. She was proud to hang on his arm walking to class, or sit almost in his lap in the truck. And Billy was teaching her all sorts of new things. Like French kissing. Ooh lah, lah, she loved to French kiss! She began to let him cop feels. She liked his hands on her; sometimes it made her dizzy. On occasion she could feel his hardness. She wanted to touch him, too, but didn't dare. She soon felt comfortable enough to tell him that she lived in a rusty old trailer. He said that he didn't care. The only thing he cared about was that she was his gal. She melted when he said that.

Rebecca finally told her parents about Billy, and that he had offered to bring her home after school. She held her breath, praying that she hadn't been seen getting out of Billy's truck at the cattle gap several times the past few weeks. Rebecca breathed a sigh of relief when neither mentioned it. Clem, her dad, said why not? Made sense to him not to be cooped up in the bus the whole afternoon. Katharine, however, wanted to meet Billy before giving her blessing. Rebecca and her mother compromised, agreeing that Billy could bring her home at the end of the week when she could meet him properly. For the whole week, Rebecca had thought about nothing else.

"Here, take a toke. It'll calm you down," Billy said, passing her the pipe. Rebecca took a big hit and, holding the smoke in, looked out over the Fenholloway River. They were at one of Billy's secret places just south of Perry. She let the smoke out.

"The color of the water looks funny," Rebecca said, handing the pipe back.

"Big time pollution from Buckeye. EPA's been after their butt and Dad says they're a real pain; but the mill's finally doing something about it now."

"Aren't you nervous about meeting my mom?"

"Nope. Adults are easy to schmooze; just gotta be polite, smile and, offer to help them do something, and you're in like Flynn. Don't worry, piece of cake."

Rebecca loved his confidence. She snuggled up to him. "How about a little schmoozing with me?"

They started making out. Their senses heightened from the pot, it soon became hot and heavy. Rebecca let Billy go farther than ever before. Finally, breathless, she broke away. "What time is it, Billy?" she asked, buttoning her blouse and re-cinching her ponytail.

Billy turned the key. "Four-fifteen. We don't have to leave quite yet. Besides, things were just getting interesting."

Rebecca laughed. "Tough! How about going to the Dairy Queen first? I've got the munchies."

"Not a problem, Milady." He started the truck and carefully turned around. It was a narrow woods road with areas of churned up sand. He needed to put it in four-wheel drive to get in and out. Once on the highway, it was a hop, skip, and a jump to the Dairy Queen. They both ordered a large cone of vanilla dipped in chocolate. Billy pulled a wad of cash out to pay for the cones. Billy always had a wad of cash; he must get a big allowance, Rebecca thought. On their way to Crescent Beach, sitting close to Billy, and devouring the ice cream, Rebecca thought she had died and gone to heaven. Twenty-five minutes later, though, Rebecca's stomach began churning when they passed the Crescent Beach water tower with the cattle gap not far ahead.

"How do I look?" she asked, brushing cone crumbs away from her blouse.

Looking over, Billy said, "Not bad, except maybe for the chocolate ring around your mouth…"

Rebecca immediately reached up and turned the rear view mirror. "Yuk!" She pulled a tissue from her daypack, wet it, and began to wipe. As they approached the cattle gap, Rebecca moved over to the window.

Billy looked at her and smiled. "Don't worry. Piece of cake." Rebecca directed him to the trailer. He parked in front. She watched him for a reaction. Nothing. They got out. They saw Katharine off to the side of the trailer taking laundry off the line. Rebecca was embarrassed because Katharine was stout, shapeless as a fire hydrant, had her old tattered apron tied around her middle, and had her scraggly black hair severely pulled back. She looked like a poor hardworking washerwoman, which, of course, was about what she was. At least hairy Sammy wasn't around, Rebecca thought. Rebecca and Billy walked over.

"Mom, this is Billy."

Katharine noted Billy's combed hair, clean clothes, and, behind him, his shiny new truck. Billy stepped politely forward and stuck out his hand. He was smiling his best smile. Katharine's face was noncommittal.

"Nice to meet you, Ma'am."

"Nice to meet you, too, Billy." Katharine bent over to pick up the blue plastic laundry basket. "Let's go inside and have a glass of iced tea, or something."

"Here, Ma'am, let me take that for you," he said, reaching for the basket.

"Why thank you, Billy." Rebecca smiled. Billy brought up the rear as they entered the trailer.

"Here, Billy, I'll take that. Why don't you sit down over on the couch? Rebecca, there's some sweet tea in the fridge. Why don't you get us all some while I put this in the utility room." Rebecca went to the kitchen while Billy sat. He looked around. He had seen worse, especially in the Old Town Hammock when he was delivering goods to his fence. He smiled at Rebecca when she brought the iced teas over. "Thanks," he said, taking a glass from her. She looked nervous. She left a discreet space between them when she joined him on the couch. Katharine returned and sat in one of the easy chairs.

"So, Rebecca tells me that you would like to give her rides home from school."

"Yes, Ma'am."

"Is that your father's truck?"

"No, Ma'am, it's mine." Katharine digested that as she took a sip of her sweet tea. Billy and Rebecca followed suit.

"What does your father do?"

"Works in the offices of Buckeye, Ma'am."

"Does he approve of your driving all the way out here?"

"Oh yes, Ma'am. He knows that Rebecca is a good friend and I explained how long the bus takes. Begging your pardon, Ma'am, but Dad thought that was ridiculous. And I was also thinking that maybe if Rebecca didn't have to take the bus, it might free up some time to study in the library for mid-term tests. Dad thought that a good idea." Rebecca looked poker faced at Billy: this was news to her.

"I see," Katharine said, obviously impressed. "How long have you had your license?"

"About a year and a half, Ma'am."

"Any accidents or tickets?"

"No, Ma'am."

Katharine noticed Billy's glass was almost empty. "More tea, Billy?"

"Oh, no thank you, Ma'am. But this sure hit the spot."

Katharine turned to Rebecca. "If I give permission, then you'll be home by the usual time?"

"Yes, Mom, I promise," Rebecca said, thinking, Far out! She's going to let me do it!

Katharine looked from one to the other. "I guess it's okay by me, then."

"Thank you, very much Ma'am. And I'll make sure I get her here on time."

Rebecca was all smiles. She stood up. "Mom, I want to show Billy the town. There's time before dinner, isn't there?" Rebecca's obvious happiness softened Katharine. For the first time, she smiled.

"Yes, Rebecca," she said, standing up. "Nice to have met you, Billy."

"You, too."

Katharine watched Billy take his and Rebecca's glass to the kitchen sink. It would never have occurred to Rebecca to take them out, Katharine thought. Nice boy, that Billy; well brought up. Billy said goodbye and thank you, and opened the door for Rebecca. They walked over to his truck and got in.

When they were a block away from the trailer, Rebecca broke into laughter. "Study at the library! Say what!"

"Spur of the moment. Nice touch, though, if I do say so myself. But, what'd I tell you? Can of corn! Easy! Just got to say your please and thank yous. Plus now we get a little extra time to kill with that library thing. Wonder what we can do with so much extra time," he said, taking a hand from the steering wheel and putting it high on her thigh. She let him keep it there as she began to show him the sights.

Rebecca pointed out everything on Main Street first: the library, real estate office, little general store, Tiny and T's bait shrimp and ice facility, the shrimp and crab boats, the Crescent Beach Club, and finally the cul de sac at the end of the road. "People come here from all around to watch sunsets," Rebecca said.

They crossed Humpback Bridge and drove along Rich Man's Row. Rebecca pointed out Snowy Key in the Gulf, a small island that had been named for the blanket of white egrets that used to roost there. Billy, however, wasn't interested in birds or islands. What caught his attention were all the expensive boats parked on trailers underneath the fancy houses lining the beach. Each boat had multiple fishing poles sticking up. Golf carts were also parked underneath the buildings. He saw riding mowers and an open garden shed with weed whackers and a plethora of power tools inside. They drove by the marina where Rebecca pointed out her father lifting a boat up from the canal and taking it with a huge forklift into the boat storage building. Even at a distance, it was easy for Billy to see where Rebecca's fair hair and slight frame came from. She told Billy to drive on by: she didn't want to have to introduce him to her dad—her mother was enough for one day. They continued on past the post office to the condo and ball field. Like Rich Man's Row, Billy noticed that each condo unit had a fancy outboard and golf cart parked underneath. Such a conspicuous display of wealth was mostly foreign to a mill town like Perry.

"Haven't been in Crescent Beach for quite awhile," Billy said. "It's changed. More upscale. Lots of nice boats and fishing gear around here. Must be pretty tight security."

Rebecca laughed. "No such thing as security in Crescent Beach: the nearest policeman is in Perry. About the only time the police are called in is when there are fights at the Crescent Beach Club." Rebecca recalled her dad coming home bloody on more than one occasion back when he was drinking. "But that's pretty rare these days. Besides, there's no real need for police because no one takes stuff around here."

Chapter Seven

Gumshoe? Private eye? Dick? P.I.? What should he label himself, Rusty mused as he headed into Perry for the fourth time this week. Sleuth would be good…but, what a joke! He'd been poking around for a couple of weeks now and nothing. Just like Smathers said, absolutely *nada*! Most of the grocery and convenience stores' employees had different jobs back then. And how many employees were there at Walmart? About impossible to track them all down; and even if he could and by chance they were working there two years ago, how could they possibly remember one face out of thousands! Crystal says I'm absolutely nuts. Captain Smathers doesn't say it, but I know he thinks it. They're both right of course: it's useless. If the F.B.I. couldn't come up with anything, how the heck could he? Especially now, two years after the fact. "I'm just pissing up a rope," he said, out loud.

He turned onto Highway 19 and soon entered the outskirts of Perry. It was late afternoon. He had pretty much finished checking out the daytime emporiums yesterday. Next up was the ton of fast food and hamburger and BBQ joints. No way was he going to do them all in one night; but then again, Rome wasn't built in a day. And when he finished with Perry, he'd branch out. Chances are, if Slater did any shopping for beer or groceries or something, it would have been in Perry. But he could have gotten gas or eaten anywhere. Captain Smathers said Slater lives in Naples. So, if he did do Jimmy, he most likely came up from the south. After Perry, he'd check Cross City,

Old Town, and Fanning Springs. At least those were all hole-in-the-wall towns with just a handful of service stations and restaurants. But how far south should he go? If Slater came up 19, then maybe Chiefland. That would be the cutoff, he thought. But if Slater came up I-75, he would have exited at Gainesville or Ocala which…forget it! They were huge! Okay, easy there. He could at least check the service stations right off the exits. But those stations probably use the pay-outside machines. But Slater wouldn't want to leave a paper trail: he'd pay in cash. Rusty shook his head. It was like looking for the proverbial needle in a haystack.

Rusty started with the Dairy Queen. He courteously waited for a new F-150 to exit before he pulled in. A kid was behind the wheel and he waved a thank you with an ice cream cone in his hand. Rusty waved back. There was a girl sitting almost in his lap. Rusty recognized Clem and Katharine's daughter Rebecca. She saw him at the same time and quickly turned away. Maybe she didn't recognize me, Rusty thought. Amazing how quickly they grow up! Seems like yesterday that she was the darling of Crescent Beach with everybody feeling sorry for her, what with her infected broken arm and leg. She was the princess of the community. And now she's a teenager riding around in her boyfriend's lap.

Rusty parked and walked up to the counter with a large manila envelope full of 8x10's of Slater. He waited until the pimpled young man behind the counter was free. Rusty pulled out the pictures. He also flashed his old trooper badge he had pulled out of a drawer and fastened to the inside of his wallet. Usually that was enough to get people to talk, and he didn't have to lie about still being with the state police. Captain Smathers, of course, would not approve; but what's a guy supposed to do?

"You ever see this guy around?"

"Nope," the kid answered, after taking a look.

"Were you working here two years ago?"

"Nope."

"How about you? Were you working here two years ago?" Rusty asked the other teenager sweeping the floor near the counter.

"No, Sir."

"Do either of you know who was working here then?"

The two young men looked at each other and shrugged. The pimply one said, "Not a clue. You'd have to ask the manager, but he won't be here until around closing at eleven."

"Okay, thanks," Rusty said, as he put the pictures back in the envelope. He returned to the truck. So, what's new, he thought, as he put the truck in gear and headed to Burger King. Close to four hours later, Rusty decided to give it up for the night. He was exhausted. He was also famished. Burger King, McDonald's, three BBQ joints, the Subway in Walmart, two restaurants in the downtown area, an oyster house a mile out of town, a Taco Bell, and a Cracker Barrel had led nowhere. He needed to eat. He liked Mexican and had saved the local Mexican restaurant with a pretty good reputation for last. He pulled up to a large, one-story faux adobe building with garish lime green and pink neon lights. It had a ten-foot smiling pig out front wearing a *sombrero* and *poncho.* Above the pig in big letters read *El Hosico del Chancho* which he had been told meant The Mouth of the Pig. It was late. There were only a few cars in the parking lot that, judging from the dings and dents, probably belonged to the employees. The letters above the pig were still lit up, so hopefully they hadn't stopped serving. He entered the front door.

It could have been a Mexican restaurant anywhere in the world with its arched interior doorways and the whitewashed walls with large cacti and snoozing Mexicans wearing *ponchos* and *sombreros* painted on them. The windows and tops of the walls were trimmed with pink and lime green lines, the same colors as the neon lights out front. Booths lined the walls and lively mariachi music came from overhead speakers. Several Mexicans were seated at the bar area that had strings of green and red pointed plastic banners hanging from the ceiling. Several soccer team photos adorned the wall behind the bar. They were watching a soccer game on TV with the sound off. They all looked over when Rusty entered. A very pretty young Mexican woman whom Rusty guessed was in her early twenties was wiping tables. She came over to Rusty as two of the men got off their barstools and headed to the kitchen.

"Sorry I'm coming in so late. Still serving?" he asked.

"*Si, Señor.*" She gestured around the large room. "Anywhere you like."

Rusty picked out a booth near the kitchen entry. The girl brought him a large plastic menu and a bowl of salsa and chips. "Sometheeng to drink?"

"Negro Modelo with a lime, please."

The waitress went off with a smile. Rusty looked at the extensive and reasonably priced menu. She soon brought a bottle of beer with a wedge of lime sticking up from the mouth. She waited expectantly.

"Number five, and make one of the *enchiladas* chicken, the other beef," Rusty said.

"*Si, Señor,*" she said, and turned on her heels. Rusty watched her walk to the kitchen. Very cute little number all the way around. He pushed the lime into the bottle and took a healthy swig. His whole body said, Aah! He took another swig before attacking the chips and dip. It was good *salsa picante* with plenty of *cilantro*. He looked over to the bar. Three of the

Mexicans were still there in front of the TV. The girl soon joined them, standing at the far end. All were intent on the game. Maybe the Mexican national team was playing a qualifier for the World Cup, Rusty thought. He went back to the chips.

The girl soon brought Rusty his meal as well as fetching him another Negro Modelo. Rusty devoured the *enchiladas, frijoles*, and yellow rice. When his mouth began burning, he soothed it by taking bites of the shredded iceberg lettuce in the center of the plate. By the time he was finished, everything on his plate—the enchiladas, the chips, salsa, and beer—was gone. He pushed his chair back and digested. Excellent, he thought.

"Dessert, *Señor*?" the girl asked, when she began to clear the plates. "A *flan*, maybe?"

"No thanks, but I've got a couple questions I'd like to ask, if that's alright."

"*Si*…" She stood there waiting curiously.

"How long have you worked here?"

She thought about that.

"Almost four years…Mostly," she added.

"Mostly?"

"*Si*. When I had my Angelita, my leetle girl, I took time off. Just over a year."

"When was that?"

"Why do you want to know?"

"I am looking for a man who may have come in here about two years ago. Maybe you were working then and saw him."

"*Señor*, many men come in here. And two years! There ees no way that I…"

Rusty interrupted her. "Please. It's very important. Were you were working here mid-August in 1998?"

"*Si*."

"How did you know that so quickly?"

"Because my Angelita was born August thirty-first that year. I worked up until a week before she was born. I was so *embarasada*, pregnant, that I could hardly walk; but I didn't want to stop because the customers, they felt sorry for me and left very beeg tips."

Jimmy had been murdered on the fourteenth! Rusty felt a tinge of hope: just maybe. Please, Lord. He reached for the manila envelope. "Here are some pictures of the man," he said, pulling out a handful. He spread them around the table. The girl put the plates down and took a look.

She answered immediately. "*Si*, I saw this man. I served heem his dinner. He came in late, like you, *Señor.*"

Rusty was thunderstruck, speechless. It took him a moment to react. The girl began to pick up the plates again. "Wait a minute! Are you absolutely sure? How can you be so sure?"

"Because, look at heem. He ees very handsome and *gringo* with his blond hair. He was tall, too, like you. So he surprised me when he spoke perfect Spaneesh. He also, how do you say *pinchando?* Flirting? *Si,* he was flirting with me even though I was so *embarasada.* He made a joke saying he met me nine months too late. He also left me the biggest teep ever in my whole life. No, I do not forget thees man, *Señor.*"

The girl took the plates away and returned with the bill. "Why are you looking for thees man, *Señor*?"

"Because I believe he killed my best friend," Rusty said, looking at the bills he was peeling out of his wallet. "He has someone vouching for him, saying he was somewhere else down south when you saw him. But now, because of you, things have changed. Now I know for sure he was in this area. Here," he said, putting the wad of bills down on the table with the bill. "Keep the change." The girl stood there silently holding the dishes while she watched Rusty cross the room to the door.

Rusty couldn't believe his luck! He was exuberant, all smiles when he got in behind the wheel. Gotcha, you son-of-a-bitch! he thought. He excitedly pounded the top of the steering wheel with both hands a couple of times before starting the truck. He pulled out of the parking lot and headed home. He would call Smathers in the morning to tell him the good news…No, maybe not yet. Maybe just call him to get the fish camp's owner's name and address down on the Little Manatee; take a little road trip to ask the guy how Slater could possibly be in two places at the same time. Rusty pulled into the combo gas station and convenience store at the turn off to Crescent Beach. He filled up with gas while debating whether or not to buy a roadie. What the heck, he thought, chances are there won't be another soul on the road between here and Crescent Beach, and this calls for a celebration! Maybe he'd stop at Crystal's to tell her before going home. Heck, maybe he'd spend the night at Crystal's! He paid for the gas and a single 16-ounce Bud. Once on the Crescent Beach road, he popped the roadie and took a sip. But why didn't the Feds catch it? They must have canvassed the restaurant. Nodding to himself, he answered his own question: because the Mexican girl wasn't there to question; she was having her baby and taking time off. Smiling, he wondered if his tip at the restaurant had topped Slater's. He had left her a whopper.

Chapter Eight

Virginia was all smiles. What a day! What a glorious day! She was out on the front deck overlooking the Gulf, drinking her morning coffee. Beau was still in bed. Last night had been poker night which meant he had got into the scotch while with the boys. That's fine! He deserves to let loose a little, she thought. Poor man was always working these days. Being mayor was so complicated what with the town growing like it has. There were more and more fires to put out. It seemed like people didn't settle their differences anymore by leaning on the hood of a pickup and rationally discussing and working things out. No, they needed to complain to the town officials about their neighbors, have the town castigate them for some minor nuisance or ordinance infraction. That, or they felt they had to hire lawyers and threaten lawsuits. My how things have changed!

Frowning, she abruptly put her coffee down. Thursday nights were also Beau's reprieve from her, she knew. She'd become such a burden! Beau hardly ever went to his office in City Hall anymore. Rather, he worked at home so he could keep an eye on her to make sure she didn't set the house on fire by leaving a burner on. Or so he could shut the refrigerator door that she'd left wide open. Or make sure that she didn't wander off somewhere from the garden. Oh, why me, Lord? Why me? Why couldn't I take care of Beau, instead? That's the way it should be!

Now don't get down on yourself, Virginia! You know Norm told you that stress can trigger it! And this is a good day! So, stand up and enjoy it while it lasts! Virginia stepped into the bedroom and walked over to Beau's side of the bed. Beau opened his eyes when he felt her sit down close to him. Seeing her smile, he smiled back. Hallelujah, one of the good ones! "Good morning, Sugah," he said.

"Yes," she smiled back, " It is a GOOD morning. Would you like some coffee?"

Beau propped himself up, rubbing his eyes. "Yes, Ma'am, please." Virginia left the room and soon returned with a steaming mug.

"Careful, it's pretty hot," she said, handing it to him. She remained standing. Beau took a cautious sip. "Beau, Skillet and I are going to take a little walk." Beau took another quick sip and leaned over to set his coffee on his bedside table. Virginia stayed his hand, and added, "Alone, Dear. You don't have to chaperone us today. You stay in bed and I'll make you some breakfast when we get back."

Beau looked at her. Her eyes sparkled. She was happy for a change. It definitely was one of her good days. Problem was, neither one of them ever had a clue as to how long it would last. Still, Norm said that exercise was about the best thing you can do to stave off Alzheimer's. "Are you sure, Sugah?"

Virginia laughed. "As sure as I can be… But don't worry; Skillet and I'll just do the usual loop. We should be back within an hour. I'll be fine. And if I'm not, Skillet will drag me home: he'll want his breakfast."

Reluctantly, Beau agreed. He looked at the alarm clock. "Does Skillet know about this? Pretty early for the old man, don't you think, Sugah?" he asked.

Virginia laughed. "He's zonked out alright, but not for long. See you in a bit."

Virginia pulled a leather leash hanging from a coat hook near the front door. She looked over at Skillet. He was indeed zonked, softly snoring, dead to the world. "Anybody want to go for a walk?" She had to say it twice before he opened his eyes. When it registered that Virginia was standing by the front door holding his leash, he stiffly got up from his beanbag. After a long, leisurely stretch with his butt up and his forelegs extended low out front, his tail began to wag and he sashayed up to Virginia in typical Lab fashion.

They followed the beach along Rich Man's Row, heading towards the marina. They didn't dawdle because there was no breeze and the winter no-see-ums were out in full force. When they approached the marina, Skillet began straining at the leash; he wanted to visit Bad Dog who was most likely inside with Louie. She let go of the leash and Skillet trotted straight to the big glass door where he planted himself and barked. Bad Dog soon appeared on the other side. With tails wagging on both sides, Louie opened the door for Bad Dog. Bad Dog streaked out. Louie, surprised to see Virginia by herself, quickly followed.

"Morning, Virginia."

"Louie."

"Beautiful day."

"It is. You're at it early, especially after a poker night. What are you up to?" she asked.

"Books. Numbers and inventory. Never ends."

They heard a forklift approach and watched Clem lower a Carolina Skiff in the water, then jump down to tie it to the dock. Virginia and Louie began to scratch their arms and necks as they watched Clem.

"One of the silent partners is coming over from Gainesville," Louie said. "Clem's getting his boat ready."

"Beau says that the Mercury dealership has really helped. All the partners, including Beau and Norm, are tickled pink with the way things are going with the marina. How's Clem working out?"

"Hasn't missed a day since he started. You'd never know that he was the town drunk for years."

"I'm glad." They were both scratching in earnest now as they watched the dogs take turns marking territory. They were very busy.

"Argh!" Louie said. "No-see-ums are awful! I've got to go back inside."

"And I've got to continue our loop. Library's next... C'mon, Skillet, time to go!" Skillet, with Bad Dog right behind, trotted over. Louie picked up his leash and handed it to Virginia.

"Thanks, Louie."

"Say hi to Linda for me," he answered, opening the door and letting Bad Dog in.

Virginia had founded the library and run it for years. When she had become ill, Louie had taken it over for her. But then when Louie began working at the marina, he didn't have the time. He talked Linda, a recent widow who moved to Crescent Beach from New Hampshire, into taking his place. Many in town considered the library a joke. No one took out books, and only a few took out movies. Lately it was becoming more like a community center with parties for kids celebrating Halloween, Valentine's Day, Easter, Thanksgiving, and Christmas. It also organized and sponsored the Scallop Festival every July, and a lady barber from Perry came once a month to cut hair. People, especially the retired folk, stopped in to hang out and gossip. Some were calling it The Chatterbox Café.

The library was next door to Ralph's real estate office. Virginia looked at her watch. Ralph wouldn't be opening up for at least another couple of hours. Linda must have just arrived because she was fiddling with the coffee maker and the small neon OPEN sign was not lit. The door, however, was unlocked and Virginia and Skillet entered. A little bell tinkled and Linda looked over. Skillet came up to her, tail wagging. She bent down to pet him while smiling at Virginia.

"Haven't seen you two in awhile," Linda said. "If you're after a book, you're the first customer of the day…and of the week…and of the month," she joked.

Virginia laughed. "I should take one out just because; but, I've already got a stack. It takes me forever to finish a book these days." It went unsaid that Virginia could only sporadically comprehend what she was reading. Most days it was impossible with the words dancing all over the page. "No, I came over to offer my help with the Christmas party."

"Why thank you, Virginia. That's sweet."

The two women's accents couldn't possibly be more different: Linda spoke like a New England woodchuck and was parsimonious with her words whereas Virginia spoke like a southern belle with her long, drawn out Charleston accent. It seemed that there wasn't a single syllable word in Virginia's entire vocabulary.

"Do you know what you'll do with the kids yet?" Virginia asked.

"Yup." Linda went to her desk drawer and brought out a notebook. She handed it to Virginia. "All laid out," she said, looking over Virginia's shoulder. "Decorate a tree, Christmas carols, pin the nose on Rudolph, candy canes and stockings, a Santa, the whole nine yards."

"Santa? Who?"

"Louie."

Virginia laughed. "I swear! How did you ever talk him into it? I could never have gotten him to do it in a million years!"

"Woman's guile," Linda said, smiling.

"Just saw him and Bad Dog over at the marina. He said to say 'hi.'"

"Nice man. He makes me laugh. I need that these days," Linda said, matter-of-factly. "He also has been helping with the library's spread sheet, such as it is. I've never seen anybody handle numbers in his head like he can."

"Linda, you're not interested in Louie by any chance?"

Linda turned pink. "No, no. He's just fun to be around." She quickly took back the notebook from Virginia and turned the page. "Here's a list of stuff we need to purchase for the party."

Twenty minutes later, Virginia and Skillet continued their walk. They stopped at the sandy path that led behind the ballfield to the condos. In the other direction was a large pond. Three mergansers flew up and passed low overhead. Skillet watched them intently. A trail bordered half the pond before leading to the edge of a vast area of swampy woods and hardwood hammocks full of snakes, gators, and critters of all sorts. It was part of the Big Bend National Wildlife Area that encompassed more than ninety thousand acres in Taylor and Dixie County. Even the most skilled and experienced hunter could get turned around quickly in the thick tangle of cypress trees, vines, sweet gum, cabbage palms, palmettos, and swamp. Skillet tugged on the leash, and they resumed their walk. They passed the condos and came up to the post office where the postmistress was just unlocking the door. She heard them approach and looked up.

"If you wait a minute or two, Miss Virginia, I'll bring out your mail."

Where else in these busy times would a postal worker do such a thing? Virginia thought. Just like the good old days! Virginia didn't wait long before the postmistress handed her the mail and bid her a good day. The duo was in the homestretch. Virginia tightened her grip on the leash when Skillet's hackles rose a half block later down the street. As much as Bad Dog was Skillet's buddy, the two ratty-looking, chained dogs near the post office were his enemies. Their barking and snarling ritual soon erupted.

"Come on, Skillet! Act your age! You know that you don't want to get in a fight with those flea-bitten mongrels!" Virginia yanked hard on the leash, and Skillet, hackles still up, allowed himself to be pulled along. They turned on to Main Street just as the school bus stopped in front of the real estate office to pick up the kids. Virginia watched them file on. Rebecca was at the end of the line. Virginia didn't remember seeing her for the longest time. My, she thought, Rebecca's blooming into a little beauty! And she's no dummy, either. Virginia recalled how Rebecca had loved to read as a little girl and was one of the few kids who had ever taken a book out. She's got promise, Virginia thought, and her whole life's ahead of her. It must be so exciting for her to be going to high school now. But what exposure, what real possibilities will a provincial high school in Taylor County offer her? And there's certainly no real incentive for higher education in Crescent Beach. It's so limited for a person her age. What a shame that Katharine said no to the Tallahassee family's offer of free room and board so Rebecca could attend school there. I guess Katharine felt it was an offer of charity and wanted no part of it. She's a proud woman. But Tallahassee is a university town with lots going on—good southern culture, the state capitol with museums, theaters, and the like. It would have broadened her horizons. Not many kids go to college from here, but Rebecca just might have. If she attended high school in Tallahassee, it might lead to enrolling in Florida State. But, who knows? Maybe she's happy here. Maybe she just wants to meet a nice guy like Tiny, settle down and have kids. "Not really my business, is it, Skillet?" Skillet looked up at her. "Anybody hungry? Anybody want some breakfast?" Judging by the way Skillet began tugging her home, he understood every word.

Rebecca went to the rear of the bus. It was a rougher ride back there, but then she didn't have to listen to the chatter and antics of all the younger kids up front. There'd be no interruption to wrapping her mind around everything Billy. She loved thinking about him: it was delicious. He dominated her thoughts. He was the best thing that had ever happened to her. She had plenty of friends now because of him. She was the envy of the other freshmen girls. He had taught her how to smoke pot and French kiss and how to better handle her mother. Everything was new and different with him. They had the freedom of his truck. She lived for the afternoons together with him. He made her life exciting. She loved him to death!

But what if he grew tired of her? What would she do? She'd die! She couldn't live without him! Billy was trying to go a little farther each time they made out. So far she hadn't put up much resistance. But, there wasn't much farther to go without doing it. Should she let him? Wouldn't she lose his respect? Was she being too easy? Didn't something like that really matter? Maybe not. Maybe everybody thinks we were already doing it because we've been an item for weeks now. Would he drop her if she wouldn't do it? But what if she let him and she got pregnant? Then what? Would he marry her? No, we're too young. Would I get an abortion? She shuddered. She didn't want to think about it and changed channels.

Wonder what he thought when he saw our rusty trailer? It didn't seem to bother him, but he must have thought it awful. And Mother! An old washerwoman! I'm glad I got Daddy's genes, not hers. At least I hope I never look like her when I get old. But Daddy; Billy still hasn't met him. He hasn't had a drink since my accident; but before, how awful was that! Drunk every night after mullet fishing. If it was bad weather and he didn't go out, he'd drink all day. He'd hide bottles from Mother, stashing them all around the trailer. I found that one in my rubber boot. I thought he was going to kill me when he couldn't find it and I told him I poured it out. And if somebody wanted to come over and play, I always had to make excuses for them to wait outside while I went in to check if the coast was clear—to see whether Daddy was passed out on the living room floor and I'd have to somehow get him into his bedroom. Oh my God, that time Mother sent Uncle Sammy to bring him back from the Crescent Beach Club! Miss Tammy had called to say that he had passed out. It was still daylight when Uncle Sammy put him in a wheelbarrow and brought him back right down Main Street in front of the whole town! Although it had been years ago, Rebecca still flushed with embarrassment at the memory. She switched channels again.

She reached out and felt the shape of the Oxycontin bottle in the small zippered section of her backpack. Wonder what Billy wants to do with it? He said it was going to be a surprise, that it would be way fun. He also said that they'd cut the last class and go over to his house because they needed time before he took her home. What did that mean, 'needed time?' Time for what? Wonder what his house is like? Probably a mansion or something. Rebecca looked herself over. No wiggling into skin tight jeans today; she thought she should put on her best slacks and a nice blouse in case she met his mother. Be neat and clean and clean your room, Billy says, and the adults will be putty and you can get away with murder. These and a thousand other Billy-thoughts occupied her mind during the long bus ride. She paid no attention to the multiple stops and bumps heading into Perry, but when she heard a car honk close by, it brought her out of her reverie. She looked out the window. Whoa, at the highway already! Only a few minutes more before the little kids get let off. That's got to be a record, she thought. She hoped her classes would go just as fast.

But they didn't; her classes dragged on interminably. Finally, the bell at two. Rebecca jammed her grammar book into her pack and joined the chattering throng in the corridor. Billy had laughed when she told him she had never cut a class before and was nervous. She hated when he laughed at her. Feeling a thousand eyes on her back, she peeled away from the rest of the students and headed off towards the parking lot. Billy was already in the truck when she arrived.

"Hey," he said, as she climbed in and scooched over to peck him on the cheek.

"Hey, yourself," she said, rubbing his thigh.

"Higher!"

Blushing, she quickly pulled her hand away. "In your dreams."

Laughing, Billy started the truck. "I keep forgetting you're just a freshman," he teased. Rebecca felt stabbed. She stared straight ahead. Billy laughed again as he pulled out of the parking lot.

It didn't take long before he turned into a paved driveway that led to a large split-level house sitting on an acre of manicured lawn. The driveway was lined with chest-high clipped hedges, and a few, very old live oaks shaded the lawn aesthetically with their thick, horizontal branches. A black man on a riding mower was carefully maneuvering around the beds of azaleas that circled each tree. Billy parked alongside the gardener's old pickup and trailer full of lawn maintenance equipment. A three bay garage was directly ahead. "Here are my digs. Not bad, huh?" Rebecca didn't answer. "You got the pills, right?" Rebecca nodded. "Good, bring'em inside. Come on." Rebecca fished them out of her pack and followed Billy out his side of the truck. She watched the black man for a couple of seconds before following Billy up the stone walkway to the front door. She thought of the thirty-by-hundred foot overgrown mix of St. Augustine grass, weeds, and sandspurs that they called lawn at home. Billy opened the thick oak front door and ushered her in. The hallway was paneled with wide, pecky cypress, the floor was large beige rectangular tiles, and besides coat hooks, there was a large mirror on each wall. Straight ahead, beyond the hall, was a step-down living room with a beige, three-quarters circular couch surrounding a low oval table with a driftwood base and thick glass top. Two large easy chairs complemented the couch. The ceilings were high with large fans strategically placed. To the left, rising up from the far wall was a raised stone fireplace fronted by another couch and pair of easy chairs. The chimney was flanked on either side by a framed watercolor of live oaks draped with Spanish moss. At the other end of the living room was a step-up to a large dining area with the kitchen beyond. An eating counter with what looked like a marble top separated the kitchen from the dining. The living room was very bright due to several large windows, and glass sliding doors led to a good-sized kidney-shaped pool enclosed within a screened-in lanai. It was a sunny day and the pool's ripples shimmered. Billy slid the glass door open.

"My room's there," Billy said, pointing to another sliding glass door beyond the deep end of the pool. "Guestroom's over there at the other end. Both got their own bathroom. Parents' room is upstairs." He bent down and pulled a floating thermometer out of the water. "Heated," he said. "Eighty-two." Rebecca still hadn't said anything. She didn't know what to say. She was blown away by all the wealth. Billy stood and took her hand. He led her to his room. It was very neat. Posters of hip hop, nu metal, and punk rock groups adorned the walls with a very large poster of Michael Jackson front and center. There was also an expensive looking sound system: the speakers alone looked like they cost a fortune. Billy flipped a couple switches and Michael Jackson flooded the room. Billy did a brief boogie before turning down the music. "Okay, Sweet Lips, let's get down to business. Let's have it," he said, reaching out. Rebecca handed him the Oxycontin. She noticed that her hand was sweaty and furtively wiped it on her slacks. She kept looking at the queen size bed. Billy frowned when he saw the size of the bottle. He said, "That's it? This is 'gobs' of it?"

"It's a full bottle," she said, defensively. "Thirty pills."

Billy grunted and set the bottle on his desk. He took out a smooth piece of quarter-inch thick plastic plus an exacto knife and a straw from the top desk drawer. After shaking some tablets onto the plastic, he set to work slicing them up and dividing the fine powder into two piles. When he finished, he handed the straw to Rebecca. She didn't have a clue what to do with it. She also had no idea that Billy had become hard, but he wasn't hard because they were alone in his bedroom. Rather, it was anticipation of the upcoming Oxycontin rush.

"What do I do with this?" she asked.

"Snort one of the piles, for Pete's sake," he said, rolling his eyes.

"I don't know how," she said, in a small voice.

"Here. I'll show you." He took the straw and snorted one of the piles. "See, easy," he said, handing her the straw. She stood there while he adjusted the sound system. A couple minutes later he returned to the desk. He closed his eyes and smiled. "Oh yes, here we go!" Several seconds later his smile broadened and he opened his eyes. "It's coming on now." Rebecca made no move to snort the powder.

"How do you know all this stuff?" she asked.

"Got friends who showed me when I was about your age."

She winced at the age thing again. "What does it do?" she asked, nervously.

"Makes you feel wonderful." She had never seen him smile like that. "Especially the first time. It's…incredible!"

Rebecca continued to hesitate. She didn't feel good about this. It looked like something serious. "I don't know, Billy, it's…"

He didn't let her finish. "That's alright, scaredy-cat. More for me. I'll save it for later," he said, reaching for the straw.

She didn't let him have it. Instead, she quickly leaned over and inhaled the powder. When she finished, she looked up at Billy, wondering what she had just done. He was still smiling, watching her closely. It took several minutes, then, Oh my God, she thought: Billy's right! She did—suddenly she did feel wonderful! Euphoric wasn't in her vocabulary, but that's what she was beginning to feel. Over the top! Better than…never! She gently, carefully put the straw back down on the desk. She smiled at Billy. She looked around the room. She didn't want to sit on the bed, so she sat down on the rug in front of the bed, and leaned against it. She closed her eyes, still smiling. Billy sat down close to her. Flying high, she thought, Billy has made me feel like this. Oh, how wonderful he is! How she loved him!

"Not bad, huh?" he asked.

In response, she leaned over and kissed him lightly on the lips. "Not bad," she said, smiling. She stayed close to him, mouth to mouth, and they began flicking and touching tongues. She leaned back against the bed, eyes closed again. At some point she felt Billy's hands unbuttoning her blouse and undoing her bra for a feel. That's fine, she thought: we've done that plenty of times. He caressed her. It felt good. She almost fell asleep she was so relaxed. Actually, maybe she did fall asleep because when she opened her eyes, her blouse and bra were completely off and Billy was toying with her breasts. She turned her head. The bra and blouse were neatly folded on top of the bed.

She didn't care that her top half was naked. So what? Billy was enjoying himself. He had made her feel good; now it was her turn. She was with her man. He was seriously contemplating one of her breasts as he gently caressed it. She reached out and pulled his head to her for the most delicious French kiss ever. Then, with his head still in her hands, she brought his mouth to her breast. He suckled like a baby. He raised his head to kiss her again. After a long, ardent kiss, they lay back against the edge of the bed again. After awhile, he said, "What do you say we skinny-dip, Sweet Lips?"

Rebecca was so relaxed. She thought about it for a little while. Eventually, she said, "I don't know. I've never done that before." She could hear the guy mowing the lawn somewhere. "What about the yardman?"

Billy laughed softly. Rebecca didn't mind this laugh. It was different. It was like soft and caressing and full of love. "He can't see in. The parents like to swim naked after tipping a few. They've made sure no one can see through those high hedges all around."

Rebecca saw that she had a hand on Billy's thigh. Good place for it. "What if your mother comes home?"

"Nope. Garden Club today. Won't be back 'til late. This is Dad's and my microwave night."

"Hmmm…" was all Rebecca could muster.

Billy jumped up. "Come on," he said, extending a hand, pulling her up. When she stood, she suddenly was shy of her nakedness. She put her hands to cover up. Billy gently pulled them down. "Please, don't. You're so beautiful." He kissed both of her breasts. Rebecca's hands fell to her sides and remained there. Still, she was feeling shy.

"Do you have a towel or a bathrobe or something?" she asked. Billy went in the bathroom and brought her out a large towel.

"Here," he said, smiling at her shyness. "Last one in is a rotten egg." He quickly stripped down, leaving his clothes in a pile, as she stood there watching. She caught a brief glimpse of his erection before he dove into the pool. Rebecca took off her slacks and panties, and draped herself in the towel. Billy was in the shallow end watching her when she came out of his room. The water barely came to his waist. She could see the darkness of his pubic area.

"Turn around, Billy, while I get in." She expected him to laugh, but he didn't.

"Okay," and he turned around. She let go of the towel and eased into the water.

"I'm in." Billy turned around, smiling.

"Meet you half-way, Sweet Lips."

Trying to keep her head dry—how would she explain that to her mother?—she breaststroked up to him. It felt wonderful—

soft and exciting and daring all in one. They met up. The water was up to Billy's chest. He supported her in his arms. She put her arms around his neck. They kissed. She soon wrapped her legs around his waist. She could feel her pubic hair touching his belly. She could also feel the tip of his manhood occasionally touch her from below. They kissed long kisses. She had no idea how long they stayed in the pool, but it was long enough that even at eighty-two degrees, she began to get goose bumps and shiver. He noticed right away. "C'mon, let's get you out of here and dried off."

They made their way hand-in-hand to the shallow end of the pool. With all the touching and kissing, she was past being self-conscious. They continued to hold hands as they walked to his room. Billy picked up the towel and, once in the room, began to rub her all over, stopping every now and then for a kiss. When he was done, she dried him. In the process, she fondled him. When they were both dry, they kissed a long kiss. It seemed the most natural thing in the world when he led her to his bed. Stretched out, touching each other, she asked, "Billy, do you have something so it will be safe?"

Billy squeezed her hand. "No worries, I'll pull out," he lied.

Chapter Nine

Sammy heard the Harley approach. Actually, he had heard Craig start the motorcycle way over at Ralph's by the cattle gap. Ain't as loud as an airboat, he thought, but has a right good rumble to it. Craig pulled up to the dock as Sammy was loading the cooler of beer onto the barge. Mid-tide, mid-afternoon, the boat was riding high without its usual load of clam seed. Craig got off the bike. He was right at six feet tall with a broad, muscular body. He looked like an ex-football player, which he was: he had played guard on the Bolles Military Academy's state high school championship team three years running. But that was close to twenty years ago. He attended the University of Florida after Bolles, but didn't play there because he was too small. Still; Craig swaggered as if he were a Division One all American jock. Riding a Harley fit him like a glove.

"'Preciate yur helpin' me out, Craig," Sammy said, while releasing the stern line from a cleat. "I figgered I better check on them clams after that blow the last couple o' days. Hopin' none o' them decided to skedaddle off somewheres."

"Charley out painting today?" Sammy nodded.

"Yup, finishin' up a picture out in the marsh while the weather's good. Says it's supposed to git nasty agin next week."

Craig untied the bow line when Sammy had the motor running. "Who would have thought that Charley, of all people, would become an artist? And a good one, too," Craig said, flipping the line onto the bow and climbing aboard. Charley had indeed become a good Florida landscape artist. Beau, Ralph, and especially Norm had all bought some of his early work, before his reputation had grown. Now, just from the sales at the big art festival each spring at Cedar Key, Charley could support himself, although it was becoming difficult for him to work up inventory even for Cedar Key because people kept showing up at his doorstep to buy whatever he had. Next March, the week before the festival, he was supposed to have a one-man show at a swank gallery across from the Cedar Key town office. Charley had no idea how he'd be able to do that plus have enough inventory to sell at the show. His success was beginning to create serious stress.

The barge slowly headed out the canal. Sammy popped open a couple of beers and handed one to Craig. It wasn't the best beer drinking weather with the wind coming out of the northwest and a mite nippy. No matter: they touched cans and took a belt. Some white pelicans were in formation, riding the thermals above them when they passed close by Snowy Key.

"You miss that ol' camp o' yurs?" Sammy asked.

"Yeah I do. A lot of history there."

Way back in the 1800's, the small island had been covered by hundreds of roosting egrets giving it the fluffy white texture that led to its first being called Cotton Island. Years later, after the Civil War, a Yankee soldier renamed it Snowy Key. In the 1940's, Craig's grandfather had bought the island for less than a hundred dollars because it stunk so much from the bird excrement. His grandfather had most of the trees cut down, the birds left, and a simple fishing camp was built. Power was eventually run out to the island and the camp was expanded and improved over the years until it evolved into a beautiful four-bedroom cypress lodge set on pilings four feet off the ground, and with a deck and railing all the way around. There had been a long dock and boathouse on the inland side of the island. However, everything had been wiped out by the twelve-foot tidal surge of the

'93 storm. Craig and Ralph had been on the island then and were lucky to have survived. Ralph had been washed away towards shore by a huge wave. Suffering from severe hypothermia, he had been hauled out of the water by Tiny in the nick of time. Craig rode out the storm freezing his butt off in the top of the island's only live oak. He, too, almost succumbed to hypothermia. After a spell for both in the Perry hospital, Craig moved into Ralph's house near the cattle gap. He never rebuilt the camp. Now, seven years later, the island had reverted back to small trees and bush. The only vestige of the camp and docks were some ragged pilings. The live oak that had saved Craig's life was still on the point. Craig brought his hand up and saluted it.

"What's that fer?" Sammy asked.

"That old oak there saved my life. I salute it every time I go by."

They passed the last of the channel markers leading to the Gulf. Without the protection of the land, it became choppy. Sitting on the cheap plastic lawn chairs drinking their beers in silence, the two men hardly felt the chop as the good-sized barge plowed the water. Occasionally over the sound of the big Merc, a panicked cormorant's flapping wings could be heard during its long takeoff as it shied away from the barge.

"Don't know why them birds is always so skittish," Sammy said, watching one of the cormorants and shaking his head. "Gulls, oyster catchers, pelicans, even osprey don't git spooked like them. And sure seems like a lot of bother, takin' as long as it does fer them to git up in the air."

"Maybe it's this boat, Sammy. Must be pretty scary-looking."

"Nah. Don' matter what yur in. They jest spook easy. Another beer?" Sammy asked, flipping his can into a cardboard box.

"Sure."

Sammy handed Craig another beer, then settled back into his chair with one of his own. He pushed the throttle lever forward a couple notches before taking a sip. He tilted his face to the sky: the sun had some nice warmth to it. "You heard anything more about Billy Boy's tennis courts?" he asked Craig.

"Only that Beau said that the petitions won't get much attention this time of year, what with the holidays coming up."

"Thought you was goin' to paste him the other night."

"Would have if the son-of-a-bitch hadn't snuck out. But, probably a good thing. I imagine I'd have a lawsuit on my hands if I had."

Craig took a long swig of beer. Sammy watched him, thinking how surprised he had been when he first learned Craig and Ralph were an item. Sure fooled me, he thought, and everybody else in town. Jest don't understand it none, boys liking boys. Wonder if we'd be friends if I'd known he was queer all along. Maybe, maybe not. Took awhile to git used to Ralph bein' the way he is, but Ralph's Ralph: he was never manly, jest a real nice guy. He'd do anything fer anybody; you couldn't help but like him. Craig's different. He used to bring them stacked blonds from Gainesville out to his camp on Snowy Key. Always ready to drink a beer. Had his airboat just like the crackers. Fished with the guys. A helluva shortstop and can hit the ball a mile. Guess you jest never know.

Sammy cut the throttle as the barge approached his lease. "When I ease up to that PVC pipe, jam in the spud, would'ya, Craig?" Craig did what he was told and the barge held firm. "Great invention, that spud," Sammy added. He put on his mask, laid down on the deck and lowered his head into the water. He surfaced almost immediately. "Was afraid o' that; water got good and stirred up by that blow. Can hardly see my hand in front o' my face." Sammy shed his clothes and began to struggle with the wet suit. "So here's the plan. I gotta git in the water and swim all around the edge o' the clams to see if any tore loose. If'n they're in good shape and I don' have to go feelin' fer any to see where they got at, then shouldn't take much more than an hour or so. If I gotta go searchin', could take awhile as murky as it is."

"What do you want me to do, Sammy?"

"I'm goin' to start this ol' hookah here and git all set. You jest feed out my hose when I ease off, then gather it back in as I come back. Don't worry about the compressor. If it gives any problems, I'll jest surface. It's less than six feet deep; ain't like I'm thirty feet down. First thing, though, is to fill her with gas."

Sammy picked up a two-gallon gas can and filled the Honda to the brim. He checked the oil. Right where it was supposed to be. He loved that old Honda: never gave him any problems. Craig was peeing off the bow. Zipping up, he asked, "What do you do if you got to get rid of some of that beer you drank?"

"Piss into my suit. That water's cold even with the wetsuit. Warms me up a little."

"Remind me to never borrow it."

Sammy climbed down the ladder and slowly eased himself in. "Brrrr!" he said through clenched teeth. He put the mouthpiece in and swam up to the PVC pipe. Grabbing hold, he pulled himself down under. Craig played out hose as the bubbles slowly went off in a straight line. It was indeed murky. Sammy slowly felt his way along. It was pretty good going. The nets were loose in a couple places, but nothing had moved. Still, with loose nets, a black drum could come up and grab the net in its mouth along with a bunch of clams and crunch down, sucking the meat out. In a couple of places, he re-anchored the lead lines that held down the nets. Diving in murky water, working by feel, had taken some getting used to. At first he always felt that there was something behind him, like maybe a bull shark. He'd constantly look back over his shoulder, but the visibility being terrible, he never knew if there was something following him or not. It gave him the creeps. He was scared, too, that by feeling around with his hands, he might find something he didn't want—like a big crab, a catfish, or maybe a stingray or Portuguese man-of-war. But, over time, he relaxed, and although it wasn't his favorite thing to be diving blind in sixty-degree water, it had to be done. At least he was out on the Gulf and his own boss again.

When Sammy came to a corner of the clam bed, he surfaced. He took the mouthpiece out and yelled to Craig, "Looks in pretty good shape. Shouldn't take too long…" Because of the compressor, Craig couldn't hear. He cupped an ear. Sammy gave him the thumbs-up. Craig smiled and, beer in hand, waved back. Sammy went below again. The lease was rectangular and this was the short side. After twenty-minutes and some more staking, he came to the next corner. Although chilled, he was in a good mood. Things were going along swell and he'd soon get out of this freezing water, sit in the sun and crack another beer. Halfway back he peed. The bit of warmth felt good. Ten feet later he came to a section of torn up net, and by feel he determined that at least two bags of clams were missing. Damnation! He hoped they were just a few feet away. He started feeling around. Nothing. He broadened his search. Back and forth he walked his hands over the muddy bottom. This is useless, he thought: damn things could be anywhere! He was about to give up when he reached out and felt a humped-up surface that had to be one of the... Suddenly, ARGHH! He felt a stabbing, burning, searing pain in his right shoulder. The mud became stirred up and he could feel a current of water as whatever he had touched bolted away from him. ARGHH! The pain was unbearable. Stingray! Goddamn huge ray! He launched himself from the bottom. When he broke the surface, he saw that he wasn't that far from the barge. Craig had moved one of the plastic chairs and was sitting in the bow with the hose coiled at his feet. Sammy spit the mouthpiece out and holding the thick hose in his left hand, yelled, "Craig, pull me in! Quick!"

Craig didn't like the pitch in Sammy's voice. He sprang to his feet and started to pull Sammy quickly to the boat. It didn't take long. Sammy began climbing up the ladder using only his left arm; his right hung limply at his side. Craig helped him up. He could see a hole in Sammy's wetsuit and blood was pouring out. Craig's head snapped around, looking for a bull shark's fin. Grimacing and breathing through clenched teeth, Sammy started the motor. He set it at a high idle. "Help me with this damn wetsuit!" Craig helped him peel it down off both shoulders. There was an ugly puncture wound over an inch in diameter.

"Shark?" Craig asked.

"No, Goddamn monster ray! Lord, it hurts," Sammy started to awkwardly climb down the ladder."

"What are you doing! Let's get you to Norm."

"The pain," Sammy gasped. "Got to put hot water on it." He splashed down and pulled himself around to the stern. Holding on to the transom, the water cooling the engine peed out from the lower unit. It was only warm, but soon became hot enough to offer some relief. He looked up at Craig who was bending over the motor, watching. "Hot water is about the only thing that can ease the sting, unless someone pisses on it. Damn barbs are covered with venom." Sammy closed his eyes for a couple of seconds. "Rip up my shirt, will you, and hand me a piece of it. I got to try to stop the bleeding, too." After a fifteen minute hot bath, Sammy climbed back into the boat. Craig pulled up the spud and they headed to Norm's at full throttle. With Sammy at the controls, Craig alternated between applying pressure to the wound and trying to carefully pull out pieces of the ray's broken barbs and tissue. Sammy's shoulder was killing him and it seemed like forever before they could see the town. They finally approached Norm's house and dock on the beach with Sammy pulling back on the throttle. He eased up to the dock.

Norm was sitting in his study, watching Sam's boat return to town. Must be in a hurry, he thought: Sammy's got to be going a good fifteen miles an hour. Never seen him run the aircraft carrier so fast! Norm had sat down to pay bills an hour earlier, but couldn't concentrate. The rough edges between him and Tammy were eating on him. Ever since he had decided to spend New Years in Sarasota, he was in the doghouse. It was like someone had tossed a handful of sand into the gears of his and Tammy's smooth running relationship. Well, he thought, maybe not that smooth for a while now; it seemed like she'd been short with him for some time. The Sarasota thing, though, certainly hadn't helped. But what the heck was he supposed to do? His son was having a serious operation, for Pete's sake! Tammy really wasn't being fair! They could go to Biloxi anytime! Hell, it was only something like seven or eight hours away. She was off the wall, wrong! But, it was really not like her. Sure, they'd had the occasional bumps over the years, but mostly silly stuff they could talk out. But this one she didn't seem to want to talk out; just gave him the cold shoulder. Curt sentences, no smiles, sleeping way over on her side of the bed, no sex since he had decided to go to Sarasota.

Maybe sex had something to do with it. They'd made love fairly regularly over the years; but, really, it wasn't like it was in the beginning, not even close. It was more humdrum these days. But that's understandable, right? They'd been together for years. Sex shouldn't be the most important part of any long term relationship, should it? How about trust, respect, companionship, sharing, just plain old love? He was older than her by more than a few years; maybe that had something to do with it. He was also a little flabby these days whereas she certainly was still a tidy number. The men who came into the Crescent Beach Club for the first time still ogled her and some hit on her. Maybe she was having a mid-life crisis, just like Bev did! She's about the same age Bev was. And he hadn't seen Bev's coming. Didn't have a clue. He had thought everything was hunky-dory. She had her Mercedes convertible, he had his Lyman on the bay. They had their big beautiful house, two bright, healthy sons in college, belonged to the Field Club, and he was a highly respected surgeon. Then, wham! She asks for a divorce out of the blue! Said it was a mid-life crisis. She had a crisis alright, but he didn't find out what it really was until they were officially divorced. Her crisis was that she was married to him and not to the tennis pro she was screwing! Friends had told him, but he hadn't believed them. No way, not his Bev! He was fooled big time! He had thought she just needed time to sort things out, that she would eventually come back to him. So, he rolled over and gave her everything she wanted in the settlement. And now, living here, no longer a big salaried doctor, the alimony was killing him. What a fool he had been!

That's what's so crazy about Tammy getting angry because she thinks Bev wants him back now that the tennis pro is out of the picture. But even if Bev did want him back, Tammy knows that he was done with her forever, forever as in big capital letters! He'd never forgive Bev, not because of the affair, but for all the lies. Deep down, Tammy knows that. So, what the hell is really going on? No way is Tammy screwing around. She's as honest as the day is long; it'd be written all over her face. So there must be something else bothering her, something deeper.

Norm saw Sammy slow down and pull up to his dock. That's a first, he thought. Craig was with him. Norm stood and walked out to the deck. Smiling, he yelled down, "Sammy, to what do I owe this pleasure?" Sammy looked up, and Norm saw the pain in his face. Then noticed the rag tied around his shoulder that was soaked in red. Norm hurried down the steps and met Sammy halfway from the dock.

"Stingray," Sammy said.

"Come on into the clinic and let me take a look."

"Want me to take her around, Sammy?" Craig asked.

"Yeah, that'd be great. I owe you."

Craig waved him off. "No problem. I'll rinse her, and then come back with the Harley."

Craig pushed the barge away from the dock as Sammy and Norm went into the clinic. Sammy sat heavily down on the stainless steel table. Norm cut the rag away with a pair of scissors.

"Must have been good-sized," Norm said, using a cotton ball soaked in antibiotics to clean out the wound.

Wincing, Sammy answered, "Was…"

"First hour the pain is the worst; but it could hurt for up to forty-eight hours. You dizzy or did you vomit or anything?"

"Nope…"

"Good. It's more the poison than the wound that causes the hurt: result of the neurotoxin that coats the barbs on the tail," Norm said, using tweezers for the bits and pieces of barb.

"Yeah, I know…Ouch!"

"Sorry. Just got to try to clean out every little bit. You had a tetanus shot lately?"

"Don' recall when…"

"Better play it safe then. This is a deep puncture. You were lucky, though."

"How so?"

"You were diving when he stuck you?" Sammy nodded. "Horizontal, reaching out?" Sammy nodded again. Norm shook his head, side to side. "Most people just step on them and get a leg wound. Could have gotten you in the neck or chest. Could have killed you, Sammy."

Sammy thought about that. After a moment he shrugged. "Guess it's what they call an 'occupational hazard.'" Norm laughed.

"I guess you could call it that."

They heard the Harley pull up. Craig came into the room. "Got him all fixed up, Doc?"

"Just about." Norm gave Sammy the tetanus shot and bandaged the wound tightly. "No stitches, Sammy. At least for now. If there's anything left in there, your body will push it out. I'll have another look early tomorrow."

"Still hurts pretty good, Norm."

"I'll give you something for that," Norm said, walking to a cabinet. He returned with a little plastic bottle.

"What, aspirin? Ain't you got somethin' a little stronger?"

"Aspirin's the last thing I'd give you: it thins the blood which allows the venom to travel farther in your body. How many beers have you had today?"

"Couple's all."

"Good. This stuff's got a kick to it. Take it easy on the alcohol, okay?" Sammy nodded. "Here, take one now. Might make you feel a little woozy, so don't go running a Skilsaw or anything. Take another if need be. Instructions are on the bottle."

When Norm had finished putting Sammy's arm in a sling, Sammy stood up. "How much do I owe you, Norm?"

"Pills didn't cost me anything. Got a pile of freebie samples from the company rep. Tetanus does cost, though. Just bring a pile of those cherrystone clams to our Christmas Party and we'll call it even?"

Sammy smiled. "Will do."

"C'mon, Sammy, I'll give you a ride," Craig said.

They hopped onto the Harley and rumbled away, crossing Humpback Bridge.

"Drop me off at my sister's, Craig. Gittin' to be 'bout suppertime an' I shor don' feel like cookin'," Sammy said, over the loud rumble of the Harley.

"Come on over to our place and eat with Ralph and me."

"Nah, thanks, but I'll jest grab a bite at Katharine's and hit the hay."

Craig dropped him off. Sammy walked up to his sister's trailer. Clem and Katharine were watching TV when he entered. They looked up.

"What happened to you?" Katharine asked.

"Big ray poked me."

"Ouch," Clem said. "Them suckers pack a punch."

"You kin say that agin," Sammy said, carefully settling into an easy chair. Sammy looked towards the kitchen stove. "Can't say as I feel much like cookin'."

"Macaroni and cheese is what we're havin'," Katharine said.

Sammy looked around. "Where's Rebecca?"

"Sleepin'," Clem said. "Seems like 'bout every afternoon after school she takes herself a nap these days."

"'Bout time I got her up," Katharine said, heaving herself off the couch. "You two set the table."

Katharine roused her daughter. When she returned, the weather was on TV. The forecast was not good.

"Charley said it was gonna git nasty agin," Sammy said. "Good time to work in the nursery, though don' know how much I kin do with this blasted arm. Maybe I kin git Rebecca to help."

"Don't bet on it," Katharine said.

They heard the toilet flush and soon a very sleepy-looking Rebecca came around the corner. Sammy said, "Darlin', you look plumb wore out."

"I am, Uncle Sammy. Don't know why I'm so sleepy these days." Rebecca had been snorting Oxycontin with Billy—she didn't realize that it was the drug's aftereffects that were making her so drowsy.

"How 'bout a big hug fer yur favrite uncle?" Sammy said, standing.

It was then she noticed the sling. "Uncle Sammy, what happened!" Sammy was warmed by her concern. It was the first time in weeks that Rebecca, the apple of his eye, had acknowledged his existence. He told her about the ray.

"Oh, that must hurt awful, Uncle Sammy!"

"Nah, ain't nuthin' but a scratch. And Dr. Norm patched me up good. Gave me a shot and some pills for the pain. Pills seem to me to be workin' purty good, too."

"What kind of pills, Sammy," Katharine asked.

"Dunno. He's got a whole cabinet packed full of 'em. Didn't charge me none 'cuz he says they're free samples," Sammy said, reaching into his pocket. He squinted at the bottle. "Says here, Oxycontin." Rebecca suddenly perked up.

Chapter Ten

Phone in hand, Rusty said, "Thanks, Captain. Yes, Sir. Will do, as soon as I get back…Right. Goodbye." Rusty hung up the phone. He turned to Crystal. "Gave me the guy's name and address of the fish camp." He began searching for pen and paper.

"You didn't tell him about the waitress."

"Nope. Want to see the guy first and try to get a handle on why he lied. If I told the captain about the waitress, he might have said, 'great job, thanks, and now we'll handle it.' I'll let the captain in on everything when I get back."

"It is their job, you know; not yours."

"Yeah, well, they came up with nothing. Now it's my turn."

Shaking her head, Crystal went out to the deck and stood at the railing. Rusty followed her out and put his arms around her waist. There was a slow-moving blanket of fiddler crabs on the muddy bank across the canal, and the marsh had already turned from summer's green to winter's amber. The tide was too low for the egrets to work the marsh, but several were congregated on one of the oyster bars in the Gulf's shallows. The clouds on the horizon looked like a string of gigantic white popcorn against the baby blue sky. "Looks like we might get a thunder-shower," Rusty said, looking over her head. Crystal turned to him.

"Rusty, I don't think it's a great idea, your getting involved like this. Slater's a professional killer. If he finds out…it'll be dangerous."

"No worries. This is all strictly behind the scenes. I don't care if I ever lay eyes on the man. It's just that I want him cooked for what he did to Jimmy. And I'm going to do my best to see that he does."

"When will you be going down?"

"Tomorrow morning. Might stay a couple nights."

"Leaving early?"

"Depends on what time I get out of bed." He lifted her chin up with a finger, and smiled. "I'm hoping it might not be first thing."

"You're just a horny old billy goat, know that?" He shrugged, still smiling. Crystal sighed. "Come on," she said, taking his hand. "Time to help me make dinner."

Rusty didn't leave until late morning. He gassed up at the little convenience store where the Crescent Beach road met U.S. Highway 19, a little south of Perry. Watching the highway traffic as he filled his pickup, he estimated that it was running sixty-forty, cars to trucks. On the mostly empty Crescent Beach road this morning, it had been a hundred percent pickups and logging trucks. He went into the store for a coffee and the Gainesville Sun. No designer coffee here, only Maxwell House. Struggling with the plastic lid, Rusty went to pay the middle-aged lady behind the counter. Bent over a Winn-Dixie flyer, she was surrounded by racks of lottery tickets, tins of chewing tobacco, cartons of cigarettes, and dried out slices of pizza in a large, heated glass cabinet. When she looked up and saw Rusty give up on the lid and throw it in the trash, she smiled, her hard face suddenly breaking into a hundred wrinkles. "Hate them things. Never go on right, and then before you know it you got hot coffee in your lap. That gas yours?" she asked in a deep, raspy voice while ringing up the coffee and paper. A smoker, Rusty thought. As if on cue, she turned away and coughed.

"Yup," he said, handing her two twenties. She gave him change and bent over the flyer again. Rusty returned to the truck. He pulled onto the highway, heading south through long stretches of forest, farm, and ranchland with the occasional billboard advertising an upcoming motel, bail bonds, or Jesus. Simple, one-story houses and trailers were scattered here and there. Rusty noticed that, understandably with the increased traffic, there was a lot more trash along the highway here than the Crescent Beach road. The towns were tiny blips on the radar, short strips with used tire emporiums, auto parts stores, tired-looking grocery stores, and a fast food restaurant or two. Large generic signs with removable vinyl letters announced the hours of worship in a bevy of churches. Rusty counted four traffic lights in Cross City, one in Old Town, zero in Fanning Springs, and a half dozen in Chiefland. By the time he entered Crystal River, close to two hours later, he felt like he had come to the big city.

Although Crystal River had a population of only thirty-five hundred, it felt bigger to Rusty, especially because he passed a Walmart, Publix, and a Home Depot. Last winter he and Norm had come down here on a field trip to see the manatees that annually fled the Gulf's chilly water to pod up in the seventy-two degree Three Sisters Spring. It was a big attraction for the town and had been well worth the drive. The boardwalk brought them up close and personal to a gigantic, blubbery, and gentle mass of over fifty manatees. From their vantage point they could see that many had scars on their backs, the result of careless or clueless boaters. Rusty recalled Norm's immediate anger. Anything that hurt the environment or disturbed wildlife—littering, airboats, fertilizer runoff causing eutrophication, unplanned development, poaching, any kind of pollution, numb noggin boaters—you name it and it upset Norm. Now, as Rusty passed the turnoff for the spring, he wondered if the manatees had returned yet, or was it still warm enough in the Gulf. Maybe after the fish camp, he thought, I can swing by and take a look.

Doing his best to skirt Tampa, Rusty headed east until he could head south again, this time on U.S. 301. Fifteen miles below Tampa, a back road finally brought him to Jack's Fish Camp that turned out to be a throwback to simpler times, an anomaly to the present day congestion of high-rises and the glitz and glamour of the beach areas of south Florida. Although only fours hours south, Tampa, St. Pete, and Clearwater were worlds away from Crescent Beach. However, the one-story, ramshackle weathered cypress bar & restaurant and bait shop were of early fifties' vintage. Several tiny cabins, also built out of cypress and each with a little porch facing the Little Manatee River, had been added in the sixties. The cabins along with a few rusty old pickups with campers in the back provided lodging for any fishermen or tourists who wanted a simple getaway. A rickety dock with several small aluminum boats tied to it, jutted out into the river. A few pickups and cars along with a half dozen Harleys were parked in the crushed shell parking area that was blinding in the afternoon sun. Rusty could hear C&W music clearly as he stepped out of his truck. He entered the bar & restaurant.

When his eyes adjusted from the glare of the parking lot, he could see ponytailed bikers and their babes up at the bar on stools looking his way. Most of the men were attired in the standard motorcycle garb of leather vests or sleeveless denim jackets with motorcycle club patches, bandanas tightly tied off on their heads, blue jeans with chain drive wallets, and Ray-Ban Aviators. Rusty wondered how they could see anything in the dim light with the Ray-Bans, but image was everything. Pitchers of beer lined the bar top. A pair of lean men wearing sweat-stained cowboy hats and shirts with snap buttons were shooting a game of eight ball on the single coin operated pool table. A flabby biker-type with tattoos and a greying ponytail was behind the bar.

"Who do I talk to about renting one of those cabins out front?" Rusty asked.

"You're talking to him," the bartender said.

"You Jack?" The bartender nodded. So, you're the lying sleazebag, Rusty thought. "Got a vacancy?" Some biker snickered. Rusty looked over. He noticed that a couple of peroxided blond biker-babes were standing at the bar looking at him appraisingly. Their skintight slacks hugged their crotch and plump thighs, and their tee-shirts exposed soft middle-aged midriffs. Not very flattering, he thought. He turned back to the bartender who was taking his time to answer.

"How many nights?"

"One, maybe two."

"One night is fifty-five bucks, continental breakfast included. Stay two or more and it's forty-five per. Pain in the ass to change sheets and clean for only one night. Only take cash, unless I know you. I don't know you."

"Fair enough. You rent those boats out front, too?"

"Yep."

Rusty dug out bills and handed them to the man. "So, thirty-five if I stay the second night…" The man nodded. "Once I get my stuff unloaded, I'll come back about a boat."

Not giving Rusty a receipt, the man put the bills in his wallet and reached for a key hanging on a nail driven into a wooden board. The key had a piece of string running through it and a small circle of wood with the number two on it. There were lots of keys on the wooden board and Rusty guessed he'd have few, if any, neighbors tonight. No surprise, being midweek with the snowbird migration a month away.

"Happy hour's four-thirty to six-thirty," the bartender said. "Kitchen's open five-thirty to eight-thirty if you want something to eat tonight."

"Thanks," Rusty said, taking the key. "Back in a bit."

Rusty brought his small leather bag, fishing pole, and tackle box to Cabin Two. It was surprisingly clean and quaint with a queen size bed, a simple table and chair, small fridge, and a colorful scatter rug in front of a rocker. No TV. The four small windows were curtained. The bathroom was tight with sink, stool, and narrow metal shower stall. The cabin was similar to the one he had rented from Tammy when he was undercover years ago. He laid down his stuff and went out to the little porch where there were two more rockers. He sat and looked out at the river. The tea colored water was flowing slowly. On the other side of the river, a pair of anhingas were perched on a big cypress branch, drying their wings. Several water lilies passed by, most likely tangled and torn out by some outboard upriver. A startled kingfisher clicked angrily and left a tree at the river's edge when someone walked out onto the dock. Although he had been sitting for hours during the drive down, it was mesmerizing to look out over the river—timeless. He could easily sit here the rest of the afternoon if he had a six-pack of beer; but instead he stood up abruptly. He wasn't here to relax. He wanted to scope out the place.

Rusty returned to the bar and negotiated for the small outboard. When he had his fishing gear on board, he yanked on the small Evinrude and putted out into the river. He anchored not far off the compound and fished into the evening, changing artificial bait and locale several times, although always within sight of the fish camp. The Little Manatee was known for all kinds of good eating fish—snook, largemouth, bluegills, black crappies, bream, and others. But he was skunked. He didn't even see a gar, nor did he get a single bite, not even a nibble. Jack had said that Slater had fished here for several days in sight of the fish camp except when he was at the Trop watching the Devil Rays. Of course the Mexican waitress disproved that. But even if Slater had fished here, Rusty doubted that Jack could have kept an eye on him. There was only limited vision from behind the bar out to the river: the parking lot, the dock, and maybe a little beyond. Slater's alibi was a real stretch. Jimmy had also been killed on a busy summer weekend when this place must have been bonkers with locals just like Crescent Beach that time of year—no way would Jack pay attention to one guy fishing out here. Slater's alibi just didn't hold water.

But now what? What do I do about Jack? Do I confront him point blank? Try to get more info about Slater out of him? Do I tell Jack he's a sleazebag liar and that perjury in a murder case is serious business? That he'd be an accessory to murder? Try to scare him into admitting he was lying? Do I tell him he'd most likely get immunity if he cooperated with the law? Why did the guy vouch for Slater anyway? Does Slater have something on him? Did Slater threaten him? What's his and Slater's connection? Maybe I should just get out of here without saying anything to the puke. Let the captain and the FBI handle it.

These thoughts and others were running around Rusty's head while he fished and watched the action around the bar. He saw Jack come out once to dump a pile of bottles in a dumpster at the side of the building. He had looked out at Rusty then. What seemed odd, though, was how quickly many of the customers came and went. Many stayed ten minutes or less, hardly enough time to drink a beer, let alone socialize. Mostly they were bikers, although at one point a couple of blacks drove up in a shiny Buick and went inside. Twenty minutes later Jack had personally escorted them back to their car with smiles and high fives all around. One of the black men was carrying an attaché case. Rusty couldn't recall if he had carried one inside. When the sun was low, two rental boats returned to the dock and the fishermen put their gear in pickups and drove off. The sun went down. Rusty looked at his watch. A little past five-thirty. He reeled in, organized his tackle box, and returned the boat. He strolled over to his cabin to take a shower, and a little past seven he sauntered over to the bar & restaurant.

Jack had been replaced behind the bar by an attractive woman with dirty blond hair and a tidy figure who looked to be in her early thirties. An older, plain looking woman waited the tables. Both wore tee-shirts with ***Jack's Fish Camp*** in big black letters on the back. Most everyone was at the bar. Rusty sat at one of the tables and the waitress came over with a menu.

"Something to drink?" she asked, handing him the menu.

Rusty smiled. "Bud, nice and cold." She scurried off. She returned with the bottle of beer, and Rusty ordered the fried clam basket with fries and hushpuppies and a cup of slaw. Not the healthiest, but burgers, hot dogs, gator bites, and fried catfish were the only other choices. He took a long pull of the ice cold beer. Ahh. He read the paper during dinner. After another Bud, he pushed his chair back from the table and looked around. The fish camp was doing a pretty fair business for midweek. Although only two tables were taken, the bar was three-quarters full and there was a foursome playing pool.

He saw the restrooms sign above a narrow hallway and headed that way. As he crossed the eating area, a biker entered the front door. Rusty stopped to let him pass. The biker swaggered towards the narrow hallway ahead of him. Rusty followed. The biker stopped and knocked on a door. Rusty waited for the biker to enter because the hallway was too narrow to get by. The door was opened by a man big enough to play center for the Tampa Bay Bucs. Behind him at a desk in the far end of the room was Jack. There were no windows in the room, only an air conditioner mounted in the wall. The big man eyed Rusty as he closed the door. Rusty heard it lock as he continued to the restroom

Back at the table, Rusty saw the biker come out of the room and leave the bar. It was pretty obvious that something was going on and Rusty had a pretty good idea what. Drugs. Cocaine, most likely. Rusty bought a six-pack from the pretty barkeep to take back to his cabin. He popped open one of the cans and dragged a rocker to the corner of the porch where he could see the parking lot. He turned off the porch light. The next two hours he spent drinking beer and watching clientele come and go, mentally tallying how many only made brief stops. Got to be drugs. What other explanation? And it made sense. Slater was involved with a Colombian cartel that trafficked big time in drugs, especially cocaine. And Jack was buddies with Slater, at least he lied for him. When a recently arrived biker exited the bar, he motioned to his waiting girlfriend to follow him to a picnic table near Rusty's cabin. Even though the table was not in a lit up area, Rusty saw the guy reach in his pocket and carefully lay something down on the table. He bent over whatever it was. In a couple of minutes he pulled out his wallet and handed the woman a bill which she rolled up. They took turns snorting the substance. Rusty had seen enough. He went to bed.

It was close to ten in the morning when Rusty walked across the empty parking lot to the bar & restaurant. A limited continental breakfast was spread out over two tables pulled together. No one was around and he helped himself. He was into his second cup of coffee when he heard a motorcycle pull up, rev once, and stop. He looked out the window. Jack was on a big shiny Harley, putting the kickstand down. Jack pulled out a half-gallon of orange juice and a newspaper from one of the chrome studded leather saddlebags, and entered the building. He nodded to Rusty as he poured orange juice into a pitcher. After throwing the empty carton into the trash, Jack went to the bar and mixed himself a Bloody Mary. He sat behind the bar reading the paper. Rusty could see that it was the St. Pete Times.

Jack looked up from the paper. "You gonna want a boat again?"

"Nope. Ain't no fish."

"You were fishing in the wrong spot. Should have asked me first. Up river a mile where the lilies are, is good for large mouth. Downriver around the pilings of the 301 bridge got a pile of snook."

Rusty took a sip of coffee. "I was told it was good fishing right out front."

Jack laughed. "What dumbass told you that? Wasn't local, that's for sure."

"Guy from Naples told me. Joe Slater."

"You know Joe?" Rusty nodded. "He must have been funning you: Joe don't fish, says it's the most boring thing in the world."

"That a fact? Then why, two years ago, did you tell a couple of law officers that he fished right out front here for a couple of days?"

Silence. Rusty noticed the faded tattoos on Jack's forearms were a matched pair of snakes. Fitting, he thought. He sipped his coffee.

"You a cop?"

"Nope, just a friend-of-a-friend."

"What's your name?"

Rusty smiled. "John Doe."

"I think maybe, friend-of-a-friend, you should mind your own business."

Rusty ignored him. "Got another question for you. How could you be watching Slater out here fishing if a little waitress in Perry says she saw him two hundred miles north of here? Mite peculiar, doncha think, Jack?"

More silence. Jack took a slug of the Bloody Mary. "What's this got to do with you?"

"It's like this, Jack. This friend was my best friend, see? Except he's not on this planet anymore. Couple years ago, thanks to your buddy Joe Slater, his ashes were spread into the Gulf. That bothered me, Jack. It truly did. And I think it's about time ol' Joe Slater paid for his sins."

Rusty finished his coffee, Jack his drink. Jack got up to make another. Stirring the vodka in, he said, "You don't want to be messing around with Joe. He's got connections. Big connections. You'll go getting yourself in deep shit."

Rusty stood up. "Do I look worried, Jack? Because I'm not. Tell you what, I think you should be worried. Plenty. Let's see: perjury, accessory to murder. That's big stuff, Jack. It's not too late to tell the truth. Think about it." Rusty walked to the door and opened it. "I don't need that boat, Jack, because I'm leaving. Have a good day." Fifteen minutes later, Rusty had his gear in the truck. Jack was watching him from the bar. Jack pulled out a pencil and piece of paper and walked to the window. As Rusty backed around, Jack saw the Taylor County license plate. He wrote down the numbers.

Chapter Eleven

"Don't worry, Jack, the waitress will be taken care of. Just stick to your story," Joe Slater said, then, frowning, added, "The only thing I don't understand is why she shows up now after two years."

"Got to have something to do with that friend-of-a-friend."

"Yeah, probably. What's his license plate number?" Slater pulled out a small leather bound notebook and combination gold and burlwood pen. He wrote down the number.

"Joe, that guy said his buddy was offed…" Slater didn't say anything. "I'm taking a big chance here, you realize that, right?"

"What's your point?"

"Bigger risk, bigger money."

"I'll talk to my people. Just hang loose. Got to go." Slater hung up. He looked out from the phone booth. The Tamiami Trail was already clogged and it wasn't even snowbird season. He picked up the phone, thinking that his eating at the Mexican restaurant and talking up that pregnant waitress had been a big mistake. Besides her being real pretty, she had looked like she was going to pop at any second. And most likely she was so poor that she had to work right up to the very end of her pregnancy. Probably unwed, too. He had left her a whopper tip which had been an even bigger mistake: it had made him stand out. A lesson in all this, he thought. He looked at the leather notebook. Taylor County. Same county he had iced the guide and judge. Got to check it out. The *Don* will be able to have the license plate tracked and get me a name and address. I'll see if he wants me to make a little trip north to take care of the friend-of-a-friend. But what a pain in the butt! All this for tipping a damn *peón!* He shook his head as he pulled coins off the stainless steel shelf in the phone booth and dropped them in the slots. He dialed. It rang twice before the *Don* picked up.

"Yeah?"

"Need to see you."

"When?"

"Can be there in two hours."

"I'll be tied up for awhile. Make it five."

"Alright." Slater hung up, pocketed the loose change, and exited the phone booth. He wasn't looking forward to meeting with the *Don* who had already been pissed off when he had shot the judge and brought attention to the cartel. He'll be pissed again, Slater thought; but it can't be helped: the *Don* has to know about that waitress.

The burgundy Porsche was parked nearby. He got in. Slater loved hearing the solid thunk when he closed the car door: nothing compared to German workmanship, he thought. He checked the gas gauge. Plenty. So what should he do with the extra three hours? A few weeks ago he had read in the Naples Daily News about the Miccosukee Resort and Gaming complex that had recently opened at the eastern edge of the Everglades, just outside of Miami. The Tamiami Trail passed right by it—be a good time to check it out. He smiled. Plus it would be a good little warm up for Biloxi. He started the Porsche and pulled out onto the busy highway. The traffic, he knew, would thin out soon.

After passing Collier-Seminole State Park and the turnoff for Marco Island, the landscape became a mix of swamp and saw grass. Gators and turtles were sunning themselves on the banks of the canal that ran along the highway. He passed some blacks fishing with long cane poles. He rarely ran up the Porsche because a deer or a panther could jump out at any moment from the Big Cypress Wildlife Management Area that surrounded him. He was in the middle of nowhere and if he smashed his car, it would be a major hassle. When he occasionally did run it up, the wildlife, even the snowy egrets, pretty much stayed put because the Porsche was gone before they knew it was there. He slowed down for the few Indian run airboat tour companies and the touristy, so-called traditional Seminole villages which weren't more than a scattering of thatched huts. Most people found this area scenic and wild, stopping to view and take pictures of the abundant wildlife. Not Slater: this wasn't his kind of world. Give him a five star hotel with a spa, or a good ski area in the mountains of Colorado, or a casino on a tropical island with fruity rum drinks.

With no cops and long stretches of straight road, it didn't take him long to cross through the Everglades and wildlife refuges. Still a ways from the outskirts of Miami and its accompanying congestion, Slater could make out the Miccosukee resort way off in the distance. Surrounded by all the flat land, the nine story, three-hundred-and-two room resort stood out like an ugly thumb. The newspaper article had been very informative. Hats off to the Miccosukee, Slater thought; they had stood up to the federal government, got themselves declared an independent nation, and are now going to make a fortune from all the gambling money.

He had read that Miccosukee tribe history predated Columbus and, although their language was similar to the Seminoles', the Miccosukee were originally part of the Creek Nation in Georgia. They migrated to Florida where during the Seminole Wars in the 19th century most of them were defeated and marched to reservations in the West. A band of a hundred, though, never surrendered or were captured. They hid out in the hammocks of the Everglades, and it wasn't until 1928 when the Tamiami Trail was constructed that they began to rub shoulders with the white man. To make sure the federal government formally recognized the tribe and they weren't kicked off their lands, Chief Buffalo Tiger led a contingent to Cuba in 1959 to apply for international recognition as a sovereign country within the United States. Fidel Castro granted the recognition which in turn led eventually to the U.S. Secretary of the Interior's official approval of their constitution and the recognition of the Miccosukee Tribe of Indians of Florida.

Slater turned off the Tamiami Trail onto a freshly tarmacked road leading to the casino. Scattered around were modest one-story Indian houses that contrasted sharply with the monstrous resort and where the four hundred Miccosukee resort employees, two-thirds the population of the tribe, lived. Slater parked his car and got out and stretched. He checked his watch. He had made good time; it was only three-thirty. It would be another half hour drive to the *Don's* walled compound, so he had almost two-and-a-half hours to play. He'd definitely have a drink or two to loosen up before seeing the *Don* who was about the only man in the world Slater was afraid of. He reached into the rear of the Porsche and pulled out a light colored linen sport coat. He put it on and began walking to the grand entrance. In front of the main doors, he stopped to admire a fountain with a large statue of a traditionally dressed Indian boy. At the boy's side were a pair of bronze egrets. Slater turned and entered the building.

* * *

About the time Slater entered the casino, Billy was parking his truck near Perry's old pharmacy with a brick façade on Jefferson Street. Rebecca, sitting almost in his lap, asked, "What are we doing here?"

"In case you didn't realize, Sweet Lips, we're out of OC and I don't know about you, but I got a bit of craving. C'mon, we'll go see what my man Virgil has to offer."

Rebecca followed Billy out his door, and they walked a couple of blocks down Jefferson before turning into an alley that ran alongside a boarded up building. In a chair propped against the rear of the building, sat a tall black man with eyes closed and facing the sun. Twenty feet away was a shiny black Chevy Malibu. Rebecca recognized the man as the one who had sold Billy pot in the sawmill parking lot.

The man briefly looked at them before closing his eyes again. Smiling into the sun, he said, "Billy, my man, what's shakin'?"

"How's inventory?"

"Grass?"

"Nope. OC."

The man opened his eyes. "Don't tell me you finally run out of your own shit?" Billy shrugged. The man slowly looked Rebecca up and down. His eyes crawled over her; she began to fidget. "You doin' this cute little number, Billy?"

"Cool it, Virgil. We're here to talk business."

Virgil turned to him. "Ain't got no Oxy. Hard to get these days and costs a lot of bread. Do got me some Fentanyl and Vicodin, and a lot of kickass high grade Horse."

"You know I don't do Horse. How much for the Vics?"

Virgil laughed. "Horse ain't no worse than the other shit. And lots cheaper…Twenty bucks for the Vics."

"You got twenty hits?"

"Can do."

"Same place?"

Virgil nodded. "Give me a half hour."

Virgil headed towards his car. Billy and Rebecca returned to the truck. When Billy turned onto Main Street, Rebecca asked, "What's Horse, Billy?" Billy rolled his eyes. God, she hated that!

"Heroin."

Rebecca's eyes bugged. "Heroin!"

Billy nodded. "Yeah. Lots of names for it—smack, snow, H. A lot of it around these days. The cops and everybody have figured out that people are snorting and smoking OC and other painkillers, so they're cracking down on the doctors and putting more controls on the drugstores. Makes it harder to score. Price has gone way up, which makes heroin seem like a bargain. People are starting to change over."

"You won't ever get me to do that stuff!" She shivered. "Needles! Yuk! And you get hooked, too."

"Maybe, maybe not. And you don't have to shoot it; you can smoke or snort it just like OC. Just takes a little longer to get high if you don't shoot it. Might be less than ten seconds when you mainline, maybe ten or fifteen minutes if you snort it."

"How come you know so much?"

Billy smiled. "Guess I just hang out with the right people."

"You ever try it, Billy?"

Billy didn't answer. Instead he turned on to Highway 98 where it split off to the west from Highway 19 on the north side of town.

"Where are we going?"

"Woods road where Virgil likes to do business. He doesn't carry anything on him or in his car until he's got a sale." They soon passed Deal's Oyster House on the left. The crushed oyster shell parking lot was already full of cars and trucks. It was always full of cars and trucks: best oysters around, fresh from Apalachicola every day. They drove a few more minutes before Billy turned onto a limestone road. There were no houses and the road soon narrowed. The oak tree canopy shaded the road; it was like driving through a tunnel. Billy turned into an old log landing and turned off the car. He pulled his wallet out from under the seat and counted out four hundred dollars. Rebecca watched him and did the math.

"He meant twenty dollars a pill!" Billy nodded. "And OC is even more expensive?" Billy nodded again.

"Going price is fifty. Virgil gives me a discount though, like on the grass. Good customer and all that." Rebecca thought of the thirty pills she and Billy had done. Fifteen hundred dollars worth! She had never even seen fifteen hundred dollars, let alone put half of it up her nose!

"Billy, where do you get all the money for this stuff? Your father give you a huge allowance or something?" The idea of an allowance was foreign to Rebecca. If she got any money from her family, she had to earn it. Like mowing the lawn.

Billy laughed. "Right! My dad's about the biggest skinflint on the planet!"

"Then where?"

Billy looked at her for several seconds. "Can I trust you, Sweet Lips?" She looked at him incredulously. She loved him to death. She had gone all the way with him several times now. She'd die without him. And he asks if he can trust me! Billy smiled and caressed her cheek. "Yeah, guess I can…I steal."

"What!"

"I case out joints, figure people's schedules, then sneak in their houses or garages and take small stuff I can peddle to a guy in Old Town."

"You're kidding," she said, although from the way he said it, she knew it was true. "Billy!"

He shrugged. "If you want to play the game, you got to have the moolah. You just found out how expensive it is." They were both silent for awhile.

"What if you get caught?" Billy shrugged his shoulders again.

"I'm real careful, I mean real careful. But if I were to get pinched, I'd get in trouble and all, but no jail. I'm a minor. Probably get some sort of probation and counseling. Big deal…Besides, most of the time I'm not looking to rip off stuff other than painkillers. I go straight to the medicine cabinets, and if I score, I'm out of there post haste. And it's not like the people can't get a refill or more of it. And for them buying it legal is cheap." Rebecca didn't say anything. She was processing the fact that her boyfriend was a thief. A regular burglar. "I got a couple ideas for some more scores. One, I'm thinking of hanging around the hospital's main entrance and see people limp out, or who have their arm in a cast, or maybe in a wheelchair. I figure they all got pain issues. And if they got pain issues, they'll probably have pain meds. So, I follow them home, figure out their routine, and then sneak in when no one's home and rip off the meds. Cool, huh?"

"I don't know, Billy. That's bad."

"Baby Doll, for weeks now I've split everything with you. Other than the stash you brought, it's all come out of my pocket. Paying twice as much these days because of you. Only way I can afford to is steal."

Rebecca felt a stab of guilt. She had been helping Uncle Sammy in his clam nursery over the past weekend. The tiny clams had to be closely monitored in the elevated tanks called the raceway where water constantly flowed through. The tanks had to be washed out every day, and the clams had to be loaded on to screened trays and shook under running water to dislodge and wash away their own defecation. If they weren't cleaned they could perish from their own filth. Because of the stingray, Sammy couldn't load them on to the screens or shake them with just one arm; so, he had enlisted Rebecca. At one point he had popped one of the Oxycontin pills Norm had given him, and left the plastic bottle on the edge of one of the tanks. Rebecca asked Sammy to get her a drink of water, and when he left for his trailer, she quickly ripped off two of the pills. It was the very first time that she had stolen anything. She didn't split the pills with Billy, either: she did them both later in the weekend.

Billy said, "I've got another scam, too, but I need your help."

"Me! What?"

"That condo in Crescent Beach is ripe for the picking! No security and all those fishing poles, fish finders, power-pole anchors, everything just sticking up out of those boats ready to be snitched. And with those people you can bet it's all top-of-the-line stuff. A slam dunk! But, you only get one shot and it's got to be done fast. I could strip the attached stuff while you snatched the rods and reels. Then I'd take them down to Old Town." Rebecca looked doubtful and a little scared. "Could buy us a lot of good times, Babe..."

They heard the low growl of a powerful engine and looked up. Virgil was coming towards them through the tunnel. Billy turned Rebecca's face back towards his with a single finger. He bussed her lips. "Think about it, Sweet Lips."

Chapter Twelve

The live oaks were spitting acorns that sounded like cap pistols when they hit the metal roofs, and the seagulls were swarming the sage palms and southern red cedars for their berries: both signs that Christmas was just around the corner. Norm was hanging different colored Christmas lights on the deck railing. Tammy was inside cleaning. They were getting ready for their third annual Christmas party which was a big deal and took days of preparation. Basically the whole town was invited and it was one of the few days that Tammy closed the Crescent Beach Club. Since Norm and Beau had decided to discontinue the bar at the marina and instead sell Mercury outboard motors, the Club had been doing a terrific business. True, it was the only show in town now, but Tammy also worked her butt off to make sure the food and service were consistently good, and that the bar was tame enough on most nights for parents to bring their kids. The Christmas party was Tammy's way of thanking the town for its patronage.

Although the party was potluck, Tammy had bought two hams and two turkeys and pounds of sliced roast beef. Crystal would help out by roasting one of the turkeys, and Katharine, Rebecca's mother, would bake one of the hams. Tammy would take care of the other turkey and ham, make two huge glass bowls of fruity punch—one with, and one without alcohol—prepare a few appetizers in case the ones being brought by other people arrived late, lay out festive table cloths and Norm's family silver serving utensils, decorate the interior of the large living room with red ribbons and bows, unwrap and put out all the Christmas-themed paper plates and cups, plus a hundred other things that were on her list. But the first thing that had to be done was a thorough cleaning.

Tammy was vacuuming the messy area around the two birdcages in the living room. Both birds were antsy with the vacuum cleaner so close. Henrietta, a green cockatiel with slicked back yellow head feathers and rouged cheeks was nervously hopping back and forth in one cage, and Huey, a baby-blue parakeet, was in the other. Tammy glanced over to the naked Christmas tree set up in a corner. Trimming the tree the night before the party had become her and Norm's custom. It was fun. First thing they'd string the lights. Then they'd have drinks as they cooked and strung popcorn and cranberries, and draped them over the trees. Many of the ornaments they hung had been gifted to each other over the years. Each conjured a warm memory. Afterwards they would turn out all the lights except for the tree's, and clink glasses in a Christmas toast. Then Norm would put their drinks down on a table. Out of his pocket would come a piece of mistletoe that he would hold over her head and they would kiss. This year, though, Tammy was not looking forward to decorating the tree, and probably Norm wasn't either: there were just too many rough edges between them.

Tammy knew that Norm had no choice but to go to Sarasota, and certainly no choice about the dates. He should be with his son. And she knew she could trust him with his ex. It was his ex that Tammy didn't trust. Although Tammy had never met her, the things she had done to Norm made her a real bitch in Tammy's book. But, if she knew the Sarasota trip wasn't his fault, then why was she holding out, being so cold to him? Was this about something bigger, she asked herself. Had something been triggered? I love Norm. Of course I do, but...okay, then what is it? We've been together eight years. Is it getting stale? Is the magic gone? Our sex, when we have it, is routine, not like before. We hardly ever talk, but that's because we each know what the other is thinking most of the time. Everything is so predictable. There's no excitement. Boring. Same old, like the Club with the same people, same drink orders, same dinner orders, same stories, same drunks, over and over again.

Maybe it's a good thing I'm going to Biloxi without him. See how I feel when we're separated for a week. Ye gads, it's been years since we've been apart more than a day or two. Maybe that's part of the problem. Really! There was just that one trip he took to visit his son for two weeks up in Alaska; other than that, we've been together. It was great after he returned from Alaska. We were all over each other, couldn't get in bed fast enough. We were apart only two weeks, yet we had new stories, both of us, to tell. Maybe it will be like that after Biloxi. Hope so. This is no fun…for either of us. Tammy turned off the vacuum cleaner, and the birds calmed down almost instantly. "All done, guys. You can relax now," Tammy said, as she wrapped the long cord around the vacuum cleaner and took it over to the closet. After she shut the closet door, she looked out towards the Gulf. Norm was on the deck, hands on hips, inspecting the Christmas lights he had turned on. A few were out. He reached into a pocket and pulled out a handful of new ones.

Norm wasn't really concentrating at the task at hand. His head was full of Tammy. He was not looking forward to this evening. He just couldn't fathom her attitude. She was so distant! Spoke only when spoken to. Basically ignored him otherwise. C'mon, like he had a choice about Sarasota! Being irrational wasn't like her. Besides being attractive, she was a no nonsense kind of gal. She had single-handedly built and run the

Crescent Beach Club for so many years. Thanks to Tammy, it had become the lifeblood of the community. The Club was so many things—a meeting place, a family restaurant, the local watering hole, a place to play poker weekly, a place to consummate business deals that varied from setting wholesale prices of crabs to Ralph's selling a three hundred thousand dollar house. The sports fishermen who came to town loved the Club. People could eat a pile of boiled shrimp or crabs, drink a beer, and choose between watching the Braves or Jaguars on TV, or watch Tiny's shrimp boat cruise by as it slowly headed out into the setting sun. They could talk fish. The Club hosted occasional parties and festivities like a Valentine's Day dinner and dance, or the annual scallop shucking contest. It was after the '93 storm when the town had almost been wiped out by a twelve-foot tidal surge that Tammy had opened the Club's doors as a sort of free soup kitchen for residents and workers alike during the cleanup. Tammy was a whirlwind who was respected and loved by most of the town.

Several times he had tried to talk rationally to her about Sarasota; but apparently she couldn't hear anything but her own mind. So, he had given up. Let it work itself out, he told himself. Maybe the weeklong separation would help. Norm frowned. But, maybe not. He just didn't understand it. And he didn't like it. Again he suspected that this was some sort of midlife crisis like Bev. God, he hoped not! It would crush him if she left!

Like it had with Bev. He had met Bev at Duke. They were both excellent tennis players and that's what brought them together. They teamed up for mixed doubles, then began to go out. It became serious and they married two years later when Norm graduated from medical school. They moved to Sarasota, and Norm began practicing medicine at Sarasota Memorial Hospital. They became members of the Field Club, the most prestigious club in town. It was a beautiful complex. The white stucco clubhouse was Spanish-Mediterranean with multiple arches, a *terra cotta* roof, and stone decks that looked out over the bay. It housed two restaurants and several multiple function rooms. Bright fresh flowers were brought in every day and put in large vases throughout. Tropical and semitropical perennials surrounded the clubhouse as well the ones in the circular, open-air courtyard inside the building, just beyond the massive Spanish oak front door and cloakroom. The foundation of the clubhouse was pierced in the center by an arched tunnel leading from the bay to a small lagoon behind the clubhouse with an island in the middle. The smaller boats could go through the tunnel and tie up to the seawall that bordered an Olympic-size swimming pool. The bigger boats were in the marina slips bayside. Beyond the swimming pool were the tennis courts.

They continued to play tennis at the Field Club and were mixed doubles champions several years running. But over the years he began to play less and fish more. Fishing was his release from the tension, hard work, and politics of the hospital, and he much preferred that to running around on a hot tennis court. Bev continued to play at the club and she was so good that everyone wanted to be her partner. Unfortunately for Norm, the tennis pro wanted to be her partner, too, but not in tennis. Those tennis courts, Norm wondered, was that where Bev's midlife crisis had begun? It was certainly where their marriage had ended.

He counted the years he and Tammy had been together. Eight. He had been with Bev for twenty-six if he included dating. He did some more calculations. His stomach tightened when he realized that Tammy was about Bev's age when Bev started playing around. He compressed his lips and shook his head. No way would Tammy ever play around, he thought for about the twentieth time. No way! Or was he just trying to convince himself? What about Bev? He'd thought she'd never play around either. On that cheery note, Norm finished changing the bad bulbs. Tammy had turned off the vacuum cleaner which meant he could bring up the Christmas tree lights and ornaments without getting in her way. They were stored in the clinic's closet below. He went down the stairs, thinking that he'd lay out the strings of lights on the clinic floor and check for bad bulbs there. He was in no hurry to be in the same room with Tammy.

It was almost dark when Norm finished checking and changing bulbs. How many years had he done this? Forever! Gets dark so early these days, he thought as he brought the lights and ornaments up to the living room. He began to string the lights. Tammy was wiping and dusting furniture. Silence except for the birds. Once the lights were strung, he said, "I'd say it's about time to cook the popcorn and have a drink." His voice sounded extra loud to him.

Tammy looked over from dusting. "You have one and do the popcorn. I'll get the cranberries out as soon as I finish dusting."

Norm looked over. Tammy continued to wipe and dust. They *always* had a toddy together in the kitchen while he popped the corn. He shrugged. "Alright." He walked to the bar and poured himself a generous dollop of Jack Daniel's over ice. Halfway through the drink, the corn was popped. Tammy came over to take the cranberries out of the fridge. They strung the berries and popcorn in silence. When two long strings were ready, Norm draped them on the tree. He poured himself another drink. He looked over to Tammy who was opening a box of ornaments. "Make you something?"

"No thanks," she said, without looking up. Norm sighed and took a slug. They began to hang the ornaments. With the tree halfway trimmed, Norm picked up the two tiny pewter clown ornaments—a him and a her—that he and Tammy had found in a Christmas store down in the Keys on a fishing trip. "Remember these?" he asked, smiling.

Tammy looked up. She smiled politely. "Yes, Norm." She went back to hanging ornaments.

Norm looked at her incredulously, saying, "Don't you want to hang yours?"

"Yes, Norm." She took the female clown out of his hand, hung it, and reached for another ornament in the box.

Eyeing her, Norm took a long, slow pull on his Jack Daniel's. He put his glass down on a coaster. "Goddamn it, Tammy! What the hell is wrong with you? What the hell is wrong with us? I've got no bloody choice about Sarasota. I've got to go there for my son."

Tammy shrugged. "I don't want to talk about it right now."

"Then when do you want to talk about it!"

They heard a car door slam. Tammy walked over to the window and looked down. "Crystal," she said, walking over to the kitchen. "Coming for the turkey."

Norm opened the door for Crystal who entered smiling, but after one look at Norm's face, the smile quickly faded. She looked over to Tammy who had pulled the butterball turkey out and put it on the counter. Tammy said, "Thanks, Crystal, for doing this. You and Katharine are lifesavers."

"How about a glass of wine?" Norm asked Crystal. The tension in the room was palpable. Crystal wanted no part of it.

"Thanks, but I've got to run. Rusty's coming over." Picking up the turkey, she asked, "What time do you want this big guy?"

"Six would be great."

"You got it."

"Let me carry it down for you," Norm said.

"No, no. I'm good. Six it is," Crystal said, smiling. "Going to be a blast," she said, over her shoulder and heading out the door. Norm had to pee and headed to the bathroom. Before flushing, he pulled the small piece of mistletoe out of his pocket and tossed it in.

Crystal was just opening the passenger door of her Accord to get the turkey out, when Rusty pulled up in his truck. "Here," he said, hurrying over, "let me help you with that." Crystal smiled her thanks, and together they went up the deck stairs. After putting the turkey away Crystal put her arms around Rusty's neck and gave him a big kiss. "Hmmm, that was nice," he said. She let go of his neck and entered the living room. Rusty followed.

When they sat down on the big couch facing the Gulf, she said, "I'm worried about Tammy and Norm."

"Oh?"

"When I went in to get the turkey, it was awful. They're like two strangers."

"The Sarasota-Biloxi thing?"

"I imagine. I think Tammy's taking it a little too far, though. Norm has to go. He's got no choice."

"A real bummer Norm won't be going to Biloxi. I'll be outnumbered."

"I think you'll be able to handle it," she cooed, and gave him another kiss.

Rusty put his arm around her and pulled her into his shoulder. Crystal put a hand on his thigh. "How did your meeting with Captain Smathers go?"

"He couldn't believe I found that Mexican girl. Although it's still just circumstantial, at least it puts Slater in the right area at the right time and should get the Feds fired up again. Smathers is also going to tell the Feds about the cocaine trafficking at the fish camp. Seeing as Slater and this Jack guy are connected, and Slater's connected to the cartel, there might be something pretty hot there. The Feds are always interested in anything they can get on the cartel in Miami. We also discussed the possibility of sending someone undercover to set up a sting at the fish camp if I'm right about the coke."

"Not you, I hope."

"Nope. I'm a persona non grata at the fish camp now."

"What's next with Slater?"

Rusty shrugged. "Dunno. Smathers thanked me for doing a great job, but says to butt out now; says he and the Feds will take care of it. So, I guess that's it for me."

"Good! Let them do their job. You stay put," she added, patting his thigh. Rusty reached for her hand and intertwined his fingers with her. He looked her in the eye. "Fine by me, as long as they do their job. I want that son-of-a-bitch hung up by his balls."

Chapter Thirteen

Rebecca leaned her bike against the back of the dumpster. The sun was down and it would soon be dark. Even in daylight, however, the bike would be hidden. It couldn't be seen from any direction unless someone went around behind the dumpster; but no one ever did because the dumpsters backed up to the woods. The dump had closed at five and the gate was closed which was unusual. Usually the gate was left open because otherwise if the good ol' boys of Taylor County came after hours, the gate would be lifted off its hinges and cast aside, or piles of trash dumped in front of it. Rules didn't mean much around Crescent Beach.

Rebecca was waiting for Billy. She walked around the gate and hid behind a red cedar off to the side. There was hardly any traffic on the highway at night, but she wasn't taking any chances. She paced around, back and forth. Within five minutes she heard something way off. The whine of the tires made her think it was a fast moving truck. Headlights appeared around Dead Man's Curve about a mile away and Billy's green F-150 soon pulled up to the entrance. Rebecca stepped out from behind the tree and climbed quickly into the cab. Billy's face had a faint green glow from the dash lights. She stayed over by her window.

"All set, Sweet Lips?" he asked, reaching over and patting her on the leg.

"Billy, are you sure about this? I don't like it. Must be another way."

Rebecca didn't see him roll his eyes. She was too busy looking out the rear window for traffic.

"Rebecca, we've gone all through this. If that condo empties out for the big party like you said, it'll be a piece of cake. If it doesn't, then we try some other time."

Rebecca kept looking around. "Okay. Okay. Let's get out of here before someone sees your truck."

"Which way?"

"Back the way you came."

When they had gone a little past Dead Man's Curve, Rebecca said, "Not far now. Limestone road on your right." Billy turned. "Just go up a little, couple hundred feet…There. Turn right into that forest road." Billy's truck rubbed against the fronds of a couple small cabbage palms as he turned in.

"More of a trail, than a road," Billy said, flicking on the high beams. "Not going to do my paint job any good."

"It opens up a little farther in."

"What about turning around?" Billy asked, looking from side to side.

"Near the condo there's a little pond. Hunters go there to still-hunt and drink beer. Plenty of room to turn around."

"Hope they're not out there now."

"In the dark. 'Course not."

Billy laughed. "Rebecca, this is Taylor County. They could be jacking deer or hunting gator by flashlight."

"True."

They came to the little pond. The truck's lights swept over it as Billy turned around. He saw the skeleton of a birddog boat in the middle.

"Pretty big boat for a mud puddle like this," Billy said.

“Ninety-three storm,” Rebecca said. “Was washed all the way up here by the surge. Too badly beaten up to salvage, so it stayed.”

Billy put the truck into park and looked at Rebecca. She couldn’t keep still; her fingers went through her hair, she folded and unfolded her hands, she began to fidget with the window crank.

“Relax, Sweet Lips,” Billy said, turning off the motor. “Here, look what I got for us. A nice fat doobie laced with a little something special.” Billy pulled the joint out of his shirt pocket and lit up. He passed it to Rebecca who took a big hit. She held it in extra long. They smoked the joint in silence. Soon Rebecca began to mellow out and felt energized at the same time.

“Nice. What’s the ‘something special?’”

“Tad of speed.” Rebecca nodded in the dark. She’d been learning a lot about drugs lately, and enjoying most of them. Mushrooms, though, had scared her. They made her feel too weird, see things she didn’t want to see. Billy opened his door. “Come on, times a’wasting. Let’s see what the scene is.”

There was enough of the waxing moon to see without much of a problem, although live oaks, slash pine, and cabbage palms cast somber shadows all around. Billy went to the bed of the truck and pulled back a heavy tarp. He pulled out a carpenter’s tool belt loaded with wrenches, sockets, pliers, vise-grips, screwdrivers: everything a cat burglar might need, and carefully loaded so nothing rattled when he moved around. As they began to walk down the trail, they kept an eye out for any crooked shapes on the ground: the last thing they needed was to get snake bit. They had gone only a little ways before they went around a bend and there, a hundred-and-fifty feet away, was the condo. Two golf carts were just leaving the parking area. Some of the unit windows were lit up, others dark. The floodlights on the balcony walkways, though, were all lit and brighter than the ones down below. Billy and Rebecca moved off to the edge of the trail where Billy looked at his watch. Seven-fifteen. Suddenly he was all business.

"Probably no more than five minutes a trip to move the merchandise. What time did you say the party began?"

"My parents said seven."

"They going, too?"

"Yeah, my mom cooked a ham. They'll stay there late."

Billy nodded as he turned back towards the condo. Another golf cart was being loaded with tin wrapped casseroles and a cooler. It soon sped away.

"People are punctual around here," Billy said.

"Yeah, that's Crescent Beach."

More people left and it became very still. They waited. A barred owl hooted off in the distance. Billy looked at his watch again. It was pushing eight. "Let's give it a couple more minutes," he said. Rebecca took a deep breath. A few minutes later they stepped out of the shadows. "Now be cool, Sweet Lips. Piece of cake, okay?" He handed her a pair of thin latex gloves. "Here, put these on in case they dust afterwards." He smiled. "An ounce of prevention and all that." She took the gloves and with knotted stomach put them on. They walked towards the condo. "You clean out the poles and any loose gear that looks expensive. I'll take care of dismantling stuff. You'll be getting a good workout hustling stuff to the truck. Make it quick, alright?" Rebecca nodded. He squeezed her hand as they stepped onto the slab under the condo. It felt funny with the gloves on. It was still except for the slight buzz coming from one of the stairway lights. Billy climbed into one of the boats and went to work. Rebecca started lifting the rods. By the second boat she had a half dozen in her hands when suddenly she heard a door slam above. Billy heard it too. Heated voices interrupted the night.

"We're almost an hour late now, goddamn it!"

"If you hadn't been doing your frigging jumping jacks, the cake wouldn't have fallen! And no way was I going to have that on Tammy's table with the whole town to look at!"

Rebecca frantically looked around. Billy wasn't in sight: must have ducked down in a boat. She was twenty feet from the stairs. The couple had started out on the top, second story, but were quickly descending. She didn't know what to do; she was frozen in place. The footsteps got louder. Suddenly they stopped. The man said, "Well, you got your new proper cake. I just hope there's some food left by the time we get there."

The woman laughed sarcastically. "Are you kidding! At Tammy's party? There'll be enough to feed an army."

The brief exchange sparked Rebecca. She scurried around one boat and as quietly as she could, shuffled the rods and reels under the next, then followed them, wiggling under until she was between the wheels. She held her breath. The couple came down the stairs. She could see their feet. They turned her way. She almost peed in her pants as she watched the feet pass not six feet away. She heard the woman grunt as she climbed up into the sole remaining golf cart. Rebecca closed her eyes, as if that might help make her invisible. The golf cart scooted away in a hurry. Rebecca waited until the whrrrr of the electric motor faded before she wiggled out from under.

"Holy shit, that was close," Billy whispered, from two boats away. "You okay, Sweet Lips?"

Rebecca didn't answer at first. She caught her breath as she pulled the rods back out. She looked over at Billy. "Yeah, holy shit is right! That was William, the head of the frigging condo association." She began jogging towards the trail with her arms full of poles. Over her shoulder, she said, "Let's get this done and get the hell out of here!"

"Atta girl," Billy said, pulling the socket wrench from his belt and going back to work.

William had the golf cart flat out. "Driving like a speed demon isn't going to help if we end up in the canal," his wife complained, as they careened onto Humpback Bridge and headed towards Rich Man's Row. They went over it so fast that the woman's stomach felt like it did on a roller coaster as a kid. "Damn it, slow down, William!" William didn't slow down until they came to the long line of carts, trucks, cars, and a few bicycles that lined both sides of the street.

"Might as well have walked over. Be just about as far to walk when we find a damn place to park."

"Quit bitching!"

William drove slowly past Norm and Tammy's house which was lit up like Times Square. The deck was absolutely packed. People were eating, drinking, talking, and laughing, which all blended into a steady chorus of seasonal merriment. William looked for a place to park while his wife with the angel food cake on her lap gazed out over the Gulf. The moonlight played on the ripples. So lovely, she thought. Why couldn't they have a view like this instead of the baseball field and swampy wildlife refuge? William drove almost to the marina before he found a space between two cabbage palms. He quickly exited the cart and started walking towards the party.

"William, you could at least carry the chardonnay," his wife said, holding up the bottle. William returned in a huff.

"I don't know why you had to bring that, too. There'll be plenty to drink." His wife struggled out of the cart; she was thirty pounds overweight.

"Because it's polite. I swear, you're the cheapest man I've ever met! Don't worry, you'll drink more than enough of their booze, most likely Norm's Jack Daniel's, to make up for it."

William took the bottle and turned on his heels. His wife dutifully followed. By the time they reached the wide open front door at the top of the stairs, she was wheezing. William impatiently waited for her panting to subside before entering. When she was breathing more or less normally, he said, "Maybe you should do some of those jumping jacks you complain about."

William headed straight for the bar. He put down the bottle of chardonnay and reached for a glass. He took some ice out of a small cooler and then looked around for Norm's Jack Daniel's. His wife made a beeline to the counter with desserts. Norm smiled at her from where he was carving a turkey. "Welcome," he said. "Merry Christmas and ho, ho, ho, and all that." William's wife returned the smile and, holding up her cake, nodded questioningly toward the dessert counter. Norm nodded yes and thanked her, and she went over to place her cake down amidst an impressive array of goodies. Norm turned back to the turkey. After a few minutes, he wiped his hands on a towel, took a quick sip of his JD, and resumed carving. Charley, a few feet away leaning against the stove and drinking a beer, had been watching Norm appreciatively for some time. He pushed himself off the stove and sidled up to Norm.

"Doc, I gotta say, yur somethin' else. I never, an' I mean never, seen anyone carve a bird like that. You do it special!" Norm smiled.

"I was a surgeon for more than twenty-five years, Charley, so I think I should be able to carve a damn turkey."

"Yabut I been whittlin' on hogs and fowl all my life and they shor never turn out lookin' like that." Norm laid a perfect slice of white meat on top of a stack of perfectly sliced white meat. There were no threads or shards of meat sticking out anywhere from the turkey: it was smooth, neat, and clean. “Looks like they been cut by one o’them meet slicers they got at Winn-Dixie.”

Tammy came over to put the pile of sliced turkey on a plate. “Thank you, Honey,” she said, with a polite smile before taking it over to the large dining table.

‘Honey,’ Norm thought. That’s the most cordial she’s been in two weeks! He went back to his slicing. On his way out to the deck, William, drink in one hand and deviled egg in the other, did not greet Sammy, Clem, or Katharine when he passed them at the end of the hors d’oeuvre table. He also avoided Craig and Ralph who were talking with Beau and Virginia. He worked his way through the crowd to the condo people at the far end. Beau saw him over Ralph’s head.

“Looks like your buddy has arrived, Craig,” Beau said. Craig turned. When he saw William, he shrugged.

“I’ll be cordial if he will.” Virginia, having a lucid day, one of several lately, patted Craig’s hand. He smiled at her before turning back to Beau. “What’s the latest on William’s petition to the state?”

“Says Tallahassee told him it’s a go, but with the holiday season and all, nothing will begin happening until well into the new year.”

“So the town may have to vote on it?”

Beau nodded. “And if you take a look around, Craig, it doesn’t bode well for your ball team. With all the condo people now and the new people on this avenue, plus bored wives who don’t fish, I’m pretty sure the majority would go for the tennis courts.” Craig frowned. Ralph put a sympathetic hand on his shoulder. There must be something that he could do, Craig thought, but didn’t have a clue as to what. Louie and Charley joined the foursome. Louie had a spiked punch in hand, Charley and Craig were drinking beer, Beau had his customary scotch, and Virginia a martini. Other than the ultra-conservative church people, none of whom were present, Ralph was one of the few teetotalers in town. He sipped from a glass of the spikeless punch.

"This party gets a little bigger each year," Louie said, between sips.

"Like the town," Beau answered.

Louie nodded. "Good for the marina…and Tammy's."

"That woman is a whirlwind," Virginia said. "How she keeps that restaurant going year in and year out, basically by herself, is nothing short of amazing. I wonder how much longer she can keep it up?"

"She don' appear ta be slowin' down much a'tall, if'n you ask me," Charley said. "Jest look at her."

They all turned towards the living room where Tammy, laughing, smiling, and chatting animatedly, was passing around the last of the hors d'oeuvres. Eventually she came up to them. "Lady, Gents?" she asked, proffering the last of the deviled eggs and little crab canapés. "Charley, I want you to know that your smoked mullet dip and Tiny's jumbo shrimp were the first things to run out. You should start a little mullet dip business."

"No, Ma'am; too much work. I'll stick ta paintin', thank ya kindly. But I will try one o' them little fellers," he said, reaching for a canapé.

"Me, too," Virginia said.

"It's good to see you here, Virginia," Tammy said.

Virginia smiled and curtsied. In her best Charleston drawl, she said, "The pleasure is all mine, Ma'am."

Tammy moved on, making the rounds. In the living room, Sammy looked at his watch. He turned to Katharine and Clem who were wolfing cheese and crackers and drinking the booze free punch. Clem had been sober for almost two years now. He had made a vow to God that if Rebecca recovered from her awful accident, he'd never have another drink. Katharine was proud of him. As for Clem, though, he had never lost the craving. "'Bout time ta pull 'em," Sammy said. Sammy walked past Norm to the stove where a huge pot was boiling away. Norm looked up.

"Did you put something in there besides seawater, Sammy? Smells kind of sweet."

"Beer," was the answer. Sammy took a wire mesh scoop and stirred the froth out of the way. The shells had all opened. He pulled the pot off to the side and began to drain the boiling water. "All done."

Norm had the turkey down to pure bone and cartilage. He picked up his greasy towel and wiped his hands. "You need some help moving that pot. That shoulder okay?"

"Don' bother none. I got it."

"Then I'll melt some butter. But before you take all those over to the table, how about putting a pile on a plate for me. I've been eyeing those clams ever since you got here."

"You got it, Doc."

Sammy's clams were a big hit; sweet cherrystones fresh from the Gulf that afternoon. There was the constant plink, plink, plink of the discarded shells into the waste can as people crowded around the table and devoured them. Sammy beamed. He had standing in the community, the entire community, for the first time in his life. He relished it. He stood there quietly while Charley, in between clams, explained in detail to all who would listen the intricacies of clamming. He also made it very clear how difficult the business was and how hard Sammy worked. Katharine stood proudly at her brother's side.

After a couple hours, most of the working folk began to leave. The temperature had dropped and everyone had come in from the deck, forming two groups in the living room. William, well into Norm's booze, was holding court with the condo people and several neighbors from Rich Man's Row. Charley and Louie had somehow gotten into another pissing contest and were surrounded by the poker regulars at the big dining room table.

"You bet yur boots I could come up with somethin' at the Scallop Festival that'd outdraw anything you thought o', Louie!"

"In a pig's ass!" Louie exclaimed, then, "Whoops! Excuse my French, Linda."

Linda smiled. "No worries. Have at it you two. Two more vendor booths just means more money for the library!" Louie turned back to Charley. Both had drunk their fair share of alcohol.

"I got an idea from the Steinhatchee Fiddler Crab Festival last year," Louie said.

"What?" Charley asked.

Louie looked smug. "I'm not telling you. All I know is that you couldn't come up with something that'd gross more money in a million years....unless you sold one of your paintings," he added quickly.

"Don't you have to tend the marina, Louie?" Norm asked. "That's about the busiest day of the year."

"But it's only putting boats in and out. Clem does all that. And last year Rusty helped out..." Louie looked questioningly at Rusty.

"Yeah, no problem," Rusty said. Crystal was sitting next to Rusty. Virginia, working on her third martini, was next to Crystal. Beau stood behind Virginia's chair. He had both hands on her shoulders.

"Louie, yur pretty cocksure, now ain'tcha?" Charley said. Louie shrugged. "Well, Mr. Smug, I betcha twenty bucks I kin come up wi' something better than you."

"You two! Don't you ever give it a rest?" Beau asked. "Sounds like the Tortoise and Hare again."

"And we know who won that, " Louie added. Charley glared at him.

Charley stuck his hand out to Louie. "Twenty bucks says I make more money at my booth than you, an' it won' got nuthin' to do with my paintings."

Louie immediately shook Charley's hand. "It's a bet. And it will give me the greatest of pleasures, Charley, to beat you…AGAIN!"

Craig and Ralph were at the table, too. Ralph knew Craig was depressed by Beau's assessment of the softball team's chances to keep the field intact. Craig's silence was loud. Once Charley's and Louie's bet was consummated, people began to notice. Charley asked Craig what was up. Craig told him what Beau had said.

"That shor ain't right, Beau," Sammy said. "It's like takin' away a tradition, or piece o' the town, or somethin'."

"All I said is that it's a possibility, Sammy. But if it comes to a town vote—which I'm sure William will try if the state comes through—then it doesn't look good."

"Looks like you're caught between a verytable rock and a hard place, Craig," Charley said.

"Veritable, Charley," Norm interjected.

"Whatever. Jest don' look none too good is what I'ma sayin'."

Silence. Virginia was looking thoughtfully at the martini glass she was slowly spinning in her hand. She put the glass down. "Craig, why not do what Charley and Louie have done?" Craig looked over at her.

"Meaning what, Virginia?"

"Beau told me that at the town meeting William called your team a ragamuffin or ragtag or something. William said that he and his cohorts could form a team and, I quote my husband, 'play better with one arm tied behind our backs.' Why not challenge him to put a team together and y'all play a game for all the marbles. If you win, you keep the entire field and then maybe they'd pursue buying those wetlands behind the ballfield for tennis courts there. If you lose, well you'd probably lose to a vote anyway."

Craig considered it. Maybe it was a long shot, he thought, but it might at least give them a chance. Of course William would have to agree to it, and why would he if the state said his petition was a slam dunk? His ego, that's why. He'd bet anything that William wouldn't want to lose face by declining the challenge. Beau beamed down at Virginia. He thought it was a good idea and was proud of her. He started to rub her shoulders. She reached up and put a hand on one of his.

"Maybe, Virginia! But, the game would be on only if the state okays their petition," Craig said.

"Of course," Virginia conceded.

Craig thought about it some more. His face began to light up. "Their players would have to be residents to qualify to play. No ringers brought in from Gainesville or somewhere out of town."

"I'd bet there ain't enough of them is residents to field a team," Sammy put in.

"Then, taxpayers! To play you have to be a Crescent Beach taxpayer."

"Fast-pitch or slow-pitch?" Rusty asked.

Craig didn't hesitate. Players like Tiny, Sammy, and Rusty could wail on a slow-pitch ball; but with velocity—fat chance. "Slow-pitch!"

Beau asked, "Aren't you forgetting something, Craig?" Beau nodded towards William and the condo crowd. "Might want to see if they'll accept before you get too excited." Craig looked over. William was gesticulating wildly, telling some story. People laughed. Craig stood. He looked around the table. "Anyone want to come with me?"

Ralph patted his arm a couple times. "Go get 'em, Coach," he said. All eyes were on Craig as he walked over. Craig began to talk to William. William said something to the others. Lots of discussion. Laughter from William and a few of the others. A shake of the head by Craig. More laughter. More discussion. Finally, after several more minutes, William and Craig shook hands. Craig hurried back to the table, a big smile on his face.

"They went for it," he said. "They thought it a joke at first, and then, when they saw I was serious, didn't want to do it until William started egging them on. William's cocked. Said when they whupped us fair and square, then there couldn't be any hard feelings about the tennis courts. I agreed." Craig's face suddenly fell. "Unfortunately, though, I had to agree to something else."

"What?" Tiny asked.

"The pitching…Fastpitch."

"Oh, Lord," Tiny muttered.

"That means stealing, too, right?" Sammy asked.

"Yeah," Craig glumly answered. "And we're not exactly built for speed…except maybe Ralph here." He looked down at his hands. Suddenly he perked up. "Practice, that's all. We just got to practice hitting fast pitching."

"Who'll pitch?" Rusty asked.

"No clue. We'll have to figure that out," Craig answered.

"When's the game?" Charley asked.

"It's only if they get the grant, mind you," Craig said, "but tentatively we'll play the same day of the first major league spring training game. End of February or early March sometime. Can I get anyone a beer?" Charley and Tiny raised their hands. Craig bounded up out of the chair and headed for a cooler out on the deck, his mind already forming possible batting orders and figuring out positions. Two beers and an hour later, Craig was still thinking softball while Ralph drove them back to their house. There was no windshield on the golf cart and the cold wind was sobering, although Craig was far from sober. He took a sip from his road beer, muttering, "Sammy at third. His shoulder will be fine and for a big guy he's got great hands…" Ralph began to turn onto their street when he suddenly stopped the cart. Craig lurched forward. "What the hell?" Something had caught Ralph's eye approaching the cattle gap. It was Rebecca peddling in the dark. Her eyes were big. She looked like a deer caught in headlights.

"Rebecca! What are you doing riding a bike with no lights in the dark?" Ralph asked. Craig was trying to focus on Rebecca. He saw two of her. She stopped her bike.

"Couldn't sleep, Mr. Ralph." She looked away for a brief second, then back to Ralph. " I'm worried about an exam I have tomorrow and thought maybe a little exercise might help."

"Well you be careful. Tammy's party just let out and a lot of people have been drinking."

"Yes, sir, Mr. Ralph. Goodnight. And goodnight, Mr. Craig." Craig smiled to a spot between the two Rebeccas. She pedaled off; the cool air felt good against her armpits that were suddenly as moist as when she was hiding under the boat trailer. Ralph turned into his driveway. He collected the hors d'oeuvre dishes he had brought to the party, and followed his swaying partner up the stairs. Craig went straight to the bathroom where he left his clothes in a pile and jumped into the shower. Ralph began to do the dishes, thinking how odd it was for Rebecca to have been out on her bike like that. He smiled when he heard Craig singing in the shower. He hoped Craig wouldn't use all the hot water. Finally, the shower stopped and Craig emerged bare ass. He made a beeline down the hallway to the bedroom. When Ralph went in to the bedroom for a pair of pajama bottoms, Craig was sitting up in his bed with his arms folded behind his head. He had sobered considerably. For appearance sake, they had twin beds separated by a small table.

"Left you some hot water," Craig said.

"Hope so," Ralph answered.

"Don't take too long." Ralph looked over. Craig was smiling *that* smile.

Ralph took a short shower. He cinched up his PJ bottoms and combed his hair before returning to the bedroom. Looking in the mirror, he saw that his chest hair was matted. He ruffled the area. When he opened the bedroom door, Craig had the sheet pulled over his head. "Oh my God!" Craig exclaimed. Feigning fear, he yanked his head out from under the sheet. Ralph played along.

"What is it!"

"You won't believe it! A snake! A huge snake! A regular Burmese python! Must have come up from the Everglades!"

"That's pretty scary, Craig," Ralph said, switching off the overhead light. "You should do something about it."

"You gotta help me get rid of it Ralph!"

"That a fact?" Ralph's body was full of anticipation. He started to get a big snake of his own. He walked over to stand before Craig. Craig smiled.

"Looks like maybe you got the same problem, Big Fella," Craig said, reaching out to tug on the pajama bottoms' drawstring. With his other hand, Craig turned out the bedside light. Ralph knew Craig was still drunk and it would be a long night. But that was okay with him…

* * *

The next morning the sheriff stood leaning against the squad car parked in front of the condo. His arms were folded across his hard, round gut as he listened patiently to William whose face was bright red and spitting mad.

"We pay more goddamn taxes than anyone else in Taylor County and what do we get for it? Nothing! Not a goddamn thing! We got a half assed volunteer fire department because the county won't provide one. If we've got a problem that needs the police, we got to call and we might get someone to show up in an hour or two…if we're goddamn lucky!"

"Cussin' won't help nuthin', Mr. Smith," the sheriff said, calmly. "Why don't you take a deep breath now, and just tell me what happened."

It wasn't easy for William to calm down. The splitting headache from his hangover didn't help. Other condo owners were milling around, checking their boats and trailers. It hadn't taken long for word to get around town about the theft. It didn't take long either for the sheriff's car to be spotted in town. Beau and Skillet were on the way to the condo in their golf cart. Behind them came Ralph in his.

"Someone, Sheriff, ripped off the entire condo last night when we were all at a party," William continued, in a more civilized tone.

"Entire condo? Every unit?"

"No, no. Just down below. Fishing gear. Very expensive fishing gear, I might add. They hit every boat."

The sheriff looked at the scattering of expensive boats. He pushed himself up from the cruiser. "Let's take a look." William led the sheriff to his boat first.

"Six poles, all graphite! Mitchell reels! Cost a fortune!"

"You have insurance?"

"Yeah, but don't know if they'll be covered. It's not as if they were locked up."

"Bingo," the sheriff said. "Couldn't have been easier pickings."

"But we've never had any trouble like this before."

The sheriff shrugged. He continued to walk around, noting where pole anchors and navigational gear had been disassembled. "Didn't take any of the batteries. Wonder why?" He turned to William. "Get the others together, would you Mr. Smith?" William gathered the other condo owners as Beau pulled up. Beau told Skillet to stay, and walked up to the sheriff.

"Sheriff," Beau said, shaking the sheriff's hand. "Thanks for coming right out."

William snickered as he pointedly looked at his watch. "Yeah, two hours and change. Not bad," he muttered.

Beau and the sheriff ignored him. The others had gathered around. Ralph got out of his cart and walked over. The sheriff cleared his throat. In his thick drawl he asked, "Okay. So anyone see anyone around? Not just last night, but maybe during the week…maybe casing the place. I think it's pretty obvious that whoever did it knew what was happening in town, that y'all were at Miss Tammy's." The condo owners looked at each other. Lots of shrugs, no one had seen anyone out of the ordinary.

Beau asked Ralph, "What about you, Ralph? Anyone coming here would have to drive right by your place."

Ralph shook his head. "Nobody before or after the party, anyway." Rusty pulled up in his pickup. Charley was with him. Whole bloody town will be here before too long, Beau thought. The sheriff walked over to his car and pulled a large yellow legal pad out of the front seat. He returned to the small crowd of condo owners and said, "Why don't y'all get together and make a list of what's missing. Put an approximate value on it, too." He handed the pad to William who took it over to his boat and began writing. When he was finished he passed it on to another.

"Mostly light stuff," the sheriff said. "Not one battery missing. Marine batteries are damn expensive—usually disappear with everything else in a case like this. Snip the cables and gone." Rusty looked across to the woods road. He walked over. A faint path had been worn in one side of the sooty soil. But there were no footprints, it looked like it had been brushed with a broom. Whoever it was had been careful. The trail disappeared around a bend. He called over to the sheriff. "You might want to take a look here, Sheriff. Might be why no batteries were taken." The Sheriff, Beau, Charley, and Ralph ambled over. William soon followed. "I'm thinking that maybe they carried the stuff this way," Rusty said, pointing to the worn path. If they had a truck parked further out, it would be a long way to carry batteries. Those things weigh."

They followed the trail. Sure enough, not far past the bend they came to a small pond. Beer cans were scattered around. "Hunters come here to hang out," Charley said. Fresh tire tracks showed where someone had turned around.

The sheriff bent down. There was a pretty good impression in the soft area at the edge of the pond. "Bald in the middle, plenty of tread on the sides. Typical wear from Florida's straight roads. 'Bout like ninety percent of Taylor county truck tires."

A recently snapped red cedar branch lay off to the side. Rusty picked it up by the needles. "I think this may be what they used to cover their tracks. Might get some prints from it."

The sheriff stood. He took the branch. "Maybe," he said. "Boats should be dusted, too. I'll get in touch with the Cross City Barracks and get someone down. I've got a kit in the squad car, but they'll do a better job than me." They headed back.

"And how long will that take?" William asked, sarcastically.

The sheriff ignored the sarcasm. "Few days, most likely."

William rolled his eyes and shook his head. "And all our stuff will be in pawn shops all over the state by that time."

"I can do the dusting if you like," Rusty said, as they stepped onto the slab under the condo.

The sheriff stopped. "And just who are you?"

"Name's Rusty McMillan. Was a trooper for more than twenty years. Worked at one point with Captain Smathers; he can vouch for me."

"Alright, Rusty." The sheriff went again to his car and pulled out a fingerprint kit. He handed it to Rusty. "Be my guest."

"Now we're getting somewhere," William said. "Finally!"

"William, you shor are wearin' yur butt on yur shoulder today," Charley said. The sheriff laughed.

One of the condo owners brought the legal pad up to the sheriff. The list covered two and a half pages. The sheriff read down through them, then the value totaled. He whistled. "Man, that sure is a chunk of change! One thing's for damn sure: someone made out like a bandit."

Chapter Fourteen

It was just past sunset when the shiny black Ford crew cab with tinted windows, gaudy spinners, and a fiberglass cap in the rear pulled up to the trailer that was lit up by multiple strings of indoor-outdoor Christmas lights. The license plate said Miami-Dade. Two Latinos were in front. Stocky with a butch cut, acne scarred, the driver looked like why mothers lock their doors at night. The man on the passenger side was thin, Latin good looking with long, jet-black wavy hair. He also had good teeth that picked up the light from the dash as he smiled and shook his head. "Why is eet, *amigo,* that the poorest people always put up the most Christmas lights, eh? Eet must cost them a preety penny, no?" He turned and reached back behind the seats for a large manila envelope. His expression hardened as he turned back to the driver. "*Nos vamos, muchacho.*"

They exited the truck and walked towards the trailer. To their left was a lit-up Santa in a sleigh pulled by reindeer. To their right was a large Frosty the Snowman. The eaves of the house were draped in clear, white-lighted icicles, and mixed color bulbs blinked around all the windows and doors. Up close they could see the lime green walls of the trailer could stand a good cleaning. *Chicanos*, the slender Latino thought, shaking his head. He rapped on the door. Almost immediately they heard tottering footsteps through the thin walls, then some fumbling around the doorknob. "*Angelita, mi amor! Espera...*" Hurried footsteps, heavier. The door opened. Holding the hand of a very cute two-year-old girl in a party dress, her other hand on the door knob, the pretty waitress from the Perry Mexican restaurant looked at the two men in surprise. “Yes?”

The slender Latino smiled his best smile. “Maria Elena?”

“Yes,” the woman said, again. She looked from one to the other. She thought the stocky guy looked Mexican. She also thought he looked scary. She looked back to the slender guy. He held up a manila envelope.

“I have a leetle present for you. Some wonderful pictures of your daughter. May we come in?” Maria Elena hesitated. She and her daughter lived alone. “We can look at them out here if you want, but the light…” he glanced around, red and blue and green reflected off both the men’s faces, “is not so good.” Being all alone except for her child, Maria Elena couldn’t stop them from entering anyway. The door scraped the floor as she pulled it all the way open and stood off to the side.

“*Pasen adelante*,” she said. The two men entered and looked around as she shut the door. No surprise. Heavy scent of cilantro, a big string of red peppers hanging in the immaculate kitchen, wicker baskets holding avocados, onions, potatoes, big crucifix on the wall, plastic red and green soccer pennants tacked to the cheap paneling, big box TV in front of two very used-looking easy chairs and a couch. By the kitchen sink was a huge demijohn of water encased in a tilting contraption so that smaller bottles could be filled. When the slender Latino saw the demijohn of water, he automatically looked to the kitchen sink. The porcelain was heavily rust stained around the spigot and drain. Dishes were draining in a rack off to the side. The woman motioned to the couch. There was a beaten up pine coffee table in front. The two men walked around it and sat down. Maria Elena sat in one of the easy chairs. Her daughter climbed up into her lap, shyly looking at the two men with eyes big and liquid dark.

"I see you are a *futbol* fan. The *Seleción*, no?" the slender man asked.

"*Si*. My husband ees a big fan. He should be home soon," she lied.

The slender man smiled. "Ees that so, Maria Elena? And me, I thought he was still in Juarez. It ees tough to sneak back in these days, no? Costs *mucho dinero*." Maria Elena didn't say anything. She suddenly became busy fiddling with the bows in her child's hair. "But, I want to show you my pictures. I took them myself." He opened the folder and carefully selected four glossy, 8x10 black and white photos. He passed them over. Immediately Maria Elena smiled.

"Oh, *mi jita*, loook! Here we are at the *iglesia! Que bonito*!" It was taken in front of the steps of the Perry Catholic church. Maria Elena and Angelita were hand in hand, each dressed in their finest. There were others in the pictures, but only Maria Elena and her daughter were sharp. It had been taken with a telephoto lens. Maria Elena quickly flipped to the next picture. It was of Angelita looking up and waving while holding the hand of her daycare hostess.

Maria Elena showed it to her daughter who, giggling, poked at her image, saying, "Angelita! Angelita!" Maria Elena flipped to the next. It was at the downtown playground. She was carefully pushing Angelita in a swing. The final picture was from the same park. Maria Elena was going down a slide with her daughter in her lap. All the photos were sharp.

Maria Elena leaned forward to hand the pictures back to the slender man. His companion still had not said a word. "These are wonderful, *Señor*, truly wonderful." The man put up his hand.

"Keep them, they are yours."

Maria Elena was ecstatic. "I will buy frames for them!" She was all smiles. "Oh, how can I thank you?" After a moment's pause, she frowned. "But why, *Señor?* Why deed you take these, and why geeve them to me?"

The man's demeanor changed. All business, no warmth in the voice. "I have other pictures to show you, Maria Elena, but first I theenk maybe you should put your daughter to bed." She looked at the slender man. Then at the other. He was spooky: no emotion, no movement, no apparent involvement. A zombie.

"Alright. Come, *mi amor*, it ees time to go to bed."

"But, *Mamá,* I don't want to…"

"Hush, *mi jita*. Come now, *vámanos*." Maria Elena lifted her daughter up and onto her feet. She took her hand and led the struggling child to the bedroom. It took Maria Elena a full twenty minutes to put Angelita down. The two Latinos patiently waited. They were in no hurry.

When Maria Elena finally sat down again, the slender man said, "Your daughter is very pretty. It would be very sad if something ever happened to her." Maria Elena's heart skipped a beat. He handed her another half dozen 8x10's. She looked down at the top picture. Her hand flew to her mouth. Her eyes were saucers.

"Oh, my God! *Por Dios! Que horor!"* The picture began to shake in her hand. *"Pobrecita!"* She thrust the pictures back at the man. The slender man pushed her hand away. His voice was ice cold.

"No! Look at them all."

Maria Elena forced herself to go through them. They were horrible, grotesque. Each was of a different little girl about Angelita's age. All looked to be Latinas. Each was horribly disfigured or dismembered in some way. In the first, the little girl was holding up her right hand. Each digit had been severed and healed over into gnarly bumps. The second was missing an arm. The third had been heavily slashed on both cheeks, the raw, sore looking stitching was as blatant as the stitching on an American football. The fourth was of a little girl with crutches. Her right foot had been neatly severed at the ankle. There were more pictures but Maria Elena couldn't look at them. She put her hands over her eyes. She felt like she was going to throw up. The slender man stood and took the pictures out of her hand. She did not look up. He returned them to the manila envelope. Maria Elena had no way of knowing, but the pictures had all been taken in Colombia. Most had been taken in hospitals there. During the drug wars, while fighting the government and other cartels for dominance, the Colombian cartel from Miami had crippled many children in a campaign of terror. No holds were barred. It was bloody, gruesome, barbaric.

"We have learned, Maria Elena, that you have been speaking with the police. You have told them that you waited on a certain *rubio* two years ago at the restaurant in Perry. Two years ees a long time, Maria Elena. I think maybe it ees not easy to remember so good, eh? I think you were wrong. I think that if you cannot remember thees man that your leetle girl will grow up to be a beautiful woman like her mother…Look at me, Maria Elena!" Maria raised her head. His eyes bored into her. "Do you understand that if you do not do what we wish, then," he shivered dramatically, "sometheeng will happen to Angelita." Maria Elena jumped when she heard a loud click. She looked at the zombie. He had a large, black handled switchblade in his hand. He began to clean his fingernails.

"You will cooperate won't you?"

No hesitation. Maria Elena swallowed and nodded. *"Sí,"* she whispered.

"Good. But we are not bad people. As an act of gratitude, we might be able to help your *marido* return to his family. We have our ways. I believe his name is Juan, eh?" Maria nodded, some life coming back to her eyes. "But it won't be right away. We want to make sure you do as you say." The man stood. The zombie folded the knife and also stood. They walked to the door. Maria Elena followed them with her eyes. The door scraped again as the slender man pulled on it. The zombie left first. The slender man said, "*Buenas noches*, Maria Elena," and pulled the door shut behind him.

* * *

Slater parked the burgundy Porsche in front of the main Naples post office and went straight to his post office box where he took out the expected brown manila envelope addressed to Jonathan White, one of his many aliases. He left the building without opening the envelope and tossed it into the car. He clicked the lock and continued on by foot to Don Pedro's hole-in-the-wall Peruvian restaurant where he bought a paper, a full roast Peruvian coffee and two *sopaipillas con miel* to go. He was a regular customer and Don Pedro smiled warmly as he handed Slater the takeout bag. Slater touched a finger to his brow, saying, "*Muchisimas gracias*, Don Pedro."

Fifteen minutes later, Slater parked in front of the *Pituca* at the Hamilton Harbor Yacht Club. He boarded the boat and put the envelope, newspaper, and breakfast bag down on a round, weathered gray teak table. He went below to the galley to fetch a ceramic cup. When he sat down he transferred the coffee from the large Styrofoam cup, pulled out the *sopaipilla*, and slapped the newspaper open. He took a big bite of the fried dough with honey and washed it down with a swig of the rich, full-bodied coffee. Pleasure before business, always.

After the simple breakfast, Slater cleaned up around the table. Taking the ceramic cup and bag of garbage below, he returned with a letter opener and slit the well taped manila envelope. There was a single sheet of paper inside. He took it out. He looked at it and smiled. Simple enough.

12/27
1900
26/38
300

Slater went to the helm and shuffled through some rolled up charts in a stand. He found what he was looking for and returned to the teak table where he removed the rubber band securing the chart. He spread out the chart and located where longitude 26 intercepted latitude 38. He put his finger on it. About halfway across to Biloxi, maybe five hundred miles east of the Yucatan. That's where he would meet up with the shrimp boat at seven p.m. on December 27, and when three hundred bricks of cocaine would be offloaded onto the *Pituca.* He smiled again. He was paid a tidy sum per brick. He did the math. His smile grew.

But they never let him know until the last minute, never gave him much time. The 27th wasn't far away—a week—and he had to prepare the *Pituca.* Fortunately he had been proactive and had the big Detroit diesels tuned a month ago. But he was low on fuel. Might as well fill her up. She took a thousand gallons which gave her a cruising range of a thousand miles—it was over four hundred to Biloxi. He had to get the hold ready, get the holding tank pumped out. Have all the electronics double-checked. Contact the casino and the warehouse in Biloxi. Set up times and dates. Going to need some uppers to make it a straight through run. And I want the *Pituca* to look her best, shipshape stem to stern. Never know who he might bring aboard in Biloxi. He put his hands behind his head and leaned back. He thought back to his last trip. Veritable orgy—coke, sex, more coke, more sex. Man, he was looking forward to Biloxi. And he was really looking forward to the new balance in his island accounts.

Chapter Fifteen

At first light the day after Christmas, Crystal slowly drove Jimmy's truck out of Crescent Beach to the limestone road that cut through the marsh. The road and surrounding wetlands were now part of the Big Bend National Wildlife Area and maintained by the U.S. Forest Service. But not always. The road had been built over the old Taylor Mainline from the glory days of logging when huge cypress had been cut out of the swamp. Spur roads every quarter of a mile went off in both directions so huge cranes set on railroad cars could enter the swamp and reach out with boom and cables, extracting logs up to an eighth of a mile away. Most of the trees were girdled ahead of time so they would slowly die, losing their sap in the process and becoming much lighter and easier to haul. There were no chainsaws back then, only heavy axes and wedges and two man crosscut saws, back when men were men living the rough and tumble life of logging camps surrounded by snakes, alligators, and mosquitos.

Crystal counted the spur roads she passed. She turned into the sixth and drove to where the road narrowed even more and ended in swamp. She reached into the glove and took out a hand drawn map, a red cast iron pipe wrench, and a tube of plumbing goop. After putting on Jimmy's old white rubber fishing boots and grabbing a short-handled shovel from the back of the pickup, she carefully waded a hundred feet or so through the swamp past tremendous cypress stumps until she came to a hardwood hammock that abruptly rose up several feet. She pulled herself out of the muck by a low oak branch and continued through the trees until she came to a very large red cedar stump. The sapwood had rotted away years ago, but the center was still solid as could be. She looked at the map. She took twenty of Jimmy-size paces from the stump directly towards a tall, large diameter water oak. Then she began to dig. She hit the sealed plastic PVC pipe almost immediately. She quickly dug it up and, kneeling on the short section of pipe, loosened the screw in cleanout with the pipe wrench. When she pulled the cleanout away, she was immediately struck by a heavy mildew odor. She reached in and pulled out a thick roll of hundred-dollar bills before turning the pipe upside down and dumping out what remained of several little packages of desiccant. She peeled off ten bills, hesitated, then five more. She rolled up the bills, put a rubber band around them, and shoved them into the front pocket of her jeans. She returned the other bills to the pipe along with a couple new packages of desiccant. She re-gooped the threads of the cleanout and screwed it back in. She put the pipe back in the ground, covered it up, picked up all evidence of the old desiccant, and kicked oak leaves over the freshly disturbed dirt. She looked around. Satisfied, she mucked her way back to the truck.

Crystal was excited about the trip to Biloxi. It would be the first time she and Rusty had taken a trip anywhere together. Of course it would be a lot better if Norm were coming, but you do what you got to do. And one thing she wanted to do on this trip was to pay her fair share. She knew Rusty would try to pay her entire way, but that wasn't right. He was not her husband and, besides, she had way more money than he did. Jimmy had suspected he was going to be killed by the cartel. No, he was sure of it…so much so that he had taken out a substantial life insurance policy. Even though he smoked, Jimmy was in good health, robust, still young enough to get a great rate. The insurance company lost big time on that deal.

But what was she to do with all that money? She had asked Beau. He suggested a sharp investor who worked for Raymond James down in Tampa. Beau told her of some fellow professors who had retired from Clemson and had moved to condos there. They had invested with this guy and he had done them proud. Crystal set up a meeting. When the investor learned the size of the insurance payout, he smiled. He told her about all sorts of possibilities, all sorts of strategies. He talked smoothly and quickly. She was impressed. They set up another meeting.

At the second meeting, she began to pay closer attention to the person himself. The first thing she noticed was the missing wedding ring, and that the two large framed pictures on his deck at the first meeting had disappeared. Maybe he was in the midst of a divorce, or maybe he had stuffed them in a drawer. The second thing was his hair…it didn't look right. She learned later, much later when they had become friends, that he had plugs of bald resistant follicle hairs transplanted from the back of his head and grafted to his balding front, a much more expensive option than a simple rug. It seemed like he couldn't keep his eyes off her body. Maybe a great investment broker, she thought, but a little creepy.

During the second meeting, they developed her investment strategy: conservative and diversified, but with enough yearly dividends and bond income to pay for a very comfortable life style, especially in Crescent Beach, without coming close to breaking into the principal. She brought all the investment papers back with her to show Beau. He read them carefully and said it was A-okay. She signed and returned them on her third meeting. That's when he began to come onto her. It was obvious. First a hand on the small of her back as he met her at the door and ushered her to the plush leather chair in front of his fancy quarter-sawn white oak desk. Still no pictures and no ring. Funny thing that the white on his ring finger still hadn't tanned after a month with the powerful Florida sun. He talked about taking her jet skiing next time she came down, then possibly dinner afterwards. Why not stick around Tampa for a few days next trip? He had never heard of Crescent Beach even though it was only four hours to the north. He did some research, learning that it was a backwater fishing village with absolutely nothing to offer. He told her of all the restaurants he knew. Choice of fifty movies. The beach. The symphony. An hour away from Sarasota with the whitest sand beach in the world on Siesta Key and the Van Wezel Performing Arts Hall. As she listened to him, Crystal recalled conversations with Norm who said he couldn't get away from Sarasota and all the hullabaloo fast enough. The broker said she should come down and he would do his absolute best to get away from the damn-so-busy office and show her around. He was so obvious. Crystal knew that maybe she was only a simple country girl and clueless when it came to investments and culture, but one thing she did know was when a guy was hitting on her. Over the span of the last two years, she allowed him to take her out to lunch on occasion, and went jet skiing with him once. She thought he was going to trip on his tongue when he first saw her in a swimsuit and she pulled the life preserver so tight it made her ample bosom even more ample. But she never stayed over, never was around at night. Over the last six months their relationship had evolved into a more comfortable friendship. The ring reappeared, the pictures of his wife and kids on the desk, too. He finally realized that he would never get Crystal into bed. But that was okay, they got along. Still, she knew that he found her very attractive, so she innocently flirted with him, still playing the game, but only so he would stay focused on making her portfolio the best it could be.

Crystal pulled into her driveway. Today was going to pass slowly because she couldn't wait for tomorrow. She would start packing right away. Norm on the other hand was dreading tomorrow because Tammy was heading out and nothing had been resolved. Christmas had been a disaster. He and Tammy had stopped giving each other extravagant Christmas presents five years ago. Instead they did only stockings, but they were some stockings! Starting about Thanksgiving, Norm would begin racking his brain, trying to remember different special little doodads that had caught Tammy's eye during the year—little items that fit in the Santa stocking like the pair of turquoise earrings from the western wear shop in Perry, a colorful beaded Cherokee belt she had admired at a North Carolina gift shop, an especially nice smelling hand lotion that she used but was hard to find, a Minnie Mouse toothbrush, some whacky, bejeweled flip-flops, a box of those milk chocolate covered caramel and pecan turtles she loved. Of course, there were also the practical items like dental floss, toothpaste, sunscreen, pairs of low magnification reading glasses, a new paperback or two. Tammy usually tried to be just as creative with her stockings. Not this year. It was pretty obvious that she had made no special effort. When he had brought coffee and the stockings into bed on Christmas morning, they took turns, as always, opening up the individually wrapped items. Norm wondered if Tammy was embarrassed. There wasn't one personal item, not one!

It was hard for him to feign appreciation for such a dismal effort. Tammy, for her part, occasionally laughed as she opened her little presents. Many of her smiles, though, seemed forced. When they were done, Tammy gave him a peck on the cheek and bolted out of bed. She cinched her bathrobe and gathered up all the wrapping paper after placing her booty on the bedside table. "Time to get cracking on the eggs benedict and sticky buns," she said, and quickly left the room. Norm was left with his coffee and pile of toiletry odds and ends. A new razor. Whoopty-doo! How would he describe this year's stocking? Sterile, plastic, thoughtless, by rote came to mind. He picked up the discarded green, red, and white wool stocking with a Santa image knitted into it. The Santa stocking had looked so jolly, so full of promise twenty minutes ago. Now it was as empty as Norm felt. He flung it towards the hamper in the corner. He slowly shook his head side to side. He took a long pull of coffee and stared straight ahead. He had absolutely no appetite.

The next morning Crystal loaded her suitcase into her Honda Accord and drove over to pick up Rusty. He was sitting at the bottom step of the broad cypress stairs leading up to the house, a suitcase at his side. Crystal was fired up and bubbly. To her surprise, Rusty was not. He gave her a forced smile as he slowly stood. Something was wrong. "What's the matter?" she asked.

She reads me like a book, he thought. "Just got off the phone with Captain Smathers. Seems our Mexican waitress has changed her tune. Can't for the life of her ever recall seeing Slater at the restaurant."

"Oh no."

"Yup. Agents say she's nervous as a cat. Won't look anyone in the eye. Something or someone has scared the crap out of her."

They sat side by side on the lower step.

"So what's next? What can be done?"

Rusty shrugged. "Don't have any effing idea. Dead end again, goddamn it."

She leaned into him, and nestled into his shoulder when he put his arm around her. They sat that way for a few minutes. Finally she broke away and stood. "Come on. Let's try to forget it, at least for the next week. C'mon, up and at 'em," she said, pulling him up. She handed him the keys. "Let's go get Tammy."

Norm and Tammy were upstairs in the living room, Tammy's suitcase by the front door. Both sensed that they were crossing some sort of threshold this morning, but neither knew exactly what it was. Last night in bed, when she thought him asleep, Tammy had curled up to Norm's back like a spoon. Norm was not asleep, far from it. Sleep didn't come easy these days. He felt her closeness. It was the first time in weeks. He wondered what was going on. He wanted to ask her right then, but he didn't dare, he didn't want to disrupt the moment. He brought a hand back and put it on the side of her thigh. He left it there. That was all.

They heard Crystal's Accord approach. They stood and walked over to the door. Norm bent over and picked up her suitcase. Tammy pushed his hand back toward the floor. He let go of the suitcase. Tammy came in close and tightly hugged him. He put his arms around her. He breathed her recently shampooed hair. He pulled away and held her shoulders at arms' length. "We have to talk," he said.

"I know," she answered. "We will. I promise. When I return." She stood on her toes and lightly kissed him. "And please give David my love and tell him good luck on the operation for me."

"I will," Norm said, picking up the suitcase and opening the door. "C'mon, they're waiting." Tammy and Norm went down the stairs. Norm handed the suitcase to Rusty who was waiting with the trunk open. Putting on a good face, Norm hugged

Tammy goodbye. Rusty opened the rear door for her. She got in. When Rusty was settled behind the wheel, Norm said, "Have fun, guys. Wish I were going with you." He reached into his shirt pocket and pulled out a fifty-dollar bill. "Put this on black for me, would you, Rusty?"

Rusty smiled. He took the bill. "You got it! Good luck with your son. See you soon." He put the car in gear and drove off. Norm watched them turn out of Rich Man's Row. Taking a deep, ragged breath, he went back up the stairs.

Rusty and Crystal had the trip all planned which was fine with Tammy. She just wanted to let go, put everything out of her mind, especially Norm, the Club, and Crescent Beach. She planned on getting a little drunk tonight. As Rusty drove through the Perry strip, he eyeballed the Mexican restaurant off to his left where Slater had eaten dinner. He wondered if he should try to talk to the girl. He shook his head shortly in disgust. No, he had done enough damage. He had blown it! Yeah, he had found the waitress, but it was more luck than anything else. But then what? He opened his big trap, telling the pony-tailed marina owner there was a waitress who had placed Slater in Perry. Jack had told Slater, and Slater must have remembered the waitress. Rusty turned left onto 98, heading west toward Apalachicola. But there was no way Slater would have come up to intimidate the girl, too risky. Most likely he told someone in the cartel and they did whatever they did. Scared the hell out of her. Probably threatened her two-year old little girl just like they did with Jimmy's twin grandsons. They passed Deal's Oyster House. Rusty tried to let it go. C'mon, nothing I can do about it now. Just enjoy Biloxi. But then they crossed the Econfina River. Only a mile or so ahead, Rusty knew, was the labyrinth of limestone roads that led to the sinkhole where Jimmy had assassinated Espantoso. The whole sequence of events flooded his mind. He couldn't let it go. He recalled a book he was supposed to read in high school. It was thick as a Bible. No way was he going to read a book that thick; but he did read the comic book version that the jocks had passed around. He got the gist of the story. It was about some sea captain in the 1800's searching for a huge white whale that had crippled him. The quest for revenge took over the captain's life. When he finally found the whale again, it ended up killing him. Rusty had thought the story stupid, chasing around the ocean for a single whale. Now, it had relevance. He couldn't get Slater out of his mind: Slater was his whale.

Soon after crossing the St. Marks River, Rusty took a spur road to the left towards the little town of St. Marks. Tammy surfaced from her reverie when Crystal said, "Lunch stop. Great Cuban sandwiches right on the river." They parked next to a few Harleys in front of a one-story, weathered gray, and very funky restaurant that immediately reminded Tammy of the Crescent Beach Club without stilts. Just can't get away from it, she thought, passing through the door and automatically checking how the restaurant was set up. Like the Club, simple Formica tables were scattered around. The dark wooden bar was across the room on the far side. Unlike the Club though, there was a long, open-air counter facing the river. A dock with a gas pump was just below them. It was Wednesday and there were plenty of empty seats. They sat at the open-air counter. They watched a sailboat motor up the river from the Gulf. When the waitress came over, they ordered three Cubans, a sweet tea for Crystal, a Bud for Rusty, and a big tropical drink with a little parasol in the middle for Tammy. Tammy had another drink for dessert.

When they got back into the car, Tammy had perked up. "Where to next?" she asked.

Crystal smiled. "Just down the road. Wakulla Springs."

"Never been there," Tammy said.

"Me neither," Rusty added.

Crystal pulled out an AAA guidebook. "Listen to this," she said, opening the book to some yellow highlighted pages. "It's a first magnitude spring that pumps between two and three million gallons daily! Its highest ever was in 1973 with one point two billion gallons in a single day!" Rusty whistled on cue. "It's three hundred and fifty feet deep, and has the longest underwater cave in the U.S.—over thirty-two miles long. Sixth longest in the world. Real popular for cave divers."

"I'll bet," Rusty said, "but you wouldn't catch me down there."

Crystal laughed. "Hard enough just to get you scalloping in four feet of water."

"Here we are, ladies," Rusty said, driving past the wooden sign with a carved heron. "The famous Wakulla Springs." They paid the admission plus bought tickets for the next sightseeing riverboat tour. When they boarded, Rusty looked down into the spring. It was like looking through glass and he saw fish everywhere.

Rusty really enjoyed the hour-long tour. It may have been a little old hat for the girls, seeing as they grew up in north Florida, but for Rusty it was spectacular. Pristine. Even though the cypress had shed their needles, they were hauntingly beautiful with the Spanish moss hanging from their branches—gaunt, bearded spirits at the river's edge. Wildlife, tamed by the tour traffic, was everywhere: anhingas dried their wings while perched in the crevices of Cypress butts, all sorts of turtles—cooters, snapping, soft-shelled—and plenty of gators looking like semi-submerged logs in the shallows. Osprey, wood ducks, purple gallinules and common marsh hens, herons and egrets, limpkins, black vultures, and more. All the wildlife and natural beauty made Tammy think of Norm. How he would love this: wildlife was his thing.

After the tour, they explored the lodge that boasted twenty-seven rooms and a fancy dining room with chandeliers and tall, wide arched windows. Crystal read from her guidebook again as they wandered around. "'Edward Ball began building the lodge in 1935. He imported only the finest Tennessee marble and sawed book-matched panels to make the longest marble bar known to exist: over seventy feet long.'" They looked up at the restored ceiling paintings as she continued to read. "'…over fifty-eight hundred square feet of original Florida scenes.'" There was marble everywhere—trim, baseboards, a wrought iron and marble art deco staircase as well as an art deco, walnut paneled elevator for the three stories. Crystal looked up from the guidebook. "In 1981, after Mr. Ball died, they opened it up as a hotel."

"Who would have thought there'd be something like this in a Florida state park?" Rusty wondered out loud.

From the park they continued on to Apalachicola where they checked in to the Gibson Inn. It was the grandest building in Apalach, built in 1907 in the midst of the lumber and shipping heyday. It dominated the main street and oozed an ambience of southern comfort and culture. After checking in, they sat on the expansive front porch on old rockers, watching the sparse traffic pass. It was so relaxing that it was tough to muster the energy to dine. Rusty told them about the one and only time he had been to Apalachicola. It was with Tiny just before the big storm in '93. After unloading shrimp at Buddy Ward's, they ate dinner at The Oasis Bar where the oystermen and shrimpers hung out. It was a wild and wooly bar and he recounted how he had almost come to blows with a shrimper after beating him in an arm wrestling match. He didn't tell them about Annie, the big-breasted woman he had slept with in Tiny's cabin on the *Never Been Beat*.

They debated whether to eat at the hotel or walk down to the nearby Boss Oyster Restaurant on the Apalachicola River. Crystal settled it. "We're smack dab in the oyster capital of our state. No way we're not going to that oyster house. Come on, Grandpa! Grandma!" They roused themselves and made the short walk down to the river. They entered the Roseate Spoonbill Lounge, rather than the main restaurant area. Tammy took up where she left off with the tropical drinks. They ate oysters and drank. The restaurant served oysters in a hundred ways and Rusty experimented, ordering a half dozen of this and a half dozen of that. He ended up eating three and a half dozen. The more oysters Rusty ate and the more drinks Tammy had, the more Tammy winked and joked that Crystal was going to get her exercise tonight. Towards the end of the meal, Tammy started to ramble. She would start to say something, then lose the thread. She was on a mission. She had planned on getting loaded. Mission accomplished.

Rusty had Tammy on his left arm, Crystal on his right as they merrily made their way back up to the Inn. After Tammy made one last crack about the oysters, they bid her adieu at her door. Rusty and Crystal continued on to their small room where the king size bed took up most of the space. The floor was a little uneven and creaked. For what they were paying, Rusty thought their room might be a little more grand. Crystal said it was quaint. Crystal changed into her nightie and hopped into bed. When Rusty climbed in, she turned to him, smiling lasciviously. "Well, Mr. Oysterman?"

Rusty yawned. "Forget it. I still have a lot of driving to do tomorrow. And I'm beat." He turned off the bedside light and was sound asleep in seconds. Crystal didn't blame him. She was beat, too. But she didn't go to sleep right away. She was too excited. Tomorrow, Paradise Hotel here we come! Huge room with a king size bed overlooking the water! Our own private Jacuzzi! The hotel boasted a spa and sauna, a heated indoor pool, not to mention all the shows and the slots. And no cooking for five days! She couldn't wait. This country girl was going to kick up her heels.

Chapter Sixteen

"All set, José?"

"*Si, Jefe. Listo.*"

"Cast off. *Empuje!*"

The stocky Colombian pushed the bow away and hopped nimbly aboard the *Pituca.* Slater slowly backed the fifty-six foot cabin cruiser away from the wetslip into the narrow channel that led to the Gulf. With a thousand gallons of fuel in her tank, the *Pituca* was less than nimble and Slater had to engage the bow thruster to keep from running afoul of the thick tangle of mangroves on the far side of the channel. Straightening out, he began to thread green and red markers out to the Gulf while José neatly coiled the bow and stern lines. It was pushing nine o'clock in the morning.

José joined Slater at the helm. He sat in the co-pilot's swivel chair and looked at all the electronic gear—radio, radar, GPS plot charter, depth sounder. He punched a button and two routes to Biloxi outlined in red instantly appeared on a small screen.

"Such a luxury, thees," he said.

Slater looked over at him. "What do you mean?"

José swept a hand in front of him. "All thees expensive equipment. When I first ran the square grouper from Colombia for the *Don*, I had maybe a compass, some charts, and a radio. That was eet." He smiled, displaying a couple of gold molars. "But I never had no *problemas.* I was goood. And I was lucky. But thees," he said, sweeping a hand again, "makes eet more easy, I theenk."

José hadn't been born anywhere near the sea. Rather, he was from the small mountain town of San Agustin, a hundred and thirty-six kilometers from the picturesque colonial town of Popayán in southern Colombia. San Agustin was mainly known for its three hundred unusual and mysterious stone sculptures dating from the first to eighth centuries AD, the largest collection of religious and megalithic sculptures in Latin America. In the early seventies, though, long-haired backpackers discovered that magic mushrooms grew everywhere out of the cow patties scattered in the pastures outside of town. Young travellers began to flock to San Agustin. Pensions and food were dirt cheap, and Colombian reefer was available everywhere. The little town soon became a gringo hangout, a regular Colombian Panajachel. José was no dummy: he knew when he saw a golden economic opportunity.

José began dealing at the age of ten. Eventually he sold marijuana by the ounce to the backpackers, and by the kilo to traffickers. He was an entrepreneur. After a rain, he would take the first morning bus out to different pastures to harvest mushrooms. Catching a later bus back, he would then go to the little San Agustin market to bargain for mushy, overripe bananas. He would wash the mushrooms, grind them up, and mix them with the bananas in little plastic containers for sale to the gringos. He marketed two brands: *suave* and *fuerte*—mild and strong. By the time he was sixteen, he spoke more than passable English and was a very rich young man by local standards. He had a truck and began to travel to Cali, Medellin, and Bogotá where he discovered that life was much more exciting than in a little mountain village. There were so many wonderful things to buy, too, like boom boxes, custom cowboy boots and gold jewelry, a shiny new Ford pickup. There were fine restaurants and beautiful women. As he spent more, he needed more. He made bigger deals. He met bigger operators. His reputation as a no nonsense, dependable dealer grew. It was in the early eighties when the *Don,* who hadn't moved to Miami yet, heard about José. The *Don* sent for him and in Bogotá offered him employment. José was impressed by the *Don*'s growing empire that was founded on marijuana and cocaine export. José also did his homework. He learned that the *Don* generously rewarded loyal employees. He also learned how the *Don* dealt with any competition. José loved life and didn't want to leave it. He quickly decided to work for the *Don*. He never regretted it.

The *Don* eventually assigned him to a shrimp boat smuggling forty-pound bales of marijuana to both coasts of Florida. After several years, the captain of the shrimp boat began to skim. One night he disappeared and José took over as captain. The *Don* moved to Miami, and more and more of the export-import business involved cocaine. Shrimp boats manned by smugglers along the coast of Florida were becoming obsolete: they were too easy to spot, too easy to track, too slow. The authorities were getting too hip. Large cargo space was no longer necessary. Small planes were being used more, landing in the ruler straight roads of the unfinished or deserted Florida developments. Pleasure crafts like the *Pituca* moored in the crowded marinas were being used more and more, too. José branched out. Unlike Slater, he was not a violent man and he had morals. While he could be depended on in any situation, he didn't look for trouble. He learned how to fly. He helped where needed. Biloxi was a long trip for one man to run a boat alone, especially the route they were taking. The *Don* had assigned José to help. It was his third run with Slater.

One of the routes highlighted on the navigational screen was a four hundred and fifty nautical mile straight shot from Naples to Biloxi. A thirty-hour trip if the *Pituca* cruised at her usual fifteen knots per hour. However, they were taking another route, heading directly west rather than northwest. They would hold a due west heading for close to a hundred and fifty nautical miles until they rendezvoused with a Cancún fishing boat carrying cocaine bricks. Once the cocaine was off-loaded onto the *Pituca,* they would make a beeline to Biloxi, another three hundred and seventy-five miles. The rendezvous added seventy-five extra nautical miles or an extra five hours, not including the time for the transfer. Slater guesstimated they would be on the water for a good forty hours. A long haul.

Two cormorants were sitting on the last channel markers before entering the Gulf of Mexico. Both took off, dipping low with the tips of their webbed feet snapping the water as they frantically flapped away. As the sun climbed the sky, the water slowly took on more color and the murky brown of the channel changed to the beautiful turquoise of the Gulf. The air temperature was already approaching seventy degrees. The sea was calm, and the sun felt good on their backs. Neither man said anything; they were too busy enjoying such a beautiful day. After awhile Slater switched on the automatic pilot and went below to make some coffee. He soon returned with two steaming mugs. He handed one to José.

José tilted the mug towards Slater. "*Muchas gracias*." They spoke in Spanish. On his first trip with Slater on the *Pituca,* José had been amazed at Slater's Spanish. Slater spoke like an upper-class Colombian.

"How come you speak such good Spanish?" José had asked.

"Because my parents disowned me. I got into some drug and credit card trouble while at the University of Miami, and they had to bail me out big time. It wasn't the first time either—far from it. After things got straightened out, they told me no more screw-ups or else." Slater smiled. "Less than a month later I was kicked out of school for cheating on final exams. My parents cut me off completely. Said I was on my own—have a good life." Slater shrugged. "So I had to make a buck somehow and the only way I knew how was to deal drugs." José could relate.

"I got pretty good at dealing and was making a bit of a reputation. I had taken Spanish in school, but never studied it. I soon found out that in this business, especially in Miami, Spanish was a real plus. So I began to study hard. The *Don* heard about me and asked if I wanted to work for him. He said he could use a guy who looked like me so he could work the fancy hotels and clubs. That's how I got my start with him. He took me under his wing and sent me to Colombia to train for all kinds of things. The time down there is when my Spanish got really good." What Slater did not tell José was that the *Don* had had him trained as an assassin. Slater had perfected his craft by taking care of several of the *Don's* Colombian competitors.

The *Pituca* droned on all day. Although periodically checking gauges and electronics, both men moved by rote. The throb of the twin diesels lulled them. They didn't see another boat, only a few sea birds, a lonely frigate gliding up high, lots of flying fish across the bow. Whether natural or from pollution, the sunset was a brilliant red. They headed straight into it as it covered the sky. The *Pituca* took on its color. It would be beautiful tomorrow. When the sun sank out of sight, the sunset became even more impressive. The few clouds took on reds and shimmering golds. It was a grand finale. When eventually darkness came, a million stars emerged, blinking and sparkling. It was just after seven p.m. when they saw the lights of the trawler. The trawler appeared on the radar at about the same time. José went below to his berth. When he returned he had a submachine gun strapped over a shoulder. He shrugged at Slater. "*Uno nunca se sabe. Muchos piratas en estos dias.*"

Slater nodded. José was right, he thought: there were a lot of pirates around these days. Although chances were slim to none that it was some other boat, Slater picked up the infrared binoculars. He made out *Reina del Mar,* Cancún, on the transom. Still, the right boat might have the wrong people aboard: in the drug business you never knew. He cut back on the throttle. "Take the wheel, José." Slater went below and opened up his gun safe. He removed a false bottom and pulled out his Heckler & Koch MP5K submachine gun. It was the same gun he had used on Jimmy and the judge. He slammed in a magazine, put an extra in his rear pocket, and returned topside. He took over the controls and the *Pituca* soon approached the *Reina del Mar*. José went aft, cradling his machine gun as Slater eased up to the larger craft. The Heckler & Koch lay in easy reach. The Mexican captain looked down at them from the bridge railing. Several crewmembers were leaning against the deck railing. The fishing boat gently rocked, its decks as well as the *Pituca's* completely lit by powerful floodlights.

"*Hola*, José*!* *Cabrón*, you meeet us weeth a gun?" said the captain, hands akimbo.

José smiled. He lowered the submachine gun and let it hang from its strap. "Aah, *Capitán*, eet ees goood to see your ugly face. How was your *viaje?"*

The captain was about José's five foot six, but much stockier. He was built like a bull with a thick, squat neck, very broad shoulders, hard gut, bulging thighs. He was as swarthy as Slater was fair. He was also dressed completely in black: Greek fisherman's hat, black sweater, black slacks. "Goood. No *problemas, gracias a Dios.* But I will be happy when you have the *drogas,* not us. Let us begeen, no?"

Slater brought the *Pituca* alongside and within minutes the boats were fendered and lashed together. Slater removed deck panels to access the engine compartment. In a far corner of the engine area was a custom, thick plastic holding tank with a large sealed inner compartment. By a series of valves, it could be used entirely for sewage, or the center could be isolated and just the outer area packed all around with twelve inches of fecal sludge that would deter even the keenest drug sniffing dogs. The holding tank had been pumped out before leaving Naples; since then, Slater and José had used a bucket. The top of the holding tank was molded so that it looked like it was fused to the plastic sides; but it wasn't. Slater pried off the top with a pair of long-handled screwdrivers. He then unbolted the interior top of the concealed compartment. When he motioned to the Mexican captain that the *Pituca* was ready for the transfer, the crew went down to the refrigerated hold of the trawler where they shoveled away the large pile of fish that covered fifteen vacuum sealed cocaine bales. Each bale contained twenty, one-kilo bricks. With the wholesale rate in Colombia at fifteen hundred dollars a kilo, there was quite a profit margin if the coke sold for as much as sixty dollars a gram stateside. The fifteen bales might fetch as much as eighteen million dollars retail, more if cut stateside by the dealers.

Slater stuck his head up from the engine area. "*Capitán*, I want those bricks rinsed off good. I don't need my boat smelling like a goddamn fish house."

The captain looked at Slater without expression before turning to his men. "*Laven los ladrillos bien, muchachos. Parece que el gringo no legusta el olor de los pescados!*" Two of the sailors began to hose off the bricks. An assembly line was formed and each brick was passed from man to man to where Slater carefully tallied and stacked them inside the holding tank.

After the last brick was carefully stowed, Slater returned topside. The captain had a big smile on his face. "Ahh, now the fun part, eh *Gringo*? We have been saving our sheeet for you all week." He turned to the sailors who lined the deck railing. Like their captain, most were smiling. "*Traigan la manga, muchachos*!"

Two of the sailors dragged over a large hose. It was brought aboard and, under Slater's direction, shoved into the holding tank. José stood where he could see both the captain on the bridge and Slater down at the tank. When the hose was safely secured, Slater signaled to José who signaled the captain. The smell of raw sewage soon filled the air. It was bad down in the engine hold. Slater, following the example of the two Mexicans manning the hose, tied a bandana across his nose and mouth. Topside the crew joked with José.

"You got some goood sheeet now, José!" said one sailor.

"*Mangos y frijoles* all week," said another. "It should geeeve the *cocaína* a good *sabor*, eh? And the color*! Que lindo*!" José smiled good naturedly, his gold molars reflecting the overhead floods, but he didn't say anything. He resisted the urge to hold his nose.

The tank filled quickly. "Slow now!" Slater yelled up. José relayed the message. The captain looked to the man running the pump. The man waited for the captain to signal. "Okay, that's it! Stop!" Slater yelled. The captain purposely took his time signaling the pump operator. The holding tank began to run over. Slater screamed, "Stop the fucking shit!" The pump stopped, but not before the area around the tank was covered in a noxious, stinking goo. Slater came up swearing at the captain who was smiling broadly.

"The lever at the pump," the captain said, " she must have stuck a leeetle." He made a face. "Whew! Even up here eet steenks! I theenk it ees a badder smell than the feesh, no, Gringo?" The captain began to laugh. He was joined by his crew.

Leaving a trail of shit as he stomped up to the helm, Slater grabbed the Heckler & Koch from where he had left it next to the radar screen. His eyes were cold as ice. The captain's smile quickly disappeared when Slater fired a short burst, the slugs chewing into the wood of the trawler's cabin door not more than a foot above the captain's head. The captain dropped to the deck. "*Coño*" he screamed. "*Ud. es loco*! " Slater lowered the gun, pointing it directly at the captain.

"Cleanup crew, *Capitán*! Clorox, buckets, mops. Now!" Slater fired another burst. The bullets sprayed the cabin door, again only a foot above the captain's head. Splinters of wood rained on the captain's hat and sweater. The captain yelled out to his crew, and four sailors, none smiling now, quickly boarded the *Pituca.* Slater kept the gun trained on the captain while the Mexicans cleaned up. They didn't waste time; in a half hour the *Pituca* was spotless except for the bilge water which would have to be flushed. Only minutes later, the trawler shoved off for Cancún.

"Eet ees a good theeng they clean up the mess, eh?" José said, looking down into the hold. It still smelled. "I do not theenk thees ees in our job description, *Jefe.*"

"That son-of-a-bitch did it on purpose."

"*Sí*, I theenk you are right.," José agreed. "I also theenk that maybe you have an enemy now…and the *capitán*, he has a long *memoria*."

Slater shrugged. "Couldn't care less. He's lucky I didn't shoot him." He put the engines in gear. "*Nos vamos*!"

They made great time. The weather continued to hold. The *Pituca* had a deep V-hull which allowed her to cut smoothly through the two-foot seas. Slater ran her up to a steady twenty-two knots. They spelled each other at the helm. Seventeen hours later they approached Ship Island, fourteen miles off Biloxi. Ship Island had been split in half in 1969, during Hurricane Camille and was part of the Gulf Islands National Seashore. Slater cut back to fifteen knots as he set a course between Ship Island to the east and Cat Island to the west. To starboard, Slater and José could see Fort Massachusetts on western Ship Island. Slater put the boat on automatic pilot. He took the cotton balls out of his ears as he walked back to finally lower the deck panels over the engine compartment. He had left it open all this time to air out. The noise had been brutal, but now at least any lingering stench was masked by diesel fumes and lubricants. He would have an even more thorough scrubdown on the boat when it was unloaded—performed with a goddamn toothbrush if need be! I should have shot that son-of-a-bitch, he thought.

The skyline of Biloxi slowly appeared. The sun, already low in the winter sky, silhouetted the scattered high-rise hotels. Gambling, although not legal, dated back to the 1940's in Biloxi, but ceased altogether in the 50's. Hurting for money, it wasn't until the early 90's that the state of Mississippi decided to legalize gambling; but the new law stipulated that the casinos had to be on water. The first two casinos were riverboats brought down the Mississippi River from Iowa, and at 10 a.m., August 1, 1991, the Isle of Capri with its four tall, black smoke stacks and multiple decks was the first casino to open. People waited for hours on deck in humid ninety-plus degree heat to get their chance to go in and test their luck. Champagne flowed and was free on opening day. It was a huge success. Two weeks later, the President Casino followed. Then the Biloxi Belle. Then others. Gobs of money were soon being made. The state of Mississippi had originally estimated that the gross revenue from coastal gambling might bring in a hundred and fifty million dollars annually.

In 1999, the gross revenue from the coastal region was over a billion dollars.

Throughout the nineties, more and more floating casinos were built on Biloxi's waterfront. They looked like boats, but most were a sham with any resemblance to a boat ending at the waterline. Essentially, the majority were casinos built on barges. When the waterfront became crowded, ponds and trenches were dug farther back on shore with barges being set in the middle. Casinos were erected on the barges, and then river water was pumped in to float them so that they complied with the gambling ordinance. The area was soon crawling with casinos.

The first casino Slater and José saw was the forty-one thousand square foot Old Treasure Island barge flying its Jolly Roger. Slater turned to starboard, heading east along the shore. Beach Boulevard, which followed the coast, was humming with traffic. It was Casino Row—the Beau Rivage, the Hard Rock, the Isle of Capri, the Grand. Interspersed were small marinas full of every pleasure craft imaginable. The *Pituca* entered a narrow stretch between the long and slender and uninhabited Deer Island to their right and the Golden Nugget Casino to their left on the mainland. They rounded the point where Beach Boulevard became the Bienville Boulevard Bridge and crossed the bay. Seafood, especially shrimp and oysters, was a mainstay of the local economy, and they soon passed long docks crowded with commercial fishing boats of all colors and sizes, their masts and booms and radio towers creating a hodgepodge look of organized confusion. Even in late December, double-decker tour boats skittered here and there like clumsy waterbugs.

The *Pituca* continued to idle along. The Paradise Hotel soon loomed to their left. Directly in front was the hotel's private marina with slips for twenty boats, one of which had been reserved for the *Pituca.* Slater lightly touched *Pituca's* siren as they passed the marina. The dockmaster dressed all in khaki came out of his office and waved. Slater waved back, thinking, if you only knew what we had on board! Not far from the Paradise, a small, double inlet separated by a narrow isthmus appeared. Several warehouses, some predating the Civil War, were set on massive wooden pilings sunk in the harbor's muddy bottom along both sides of the isthmus. A few small river and coastal freighters and barges were being unloaded. Forklifts scurried around like ants. Slater turned into the second inlet and immediately approached an older warehouse with

CREOLE SEAFOOD COMPANY, INC.
Wholesale Seafood Since 1968

painted on the very large door in front. Slater sounded his siren twice. Almost immediately the door was raised up, revealing a long interior dock. Slater brought the *Pituca* in, and the door quickly lowered behind them. José tossed the lines to two men as Slater shut down the engines. Several other men were moving to and fro. At the far end of the building, freezer sheds cooled by large compressors flanked two more large doors. The two sidewalls were lined with bubbling holding tanks. The area had a very strong fishy smell. Slater and José didn't waste any time. José went down to his V-berth in the bow, Slater to the master stateroom aft. They soon disembarked, each with suitcase in hand.

A stocky Latino approached Slater. "Any problems?" he asked.

"Clear sailing. Our taxis?"

The man gestured towards the doors. "Out back."

After clarifying that the engine area of the *Pituca* should be thoroughly cleaned with absolutely no odor before moving her to the Paradise marina, Slater exited the building with José at his side. There was no reason for them to stick around, plus they were exhausted and had smelled enough Mexican sewage for one trip. The two taxis were parked next to a fleet of Creole delivery trucks. "Don't know why you're in such a hurry to return to Miami," Slater said. "A man can have a lot of fun around here."

José shrugged. "The *Don* wants me back."

The two men got into the separate cabs. "Airport," José told his driver.

"Paradise Hotel," Slater told his.

Chapter Seventeen

"Mostly they just make a mess," Norm told Rebecca, as he vacuumed around the birds' cages. "But check their water and make sure to cover them at night and uncover them in the morning."

"Yes, Dr. Norm."

"And Tammy's plants just need to be watered once. We'll both be back sometime the beginning of next week."

Norm put the vacuum cleaner away and went into the kitchen. Rebecca followed. He opened a large catch-all drawer. A myriad of keys, most with tags, were jumbled together in small, open plastic food containers. Norm began to go through them—extra car keys, boat keys, padlocks with keys, a key to the clinic under the house. Norm found the extra house key and handed it to her. "Here you go. Any questions?"

Rebecca put the key in her pocket. "No, Dr. Norm."

Norm reached for his billfold. "I'll be leaving sometime in the morning. Thank you for looking after things." he said, handing her some bills. The money joined the key in her pocket. Norm opened the door for her and she made her way down the stairs. School was closed for the holidays and Rebecca felt like a prisoner. Billy had gone with his parents to visit relatives somewhere down on the east coast and wouldn't be back until late in the day on the first. The plan was for him to take her mudbogging the next day. She continued down Rich Man's Row to Humpback Bridge, wondering what she could possibly do for the rest of the day. Boring! At least tomorrow she could watch satellite TV at Dr. Norm's. She crossed over the creek and headed home. Beau tooted when he passed by in his golf cart on the way to City Hall.

The book title "All Quiet on the Western Front" popped into Beau's mind as he drove down Main Street. Other than Rebecca, the street was deserted. The TNT Shrimp Company was closed up tight, and Tiny, T, and Boda had gone to visit T's folks in Trenton. The Club would be closed until New Year's Eve—a first. Most of the crabbers and clammers were taking time off, too; their boats were out on trailers in the country where most of them lived these days. Rusty, Tammy, and Crystal were in Biloxi for New Year's, Norm leaves tomorrow for Sarasota, and Sammy and Charley, as well as most the other men from town, were deer hunting. Louie and Clem were most likely at the marina, although Beau'd bet they'd be twiddling their thumbs with the weather cooling off like it had. It was also an excellent opportunity for him to catch up on the town business he'd been ignoring for the last couple of weeks, although he was not looking forward to troubleshooting why the bacterial count was high at the water plant again. The last thing he wanted to do was go through all those gobbledygook tech manuals to figure out the problem. He was an historian, not a bloody chemist. He slowly unwound his long, lanky frame from the golf cart, pulled a ring of keys from his pocket, and unlocked City Hall.

As he entered his office, Virginia and Skillet were setting out on their afternoon walk. Virginia was in a great mood. It had been over two weeks since she had one of her, as she called them, "spells." She knew she shouldn't get excited, but wondered if, for whatever reason, the dementia could be curing itself? Norm said it was highly unlikely, but added that you never knew what the brain was capable of; stranger things have happened. There was still a lot not known about Alzheimer's, he said. One thing was for sure, Virginia thought, Beau's much more relaxed these days now that he doesn't have me, the albatross, around his neck. Life's almost back to normal—cooking without Beau looking over my shoulder, doing the laundry and gardening, getting plenty of exercise with Skillet, and most every sunset we have our pitcher of martinis in the hot tub. Maybe these really will be the Golden Years after all!

Craig and Ralph were out front of Ralph's house tossing a softball. It was a cool sunny afternoon in the high-fifties; the climate in these parts was more like south Georgia than south Florida. "Don't tell me you're practicing already for the big game!" Virginia said, laughing. Skillet was tugging hard on his leash; Ralph was one of his favorite people. His tail was going a mile a minute. "Oh, alright, Skillet!" Virginia let go of the leash and Skillet bolted up to Ralph who put his mitt down so he could better pet him.

"Game's a couple of months away and Craig's already put together a half dozen lineups," Ralph said. "You'd think it was the World Series."

"More important than the World Series," Craig muttered. He began throwing the ball up in the air and catching it while Ralph scratched Skillet's back. Skillet almost smiled. After a minute or two, Virginia grabbed Skillet's leash.

"C'mon, Skillet. You've had your fix."

"You two out and about on your usual?" Ralph asked.

Virginia nodded. "While Beau's slaving away at City Hall."

"Bless his heart," Ralph said, putting his mitt on again and pounding it a couple times with his other hand. "Don't know what this town would do without him." Craig threw Ralph the ball and they resumed their game of catch while Virginia and Skillet walked to the ballfield. Virginia unhooked Skillet's leash so he could run around. While Skillet was checking out all the smells, Virginia moseyed over to the pond in the spoils. She didn't see any mergansers; must be out in the Gulf fishing, she thought. Skillet came trotting up to her. They continued on the path along the pond until it entered the Big Bend Wildlife Area. They usually turned around here and headed for the condos, but today, feeling totally invigorated, Virginia continued on into the swampy woods. Skillet stopped at the woods edge and watched her.

"C'mon, Skillet. Little nature walk today." Skillet hesitated, but when Virginia kept on walking, he trotted after her. The jungle-like woods quickly closed around them, and the overstory of live oaks, cabbage palms, red cedar, pine, and cypress blocked out much of the late afternoon sun as well as any town noise. They stuck to the path which became fainter as it began to knife through prickly vines, saw palmetto, and baby cabbage palms. The gardener in Virginia took it all in. So incredibly organic and unspoiled! "Must be what it looked like when the conquistadores were here," Virginia told her dog, as she pushed a few branches out of the way. They continued for another twenty minutes before Virginia sat down on an uprooted cabbage palm. It was noticeably darker than when they had entered. She looked at her watch. Almost five-thirty. A little rest break and then scoot out of here, she thought. We've got to be home before dark or Beau will worry. Skillet came over and put his head in her lap. "Okay, okay," she said, scratching his ears. "We'll leave in a few minutes."

Virginia stood up. With the vines hanging from the trees and palmetto most everywhere, everything looked the same. The palmetto fronds had closed in behind them. Virginia looked in all directions. Trees, vines, palmetto, scrub bushes. No sign of the trail. She got a queasy feeling in her stomach. Relax, she told herself, relax! Let's see, I came over from the path to sit on the tree. She retraced what she thought were her steps. She pushed aside some of the palmetto fronds. No sign of the trail. She started pushing aside palmetto fronds all around her. The groundcover looked undisturbed everywhere she looked. She began to panic, walking first this way, then that. It only served to disorient her further. She was in the primeval jungle. It was getting dark. Trees and stumps were taking on all sorts of macabre shapes. There, that large pine. Hadn't she walked right by that tree? She was sure of it! The path should be right at its base. She pushed aside some young cabbage palms and walked up to the tree. The ground all around was undisturbed.

She looked at her watch. Twenty minutes she'd been searching around and she had absolutely no idea where the path was. She was lost. It was early evening. She was confused, agitated. She saw a black shape out of the corner of her eye. She turned, startled. Her stomach was in her throat. Was that a bear? A panther? No, no. Only a stump. Take it easy! There, up in the top of that cypress. Something moved, I'm sure of it. A buzzard? No. It's a monkey, for Pete's sake. She suddenly saw monkeys all over the place. There aren't supposed to be monkeys here! As agitated as she was, Skillet was sitting calmly, watching her; but she was in a panic, scared to death. She looked frantically this way and that. Everything that she had thought beautiful in daylight, was becoming sinister and evil as the light dimmed. She started to push her way through some vines towards another cypress tree that looked familiar. The soil turned wet, and she realized the cypress was in a swampy area. She looked at a log in the swamp. No, it wasn't a log. It moved! It was a ten foot gator and coming at her. Virginia screamed and took off in the opposite direction. She ran wildly; her light sweater was being shredded by the prickly vines, and her face and hands were scratched in several places and began to bleed. She saw small, dark stumps off to her left. Were they really stumps, or boar? She heard their grunting and snarling as they chased after her. Totally out of breath, she came to a stop in front of a large fallen pine that blocked her way. She looked back over her shoulder. No gator. No boars. But that noise? What was that? She looked down. The largest Eastern Diamondback rattlesnake she had ever seen, lay coiled and rattling less than three feet away. Virginia froze. She had hallucinated the monkeys, gator, and wild pigs, but the snake was real. It was close to eight feet long which meant it could strike from at least four feet away.

Skillet, who had followed Virginia at a trot, saw the snake at the same time. He didn't hesitate, he streaked forward and pounced. Virginia screamed and backed up out of the way as Skillet violently whipped the snake back and forth. He lost hold of it temporarily and the snake struck out, not once but three times before Skillet had hold of it again. He shook it and shook it. It was a lot of snake to shake. It was a battle, but Skillet was a big dog and ferocious. Still, the snake got in a couple more licks before it died. When Skillet finally dropped the snake, he had snake blood all over him. He was also bleeding from the snake's punctures. Each bite was like being stabbed with two curved, quarter-inch diameter screwdrivers. Because rattlesnake venom prevents coagulation, Skillet's wounds continued to bleed. He had two wounds in the face which was good because the swelling would be extreme there which in turn would slow the uptake of the venom. However, he had two punctures in his chest which was bad because there the venom would be absorbed more rapidly. But what was worse was that the snake had bit Skillet's tongue, the worst of all possible places. Skillet needed a vet and a large dose of antivenom and to be perfectly still. The last thing he needed was to move around and spread the venom throughout his body.

While Skillet was killing the snake, Virginia freaked. She started running blindly through the woods again. Skillet picked up the snake for one final shake, then followed Virginia. He started off at a trot, but soon slowed to a walk. The wounds in his face began to swell as the venom destroyed cells. His face was on fire; he began to whimper. Skillet had gone maybe a hundred feet when the muscle tremors began. His whole body began to shake. His breathing was soon labored. His front legs were hard to control, then his rear legs. He wobbled unsteadily along, trying to catch up with his mistress, following her scent. His rear legs collapsed. He tried to drag them along, but didn't get far. He whimpered in pain and frustration. Finally, he collapsed.

Chapter Eighteen

It was completely dark in his office when Beau woke up. He switched on the overhead fluorescent light. The incredibly boring technical manual that had put him to sleep lay face down on his desk. He looked at his watch. Quarter to seven! He was surprised that Virginia hadn't called or come over to get him. Almost dinnertime. He put the manual away, shut off the lights, closed down City Hall, and was soon scooting down Main Street towards Rich Man's Row. He looked at the six-foot-tall ocean-themed Christmas lights hanging from the power poles along Main Street—a dolphin, an anchor, a sea turtle, a stingray, a horseshoe crab, a seahorse. Wonderful to look at.

It was getting downright chilly. He zipped up his light-weight jacket before crossing Humpback Bridge and turning onto Rich Man's Row. Something was wrong! No lights were on at the house! With Virginia's disease, he always imagined the worst. He climbed the stairs as fast as his septuagenarian body would allow. He turned on the lights. Skillet's empty beanbag bed was the first thing he saw. He checked the bedroom. No note on the kitchen counter. He checked the answering machine. No message. They had been going for a walk. He knew the route. Back down the stairs in a flash and out of breath, Beau hopped into the golf cart. It didn't take more than ten minutes to drive the entire route. Not a sign. Who was in town that lived along their route? Ralph and Craig! He drove over. Ralph was cooking, Craig was watching the news when he burst through the door.

"Have you seen Virginia?" Beau blurted. Craig and Ralph looked at each other.

"Few hours ago," Ralph answered. "She and Skillet were off on their walk."

"She never came home."

"Maybe she's visiting somebody," Craig said. Because of the hour and because of the Alzheimer's, they knew this highly unlikely. "Let's call around before we panic."

They broke out the single page Crescent Beach directory, calling people along the route as well as Virginia's best friends. William said that he had seen them from his condo window walking towards the pond in the spoils. He hadn't seen them return, but then again, he hadn't been watching for them either. No one on the walking route beyond the condo had seen them. Ralph shut down his cooking and went to the closet where he kept his flashlights.

"Let's zip over to the spoils and take a gander."

The three men hopped into the golf cart and sped off. They had to park the cart some distance from the pond because there was no way the cart could make it through the sugar sand churned up by four-wheelers and good ol' boys testing the mettle of their 4X4 trucks. They found plenty of tracks in the sandy path, but they were hard to make out. Off to the side, though, the wanderings of a large dog were obvious. They continued past the pond. "Virginia likes to watch the ducks here until Skillet scares them off," Beau said, unnecessarily. They followed the tracks to the National Wildlife Area. In the moist soil of the woods, the tracks were distinct—the paw prints of one large dog and prints made by a pair of woman's size eight hiking boots. The tracks headed in. There were none coming out.

"Virginia!" Beau yelled. No answer. They walked in fifty feet. Beau yelled again. Again, no answer. Beau yelled several more times. He whistled for Skillet. No response.

Craig said, "We need to get Charley, or Sammy. They're the only ones who could find her tonight without getting into trouble in this, this jungle."

Beau quickly agreed. "You two take my cart, and get Norm, too. He hasn't left for Sarasota, yet." Ralph and Craig hurried off. Beau flashed the light all around. It was spooky. Poor Virginia! She must be scared to death. That I let her and Skillet walk without me, or without someone else, is criminal! If something's happened to them, it's my fault!...But nothing's happened, they're just lost, that's all. Happens all the time. Only a few hours. Not a big deal. They came here late and it got dark and they lost their way. Nothing more than that. He heard a barred owl off in the distance. Another answered. Critters! Lots of critters in these woods. Alligators, at least four types of poisonous snakes, even panthers! What was she thinking! Why would she even consider entering these woods, especially so late! She'd never done that before. No worries, though. Skillet will take care of her. He won't let anything near her.

* * *

In sheer terror Virginia had run away from the gargantuan snake being mangled by the wild cur. She ran for all she was worth, splashing through swampy areas, slipping on dried oak leaves in the hammocks, being pricked by a thousand vines. It was almost dark and all sorts of things were chasing her. She couldn't stop or they would get her. It was as if she were swimming in a dark, shark-infested sea. She couldn't see the sharks, but knew they were all around her, knew that sooner or later, one would pull her under.

If she wasn't lost before, she certainly was now. She had no idea how far she had been running and no memory even of Skillet being with her. Her breath was coming in ragged gasps and she had a stitch in her side. She knew she'd have to hole up somewhere soon before it became so dark that she'd run into something. Unexpectedly, she suddenly burst out of the trees into a grassy section at the edge of a large salt marsh. She was surprised to see that the sun was still up, barely. The marsh was huge, its amber grasses waving in the cool evening breeze. The temperature, though, was dropping with the sun. Virginia, standing at the edge of the marsh looking out, began to shiver.

The marsh was nowhere near as spooky as the woods she had left. For one thing, she could see clearly. She began to calm down. Two herons passed overhead heading for their roost. A group of snowy egrets did the same. Birds were a definite improvement over panthers, gators, monkeys, and boar! She walked along the edge of the marsh. She didn't go far before the water and mud deterred her and she returned. It was like she was on a tiny island. She was still terrified, did not know what to do, did not know what might spring out of the woods at any moment. But, she did feel more comfortable here than in the deep woods. She paced around. She found a stout stick and picked it up. It would be her war club if anything came at her. She pushed the needle-like marsh grass down flat along the edge of an uprooted red cedar. She sat down on the flattened grass and leaned back against the cedar. She kept the stick close by as she watched the sun sink into the sea. Her eyes became heavy and her eyelids fluttered. She was exhausted. She fell into a deep sleep almost immediately.

* * *

Beau impatiently waited at the edge of the wildlife area for the others to return. After what seemed like forever, he finally saw beams of lights bouncing off the trees. Soon Craig, Ralph, Charley, and Norm walked up. Norm was carrying a blanket and had several plastic bottles of water sticking out of his coat pockets.

"Thanks, Norm, Charley," Beau said, sincerely.

Charley said, "Alrighty, then. Let's git at it." He pulled a full roll of fluorescent flagging out of his pocket. He led the way for about twenty feet before he stopped to tie off some flagging on a bush. "Now keep them lights on the ground. Snakes like to come out at night and they ain't got no friends, jest enemies." Charley had no problem following the tracks and broken branches and fronds of Virginia's and Skillet's trail. He continued to flag bushes and trees. The others were silent and gave Charley plenty of space. The sun had long since gone down. Without the flashlights, you couldn't see your hand in front of your face. But Charley was in his element. He had hunted and tracked his whole life. He had no problem following Virginia's and Skillet's route; to his eye, it was a veritable highway.

It did take Charley a little while to figure out where Virginia had gone after she had sat briefly on the uprooted cabbage palm. Things were disturbed every which way he looked. Charley came up to the large pine tree Virginia had thought she recognized. He followed her footsteps from there toward the swampy area where she had mistaken the log for a large gator. Charley closely examined Virginia's tracks leading away from the marshy area. They went in a straight line and the length of stride plus the little kick-ups of soil and leaf matter indicated she was running. As Charley tied yet another piece of flagging on a branch, he said, "Believe she was spooked here. Took off a-runnin'." Beau swallowed. The farther Charley brought them into the woods, the guiltier he felt. What had he been thinking to let them walk alone? Never again!

Charley quickly surged ahead of the others. Thrashing through the woods like she had, there were indicators everywhere. Charley soon came to the fallen pine where the snake had been coiled. Charley shone his light in all directions. "Looks like there was quite a ruckus here, alright…Holy shit!" he exclaimed. "Lookee here," he said pointing at the huge, mangled rattler.

"Oh my God! Virginia!" Beau said. He frantically began shining his flashlight around. He yelled out for Virginia. He whistled for Skillet. Nothing.

Charley picked up a stick, and poked and prodded the snake. "Biggest rattler I ever did see." He bent close to examine it. "Don' know 'xactly what happened, but one thing's fer sure: Skillet done killed it." Charley stood up quickly. "Think we better move double time from now on."

Virginia opened her eyes. Had she heard something? Had someone called her name? She listened intently. Nothing. There was faint light coming from the west on the horizon. She reached for her stick. Good. Still there. She looked up. A zillion stars in the sky. How beautiful! But it also meant it was clear. She could see her breath. The temperature was dropping fast. She shivered and hugged herself. She was so tired. She closed her eyes again.

Charley saw Skillet first. It stopped him dead in his tracks. "Oh Lord!"

"What, Charley!" Beau asked.

Charley didn't answer. He knelt besides Skillet. Beau looked down. A sob escaped from his very soul and he collapsed to his knees. Skillet's face was grotesque. The venom had been working in each puncture, causing everything to swell to prodigious portions. Skillet looked more like something out of a circus freak show than a lovable black Lab. Beau, tears suddenly streaming down his cheeks, reached out. Charley grabbed his hand. "Don't, Beau," he croaked. "The venom. You don' wanna touch it." Charley stood. He helped Beau up. "C'mon," he said, swiping at his eyes that, like Beau's, had filled. "We've got to find Virginia pronto!"

Charley took off almost at a run. Craig and Ralph quickly followed. Beau remained where he was, his flashlight shaking as it trained on Skillet's face. Norm gently put a hand on his shoulder. "C'mon, Beau." Beau let himself be led away.

Rushing through the woods, Charley and the others were making a lot more noise. They were also close enough that they woke Virginia. She had no idea what was going on. Were those animals? She soon saw moving lights a ways off, flashing here and there, a soft glow in the overstory. Animals didn't have lights. People did. Jungle people! Savages! The lights were coming closer. Virginia quickly stood. She picked up her war club. She had to hide. Where! Only place was behind the roots of the fallen cedar. She pushed the marsh grass out of the way and ducked down behind. She peered out through an opening in the root ball. The first to appear was Charley, dressed in camouflage, unshaven, large hunting knife on his belt. She had never seen this man before. Craig and Ralph were next. She didn't recognize them either. Virginia tightened her grip on the club as they shined their lights around. Norm and Beau emerged. The tall man looked familiar. "Beau?" she whispered, not sure. Recognition surfaced from the depths of her mind. "Beau!" Virginia exclaimed. She stood, suddenly materializing from behind the root system. Ignoring the others and still holding her war club, she rushed up to Beau. Beau's face was a mixture of relief and alarm. Virginia's face was scratched and bleeding. Her gray hair was all tangled up like a bird's nest, full of twigs, leaves, and pieces of vine. He reached out and gently took the club from her. He tossed it away and drew her in close.

There were no flies on Charley! As Beau and Virginia fiercely embraced, Charley began snapping off dead cabbage palm fronds. He made a pile of them and soon had a white blaze going that could thaw out a hockey rink. Norm put the blanket over Virginia's shoulders, and examined her hands and arms in the bright firelight. "Virginia," he asked, noting the confusion in her eyes. "Were you snake bit?"

Virginia stood as close as she could to Beau. "Snake bit?"

Norm took another look at her hands and arms. He bent down to examine her trousers and boots. He pulled up her pants' legs. Other than some minor scratches, she was clean. He stood back up. "Everything looks okay."

"Thank God," Beau said, arms again protectively wrapped around his wife.

Norm made her drink from one of the bottles of water. "Do you think you can make it out of here okay, Virginia?" Norm asked. More confusion. Norm bet she had no idea where she was.

Beau answered for her. "She'll be fine. Just got to take our time."

Charley spoke up from the other side of the fire. "Talk to you for a sec, Beau?" Virginia clutched Beau to her.

"It's okay, Sugah. Just going to talk to Charley. Norm's right here." Beau walked over.

"Figger I should go ahead of y'all. Figger Virginia don' need to be trippin' over Skillet and that ol' snake right off."

Skillet's swollen, distorted face flashed in front of Beau's eyes. He nodded. "Once we get Virginia safely home and in bed, I'll come back for him. I'm not leaving him out here for something to chew on. I'll bury him tonight."

"I'd like to help," Charley said. "He was my bud, too."

"He'd like that, Charley." Charley turned and disappeared into the woods. Beau rejoined Virginia. "What do you say, Sugah? I think you've had enough excitement for one night. Let's go home."

Charley was waiting for them at the fallen pine. He said, "I'll meet you later where the path enters the woods. Take your time, Beau, but might want to bring a blanket or somethin'." Beau nodded. Charley watched their flashlights slowly fade as they followed the flagging out of the woods. Time to get to work, he told himself. He unsheathed his hunting knife and began to cut saplings and vines. When he had a rough *travois* lashed together, he brought it over to where he had hidden Skillet. He carefully loaded the hundred pound dog on the *travois* and began to drag him out of the woods.

* * *

Norm shut the bedroom door softly behind him. Beau was on the leather couch across the room, staring at Skillet's empty beanbag bed. He looked at Norm. "How is she?"

"Resting comfortably. I gave her something to calm her down."

"Was she still talking about alligators, wild hogs, and monkeys chasing her?"

Norm nodded. "Hallucinations. Another sign, I'm afraid, of Alzheimer's. Common, really, especially given the time of day and situation."

"What do you mean?

"There's a study that says two-thirds of Alzheimer patients are affected by what they call *sundowning.* A patient tends to get more confused or agitated late in the day or early evening when light is low and there are lots of shadows around. Virginia's confusion and agitation were most likely triggered by getting lost in the first place, but the dimness of those woods full of all those strange shadows and shapes certainly heightened her anxiety to the point that she began to hallucinate."

"Did she say anything about Skillet?"

"No. And I don't think you should. I don't believe she has a clue as to what happened. Better feel her out on that."

Beau nodded. He looked back towards Skillet's beanbag bed. Norm followed his gaze. "Beau, I can stay here as long as you need. I know you want to take care of him."

Beau stood. "Might take awhile."

"You go on." Norm ushered him towards the front door. Beau went down to the garage where he pulled out a blue plastic tarp and a couple pairs of gardening gloves. He put the tarp on the rear seat where Skillet usually sat and slowly drove off. He was in no hurry.

Charley was waiting at the edge of the wildlife area. They transferred Skillet onto the tarp and together they pulled him to where Beau had left the golf cart. As they drove off, Charley asked, "Know where you goin' to put 'im?"

Beau nodded. "There's a corner of Virginia's flower garden near the hot tub where Skillet used to bury his bones. I think he'd like it there." They rode in silence to Rich Man's Row. Beau went into the garage for a pair of shovels and carried them out towards the hot tub. Charley followed. For the next half hour they dug. When they were satisfied the hole was wide and deep enough, Beau drove the golf cart over. They were about to unload Skillet when Beau suddenly said, “Wait a minute!” Beau quickly climbed the stairs up to the house and returned with Skillet’s beanbag bed. It didn’t quite fit in the hole, so Beau widened it until it did. They carefully lowered Skillet onto his bed. Beau knelt and futzed around until he felt that Skillet was positioned just right. Other than the swollen face, Beau thought Skillet looked comfortable enough. Beau stood. He and Charley looked down in silence.

“Fourteen years,” Beau said, his eyes misting. “Couldn’t have asked for a better dog and companion. Hell of a lot of good memories.”

“Your best friend,” Charley said.

“Amen.” Beau picked up the blue tarp and carefully arranged it over Skillet so no dirt would fall on him. The two men picked up their shovels and filled the grave.

Chapter Nineteen

Rusty had both showerheads adjusted to a concentrated torrent and trained on the small of his back. His muscles, tight from the road trip, began to relax under the steady stream of hot water. How had he ever been able to sit all those years in a cruiser for eight, ten, twelve hours a day? Running the length of the shower's rear wall was a two-inch-thick teak bench. To his right was a marble shelf with a healthy selection of complementary body lotions, shampoos, and soaps. Once his muscles loosened up, Rusty switched the shower settings back to normal and reached for one of the little boutique plastic bottles. Why do they make the print so damn small on these things! He looked through the opaque glass door. A semblance of Crystal was in front of the sink. He opened the door and held the bottle out. "Crystal, is this conditioner or shampoo?" Crystal was wearing a white terrycloth bathrobe with *Paradise Hotel* emblazoned on the chest. She read the label.

"Shampoo. Here, give it to me." Bottle in hand, she disrobed and joined Rusty in the shower. "About time you go to the Dollar Store for reading glasses don't you think, Grandpa?" she said, as she squeezed a generous dollop of shampoo onto her hand and began to massage it into Rusty's scalp. He closed his eyes. Life doesn't get much better than this, he thought. After rinsing, Rusty opened his eyes. Crystal was training one of the showerheads on her full, classically curved body. She selected a little bottle of her own.

"Body wash," she said, smiling at him while removing the cap.

Rusty reached out. "My turn." He started lathering her back. Soon he was kneading her neck and shoulders. He could feel her relax under his hands. He worked his way around to her stomach. Then her chest. He put more soap on his hands and concentrated on her chest. When he began toying with her nipples, Crystal sighed and leaned back. She could feel his hardness. Rusty turned her to him and they kissed long and deep. After more touching and kissing, Rusty sat on the edge of the teak bench and gently drew Crystal down to him. She straddled him and he entered her. With his hands holding her waist and hers on his shoulders, they rocked in rhythm under the shower's warm embrace.

While Rusty and Crystal were drying off, Tammy was making her way to the elevator. She was supposed to meet Rusty and Crystal at the casino bar at six. She looked at her watch. Twenty of. So she'd be a little early and get a head start: no problem there. With Norm in Sarasota, alcohol was going to be her companion for the next several days. The elevator was three-quarters full. Tammy noted that dress code was all over the place, from jeans to jewels. She was somewhere in between with her new slacks and blouse and bright silk kerchief. The elevator was quick and soon spilled everyone out into the plush lobby. Tammy walked down the garishly carpeted corridor that exited out to the casino walk bridge. Even though the floating casino was on the other side of the bridge, Tammy could clearly hear the slots. She smiled at her internal reaction: somehow that sound signaled fun and that she, along with everyone else, was here to have a good time.

Happy hour was in full swing. No booths or tables were open, but there were several vacant spots at the bar. Tammy pulled out a stool. The bar was long and the bartender was at the far end with his back to her. Tammy watched him shaking some concoction. Some bod! Shaped like a V—broad shoulders and narrow waist. Sexy butt, too. Hair in a short ponytail. Whoa, girl. Enough of that! She reached for the bar menu. Quite a selection of tropical drinks. Ten in all. They all looked good. Let's see. The usual Mai Tai, Piña Colada, Margarita, Planter's Punch, Daiquiri. She knew all those. But there were several others she didn't know like the Rum Runner and the Bahama Mama. The Hurricane was a specialty of the house. The Pain Killer sounded good with rum, pineapple juice, cream of coconut, orange juice, and a pinch of nutmeg on top. With her nose in the menu, Tammy didn't notice the smiling bartender come up to her.

"Tough choice, huh, Tammy?"

Startled, Tammy looked up. Her mouth dropped. "Bobby!"

"The same, Babe." Tammy was speechless. Bobby laughed. "You should see your face. Funny isn't it? Last time we meet up in a bar, you were the bartender."

"What are you doing here?"

Bobby held his hands apart. "What does it look like?"

Tammy shook her head. "No, I mean, like how'd you end up in Biloxi?"

"Was just passing through two years ago after I left Crescent Beach and took a shine to it. There were several openings for bartender, so I applied. Considered putting Frank and BeeBee down for a reference, but thought better of it."

Tammy laughed. "Smart man."

"Anyway, been here ever since."

Tammy shook her head. "Unbelievable."

"When are you going to realize that it's in the stars, Babe? You and me, it's destiny!" Bobby looked down the bar. Several new patrons had sat down. "Gotta go tend the customers. What can I get you?"

Tammy tried to focus on the menu. "I guess the house specialty: the Hurricane."

"You got it. Back in a jif."

Unbelievable! This was the second time her ex-husband had almost made her pee in her panties. The first was at the Club when he showed up unannounced after serving seventeen years in prison for putting a state trooper in the hospital. They had divorced right after he had been sentenced and there had been no contact between them in all that time. Then, out of the blue, he shows up at the Club and wants to get back together! No way, she had said, Norm was her man.

Bobby placed her drink down. "So, where's the doctor?"

"Sarasota. His son is having an operation."

"You're here alone?"

Tammy shook her head. "Nope. With Rusty and Crystal. They should be here any minute. They're an item now."

"What about Jimmy?"

"Long story."

"I'd like to hear it. So, you're here, single, for New Year's?" Tammy nodded. "I might have to do something about that."

Tammy laughed. "You don't give up, do you?"

He looked her in the eye. "No Babe, I don't. Like I say, we're destined." He left again to tend to business.

Halfway through her drink, Rusty and Crystal arrived. After a customer accommodated them by moving over a couple of stools, the three were able to sit together. Crystal reached for the cocktail menu while Rusty eyed the different beers on draft. Tammy blurted out, "You're not going to believe this, but check out the bartender."

Bobby's chiseled back was to them, mixing drinks. When he turned around, Crystal said, "Oh my God. It's Bobby!"

"Now that's what I call a hell of a coincidence," Rusty said.

"Bobby calls it destiny."

Rusty laughed. "He already put the moves on you?"

"No, not really. But you're right, some coincidence!"

When Bobby saw them, he marched over. "Crystal, Rusty, long time no see. Here to celebrate New Year's, I understand." He extended his hand to Rusty who shook it.

"Yup," Rusty said. "Rednecks come to the big city."

"Biloxi's not that big," Bobby answered.

"A lot bigger than Crescent Beach."

Bobby laughed. "Most places are." He looked down the length of the bar, then back at Rusty. "Get you two something?"

"Bud draft would be good," Rusty said.

"What are you drinking, Tammy?" Crystal asked.

"Called a Hurricane. Take a sip."

Crystal took a sip. "Yumm. I'll have one of those, Bobby."

"You got it."

When Bobby returned with the drinks, he asked, "How long are y'all here for?"

"Until the second," Crystal said.

Bobby hesitated, then said to Rusty, "As I recall, people in Crescent Beach said you were an ace mechanic."

Rusty shrugged. "I tinker some."

"Know anything about diesels?"

"About everything. Why?"

"Bought me an old F350 to pull a camper I've been working on. Can't get that motor to run right. Smokes and doesn't have the power it should. Took it to one place, but they, excuse my French, ladies, didn't do jack shit. Any chance you could take a gander?"

Rusty quickly looked over at Crystal who laughed and said, "Tomorrow we're supposed to take a tour on *The Shrimp Train* to see the Biloxi sights, like the antebellum houses along the waterfront, some civil war memorials, Jefferson Davis' Post-Civil War home, and other stuff that would bore the stuffing out of Rusty. Believe me, he'd much rather take a look at that oily old diesel."

Rusty smiled at Crystal, and turned to Bobby. "She's right, Bobby. Tomorrow morning if you want. Do you have tools?"

"Affirmative. Ten okay? I get off at one, so that'd let me get some shuteye. I'll write down the address and draw you a map."

Rusty nodded. "Ten's fine."

"Planning on a little camping trip, Bobby?" Tammy asked.

"More than that. I figure that I spent seventeen years staring at prison walls, and it's about time I saw this country of ours. And I'm not going to rush it; might take me years."

"Bobby dear, what do we have to do to get a refill around here?" asked one of two middle-aged women several seats down the bar, both in tight sequined dresses that pushed their boobs up."

Bobby sighed and smiled pointedly at Tammy. "Duty calls." To Rusty, he said, "I'll be back as quick as I can with that map and address. And, thanks." Tammy watched Bobby walk away. She was thoughtful. How exciting! Travel around the country, free as a bird, new sights whenever you wanted, no same old. Good for Bobby.

When Bobby returned with the map and address, he asked, "Another round?"

Rusty looked at the ladies. They shook their heads. "Guess we'll head out for some dinner." He pulled out his wallet. "What do we owe you, Bobby?"

"On the house." As he collected the glasses, he added, "And Tammy, FYI, I'm here all week from four to one in case you want to visit." Tammy didn't respond, her face was a mask. Rusty and Crystal looked at each other. "See you tomorrow, Rusty," Bobby added. He took the glasses away as the trio stood up and left.

Less than five minutes later, a tall, handsome, blond-haired man walked into the bar. He took one of the three seats recently vacated. Bobby came up to serve him. "Bobby," the man said, "Good to see you again."

"Likewise, Joe. Been awhile. What can I get you?"

"The usual."

Chapter Twenty

Rebecca went into the kitchen and opened the catchall drawer full of keys. It took her less than a minute to find the one she was looking for. She took it and went straight down to the clinic. After glancing innocently around to make sure no one was in sight, she unlocked the door and entered. Safer going in during the day, she thought, with no lights shining out. Anticipation coated her stomach. She opened the large cabinet above the sink and *voilà,* just like Uncle Sammy had said: Oxycontin sample bottles were lined up on two shelves like fat little soldiers. She opened one of the bottles. Look at all those beauties! She became so excited that for a moment she thought she might have to rush back upstairs to the bathroom. She made herself calm down. What to do? Swipe them all? Buy a big bottle of aspirin and swap out the Oxycontin? Take only a couple bottles? Maybe open them all and take a few out of each? But if she took them all, think how many highs she and Billy could have! This was the chance of a lifetime! What a score! Billy's never made this big of a score! But if she took them all, wouldn't Dr. Norm suspect me? No, not me. Duh, are you crazy? Of course he would, you ninny! You were taking care of his house! You had the opportunity! But why would I take them? Where's the motive? He would never suspect what we're doing with them. I'll bet he doesn't know anything at all about that. Like Billy says, adults are clueless. No, he'd think there'd be no reason for me to rip off pain meds. It'd just be a mystery. And who knows how long before Dr. Norm even noticed. It's not like people line up for his pills every morning. Could be months. And just think of all those highs! Billy's going to be blown away!

Ripping off Dr. Norm, girl! That's pretty low! He's been your doctor since forever! How many of your scraped knees and colds and such has he taken care of? How many times did he visit you in the hospital after the accident on Humpback Bridge? How many house visits after you got out? He never charged us, only took some fish from Daddy sometimes in payment. Rebecca looked at all the little bottles lined up. But Billy would think I was an absolute idiot to let an opportunity like this go by! All these could keep us high for a couple weeks easy! C'mon, it's a no-brainer!

Rebecca stuffed the bottles in her pockets and under her shirt. She returned upstairs where she lined them up on the coffee table in front of the TV. Dr. Norm said she could watch as much TV as she wanted. So she had, almost non-stop since he had left. She loved the TV because it was three times bigger than theirs in the trailer and it got a ton of stations. The picture was never snowy. She turned it on and flicked through the stations until she found an old movie. She sat down to watch. It wasn't long before she began looking back and forth from the TV to the line of bottles. Abruptly she stood and marched into the kitchen for a knife. Shaking out a pill, she ground it up into a fine powder. She found a small notepad by the telephone. She ripped out a page and rolled it up like a straw and snorted the powder. Within minutes she was smiling. She began to do a succession of pirouettes around the living room which excited the birds: Huey and Henrietta began to chatter and jump back and forth in the cages. Oh, life was wonderful…even here in Crescent Beach! She returned to the couch. Oh, what a score! Wait 'til Billy sees all these. Her eyes narrowed. *All*? Maybe

Billy doesn't have to know about *all* of them. She floated to the kitchen for a plastic bag to put all the pills in. No, she decided, shaking her head slowly. Not all of them. Gotta keep some for my own stash.

* * *

About the time Rebecca was dancing around the living room, Norm was exiting Interstate 75 in Sarasota. He turned onto Fruitville Road, heading west towards the Tamiami Trail and downtown. Originally he thought he should stay at a motel, but Bev convinced him to bunk in one of the boys' old rooms. No reason to throw away money, she said. She had been very cheery and said that they would all get together for a New Year's Eve dinner at the house. It would be just like old times. Don't bet on it, he thought. He hadn't seen his sons John and David in quite awhile. John, the eldest, had followed in Norm's footsteps—Duke Medical School, followed by a residency at Sarasota Memorial Hospital. Like his father, John had become a surgeon, although knees and shoulders were his specialty, not the heart like Norm. These days, though, their shared medical history was about all Norm and John had in common. John could not fathom why Norm had left an illustrious and extremely lucrative career to live in a backwater fishing village. What a waste, he had told his father over and over. David, on the other hand, lived off-grid in the bush of Alaska. The only way to reach the cabin he had built was by walking or four-wheeler in the summer, and by snowmobile or cross-country skiing in winter. Although he supported himself as a bush pilot flying wealthy people into sporting camps, David also hunted and fished and trapped for a good percentage of his and his girlfriend's food. David had never been to Crescent Beach, but Norm believed he would like it. David was an outdoorsman, and the outdoors was what Crescent Beach was all about.

Norm turned south onto the Trail, heading straight to Sarasota Memorial where David had already been admitted. Through his connections, and hoping to minimize any chance of infection, John had made sure that David would be the first person to be operated on in the morning when the operating room was squeaky clean. The hospital was not far and Norm soon pulled into the parking lot. Everything was so familiar. Over there was the doctors' parking lot; he could see his old spot. Inside hadn't changed either. Although he didn't recognize any of the staff, the smells, the noises, the bustling around, the fluorescent lights were all too familiar. There was no nostalgia, however—the hustle and bustle did not make him feel warm and fuzzy in the slightest. He took the elevator up to his son's room.

Norm knocked softly and entered. David was asleep. The last time Norm had seen him, David was tan and fit and glowed with good health. Norm was shocked. His face, neck, and arms were pale, and there were tight lines around the mouth and eyes. David looked like he had aged ten years. Indoors night and day, and in chronic pain would do that, Norm knew. David woke when Norm pulled a chair up to the bed.

"Hello, Dad," David said, with a tired smile. Norm bent down to lightly kiss his cheek, and squeeze his hand.

"You look awful," Norm said, sitting.

"Feel awful."

"How'd it happen?"

"Going too fast. Came around a bend in the trail and a moose was right there. When I swerved to miss him, ran into a log and flipped. Snowmobile landed on top of me."

"How'd you get out."

"Crawled. Friend's cabin wasn't all that far away."

"You're lucky. Could have frozen to death."

David tried to get more comfortable. Norm jumped up to help. "I don't feel lucky. I feel like shit," he said, as Norm helped him with the pillow.

"In pain?"

"Not so much. Just drugged up. Hate the feeling. Just hope I don't get hooked. Easy to do with the crap they've been giving me."

David was all about eating and living healthy, Norm knew. He hated to poison his body. "What have they been giving you?"

"Painkillers like Oxycontin in honker doses."

"Oxycontin's addictive?"

"Hell, yes. Big time."

"All the promo stuff I've read doesn't say anything about that. Says with time release capsules there's no danger."

"Bullshit. If you take enough of it, long enough, it'll get you. Not to mention what the kids are doing with it."

"What kids?"

"Back in Alaska, especially this time of year when it gets dark so early. Kids get bored and want to party. If you snort the stuff, you get real high real fast. Instead of that time release, they get a massive hit all at once. Big, euphoric rush. It doesn't take long before their bodies begin to crave those big hits. The body also gets used to it and builds up a tolerance so it takes more and more to get that same big high. It's becoming a real problem. Besides the occasional overdose, kids get hooked so bad that they begin stealing to pay for their habit."

"Pharmaceutical reps sure didn't tell me any of that...Kylie didn't come?"

"Couldn't. Not this time of year. Has to keep the fires going." Norm shook his head, thinking his son and girlfriend were so hardcore. He wondered if he could have ever done that, lived like that off-grid, especially in Alaska. He was proud of his son and respected his lifestyle. But if the operation wasn't successful, David was going to face some big changes. "You staying at the house?" Norm nodded. David smiled. "When was the last time you saw Mom?"

"Long time; way before I learned the latest about the tennis pro."

"That's all over now."

Norm shrugged. "Doesn't matter. What time you going in?"

"Six-thirty."

"Prognosis?"

"Should be a piece of cake. Doctor's the best and done a lot of these with a good success rate."

"That's what I understand." Norm stood up. "I came straight here. I better go see your mother and get settled in. I'll come back after your dinner."

David smiled again. "Good luck."

"That's what I'm supposed to say to you."

Chapter Twenty-One

"Thirty-seven of them. I counted," Crystal told Tammy. Each of the toilet stall doors had a large oval photo of a 1900's woman. Just outside the stalls was the ladies' lounge with stuffed couches, marble end tables, and tall ornate birdcages. Tammy was more interested in the birds than the ladies' room stall doors. There was a cockatoo in one of the cages that could have been Henrietta's twin. The entire lounge ceiling was flowered; the floor was marble. Tammy and Crystal had never seen anything like it; it was beyond over the top. After powdering their noses, they returned to the gambling area of the Grand Casino Biloxi where Rusty was playing three card poker. Judging by the diminutive pile of chips, he wasn't doing so well. He looked up at the two women. They had been ready to go for some time.

"Easy come, easy go," Rusty said, smiling. He shoved the remainder of his chips out in front of him. "I'll put everything on this last hand, and then we'll go."

There were three others playing at the table. The dealer dealt. Rusty ended up with a pair of queens and a 10. The dealer had a pair of sixes, ace high. Rusty raked in the chips. He was ready to start over.

"No you don't, Bucko," Crystal said. "A deal's a deal." Rusty nodded and collected his chips. After cashing in, they returned to the Paradise Hotel via the Casino Hopper, a round-the-clock faux trolley that stopped at all the casinos.

When they got off the trolley, Tammy asked, "How about a nightcap?" Tammy hoped she didn't sound too eager, but she wanted to see Bobby again. He seemed so different now. When she and Crystal had dropped Rusty off to tinker on Bobby's truck, Bobby had given them a tour of his camper.

"Twenty-eight foot, 1964 Ambassador Double. Good solid old Airstream, made back when they really used thick aluminum," Bobby said. He opened the door for them to climb in. "I met a guy who told me he was a campground host in Florida in the winter, and in Minnesota in the summer. He passes through here on his way north and south. He told me that one summer there was one of those Airstream jamborees at the campground when a freak hailstorm hit with almost tennis-ball-size hail. Most of the newer airstreams were trashed, but the surface dings decreased in size with the age of the camper. There was negligible damage to the old ones like this baby."

Bobby showed them the custom shower he had fabricated, explaining that it was twice the size of the original. He had also yanked out the twin beds and built a custom queen size bed with drawers underneath. New appliances were in the kitchen, as well as a new AC unit in the ceiling. He had opened up the interior as much as possible, and painted the walls and ceiling an off-white. It was bright and spacious. "Been working on it for over a year now. Bar tips paid for the whole thing."

"I didn't know you could do stuff like this, Bobby." Tammy said.

"Lots of things you don't know about me now, Babe."

Tammy sat on the bed. "Comfy." She began to imagine the nomadic life—take off and go wherever you wanted, when you wanted. Find a beautiful spot and hang out. See new country. Mountain and lake sunrises and sunsets. Meet new people. Heck of a lot more exciting than running a bar and restaurant.

How many years had she busted her butt at the Club? Almost twenty-five! Twenty-five years of employee hassles, putting together food orders, repairing storm damage, wiping bloody noses from fights, mopping up vomit, listening to the same stories told by the same drunks year in and out.

The threesome entered Bobby's bar and sat on the same stools as the night before. Soon Bobby came smiling up to them. "About time you showed up. Two Hurricanes and a Bud?" They nodded. When he returned with the drinks, he asked the girls, "So how was the Biloxi tour?"

"Learned all sorts of stuff," Crystal said, after a sip of her drink. "Biloxi's named after a tribe of Indians. It was colonized by the French in 1699, turned over to the British in 1763 after the French and Indian War, then it was Spanish from 1779 to 1810. Finally, it was United States, briefly Confederate, then Union. A regular flag gumbo."

"I'm impressed. See what you missed working on the truck, Rusty," Bobby said, grinning.

Rusty rolled his eyes. "Did you get those parts?"

"Yup. What are you girls doing tomorrow while Rusty and I finish playing grease monkey?"

"Indoor pool and spa," Tammy said, smiling. "Going to be a tough day at the office."

Rusty was about to take a swig of beer when he stopped in mid motion. He put the mug down. When Crystal saw his expression, she turned to see what he was looking at. A tall blond man was escorting a woman past the bar. She was a knockout—tall, elegant, well endowed, tightly wrapped up in a velvety outfit that didn't leave much for the imagination. Crystal turned back to Rusty, laughing. "Easy, Grandpa. She's much too young for you."

Rusty shook his head impatiently. "No, not her. Look at *him,* Crystal."

Rusty's tone erased her smile. The man and woman had sat at a table in the middle of the room. The knockout's back was to her, but Crystal had a clear shot of the man. Crystal's head whipped back around to Rusty. Rusty nodded. "Oh my God!" she said.

Tammy and Bobby looked at each other. Tammy was mystified. Bobby asked, "You know 'Good Blow Joe?'"

"Let's say I know *of* him. Slater's his last name." Bobby nodded. Rusty couldn't take his eyes off Slater. Slater looked their way and signaled Bobby.

Bobby almost jumped. "Best tipper in the hotel," he said, before hurrying off.

Crystal began telling Tammy what Rusty had learned about Slater. Tammy's eyes got real big: this was all news to her. Rusty watched Bobby take Slater's order. When Bobby returned, Rusty asked, "So why 'Good Blow Joe?'"

Lowering his voice, Bobby said, "One of the jobs of barkeeps in Biloxi is to know where people can get stuff." Bobby knew that Rusty used to be a trooper. He held up his hands. "Me, Rusty, I'm clean. With my record, I don't want or need any trouble. All I do is carrot juice these days; but, like I say, part of my job is to direct customers to where they can get what they want…usually drugs or," he looked apologetically at Crystal and Tammy, "sex." Bobby cleared his throat. "Anyway, Slater comes over a few times a year in his boat from Naples. Keeps it at the hotel's marina. Funny thing is, just before he comes, coke is real hard to score. And what there is, has been cut big time. Then Good Blow Joe shows up and suddenly coke is plentiful and pure again. Now I don't know if the owner of the Paradise is involved, but everything's connected around here…not to mention that Slater's comped each time he comes—bar bills, hotel suite, food, the works. The scuttlebutt is that Slater must be bringing in the coke, hence the nickname." Bobby shrugged. "But, what do I know? I'm just a simple bar-keep trying to stay out of trouble."

"That's not all he does," Rusty said. "I'm pretty sure he's also a hit man for a Colombian cartel. Crystal and I think he's the guy who whacked Jimmy."

"Whacked, Jimmy!" Bobby looked at Crystal. She was looking down at her empty glass.

"Later, Bobby," Tammy said, looking at him and squeezing Crystal's hand.

After ordering another round of drinks, Rusty, his mind working overtime, continued to stare at Slater. Funny how things work. This could be the opening we need. If Slater's smuggling coke for the cartel, it must be in large quantities. Wouldn't be worth it otherwise. Catch him in the act and he'd be put away for a long time…probably just as long if he were convicted of killing Jimmy. When Bobby placed the beer in front of him, Rusty asked, "You say he keeps his boat here?"

Bobby nodded. "A beauty, can't miss it. Got a funny name I can't remember, but it's a real sleek cabin cruiser. Only cabin cruiser I've ever seen painted yellow."

"Think I'll check it out after we finish with your truck." Rusty continued to stare fixedly at Slater. How he wanted to nail that son-of-a-bitch! Slater looked over. They locked eyes. Probably not the best thing to draw his attention. Rusty tore his eyes away. He turned to Crystal. "How about we call it a night after I visit the little boys' room? I don't trust myself not to do something stupid, like kick the you-know-what out of that guy."

"Good idea; leaving I mean," Crystal replied.

Rusty stood and made his way to the men's room. Slater came in as he was standing at the urinal. Slater leaned against a sink. "Do I know you, friend?"

Rusty looked over. "Afraid not."

"Then why have you been staring at me for the last half hour?"

Rusty shrugged. "No reason…other than maybe wondering how you scored a dish like that."

Slater didn't say anything. Rusty gave himself a couple of shakes and zipped up. He went to another sink to wash his hands.

"I don't like being stared at, Red."

Drying his hands, Rusty said, "Last I heard, it was a free country, Bub." The wastebasket was next to Slater. Rusty calmly walked over to pitch in the paper towel. Only inches separated the two men. They were about the same height, but Rusty outweighed Slater by a good thirty pounds. How Rusty wanted to slam Slater against the wall! Instead, he said, "Have a good night," and left the bathroom.

Back at the bar, Crystal said, "Slater followed you into the bathroom…"

"Yeah, little bit of a pissing contest, but not in the urinal. Slater didn't like being stared at. You ready, Tammy?"

"Think I'll stay and have another drink."

Rusty and Crystal left. Tammy ordered her drink, and watched Bobby tend bar. He was a good bartender: efficient, attentive, played the patrons well. Could use him at the Club. The Club! It was the first time she had thought about work since she had arrived in Biloxi. Maybe she really could have something in life besides work. She watched Bobby mix drinks. He really was a hunk. He wore one of those polo shirts with a little crocodile on the chest. She could see the muscles work in his V back. So different from Norm who was softer, a tad overweight maybe, with no real muscle definition. I wonder how his son's operation went and what he's doing now. Probably having a glass of wine with Beverly celebrating old times. I wonder if that's all they're doing for old times sake. Tammy suddenly realized that, like the Club, this was the first time she had thought about Norm. She watched Bobby again. He was flirting with a bevy of drooling middle-aged women in their cups who looked like it was their out-on-the-town ladies' night. Tammy finished her drink. Another? Shouldn't. Why the hell not? She caught Bobby's eye and pointed to her glass. He motioned for her to come around to the other end of the bar.

When she was seated with the fresh drink in front of her, Bobby said, "It'll be slowing down soon and I've got glasses to wash. Figured maybe we could talk."

"Are you sure you wouldn't rather talk to your fan club?" Tammy said, nodding in the direction of the women. She also realized she was slurring a little.

Bobby smiled. "My, my. Jealous, Babe?"

"Hardly." Tammy sipped her drink. She looked over to the women again. "I imagine you get all the action you want around here."

Bobby stopped drying a glass. "I could have a different woman every night. Problem is, there's only one woman I want. I'll give you a hint: she used to be my wife."

They looked at each other for a long moment. Even with all the alcohol coursing through her veins, Tammy felt a stirring in her loins. She hadn't felt that in a long time. Bobby began to dry the glass again, his biceps flexing. "So tell me what happened to Jimmy, and how Rusty and Crystal got together."

* * *

The next afternoon Rusty watched from a bench as the *Pituca* eased into the only vacant slip at the marina. A man wearing khaki pants and shirt caught the bowline, and soon had bow and stern secured on both sides. Must be the dockmaster, Rusty thought. Two short, stocky men who only could be Latinos jumped down and spoke briefly to the man. When they passed Rusty, they were speaking Spanish. Rusty walked over to the *Pituca*. "Boy, she's a beauty," he said. The dockmaster looked up.

"That she is," he agreed. Rusty walked the length of the craft.

"I thought she was Joe Slater's boat."

"She is."

"Sure wasn't Joe who brought her in."

The man laughed as he stood. "Nope. Those two guys brought her over from the Creole Seafood Company just on the other side of that isthmus," he said, pointing. "Don't know why, but Joe always takes her over there first." He picked up a clipboard, looked at his watch, and filled out a form. Rusty slowly walked the length of the boat again. When the dockmaster finished, he asked, "So, how can I help you?"

"Just sightseeing. Staying here at the Paradise and the bartender told me about the boat." Rusty smiled disarmingly. "I'm a boat nut and wanted to take a gander."

"Sorry, but I got to go back to my office, and only owners and crew are allowed on the docks."

Rusty raised his hands, palms out. "Not a problem. Maybe I'll run into Joe at the casino tonight and see if he'll give me a little tour. Would love to see what she looks like inside." At the office door, Rusty said, "Have a Happy New Year."

The dockmaster smiled. "Likewise."

Rusty circled around the hotel and started walking down Cedar Street which he hoped would take him past the isthmus. The *Pituca* wasn't the only thing he wanted to take a gander at. It didn't take long before he came to a narrow inlet that wasn't more than a hundred and fifty feet across in the widest spot. To his right was the isthmus, and to his left the mainland curved out and around. There were warehouses on both sides of the inlet. Gate and a tall fence kept him from walking out the isthmus, so he continued down Cedar Street which followed the edge of the mainland and serviced the other warehouses. Although there were fences here, too, at least he could get closer to the buildings.

He soon came to the Creole Seafood Company. Two beefy security men sat in plastic chairs in front of a partially open gate. Beyond them, the macadam around the warehouse was full of potholes. Several fish delivery trucks with the company's logo and showing various stages of rust were scattered around. There were two large, wooden doors at the rear of the building. A different Latino from the two who had brought the *Pituca* over, came out a smaller door and started one of the trucks. He backed it up to the large doors which swung open. Rusty walked up to the gate, catching a glimpse inside the warehouse of a long dock with a shrimp boat tied to it just before one of the security men stood and came over.

"Sorry, but this area is restricted."

Rusty gave him his best 'aw shucks' smile. "What kinda seafood do they sell, if you don' mind my askin'?"

The man wasn't sociable. "Shrimp."

Rusty's smile was glued. "If I come back with a cooler, kin I buy some?"

"See what those trucks say? Wholesale. No you can't buy any goddamn shrimp. What you can do is move along."

"Geez, sorry; but you never know until you ask." Rusty started walking away. Muttering loudly enough for the man to hear, he said, "Shor woulda loved some of them shrimp."

"Damn moron," the man said to his partner as he sat down.

Chapter Twenty-Two

Returning from a cocktail party, Norm turned the Mercedes onto Orange Avenue. He and Beverly soon crossed a small humpback drawbridge. Trophy snook, Norm knew, hung out under that bridge, or at least they had fifteen years ago. Beverly touched his shoulder.

"Did you enjoy seeing your old friends, Dear?"

'Dear?' Where had that come from? Probably the alcohol: he had counted three glasses of Chardonnay. Not that he had been a saint; he'd *needed* two Jack Daniel's just to make it through. "Awkward," Norm said. "We don't have much in common anymore. Maybe we never did."

"Nonsense!"

Norm came up to the light at the Hillview Drive intersection and turned right into Harbor Acres. They wound their way around to their old house on the bay; Bev's house now. God, how it's changed around here, Norm thought. Harbor Acres had always been exclusive with some of the nicest, albeit one-story, houses in Sarasota. But many, especially those by the water, had been torn down, replaced by hideous multistory McMansions. What a shame! Thorstein Veblen came to mind. *Conspicuous consumption!* It seems that the people around here now have to show how much money they have…or pretend to have. Bigger's better! If it glitters, it's got to be gold! He pulled into Bev's house and parked next to his Subaru wagon in front of the three-bay garage. They had to pass the pool on their way to the front door. In the shallow end was David, the middle of his back heavily bandaged, slowly walking back and forth. His walker was parked next to the chrome pool ladder. Norm sat at the edge of the pool. Bev said she had to check the roast beef.

"Should you be in the water?" Norm asked.

"Don't worry: the incisions are staying dry."

"Fifteen years ago you'd still be in bed in the hospital. They wouldn't have you moving around like that for over a week at least."

"Let's hear it for modern medicine."

"Where's your brother?"

"Coming over at seven."

Norm looked at his watch. "Twenty of." He stood. "Think I'll see if your mother needs any help."

"Things seem to be going okay with you two."

"We're tiptoeing."

David nodded. Norm left him with his exercise.

As Beverly, David, and John sat down to dinner, Norm began to make the rounds with a nice Pinot Noir. He filled Beverly's glass first. "Thank you, Dear," she said. 'Dear' again, thought Norm. John and David looked at each other. Norm filled their glasses, his, and sat down. He raised his glass.

"Here's to David's new back; that it mend with ease and last a lifetime!"

They all drank.

"And here's to having our family back together again," said Bev. Norm avoided Bev's eyes and took the smallest of sips.

Quite a meal: rare roast beef, Yorkshire pudding with gravy, broccoli with hollandaise, and tossed salad. Bev had made quite an effort. They had another bottle of wine. When Norm started answering David's questions about Crescent Beach, John couldn't help himself: he began ragging his father. "Crescent

Beach," he said, derisively. "What a waste of your God-given talents, Dad! It's absurd!"

"Don't. I've heard it all before."

"And you'll hear it again! One of the best damn cardiac surgeons in the state, hiding out in Hicksville, fishing and God knows what else you do in that pimple of a town."

"It suits me."

"It suits him!" John exclaimed, looking around the table. David was pushing a piece of Yorkshire pudding around with his fork. Beverly got up to clear. "How the mighty have fallen!"

Norm put his napkin on the table and stood. "Here, let me help, Bev."

"That's it. Get up and walk away. Don't face your… your crime!"

Norm turned angrily to John. "Enough!"

Out in the kitchen, Beverly was slicing up a Key Lime pie. Norm waited to take the plates out. Bev said, "He's right, you know."

"Don't start."

"Are you still with the saloon keeper?"

'Saloon keeper!' "You mean, Tammy? Yes I am. I should be with her now."

"You should be with your family!"

"Oh, but of course—our tight knit family! Actually, it *was* tight-knit once; but that was before…" Norm didn't finish; he let it hang. He took the pieces of pie out. They ate in silence until Beverly asked, "When are you going to settle down and get married, John? Your father and I want some grandbabies." Norm couldn't care less about a grandbaby, but at least John was on the defensive now.

"Don't start, Mother, please."

"You're almost thirty years old," she persisted. "I want to have grandchildren before I'm an old woman!"

"Maybe John's gay," David put in, eyes smiling. Beverly looked shocked, Norm amused. John laughed.

"Yeah, that must be it," John said. John had a solid reputation of hitting on every good looking, single nurse at Sarasota Memorial. He was one of the most eligible bachelors in Sarasota. "Maybe my clandestine boyfriend should be here. We could have a contemporary version of 'Guess Who's Coming to Dinner.'"

"Oh hush," Beverly said. She went back to eating her pie.

When they finished, Norm asked John, "Are you going to stay and watch the ball fall with us."

"Are you kidding! Big party at Marina Jacks. I'll be leaving as soon as I do the dishes."

After John left, Norm wondered what they'd all do for the next two hours. He hoped Tammy was having a better time than he was.

"Dad, I want to go outside. Come with me?"

"Sure."

Norm held the door open for David to shuffle through with his walker. Negotiating the thick tendrils of St. Augustine grass, David slowly made his way to the dock. They could see the lights of downtown Sarasota off in the distance. Norm thought back to when his Lyman was tied up here, and when there were no high-rises.

"Sure has changed, hasn't it, Dad?"

"Too damn crowded."

David laughed. "Got that right."

"How long before you return to Alaska?"

"Giving it a month."

"Maybe you could visit my 'pimple of a town' before you leave. It's old Florida."

"We'll see."

The walk to and from the dock had tired David. He begged off watching the new year come in and went to bed. Beverly mixed Norm a drink. They sat in the living room in front of Times Square. Norm didn't know what to say because there was nothing to say. How he wished he were in Biloxi!

"What did you mean that you had nothing in common with your old friends?" Beverly asked.

"Just that. We live in different worlds. All the one-upmanship here. Everybody trying to be cleverer than the next person. And all the glitter! The big houses, the fancy cars, the cabin cruisers. I live in a town full of rusty pickups, with people who don't play games and where life is real…work is real. They say what they mean and they use their hands to make things, real things that are practical and useful. They…"

Beverly interrupted. "You used to use your hands, too…to save lives." Silence. She left the room. Norm picked up his glass. He took a sip. Whoa, that's strong! Beverly returned in her bathrobe and bare feet. He watched her pour a glass of wine. She was still a very goodlooking woman. Classy, too. Sure, a bit of crow's feet, but a very tidy figure for someone her age. The tennis kept her in shape. Tucking her feet under her, Beverly sat a little away from him on the couch. She looked at him over the rim of her glass. Norm didn't want her that close. He didn't like that look. He cleared his throat.

"Still playing tennis at the Club?" Beverly nodded and leaned forward to put her glass down on the coffee table. Her bathrobe parted and Norm could see she was wearing a black nightie. That wasn't all he could see. He looked quickly away. The exposing of her breasts had been no accident.

"Norm?" Her tone was soft, inviting. He turned to her. She hadn't covered up. He could see her breasts through the sheer fabric. Norm put his drink down next to hers, shaking his head.

"No way, Bev."

"Why not?"

"Because you killed it."

"I'm all done with him. It's been over for some time."

"You really don't understand, do you? I don't care about him. You killed it with the lies. You swore to me you weren't messing around; said it was a midlife crisis. You played me like a trout to get the house and huge alimony payments, then once everything was legal you moved in with him the next day. That, Bev, was when I stopped loving you. Nothing you can do or say can change that."

"You're a fool, Norm," she said, and drew in her bathrobe. She smiled thinly. "Guess there's no reason to wait for that ball to drop. I'm going to bed." She stood and walked towards her bedroom.

"Speaking of alimony, I'm not a highfalutin surgeon anymore making big bucks. I don't suppose there's any chance I could talk you into negotiating something a little more reasonable?" Bev laughed. It wasn't a pretty laugh.

"Fat chance. Go back to work if you need money."

"You don't need this big house on the water. You could sell it for a lot of dough and get something smaller. Something more manageable, like maybe a condo.

She stopped at her bedroom door and turned to him. "Don't you remember the wording of the settlement? Something like, 'she will be supported in the manner she's accustomed.' Well, Doctor, I'm accustomed to this," she said, swinging her arm around. She slammed the door behind her.

Norm finished his drink. He didn't notice the ball had dropped until he heard *Auld Lang Syne.* Maybe Tammy hadn't gone out. He went into the kitchen to use the phone. He called the hotel and they rang her room. No answer. Well, good. Glad she's having a good time with Rusty and Crystal. He returned to the living room. He watched the people partying at Times Square for awhile, then looked at his watch. Twelve thirty-five. He tried calling again. No luck. Time to hit the hay. He went into John's old room and went to bed. Before he fell asleep, he couldn't help hoping that Tammy wasn't having *too* good of a time.

* * *

Tammy, covered in confetti, was having a very good time. Crystal and Rusty were dancing cheek to cheek while she was watching Bobby trying to keep up with drinks. According to the clock, it was quarter past. People were still blowing on noise-makers. A middle-aged man more than a little tipsy asked her to dance. She turned him down. Bobby came up to her. "Sorry I didn't wish you Happy New Year before this, but I've been kinda busy."

Tammy laughed. "I know, I've been watching. You're really good, you know."

"For your information, I'm good at a lot of things." Tammy laughed again. She was feeling no pain.

"Anyway, Happy New Year..." He leaned halfway across the bar. Tammy hesitated, then met him halfway. It was no peck on the cheek. Their lips lingered. Tammy pulled away.

"And a Happy New Year to you, too." She had that feeling in her loins again.

Bobby looked at her, into her. "I get off at one, Babe..." He saw her hesitation. He took that as a good sign. "Think about it." He went to refresh drinks. Ten minutes later, he returned. He didn't say anything, only looked at her.

"Room 812."

Bobby smiled. "That's my girl."

Rusty and Crystal came up hand-in-hand. "Can't believe I made it 'til midnight," Rusty said. "But, I'm beat. What do you two say?"

"Me, too," Crystal said.

Tammy stood up from her stool. "Ditto." She stuck her hand out across the bar. Bobby took it. A flicker in his eyes. "Happy New Year, Bobby."

Bobby palmed her extra keycard and put it in his pocket. "Happy New Year, yourself." He shook with Rusty and Crystal before returning to the other customers.

Up in her room, Tammy's loins were almost throbbing with anticipation. She couldn't decide if she should put on a nightgown. Was she really going to sleep with him? She shouldn't! She couldn't! What about Norm! She'd never been unfaithful, not even close. They had been rock solid for so many years! No, no nightgown. She and Bobby would just talk. But maybe Norm's sleeping with his ex. She shook her head. No way. Not Norm. The feeling between her legs wouldn't go away. The minutes dragged on. She went and brushed her teeth. She sat back down. It was after one-thirty when the knock finally came on the door. Tammy jumped; she had nodded off. Smoothing her hair, she let Bobby in. He had a bottle of champagne in one hand, and a clear plastic container with some sort of orange drink in the other.

"Sorry it took me so long, Babe, but my replacement was late." Tammy felt awkward. She didn't know what to say.

Bobby smiled and held up the champagne. "Something special for a special occasion."

"What's the orange stuff?"

"Carrot juice."

"You're kidding!"

Bobby began opening the champagne. His biceps bulged. "Nope. Haven't touched alcohol since leaving Crescent Beach."

Tammy was impressed. "That's over two years!"

Bobby uncorked the champagne. "Yup." Tammy came over with two glasses. Bobby filled one with champagne, the other with carrot juice. "Here's to happiness."

"I can drink to that." She took a sip of champagne, but continued to feel awkward. "Um, let's sit down." There were two easy chairs in front of the TV. They sat there. Silence. Tammy looked everywhere but at Bobby. Finally, Bobby stood.

"Babe, maybe I better leave." Tammy reached up and put her hand on his forearm. Touching him was electric. Her whole body tingled.

"I'm sorry, Bobby. It's just…"

"I know. The doctor. You feel guilty as hell. I'll go…"

Tammy stood up. "No, don't. Oh, I don't know what to do. Norm's such a good man. Too good of a man. I don't deserve him."

"That's right, you don't. You deserve me. I'm telling you, Babe, there's nothing you can do about it. It's in the stars." Bobby reached out and encircled her slim waste with his hands. He drew her to him. She didn't resist. She couldn't. This time they really kissed, long and hard. They undressed each other. He pulled her close again. She ran her hands over those dinner plate pecs. He ran his over the smooth, round cheeks of her rear end. "Still got that world class butt." He reached down to feel her womanhood. Damp was an understatement. He lifted her up as if she weighed no more than a feather and carried her to the bed. She had forgotten how good a lover he was. The sun was coming up when they finally fell asleep.

Chapter Twenty-Three

If it weren't for the pot and an occasional sip of Billy's Southern Comfort, Rebecca would have been bored out of her mind. She just didn't see the point of driving a pickup with a jacked-up body and huge tires around and around in what amounted to a gigantic mud puddle. She watched as each driver took his turn revving his engine and driving slowly down into the mire, spinning his wheels and splattering mud and water all over. The muddier the truck, the better: it was status, a badge of *machismo*. When school started up again in a week, the student parking lot would be full of filthy trucks.

Not Billy's. Billy thought the event was as ridiculous as she did. His truck was stock, no huge tires; you didn't need a step-ladder to get in and out. He also kept it immaculate. But Billy was social and the January 2nd mud bogging was an annual event. Originally it had been held on New Year's Day, but with the dominance of Florida college football teams, it had been changed to the second: no way the young men of Taylor County would miss watching their teams in the bowl games. Even she had been sucked in this year with all three Florida universities playing in major bowls. Each had won easily, including Miami's winning the national championship.

"Look who's here," Billy said. Rebecca followed his gaze. She saw a shiny black Chevy Malibu slowly circle the bog. It stopped close by. Billy yelled over. "Virgil, you going down in there to show us how it's done?"

Virgil's teeth flashed white. "Billy boy, I don't see no mud on that truck o' yours."

"And you won't. Why don't you come over and partake of some recreationals and tell me what's shaking." Virgil got out of the car. He was all duded up with a black silk shirt, tight black Chinos, and black high top Nikes. He wore wrap around sunglasses and his head was a cornucopia of dreadlocks. He sauntered over. "Virgil, I swear I don't know why you've never been busted, going around dressed like that. If you don't look like a drug dealer, I don't know who does."

Virgil tapped his forehead. "Because I'm cool, that's why…So, is this social or business?"

"Both. Come on, Man, get in." Rebecca gave Billy a look like, 'are you crazy!'

Virgil laughed. "What's the matter girl? You don't like black?" Rebecca looked the other way. "Don't mind if I do, Billy." Virgil walked around to the passenger door. Rebecca scooched closer to Billy. Virgil laughed again. He climbed in and sat so their thighs touched. Bobby pulled out a thick doobie and lit it. He passed it to Virgil who took a big hit. "Here, pretty Missy," he said, handing Rebecca the joint. Virgil eyed the pint of Southern Comfort between Billy's legs. "Whacha got there?"

"Help yourself," Billy said, passing over the bottle. Virgil took a swig.

Virgil grimaced. "Ain't nuthin' more than kick-ass cough syrup," he said, and passed the bottle back. "That be the social. What be the business?"

"How are you fixed for Oxy?"

"Told you while ago. Hard to get. Inventory low."

"Want some—wholesale?" Rebecca looked at Billy. News to her. And the only Oxy they had was Norm's. What was he doing?

"How many?" Virgil asked.

"What's the price?"

"Twenty."

"That's less than half street price."

"It *is* half. Price come down. No one want to pay fifty."

Billy thought about it. "Alright." He handed Virgil one of Norm's little bottles. "You got fifteen there." Virgil examined each capsule. He reached into a front pants pocket and peeled three bills from a wad. He handed them to Billy.

"Why you don't sell them out there? Make more money."

"I want to keep this between you and me. And you don't want the competition."

Virgil flashed that big smile. "Amen, Brother. Good doin' business with you." He gave Rebecca's thigh a quick pat. "Any time Billy here treat you wrong, Missy, you just come and see ol' Virgil. Once you go black, you ain't never goin' back." Rebecca recoiled like she'd been touched by a snake. Virgil laughed and opened the door. "Be seein' you."

They watched him drive the Malibu to the other side of the mud bog. "Setting up shop," Billy said. "He likes you, Sweet Lips."

"Billy, why did you sell those? They were for us."

"Spending money. C'mon, let's blow this popcorn stand." They weaved their way around the rumbling trucks to the wide open pasture gate. A town road was on the other side. He gave her thigh a squeeze. "Missed you, Sweet Lips. What say we go get reacquainted?"

* * *

Once they entered Florida on Interstate 10, both sides of the highway became thick forest. Traffic was light and Crystal was soon lulled to sleep. Not Tammy, she was wired. Guilt and confusion permeated her being. How could she face Norm? What was she going to say? What could she say! She had cheated on him! Crystal and Rusty didn't know, or at least she didn't think they did, so maybe she just shouldn't say anything to Norm. Pretend nothing happened. But it did. Hiding it would be worse. At least for her. But what did she want to do with her life, with Norm, and now with Bobby? And the Club. She was more mixed up than ever.

She had enjoyed both times Bobby had come to her. Last night had been better than New Year's. No booze for her and still it had been exciting. Bobby's mellowed, he really has. It was comfortable, relaxed, fun. They had talked into the wee hours after making love. He said she should go with him in the fall. It jolted her—the idea. Take off and don't look back! So tempting, but how could she? The business. Norm. Oh, what was she going to do about Norm? Tammy looked out the window at all the trees rushing by. She didn't see any of them.

She had told Bobby no way, she couldn't. Norm was too good a man, plus she had twenty years into the Club; she couldn't just leave it. He said that's exactly why she should. Said she was a prisoner just like he had been for seventeen years in Raiford. Said it was time to set herself free. And he said the magic was gone between Norm and her, that it was time for a change. It made sense the way he put it. He saw her hesitation. Think about it awhile, he said. There's no hurry. Maybe come visit a couple times. Now that Rusty's got that old truck purring, we could give the camper a test run. See if you like it. One thing's for sure, Babe, we're destined, always have been. And we've got the magic now.

Rusty had set the cruise control to seventy-five on the interstate, and the Honda Accord ate up the miles to Tallahassee. From there they would drop down to Hwy 19. With no stops other than gas and snacks, he calculated it would take close to eight hours to reach Crescent Beach, which was a heck of a lot faster than following the coast through the Panhandle like they had on the way over. He drove by rote because he was as preoccupied as Tammy, though his mind was full of Slater. What were the odds of Slater staying at the same hotel? A million to one? Probably about the same as the sea captain in the comic book finding that white whale! And Bobby's scuttlebutt, too! 'Good Blow Joe!' If it's true, we've got a whole new ballgame! More than once Bobby said that Tammy's coming into his bar was in the stars. Don't know about that, but it sure looks like Slater and I are destined.

Crystal woke up and stretched. She put a hand on Rusty's thigh. "Want me to drive?"

Rusty shook his head. "I'm fine."

Crystal watched him for a while. "What are you going to do about you-know-who?"

"I'm going to meet with Captain Smathers. See what he says. The FBI and DEA will be brought in. The coke thing may or may not be true, but they can't pass on the possibility." Rusty turned to her. "But it's going to be a trade: my info for my participation in the bust…if there is one."

"That's crazy! Let them handle it, Rusty."

"Nope."

"They won't let you, anyway."

"We'll see."

Tammy piped up from the backseat. "How's the gas, Rusty?"

"Quarter tank."

"Just so you know, I can pee anytime."

Rusty smiled. "Rest area in ten miles. Will that work?"

"You betcha."

The sun was low when they passed through Perry and turned onto the Crescent Beach Road. The closer they got, the more nervous Tammy became. She had had a hundred conversations with Norm in her head. None of them went well. They crossed the cattle gap and headed down Main Street.

"Christmas lights have been taken down already," Crystal noted. Tammy didn't even look up.

They crossed Humpback Bridge and turned down Rich Man's Row. Tammy's stomach was full of writhing snakes. They stopped in front of Norm's. The Subaru was in the carport. Rusty got out and opened the trunk. He pulled out Tammy's suitcase and put it on the ground. Tammy hugged him and leaned in to kiss Crystal's cheek. "Heluva good time. Thank you both."

"Say hi to Norm, and tell him we'll catch up later," Rusty said, from the driver's seat. He put the car in gear and drove off. Tammy picked up her suitcase and looked up the stairs. The door opened and Norm came out. He had a big welcoming smile. It vanished when he saw Tammy's face.

Chapter Twenty-Four

The walls of the Cross City State Police barracks were still grimy and the same two cruisers were parked out back. This time, though, a late model black Ford sedan with Georgia plates was parked in the small front parking lot under one of the live oaks. Rusty entered the building. The corporal at the desk quickly ushered him into Captain Smathers' office. Captain Smathers was talking to two men in suits.

"Rusty, Special Agents Hamilton and Morales of the FBI." The pair nodded to Rusty. "They'd like to hear what you told me about Slater." Captain Smathers pulled a chair over from the sidewall. Rusty sat and began to tell the special agents everything except his source. He also didn't specifically name the Creole Seafood Company. When he had finished, Special Agent Hamilton spoke up.

"When do you think the next shipment might be."

"No way of knowing, but my source thinks in a few months. He's got big ears and will contact me when he hears something."

"Who's your source?" Hamilton asked.

"Sorry."

The two special agents looked at him.

"Why not?" asked Morales.

"Couple reasons. One, he wants to remain incognito. Two, I figure it's my ace in the hole."

"Meaning?" Hamilton said.

"Meaning I want to take part in the action."

"Forget it," Morales said.

An ‘I told you so’ expression was on Captain Smather’s face. Rusty shrugged. He stood and, looking down on the two special agents, said, “Sorry if I wasted your time.” He turned to leave.

“Legally we can force you to tell us,” Morales said.

“Tell you what? I don’t know a thing.” Rusty left the room.

He got as far as his car before the corporal motioned him back. In the office, Hamilton asked, “What’s your involvement?”

“The fishing guide with the judge was my best friend.”

“So you’re emotionally involved,” Morales said.

“Might say that.”

Morales rolled his eyes. He turned to Hamilton. “No way.”

Smathers spoke up. “Rusty here was a state trooper for over twenty years. Before that he was an MP in Vietnam for three tours of duty. His record is commendable. And he was the lynchpin for our making the biggest dope bust on record in this area. The dope, incidentally, was smuggled in by the cartel Slater works for. I might add that he also found that Mexican waitress after you guys came up empty-handed. Sergeant McMillan would be a help, not a hindrance.”

The two special agents looked at each other. Hamilton looked at Rusty. “Highly unusual. I don’t know if it’s ever been done.”

“Legalities, too; especially if it gets rough. It’s nuts to even consider it!” Morales said.

Hamilton continued as if he hadn’t heard Morales. Looking at Captain Smathers, he said, “Maybe if he were reinstated with the state police, then loaned to us on special assignment? Or maybe he could be deputized like in the old days.” He looked back at Morales. “Coke trafficking is out of control and the

Bureau wants some results pronto. We bust Slater on a major coke deal and we can put him away for a long time. It might even lead to someone higher up in the cartel." To Rusty, "I'll broach it in Atlanta. We'll be in touch." The two special agents stood and left the room.

"Thanks for the kind words, Captain," Rusty said, standing up.

"I hope I don't regret them."

Rusty left the Cross City barracks. He felt encouraged. He looked at his watch. It was already after five and it was Thursday—poker night. He didn't feel like cooking. He'd go straight to the Club, grab a cheeseburger and a beer. Other than a few logging trucks hauling tree-length slash pine to the mills in Cross City, there wasn't much traffic on Highway 19. A half hour later when he turned onto the Crescent Beach Road, he thought back to when he had returned from Biloxi two weeks ago. The big news had been Skillet and the rattlesnake. The town still hasn't gotten over that dog's death, not even close. Skillet was beloved by the whole community. But that news was dwarfed days later when Tammy moved out of Norm's into one of her cabins. Totally unexpected. The talk of the town. Norm only comes to the Club on Thursday nights now. Rusty shook his head. Trying to play poker with those two in the same room is like having two live wires dangling from the ceiling next to each other: you never knew when they'd touch and shower you in sparks.

* * *

Norm guzzled the last of his drink and debated making another. He was drinking too much, especially on Thursday nights. But it bolstered him. He didn't know if he could face her without the alcohol. And it had to be better than hiding at home like he did the rest of the week. She said she was confused. Said it must be some sort of midlife crisis. He'd heard that before. That's what Bev had said, although Bev had omitted the part about the tennis pro. At least Tammy told me about Bobby. Bobby! What were the chances! And that's why she said she had to move out, that she couldn't share my bed after what she'd done. She needed time to think, to sort it all out. It was for the best, she said, at least right now. Norm stood and walked over to the bar. He made himself a short drink.

He had known right away from the expression on her face. Tammy couldn't hide her emotions. She said we should have that little talk and began crying as she exorcised the guilt of her infidelity. She said it wasn't me, it was her; that she felt trapped, that she wanted a change, that she didn't know if Bobby was just an infatuation or what. One thing she did know, she said, was that I was too good for her. Guess the bottom line is that nice guys finish last.

She said Bobby was just part of it. That has to be true because things weren't good before she went to Biloxi. But if she was just tired of work and feeling trapped, we could have spiced things up. If she wanted to see more of the country, hell, more of the world, then no problem—we'd travel. But now Bobby's entered the picture! I asked if she had forgotten how many times he had beaten her up when they were married. What about the time he broke her jaw? That was when he was drinking hard alcohol, she had answered. He doesn't drink any kind of booze now. And that was twenty years ago; he's changed. Maybe that's what I have to do, Norm thought. Be more of a bad guy. Maybe women expect that. Need that. Maybe that keeps relationships from getting too humdrum. Keep them on their toes. He looked around the living room. It was so quiet! He never would have guessed how much he would miss the birds, especially Huey. There was no chatter, no seed to sweep up, no little buddy to talk to. Norm sighed and walked over to put his glass in the kitchen sink. He pulled his jacket from the back of a chair and left for the Club.

Entering the Club, Norm saw Tammy behind the bar. He walked straight to the poker corner. He was the last to arrive. Nods of greeting from Rusty, Beau, Craig and Ralph, Charley, Louie, Tiny, and Sammy. Beau was shuffling the cards. Norm made little stacks of the quarters he emptied from his pockets. Tammy set his customary Jack Daniel's in front of him. Norm, eyes straight ahead, didn't acknowledge it. Tammy walked away. Beau cleared his throat. "Five card stud, deuces wild, quarter ante." Quarters plinked onto the center of the table.

A couple hours later, Beau said, "I'm dropping out early tonight. Think I'll let T and little Boda get a regular night's sleep."

"They git jest as much sleep at your place as they do at home," Tiny said. "Besides, they like to visit Miss Virginia."

"Still, I should go. These last few days, since Virginia realized what happened to Skillet, have been tough. She feels so guilty! I wish people would stop coming up to her with condolences! I know they mean well, but each time it triggers the guilt. She withdraws more and more. Some days she sleeps around the clock; never even gets out of bed." Beau cleared his quarters off the table and stood. "Besides, you gents have about cleaned me out." Charley and Louie were the big winners. They were almost always the big winners.

They watched Beau leave. Charley said, to the table, "What he needs is a new Lab puppy."

"I suggested that," Louie said, "but Beau says that he and Virginia are too old. Says that it wouldn't be fair to the dog."

"And he probly don' wanna clean up messes, and git his shoes and socks all ate up," said Sammy.

Tammy had been listening. She came over to the table. "I think it's a good idea. I think it would give Beau a break from worrying about Virginia. You know he'd bond with it. And I think a puppy might be good for her, too. Put a smile on her face...What do you think, Norm?"

Norm had been quiet most of the night. He looked blankly at Tammy. "Well, well, who'da thunk my opinion still mattered." The room became very quiet.

"Of course your opinion matters! Do you think I'd have lived with you for seven years if it didn't?"

"But then you got the seven year itch and hadda be scratched." He smiled sarcastically at the others. He was slurring. "First I lose my wife to a tennis pro. Now I lose Tammy to a goddamn barkeep!" All eyes, except Tammy's and Norm's, were suddenly interested in the floor.

"Don't be a snob, Norm! For your information, you've been living with a 'barkeep,'" Tammy countered.

"Guess water seeks its own level."

"I guess it does."

Norm threw some bills onto the table. "Keep the change." He stood up unsteadily and left the room.

Chapter Twenty-Five

Billy drove up over the curb of the *cul-de-sac* and parked at the woods' edge, out of range of the streetlight. There was no moon which was good, but Billy could do without that barking dog. He heard the yapping as soon as he turned off the truck. It was non-stop. Owner's probably inside watching TV, he thought. Billy pulled out a small flashlight and quickly found the trail leading into the woods. He kept a close eye out for snakes. The hardwood hammock of mostly water oak, sweet gum, and cherry, butted up to a new middle class housing development. Several narrow footpaths diverged off the trail leading to the various houses. The second house Billy passed had the little yipping dog. The fourth was his destination.

The house was dark except for the lights above the front door and wheelchair ramp. There was no vehicle in the carport. It was Wednesday night and Billy knew that the owner was playing bingo at the local VFW post. Billy put on latex gloves and stepped out of the woods. He tried a rear door. Locked. The first two windows wouldn't budge, but the third grudgingly slid open. Billy climbed in. Billy had followed the man home from the Perry hospital weeks ago, thinking that if there were ever a candidate for pain meds, this guy was it: the man was legless and wheelchair bound. Billy had staked out the guy's house for several nights and it was then he learned of the bingo. He shone the light around. The furniture was arranged to accommodate a wheelchair. Pretty Spartan except for a huge flat screen TV. Billy located the master bedroom and bath. He went straight to the cabinet above the bathroom sink. He was excited. It was like being on a treasure hunt. He opened the cabinet and smiled.

The shelves were full—percoset, fentanyl, vicodin, and other meds he had never heard of. He had hit the jackpot! He shoveled every med he could find into a small plastic bag. What a coup! He and Sweet Lips would party tomorrow! He'd do some research tomorrow, too, on the mystery meds. He left the bathroom. He shone the light around the bedroom. Framed pictures and medals were on the wall above a large bureau. One was the service picture of a young Army corporal. The gold, red, and blue triangular patch of the First Armored Division was also framed, as well as a Purple Heart. Sitting alone on top of the bureau was a large framed black & white of the same corporal in a wheelchair shaking hands with President George Bush.

Billy knew he should leave, but he might as well poke around a little. There was no hurry. He went to a bedside table. The drawer was full of skin mags. Poor sucker, Billy thought, bet it ain't easy to get laid with half a body. He went to the other bedside table. Another score! There was a small wad of cash and a service revolver. He counted the bills before he put them in his pocket. Seventy bucks. He picked up the handgun. A Beretta M9 semi-automatic. He hefted the gun. Good feel to it. Should bring a good price in Old Town. He poked around a little more before returning to the open window. He climbed out. The dog was still barking.

* * *

"It don't take two of us to shut up some damn poodle, Sarge!" the young patrolman said.

"That's alright. It'll give you two something to do."

The detective and Perry patrolman left the stationhouse and climbed into the squad car. The patrolman was behind the wheel. Although young, he already had a tumescent tummy pressing against his heavily starched shirt.

"Finally graduate from the academy and ready for some real police work, and what do I get? Doggy duty!" the patrolman complained.

"Would you rather be digging ditches?" the detective asked.

The patrolman started the car. "Where we going anyway?"

"That new subdivision to the east of town, not far from the Buckeye Mill."

Fifteen minutes later they drove through a gate with a pompous lion sculpture on each side. They slowly cruised past the houses until they came to the *cul-de-sac* at the end of the subdivision. The patrolman turned off the motor. Sure enough, they could hear the dog barking.

"Sounds like it's coming from that one," the detective said, pointing. The driver started the cruiser and began to turn around. The headlights just reflected off Billy's truck. "Hold it!" The detective reached for the powerful spotlight charging in the cigarette lighter. He shone it over to the woods and Billy's truck. "What's a truck doing there this time of night?" He shone the light on the license plate. He called in the number.

The sergeant chased it down. "Registered to George Streeter here in Perry. I think he's a Buckeye big shot."

"Odd place for a truck. Any report of it being stolen?"

"Nope."

"We'll check it out."

"That's a ten-four."

They got out of the truck and approached Billy's truck. It was locked. They shone the light into the interior. Nothing suspicious. "Maybe this Mr. Streeter's having an affair," the detective said. The dog was still barking. “Why don’t you disappear the squad car and we’ll see if anyone shows up. Maybe there’s a reason why that dog’s barking.”

They didn’t have to wait long. Only a few minutes after the squad car was parked behind a half completed house, they could see Billy’s flashlight winking in the woods. They waited behind a bush. The patrolman had his gun in hand. When Billy cleared the woods, they jumped out with the detective turning a big heavy flashlight directly on Billy’s face, yelling, “Stop! Police!” Billy was carrying his flashlight and bag of drugs in his left hand. He held the pistol in his right. He was blinded by the light and quickly raised a hand to shade his eyes. Unfortunately, it was his right.

“Gun!” yelled the patrolman. The detective snapped off the light and ducked as the patrolman fired three quick shots at Billy. Two of them missed. The third hit Billy in the head and he crumpled to the ground. The detective turned on the light again. Billy was in the death throes. They carefully approached, both had guns drawn. The detective turned him over.

“Oh lord! Just a kid!”

“Yeah, a kid with a gun!” the patrolman said.

The detective kneeled by Billy. He tried to find a pulse. There was none. “Oh lord,” he repeated. Neither the patrolman or the detective noticed that the dog had stopped barking.

Perry was not that big of a town and the news of Billy’s death traveled fast. The next morning Rebecca hadn’t made it halfway across the parking lot from the school bus when a girlfriend ran up to tell her. She didn’t believe it. No way! But then others came up. Rebecca was soon surrounded by a circle of faces etched with sympathy and the morbid glee of delivering horrid news. He had been shot by the police. In the head. He was dead. Billy had a gun. Rebecca screamed.

She could not be consoled. She was hysterical. A torrent of tears. She tore at her hair. She started lashing out at the circle of girls. She pushed away anyone who tried to touch her. A girl ran for a teacher. The teacher couldn't control her. There was quite a crowd now. Other teachers came out and together they were able to bring her to the infirmary. When she had calmed down enough, she was taken to the principal's office. Her parents were called. Clem left work and drove in with Katharine to get their daughter.

She spent the next two days in bed. She wanted to die. She began to have terrible insomnia. Katharine tried her best to get her to eat. Clem came home from the marina several times daily to check on her. Rebecca asked him to find out when the service would be. He made some calls from the marina. Billy was to be cremated. There would be no public service. Only family. Other details surfaced. Billy had been stealing drugs from a crippled Operation Desert Shield vet when confronted by the police. He had stolen the gun, too. The young patrolman was put on paid leave. Billy's father was suing the police department.

Katharine thought that all the stress had compromised Rebecca's resistance because she came down with the flu. All the symptoms were there—runny nose, sweating, chills, fever. Norm came over. He thought it was the flu, too. Told her to drink plenty of fluids. But it wasn't the flu. With her mother hovering over her every second, Rebecca couldn't do drugs and she had started going through withdrawals. She and Billy had been doing a lot, upping the ante to sometimes a dozen in a day. Their tolerance had grown; it took more and more to get that real good high. That was why Billy had ripped off the army veteran: their supply was dwindling. And now Billy was gone.

She still had her stash of some of Billy's grass and some of Dr. Norm's pills. But it wouldn't last long. And Billy would never score any more. It was up to her now. She needed money. But how? Where? Rebecca stayed home for a week. She went through her mother's purse. Ten lousy bucks! She walked around town, developing an eye like Billy's. The condominium people were beginning to leave fishing gear down below in their boats again. But even if she stole that stuff, what would she do with it? She had no contacts. She had no transportation. What she needed was cash. She walked down Main Street towards the point where she would smoke a joint. She passed Tiny and T's bait shop. She walked another fifty feet before she stopped. She returned to the bait house. The tank was bubbling away. It was full of shrimp. Midweek Tiny and T had other things to do besides tending to sales. There was an honor system: people could help themselves to shrimp or ice, and leave the money in a big plastic jar. Rebecca saw the jar on the counter next to the shrimp tank. It was half full of bills. She continued her walk to the point. That night she returned to the bait house. She took all but a few of the bills from the plastic jar.

The first day back in school, Rebecca walked to the downtown during lunch break. She turned into Virgil's alley off Jefferson Avenue. Virgil's Malibu was parked in its usual spot. And so was Virgil, leaning back in his chair, reading the Perry News-Herald. He looked just like he did at the mud bog. He put the paper down when he heard Rebecca approach.

"Sorry about Billy boy. Messy business." Rebecca, numb from commiseration, shrugged. "Why you here, Missy?"

"Want to buy."

"How much you got?"

"Ninety dollars."

"Won't get you much."

"What will it get?" Virgil told her. She agreed. "C'mon then, let's take a ride." Virgil drove to a copse just north of town. “Be right back.” Virgil disappeared among the trees. Ten minutes later he returned with an assortment of pills in a baggy. He handed her the bag, she handed him the money. He drove her back and parked across the street from the high school. “Missy, you’d get way more bang for your buck if you buy some Horse.”

“Don’t like needles.”

“Smoke it or snort it then.” Rebecca shrugged and started to get out. “Wait.” He reached into his shirt pocket for a tiny packet. “Here’s some Horse. On the house, sorta like an introductory offer. See if you like it.” He passed the packet to Rebecca. “An’ Missy, you come see ol’ Virgil anytime you want. An’ don’t worry none if you’re short of cash,” he added, smiling and putting a hand on her thigh. “I’m sure we could work something out.” Rebecca couldn’t get out of the car fast enough.

Chapter Twenty-Six

It was Tiny's turn to shuffle. The cards all but disappeared in his meaty hands. He talked while he dealt. "So I think I'll be putting up a game camera."

Louie was arranging his cards. "You sure you're being ripped off?"

"All I know is we usually clear aroun' a hundred or more a week unless the weather's nasty or the winter low tides keeps people away. Ain't been neither the last three weeks an' been averagin' about twenty bucks. T says someone's got their hand in the till fer sure."

Tammy overheard Tiny and walked over. "Just last week a woman said her wallet was swiped out of a purse she left below in the front seat of her car."

"The condos, Tiny and T's, and now robbing cars in front of the Club. This is not good," Beau said. He threw a quarter into the center of the table. "I'm betting twenty-five."

"I'll bump it twenty-five," Louie said.

"I'm in," said Sammy.

"Me, too," said Tiny and Rusty. Craig and Ralph stayed in; Norm and Charley bowed out.

"How's Rebecca's flu, Sammy?" Norm asked.

"Gone almost overnight, though she does seem real tired all the time. Fell asleep at the dinner table the other night."

"Got to be the quickest flu on record. Clem and Katharine okay?"

"Yup…I'll take three, Tiny." Everyone drew multiple cards. Only Beau drew one.

Beau raised another twenty-five. Louie bumped him again. Beau eyed him over his cards. "Must have something pretty good, Louie."

Louie smiled. "Bet on it."

"I already have."

The others all stayed in. Big pot. Sammy called. Beau was the first to lay down his cards. "Straight flush," he said, looking around the table. Everyone, including Louie, threw in his cards. Beau rubbed his hands together and raked in the quarters.

"Starting softball practice in a couple weeks, fellas," Craig said.

"So, there's going to be a game?" Charley asked.

"Looks that way," Craig answered. "William's already received verbal approval from Tallahassee. Said the paperwork should go through in another week."

"So when's the game, Craig?" Tiny asked.

"William and I had thought it appropriate to have it on opening day of spring training; that's March second. But that's a Thursday, so we agreed on the following Saturday, March fourth."

"I'll bring a case of beer for the team," Charley said.

"You do that, Charley," Craig said. "But no beer until afterwards. Then we can either celebrate or drown our sorrows."

"But we always have beer during games," Sammy whined.

"Not this one."

"Who's going to pitch?" Norm asked. "No one in town's ever pitched fast-pitch before."

"Except apparently William," Craig mourned.

"Yur wrong there," Tiny said. He looked at Craig. "I'm tellin' you, Craig. You should give T a look. She was all-state as a pitcher in high school."

"We'll see."

They played another hand. Charley took the pot. "Think that kid's father will win his suit against the police, Beau?" Charley asked, while stacking his quarters.

"Doubt it. The officer may have been fresh out of the police academy and overzealous, but the kid had a damn gun in his hand. I'm guessing that alone will squelch it. Just a damn tragedy."

"Seventeen years old," Louie said, shaking his head.

"Stealing drugs. There's more and more of that," said Ralph.

Norm looked up. "What kind of drugs."

"Opioids," Ralph said. "That's the rage these days." Norm thought of what David had told him.

"I understand the kid was Rebecca's boyfriend," Craig said, to Sammy.

"That true, Sammy?" Norm asked.

"Yeah. Shor fooled us. Katharine said he was polite, a real gentleman. Come from a good family, too. Father's one of the top dogs in Buckeye. The kid always brought Rebecca home when he said he would. Guess you jest never know."

The group played several more hands before calling it a night. On the way back to Rich Man's Row, Norm decided that he'd do some research on opioids. He thought about the kid that got shot. He was Rebecca's boyfriend. He was three years older than her and she's at an impressionable age. What are the chances she did drugs with him? Pretty darn good! And what did David say? That kids get hooked so bad that they begin stealing to pay for their habit. And now we've got the Condo,

Tiny's, and that lady's purse! Norm arrived at his house in what seemed no time. Amazing how quick that walk is when you're thinking about something else. He didn't go up the stairs. Rather, he unlocked the clinic and went straight to the medicine chest above the sink. He wasn't that surprised to see all the Oxycontin gone.

That weekend Tiny rigged his game camera up on top of the icehouse, camouflaging it by putting it in a three-sided aluminum box he fabricated and screwed into the icehouse roof. The open side of the box faced the oxygenated shrimp tank. He checked it a week later when he came in from shrimping. The video clearly showed Rebecca digging bills out of the plastic jar and walking away with them. He showed the footage to T. She was flabbergasted. They didn't know what to do. They decided to show Beau the tape. Beau set up a meeting with Tiny and T, Clem and Katharine, Sammy, and Norm in his office at City Hall.

Rebecca's family was shocked. They couldn't believe it. They had never suspected. Katharine was furious. Clem and Sammy totally mystified. Where had they gone wrong? Norm told them he suspected Rebecca stole the money for drugs, and that he also believed she stole Oxycontin from the clinic. "I have done some research," he said. "Rebecca's falling asleep at the dinner table, Sammy, could be a sign of opioid drug abuse. When someone comes down off a high, they are extremely drowsy." He turned to Katharine. "And when you were taking care of her round the clock a few weeks ago, she couldn't do any drugs. Those flu-like symptoms may have been early signs of withdrawal. I've never heard of a flu coming and going in a matter of hours. All she had to do to get rid of the symptoms was to ingest more opioids.

"If she is doing drugs, the first thing to do is to get her off them a.s.a.p. It won't be easy. She'll go through serious withdrawals. Depending on how severe they are, she might need some meds to help her through."

"What happened to my little girl? A thief and a drug addict at fourteen!" Katharine said.

"Was hangin' out with the wrong people. Maybe it's better that boy ain't aroun' no more!" Sammy spat.

"But Billy was so polite." Katharine looked miserable.

"Can't judge a book by its cover," Sammy said. He looked at Clem. He had his head in his hands.

"What should we do, Norm?" Katharine asked.

"Talk to her, all of you together. First, see if she'll fess up. Then see if she'll try to quit. Be patient, be kind. Support her."

Clem raised his head. "Norm will you help us?"

"Anyway I can."

Clem looked at his wife and brother-in-law, then back to Norm. "I think all three of us would like you there when we talk to her." Katharine and Sammy nodded.

"If you want." Norm looked around the room, his gaze stopping at Tiny. "One last thing. Tiny, have you told anyone? Charley?" Tiny shook his head. "Good. Let's keep this quiet. Rebecca needs help, not to be ostracized by the town." Tiny nodded. So did the others.

"Tiny, we'll pay you back."

"I ain't worried about some little ol' shrimp money, Clem. We jest gotta get Rebecca right."

That evening after Rebecca had returned from school and before dinner, Norm walked over to the trailer. He took a deep breath before knocking on the door. Katharine opened it immediately. Sammy and Clem were seated in the living room. They looked uncomfortable. Katharine went to get Rebecca from her room. Norm watched Rebecca closely when she came in. Her hair was stringy and unkempt. It looked like it hadn't been washed in a while; there was no sheen. She also looked drowsy, like she had just wakened. But it was her eyes that most interested him. The sun was close to setting in the west, and the living room windows were on the east wall of the trailer. No lights had been turned on yet and the room was dim. Pupils, Norm knew, continually adjust to lighting conditions, normally dilating in dim light, and shrinking in bright. Rebecca's were just the opposite. They were pinpoints: a classic opioid telltale. Rebecca was stoned.

"Hi, Dr. Norm."

Norm smiled. "Hi yourself."

"Sit down, Dear. We'd like to talk to you," Katharine said.

Sammy patted the couch. "Come sit next to me, Darlin'." Rebecca looked from one to the other. Something was up. She sat on the couch and folded her hands in her lap.

"Rebecca, we know that you have been taking the shrimp money from Tiny and T," Katharine began. Rebecca's stomach flip-flopped. But how could they know? She was sure no one had seen her.

Eyes wide in feigned surprise, Rebecca asked, "Someone's been stealing their shrimp money?"

Katharine looked at her with a mixture of disappointment, anger, and impatience.

"Yes, you! Don't deny it! Tiny set up a video and got pictures." Rebecca, suddenly sullen, shrugged. "Why did you do it?"

She shrugged again. "Why do you think? I needed the money."

"For what?"

"This and that."

"Do you think you could be a little more specific?"

"Just stuff."

Norm spoke. "Rebecca, did you take the Oxycontin from the clinic when you housesat?"

Eyes wide, she said, "Of course not." Norm didn't say anything, only looked at Rebecca. She turned away.

"Was that money for drugs?" Katharine asked.

"No! Just stuff." She hesitated, then added, "And food. You know, like McDonald's and Dairy Queen."

"That's a heck of a lot of ice cream sundaes," Katharine said, sarcastically.

"Rebecca," Clem said, softly, "we're on your side here. We want to help you. We can't help you if you don't tell us the truth." Atta boy, Clem, Norm thought.

Rebecca couldn't look at her father when she said, "I told you the truth."

"Then if you told us the truth, you won't mind if we search your room," Katharine said. She stood up.

Rebecca looked at her in alarm. "Of course I do! My room's private!" Katharine left the living room. Rebecca started to stand, but Sammy reached for her hand.

"Darlin', like your dad says, we're jest tryin' to help." Rebecca fidgeted. "You're gonna have to pay Tiny and T back. Gotta git a job this summer. I kin hire you if'n you want…"

"I don't want anything to do with those stinking clams, Uncle Sammy! I don't want anything to do with this rusty old trailer! I don't want anything to do with this boring town!" Sammy felt like he had been slapped. He didn't know what to do.

Rebecca started crying. Clem came over and squeezed in between her and Sammy. He put an arm around her shoulders. She buried her head into Clem's chest and really let loose: tears for Billy, for getting caught, for the dependence she knew she had, for the lies, for her lousy life.

"It's okay, Sweetheart. It's okay," Clem cooed. Katharine returned, triumphantly holding two small plastic bags. One was pot, the other was a collage of colored pills and little folded paper packets. She dropped them on the coffee table for all to see.

"Look what I found."

"You had no right! I hate you!" Rebecca said, bitterly. "Those are mine, I bought them!"

"With someone else's money," Katharine said, as she scooped up both bags and left the room. Seconds later they heard the toilet flush. Rebecca deflated like a leaky balloon. She looked down at the stained carpet.

"Rebecca, do you think you can stop? Do you want to stop?" Norm gently asked.

She looked at Norm. He had such a kind, caring face. "I…I don't know, Dr. Norm. They make me feel so good. It's the only time I feel good anymore."

"That's what it was like when I was drinking," Clem said. "It was the only time I felt good, too, Sweetheart. But if you can get clean, you can start over like I did. The Lord and I both know it won't be easy. You gotta take it one day at a time."

"Oh, Daddy, I don't know…I'm…I'm just so tired."

Clem stood. "C'mon. Why don't you rest. If you don't mind, I'll sit with you a spell." He took her hand and led her into her room. Katharine passed them in the hallway. Rebecca wouldn't look at her.

Rebecca made it almost three days before her withdrawal symptoms worsened. She began to get abdominal cramps and diarrhea. Her arms itched. She'd begin shivering and got goose-bumps. Her mood changes were all over the map. She couldn't sleep. And then there was the incessant craving. She was so fidgety—it felt like something was crawling around insider her. Her mother watched her like a hawk. Followed her around. Spied on her. She was driving Rebecca nuts. It was a relief to get back on the bus for school.

She couldn't concentrate in the classroom. The voice of the teacher faded. All she could think of was a hit of something, anything. She had tried the Horse, Virgil had given her. She liked it. It was cheap. She had bought more the next time she saw him. All morning she thought about the heroin highs. When the bell sounded for lunch, she was on some sort of weird cruise control. Her body knew where it wanted to go. It led her past the cafeteria, out the school parking lot, down to Jefferson Street. Virgil was in his usual spot.

"Missy, I didn't think I'd see you for a few more days. You must be hittin' it hard."

"My asshole mother flushed my stash down the toilet."

"A little strung out, are we? That be bad for you and good for business. What's your pleasure?"

Rebecca looked at the pavement. "I don't have any money, Virgil."

Virgil didn't say anything for a second. He reached out and lifted Rebecca's chin so she had to look at him. "Then maybe it be *my* pleasure we be talkin' 'bout, girl. You understan' what I'm sayin'?" Rebecca nodded. Virgil got up out of his chair. "What say we go for a little ride?" They drove to the copse north of town. Before he disappeared in the woods, Virgil asked, "What you want?"

"Horse."

Virgil smiled. "You smartened up, girl. Be right back."

When he returned, Rebecca said, "I want some now…before…"

"Sure thing, Missy, when we get to where we gonna play."

Rebecca didn't pay attention until she recognized the limestone road with its tunnel of live oak trees. It was the road that led to the old log landing where she and Billy had bought the Vicodin. It seemed like years ago. Virgil parked in the abandoned log landing and turned off the car. He put his arm on the back of the seat and looked Rebecca up and down while she fidgeted. She started scratching her arms. "C'mon, Virgil, let me do some."

"Sure thing, Missy." He unfolded a little packet of heroin and placed it on the dashboard. He pulled a bill from his wallet and rolled it up. He handed it to her. "This'll fix you right up."

Minutes later, she was wasted. Flying high! Oh yes, life was good again! She was smiling. She smiled at Virgil who was watching her. He reached over and unbuttoned her shirt. She didn't care. She wasn't even there. She was on a cloud. She was up high, looking down on what was happening. She moved so he could take her shirt and bra off. She watched his hands caress her. Black hands. Black on white. So unusual. The black hands pulled away. She watched Virgil get out of the car and walk around to open her door.

"C'mon, Missy." Rebecca got out of the car. "Kick them sandals off." She watched the black hands undo her pants. She stepped out of them, naked except for her panties. The black hands threw the panties onto the hood and began to gently touch her. She was infatuated with those hands. They felt good. She closed her eyes. The hands knew what they were doing. They were her friends. The hands pulled away. She wanted them back. She opened her eyes. Virgil began taking off his clothes. She had never seen a black man naked before. So interesting. Lean and mean. Way more muscles than Billy. Virgil removed his underwear. Oh my God, he's huge. Was it real? She reached out to touch it. It was real. Oh my God! Suddenly she was laughing.

"What's so funny?" Virgil asked. Rebecca was almost in hysterics. She caught her breath.

"I just snort some Horse, and now I'm about to do it with someone hung like a horse." She started laughing again. Virgil smiled.

"You know, Missy, I like you." He leaned back against the car. He spread his arms out wide with his fingers motioning her towards him. "Come to Papa…"

Chapter Twenty-Seven

Sammy was filling in at shortstop for Craig. Craig, bat and ball in hand, yelled, "Louie, you got to hit your cut-off man. Try to hit Norm in the chest. Norm, you should be halfway out in a straight line between Louie and Sammy. Let's try it again...Okay, nobody on and a base hit to right. Play's to second." Craig hit the ball hard between first and second. Louie fumbled the ball in right field before throwing to Norm who spun and whipped it to Sammy covering second. Louie's throw had about as much steam as a lob. "That's better, Louie. Good job." Craig sighed inwardly. He was trying to instill confidence in Louie who, aside from some of the women, was the weakest player on the team. Right field was definitely their Achilles' heal.

At the first practice, Craig had laid it out straight. "You all know our field's at stake. So, if the score's close or we're behind, I'm not going to play everyone; we need the best players on the field." Since then Craig had filled out his roster: Tiny was catcher, Rusty at first, Norm at second, Craig at short, Sammy at third. Tony the cement contractor was in left, Ralph in center, and Louie in right. T would pitch. Dave, a crabber from out in the country, would have been in right instead of Louie, but he had cut his hand pulling traps and it was badly infected. Norm said there was no way he'd be able to play. That meant Crystal, Linda from the library, and Dave's wife would be the benchwarmers. None of them had a problem with that and, under the circumstances, were relieved to leave it up to the men.

"Okay, everybody," Craig yelled, "time for BP and then we're done. Ladies first." T remained on the field. Tiny put on his mask. He set up behind the plate and T began to warm up. Craig watched her. He was tickled with T. Tiny hadn't been wrong—that girl can pitch! She was just what they needed to get used to fast pitching and there was a good chance she'd mow down the opposing players, too. Unfortunately though, so far he and Tony were the only ones who could hit her. Tiny and Rusty who pummeled the ball in slow-pitch, mostly flailed against her. But it was early yet, he told himself. Got three weeks. Those two will come around. Sammy will whack that apple at some point, too. Ralph's speed makes up for his lack of punch, so he should at least get some infield hits. Norm should do okay, but then there's Louie. Craig shook his head. He bails out on almost every pitch; even steps in the bucket if the pitch is way outside. He'd probably do better throwing his bat at the ball. Maybe I should tie an anchor to his left foot to keep it in the box.

Crystal, Dave's wife, and Linda took their ten swings before running out to help shag. The others came in and took their turn. Rusty was first. The outfielders backed up. It turned out that there was no need because Rusty's farthest ball was a lazy fly to shallow center. Craig and Tony hit some hot shots and long balls. Tony, like Craig, played high school ball for four years; Little League and Babe Ruth before that. He said that if it weren't for baseball, he would have quit school. He was drafted into the Army right after high school and did a tour of duty in Vietnam. He was in the infantry and saw the nasty. He felt lucky to have returned alive and was doing his best to enjoy life every day since. He became a cement contractor and did real well after the '93 storm leveled Crescent Beach. Houses needed to be raised eighteen feet up on cement piers, and new slabs, driveways, and seawalls had to be poured. Whenever there was a bad storm surge, there was more to do. Everyone liked Tony and he got all the work in town, even if it meant people had to wait. He was in his fifties and could retire anytime, but there were two things besides baseball he loved: work and beer. He and Charley got along great.

Tiny was the last guy to bat. He handed his mask to Rusty who replaced him behind the plate. He grabbed a bat and faced his wife. Like most of his teammates, he had trouble hitting T. He fouled off most of the pitches. After whiffing on a couple of fastballs, T threw him a changeup. Tiny swung well out in front and his six-foot-four frame got so tangled up he fell to the ground. Everyone, including T, laughed. Tiny didn't smile. He didn't say a word, just dusted himself off, and stepped back in for his tenth swing. T threw a strike right down the middle. Tiny hit it square. Rusty had never heard a softball come off the bat like that. The ball kept rising. The girls in the outfield craned their necks. The ball must have cleared the fence by a hundred feet. "There!" said Tiny. He dropped the bat on the plate and walked over to the bench.

Coolers were scattered around. Sammy and Tony had already cracked beers. Ralph was drinking a Coke. Charley had come over from the stands and helped himself to a beer. Craig was pitching to T with Rusty still behind the plate. Tony asked Tiny, "Did you get all of it?"

Tiny couldn't help grinning. "Not likely."

T sprayed line drives all over the field. When she finished and everyone was standing around the bench, Louie asked, "You been watching them practice, Coach?" Craig nodded as he popped a beer. "Who's that guy bats lefty?"

"Don't know his name, but he's from the north Gainesville area. He bought that half lot just off Main St. on 6th Avenue East. Says he's going to put a little camper on it."

"When did he buy it," Tony asked.

"About a month ago."

"William's from that area of Gainesville, too. Kinda suspicious, doncha think?" Tony said.

"Same thought crossed my mind, but what are you going to do? He's a bonified tax payer." Craig took a slug of beer.

"Louie and I watched him take BP," Tony added. "Hit a half dozen over the fence. Smooth swing…like Redford in 'The Natural.'"

"Regular Splendid Splinter," Louie put in.

Charley looked at Louie. "Say what?"

"Ted William's nickname, Charley. September 28, 1941, he became the last player to hit 400 in the majors." Louie was a die-hard Red Sox fan.

"Never claimed to know nuthin' about baseball. Jest like watchin' an' drinkin' beer."

"I'll drink to that," Tony said, clinking his can with Charley's.

Craig put his empty beer down on the bench. "Hey everybody, I got something to say." When he had everyone's attention, he said, "It's pretty obvious we need to work on hitting. How about another BP day after tomorrow, same time?" Everyone agreed. Only Rusty said he couldn't make it.

"Like to, Craig, but I'm heading up to Atlanta for a couple of days."

"What fer?" Charley asked.

"Business."

"What in the tarnation business you got up in them parts?" Rusty didn't answer. Sammy spoke up.

"Now ain't you the Curious George, Charley."

"No, just the *usual* Curious Charley," Louie said. "Charley can't help being a busybody, Rusty. Just his nature."

Rusty finished his beer and squished the can before dropping it in his Igloo. He picked up the cooler. "Sorry, Charley; if I tell you, I'll have to kill you." Charley's eyes widened. Rusty laughed. "Just kidding…Hate to miss BP, though; I sure as heck need the swings."

"Then how about we have it Friday?" Craig asked.

"That should work."

Craig looked around. No one said anything. "Friday it is, then."

Following Rusty's lead, everyone began to pick up empty cans and close up coolers. Craig and Ralph picked up the softballs and bats and shoved them into the canvas bat bag. Crystal put her arm through Rusty's and they walked to his pickup. Everyone began to leave.

* * *

Rusty had missed the worst of Atlanta's rush hour and he only made a couple wrong turns before he found the FBI Atlanta Field Office on Flowers Road just off the North East Expressway. He parked his truck and looked at his watch: it had taken a little over five hours and he was twenty minutes early for his meeting with Hamilton and Morales. He got out and stretched for a few minutes. The building looked like a high school, three stories, brick with large windows delineating each floor, and L-shaped. The grounds were immaculate with manicured bushes along both the entry drive and a circular grass island near the front door. He passed the American and FBI flags fluttering in the breeze. He looked at his watch again. Better a little early than late. He entered the building.

He walked up to the information desk and stated his business. The woman made a call and was told that Special Agent

Hamilton would be down shortly. She pointed to a line of chairs and said he could wait there. Rusty watched the staff, agents, or whoever they were, scurry around. The women wore conservative business skirts and blouses. The men had short, neat hair and wore ties. Rusty was wearing jeans, a sports shirt, and light jacket. He had worn a necktie every day for over twenty years with the state police. He didn't miss it one bit.

Hamilton strode up. "McMillan," he said, extending his hand. "How was the traffic?"

"Not bad."

"Lucky you. Follow me."

They took the elevator up to the third floor. Hamilton's office was the third on the right. Morales was looking out the window when they walked in. He turned and nodded curtly to Rusty. The room was antiseptic—beige wall-to-wall carpet, recessed fluorescent lights in the ceiling, and bare white walls except for a single large map of Georgia showing all the counties. Along each of the two sidewalls was a long, black Formica topped desk with square chrome legs that looked like something out of Staples. Several computers and printers were on the desks and underneath were filing cabinets. Two padded leather desk chairs were in front of each desk. In the center of the room were four more chairs surrounding a circular coffee table similar to the desks. The three men sat around the coffee table.

Morales was the first to speak. "I think you should know from the git-go that I wasn't in favor of this, McMillan, but I was overruled. If you stay out of my way and don't screw up, maybe we'll do okay."

"I'll do my best."

"You and Special Agent Morales will be working in conjunction with our field offices in Tampa and New Orleans. Also with the Coast Guard out of Tampa, New Orleans, and Gulfport,

Mississippi. I think you know," Hamilton added, "that the only reason the Atlanta office is involved at all is because the federal judge was from here. Normally the Tampa or Jacksonville Field Offices would handle everything in that area of Florida.

"Your suspicions of the fishing camp on the Manatee River were recently confirmed by an undercover Tampa agent. Consequently, we want to coordinate a sting there with Biloxi and we'd prefer, McMillan, that you assisted in that operation."

"Not a chance. The deal's Slater."

Hamilton sighed. "Figured as much. Okay, here's the scoop. When your contact tells you he expects another shipment, we will have a man watch Slater day and night. When he leaves for Biloxi, you and Special Agent Morales will monitor him from a Coast Guard reconnaissance plane that will be brought from Miami to Tampa. Be interesting to see who Slater meets up with and where. You and Special Agent Morales will return to Tampa where you'll hop on another Coast Guard plane that will take you to New Orleans to hook up with our S.W.A.T. team.

"Hope you don't have any plans for the next several days. You and Morales are going to fly this afternoon to New Orleans and meet the members of the S.W.A.T. team. They're going to give you some basic training, McMillan, so you don't embarrass us. Then you and Morales and someone from S.W.A.T. are going to drive to Biloxi to logistically check out the warehouse you told us about. Finally, on your way back to New Orleans, you'll meet with the Coast Guard commander in Gulfport to coordinate backup. How's that sound?"

"Guess I'll miss BP."

"What?" Morales asked.

"I play for a softball team and I have batting practice on Friday."

Hamilton laughed. Morales rolled his eyes and said, "Lord have mercy!"

Chapter Twenty-Eight

Norm rubbed his eyes and put the book on opioid addiction down on the table. He just couldn't concentrate. He looked over to where Huey's cage had been. He couldn't shake it: he missed Tammy. He pined for her. These last few weeks his anger towards her had been replaced by a stiff civility. She was equally polite. An improvement of sorts, he supposed. And his concern for Rebecca gave him something else to think about for a change. But yesterday Tammy came by the house to talk. When she told him she was returning to Biloxi for a few days, he felt like he had been kicked in the stomach. She said she wanted to be honest with him. He had lashed out, saying, "Honest, Tammy? Honest with me like you were on New Year's Eve?" She had spun on her heels and left. Norm had wanted to punch a wall.

But that wasn't all. He had the same feeling of evisceration as he did when he and Bev had separated back in Sarasota. He no longer had felt like the shining surgeon that the gods smiled upon. His confidence had been eroded with her rejection, his foundation had been pulled out from under him like a rug. It was the same with Tammy. When one's mate, Norm thought, the person you were closest to, the person you depended on and shared your innermost life with, suddenly and inexplicably didn't want to be a part of your life anymore, it felt like your innards were yanked out: you were no longer whole, there was a huge void, you doubted yourself.

He sighed and picked up the medical book again, flipping the pages until he found his place. He began reading when there was a light knock on the door. He hadn't heard anyone come up the stairs. "Come in," he said, putting the book down. Rebecca entered. Her face was tear-streaked.

"Dr. Norm, I have to talk to you…please."

"Of course. Come sit down." He led her by the arm to the couch. He sat beside her. She didn't look any better than when he last saw her. "What's up?"

"Dr. Norm, I…I…" She couldn't go on; she began to sob.

"Have you been taking more drugs?" She nodded wiping at her eyes, trying to stop crying.

When she settled down, she said, "I tried, Dr. Norm. I really did. I made it a few days, but then it got so bad I wanted to die. I felt like ants were crawling all over me, chewing on me…but I feel much better now."

Norm noted the tiny pupils. "You're on something, aren't you?" She nodded.

"That's not why I'm here…I'm here because I think…" She couldn't continue, she started sobbing again. Norm put an arm around her shoulders.

"It's okay, Rebecca. It's okay…" He let her cry herself out. "Now tell me what's going on." Rebecca looked at the floor. She took a deep breath.

"Dr. Norm, I'm pregnant." Lord, fourteen years old, was Norm's first thought. And a junkie, was his second.

"When did you have your last period?" She looked up.

"I'm not even sure. A long time now. I guess I haven't paid attention. Maybe months. I started thinking about it when I was feeling so awful."

He saw her confusion. "Rebecca, you could easily be late because of the drugs. We can find out easy enough. I'll go into town and get a home pregnancy test…Was the boy who was shot your partner?"

Rebecca started sobbing again. Norm went to get a box of tissues. When she had wiped her eyes and blown her nose a couple of times, in a small voice she said, "I'm not sure."

"Not sure!"

"There were two. Billy and…and a Negro man."

"Oh, Rebecca!"

Again the tears. "I know, I know. I am an awful person! Awful!"

Norm put his arm around her again. She turned into his shoulder. A muffled, "Oh, Dr. Norm, I just don't know what to do. I can't tell my parents, I just can't. Mother will kill me and it'll…I don't know what it would do to Daddy!"

They were both silent for awhile. Norm could feel some of the tension go out as he held her. Finally, he said, "First things first. Here, stand up. Atta girl." He ushered her towards the door. "I'll go in and get that test and bring it to you later this afternoon. You just pee on the pregnancy test stick and you'll know right away. But, it's best to do it first thing in the morning." Norm opened the door for her. "Okay?" She nodded. "And don't worry; if it's positive, we'll figure out the best thing to do." Her face fell. Norm thought, I shouldn't have said that! "Come on now, give me a smile." She made a pathetic attempt, but looked ready to break into tears again. She turned and walked down the stairs like a seventy-year-old woman with a heavy pack on her back.

When Rebecca entered the trailer, Katharine was all over her. "Where have you been? Sneaking off some place for more drugs?"

"I went to see Dr. Norm."

"Why?"

"Just to talk."

Rebecca entered her room, hoping to leave her mother behind. Katharine followed her in.

"What about?"

"Things."

"Like what?"

Rebecca turned furiously on her mother.

"None of your fucking business!"

Katharine slapped her. Rebecca put a hand to her face and stood there looking at her mother. "Get out of my room!" she screamed.

"Sweetheart, I'm sorry. I didn't mean to…"

"Get out! Out!"

Katharine left the room. Rebecca slammed the door, locked it, and threw herself onto the bed. She cried herself to sleep.

She had no idea how long she slept. She got out of bed and went to the door to listen. The TV was on. She unlocked her door and tiptoed to the bathroom to pee and splash water on her face. While on the toilet, she thought of the pregnancy test. Nice of Dr. Norm, but it had been months: no way she wasn't pregnant. She returned to her room and locked the door again. What she needed was a little pick-me-up. She went into her top drawer and took out a pair of clean socks rolled into a ball. She pulled the socks apart and withdrew a tiny baggie full of heroin. As she tapped the powder out onto a hand mirror and chopped it up finer with a razor blade, she thought of what Dr. Norm had said: "If it's positive, we'll figure out the best thing to do." Abortion is what he meant! Scary! But, I don't want to have a baby, even if it's Billy's. Will it hurt? Everybody will find out! Oh, Daddy will hate me! What if it's black? She shook her head. Don't think about it!

Look at all that beautiful powder! Yum! Yum! She divided up the pile with the razor blade. Virgil was quite generous these days. With good reason! She began to laugh, then almost cried. She thought of her mother in the other room. Bitch! She looked at her hit. It wasn't enough, not nearly enough. Time to fly high! She doubled it. She put the remnants back in the baggie and rolled up the socks like before, and returned them to the drawer. She snorted the four lines. She pinched her nose and waited for it to kick in…She smiled. Here it comes! The euphoria hit her like a sledgehammer. Whoa, baby, whoa! This is big time! But it was also different. She began to feel dizzy, then confused and disoriented. The room started spinning. She stumbled over to her bed. She lay down. The room was topsy-turvy. She closed her eyes. Her breathing slowed. So did her heart. She was in Never-neverland. She passed out.

Norm had taken advantage of the trip in to Perry to do a little shopping. It was late afternoon when he pulled up in front of the trailer. He knocked on the door. Katharine answered. She looked upset.

"Anything wrong, Katharine?"

Katharine stepped aside. "Me and Rebecca had another fight. I didn't mean to, but I slapped her."

"Where is she now?"

"Her room. I'll go get her."

Thinking of the pregnancy test in his coat pocket, Norm said, "Maybe I should go in to talk with her."

Norm knocked on Rebecca's door. No answer. He knocked again. "Rebecca, it's me, Dr. Norm." No answer. He returned to the living room where Katharine had settled in to watch TV. "Are you sure she's in her room?"

"She ain't left this trailer. Gotta be." Katharine glanced down to the bathroom as they walked up to Rebecca's bedroom.

The door was open and it was empty. In a loud voice Katharine said, “Rebecca, Dr. Norm’s here to see you.” No answer. “Rebecca, open up!” Still, no answer. Katharine tried the door. It was locked. She pounded on the door. She turned to Norm; she looked worried. Norm *was* worried. He tried the door handle again, then banged hard on the door.

“I’m going to bust in!” He didn’t wait for approval. He stepped back and kicked the door. On the second kick the door broke free of its flimsy frame. Norm rushed in with Katharine right behind. Norm roughly shook Rebecca’s shoulder and yelled her name. No response. “Call 911! Quick.” He felt her pulse. Very slow. She was breathing, but it was severely depressed. He noticed her lips and fingernails had a bluish tint. He turned her on her side so she wouldn’t choke on her vomit if she threw up. He loosened any tight clothing. Without meds and equipment, there was nothing else he could do. He rushed out and grabbed the phone from Katharine.

“This is a doctor speaking. We have an opioid overdose! We need Naloxone fast! A young girl’s life is at stake! …Yes, I’ll stay on…Yes, I’ve done that….Yes….About five foot two…” He looked at Katharine. “What does Rebecca weigh?” Katharine shrugged her shoulders. “I’m guessing around a hundred and ten…Yes, we’ll stay on the line, but hurry.” He handed the phone to Katharine. “Ambulance is on its way.” Norm returned to Rebecca. He felt her pulse again. Even slower. He knew she could just stop breathing. He wondered if he would have to perform CPR. It was the longest twenty minutes of his life, and maybe Rebecca’s last.

Rebecca was taken to the Perry hospital after the EMTs injected Narcan to reverse the overdose. The EMTs thought she would be okay, but it had been close. Norm accompanied Rebecca in the ambulance. Clem and Katharine followed in

Norm's Subaru. Rebecca stayed in the hospital for three days. When she began to go through withdrawals, she was given small amounts of clonidine, a generic drug used to treat high blood pressure. It would act as a sedative to reduce the symptoms. Norm and Clem visited her everyday, but Rebecca didn't want her mother anywhere near her. Norm queried Rebecca on what drugs she had taken, for how long, and what quantities. He conferred with the doctors and made some calls to his ex-colleagues at Shands in Gainesville. Norm convinced the Perry doctors not to put her on some program using drugs like Suboxone, Naltrexone, or Methadone. Such programs were lengthy and could be abused. Methadone particularly spooked Norm because if Rebecca slipped up and took a hit of heroin while on Methadone, it could result in a fatal overdose.

Norm's heart went out to her as she bravely struggled with the increasing withdrawals. She fiercely maintained that she wanted to quit and would do whatever Norm prescribed. But, she said, she needed his help. They talked of school. She told him about all the classes she had cut, assignments she hadn't done, and that she had intercepted letters from the school informing her parents of her pitiful grades and requesting them to come in to Perry and talk with her teachers.

Norm thought it best to pull Rebecca out of school. Clem and Katharine agreed. Norm also, considering the mother-daughter relationship, thought it best for Rebecca to get out of the trailer. She could stay with him. He ran the idea past Rebecca. "And you could stay in the spare bedroom, Rebecca. What do you think?" Rebecca's smile was as big as a beachball.

"Oh, Dr. Norm! Yes! Yes! Yes!"

"One thing, though, I demand."

Rebecca's smile faded. "Yes?"

"No lies. Not one."

Rebecca solemnly extended her hand. Norm took it and they shook. "Deal," she said. Norm broached the idea with Clem and Katharine. Clem was all for it. It was obvious to him that Rebecca needed a calm environment, and that wasn't going to happen with Katharine around. Katharine dragged her feet, but finally agreed. Norm hoped he was doing the right thing.

Norm arrived at the hospital early on the third day. Rebecca was to be released that afternoon after the doctors made their rounds. He had the home pregnancy test kit in his pocket. Rebecca did not look good.

"How goes it?" he asked.

"Feel kinda awful, Dr. Norm. Didn't sleep much." Rebecca's nose was runny. She smiled weakly. "Plenty of cramps, too, but no period."

Norm reached out and squeezed her hand. "Just keep on plugging. You'll feel better soon."

"Hope so."

"Speaking of periods, here you go." He handed her the pregnancy test kit. Rebecca suddenly looked spooked. "Think you can pee?" Rebecca nodded nervously. She got out of bed and walked slowly to the bathroom as if to the gallows. While waiting, Norm thought of the conversations with his ex-colleagues from Shands. They had discussed more than opioid addiction and withdrawal. He had asked whom to contact if Rebecca wanted an abortion. He heard the toilet flush. Suddenly he felt as nervous as Rebecca had looked. The door opened. Although her hair was scraggly and there was sweat on her brow, Rebecca was smiling. She shook her head. Norm quickly stood and hugged her.

Chapter Twenty-Nine

"Play Ball!" Beau said. William had won the coin toss for home field. Top of the first and Ralph was leading off. He took a couple of practice swings before stepping into the batter's box. William was on the mound, glaring in. He went into his windmill windup and the ball whistled in. Ralph fouled it weakly down the third base line. "Foul ball, strike one." For someone in his late fifties, William can sure pitch, Ralph thought: that ball was humming! Craig shouted out encouragement from the bench. The next pitch was high and inside, moving Ralph off the plate. "Ball!" William went into his windup again. Fastball down the middle. Ralph hit a slow grounder to *The Natural* at short who fielded it cleanly and whipped the ball to first in plenty of time. *The Natural* could not only hit; he had a gun for an arm.

The stands were mostly full and a few others stood along the chain link fence that surrounded the ballfield. It was sunny, but windy enough so that the ballgame had enticed many to forego bouncing around in the Gulf fishing for trout and redfish. The wind was also doing a good job of keeping the no-see-ums at bay. Charley was in the top row of the stands with a small cooler of beer. As promised, he had brought a case for the team, but it was in another cooler strapped to the lawnmower he had driven over from his place. Rebecca was sitting in the front row. She looked much better than she had in the hospital. Hollow-eyed and pale maybe, but at least her clothes were neat and her hair clean and shiny. The tranquility of Norm's house the last couple of weeks, away from her mother and the rusty trailer scene, enabled her to bravely face each day. Norm made sure she helped in the kitchen, with the laundry, and with cleaning the house, believing her participation could plant the seeds of some well-needed self-respect. Clem visited her often. He'd take his lunch break every day at Norm's. He told her he understood what she was going through because it was the same for him to stay sober. He repeated his earlier advice. "You just have to take it one day at a time, Sweetheart."

Sitting next to Rebecca was Virginia who was having one of her good days. On Rebecca's lap was little Boda who fidgeted and squirmed. A stroller was parked in front of them by the fence. The first week after moving into Norm's, Rebecca had gone over to Tiny and T's to confess to stealing the shrimp money. It hadn't been easy, but necessary. With tears in her eyes, she swore that she would pay back every cent. T had given her a big hug. T had also suggested that babysitting Boda occasionally could go towards reducing that debt.

T was up second. She lined softly to third. Craig tied into one, but it was just a long fly out. Three up, three down. Team Condo came in off the field. Beau ambled back to check on Virginia. When T began her warm-ups, Boda got all excited. "Mommy! Mommy!"

"Hush, Boda," Rebecca said, thinking the last thing T needed was the distraction of her daughter.

Like Ralph, T was nervous, if for no other reason than she was the only female on the field for both teams. She walked the leadoff man. She did better with the second batter who hit a tailor-made double play ball to Sammy on third. Sammy fielded it cleanly, but had trouble digging it out of his glove. He got the man at second, but even with Norm's quick pivot, the batter beat the throw to first. The next batter was William. He bunted. T picked it up. Her only play was to first. She threw William out. Man on second, two outs, with *The Natural* coming to the plate. Craig had been in a quandary about whether he should put Tony in right instead of Louie because *The Natural* was a dead pull hitter. But, he was also the only left-hander in their entire lineup. He kept Louie in right.

T pitched to *The Natural* very carefully. She went for the corners. He was patient and waited for his pitch. With the count full, she gave it to him. Fastball down the middle. He launched it! Louie ran back, but there was no need. Even with the wind blowing in from the Gulf, it cleared the fence by twenty feet. There was hooting and hollering from the Team Condo bench. Their players lined up to high five their shortstop as he crossed the plate. Two to nothing, Team Condo.

No one scored in the second inning and top of the third. In the bottom of the third *The Natural* came up again, this time with two on. Charley yelled from the stands, "Let's see you hit another one out, Ringer!" *The Natural* stepped out of the box and smiled towards the stands. He stepped back in with a three and one count. T pitched a strike on the inside corner. *The Natural* turned on it. It was a rocket that landed farther than the first. Five to nothing, Team Condo.

Craig paced back and forth in front of the bench while William was throwing his warm up pitches. "We got to get some runs back. Whadyasay? Chip away! One at a time. We can hit this guy! He doesn't throw much faster than T." Unfortunately, they couldn't hit T much better than they could William. Craig had made the last out. "You're up, Tiny," Craig said. "Start it off!"

While Tiny was taking swings in the on deck circle, Louie came up to him. "Tiny, this guy's first pitch is almost always down the middle. He likes to get ahead of the batter. I guarantee it'll be the best pitch you'll see." The catcher threw down to second, and the infield threw it around. Beau straightened up after sweeping off the plate. "Batter up!" Tiny strode to the plate and dug in. Just like Louie had said, the first pitch was right down the middle. Tiny slammed an absolute rocket that ate up the third baseman. The ball careened off his chest and rolled into shallow left field. Tiny ended up at second to the cheers of his teammates.

Rusty walked up to the plate. Louie had talked to him, too. Rusty slowly put one foot in the batter's box, then the other. He looked out at William as he pulled his bat back. The first pitch was fast but fat, and Rusty got all of it. It sailed over the center-field fence. Charley went wild, and in the process dropped a three-quarters full beer. He didn't care and pulled out another. *The Natural* came in to confer with William as Rusty trotted around the bases. The whole team greeted Rusty at home. Crystal squeezed his hand and gave him a big smile.

"They're beginning to figure you out, William. You got to keep them off balance! Back 'em up off the plate before throwing strikes," *The Natural* said. Sammy was next up. William windmilled his pitch high and inside, just under Sammy's chin. With home plate sixty feet away instead of ninety like in baseball, the ball seemed to be going a hundred rather than sixty. Sammy dropped to the ground. Glaring at William, he dusted himself off as he got back up. He stepped into the batter's box. The next pitch was even closer to his head. Sammy hit the ground again. He sprung to his feet, tossed the bat aside, and started marching out to the mound. Beau quickly interceded.

Sammy let Beau stop him, but not before yelling, "One more of them, Billy-boy, and you're goin' to eat a softball."

"You tell 'im, Sammy," Charley yelled.

The next two pitches were borderline outside corner. Beau called both strikes. Sammy whiffed on the third. Tony followed, and also struck out. Score five to two, Team Condo.

The score stood for the next two innings because of key defensive plays. In the top of the sixth with T on second, Craig hit a screaming line drive headed for William's head and centerfield. William flung his glove up in self-defense as he ducked. Somehow the ball found the glove to retire the side.

"Look what I found!" Charley yelled. "You can open yur eyes now, Billy-boy!"

In the bottom half of the inning, *The Natural* came up to bat for the third time. Craig walked to the pitcher's mound. One down with a man on second. "Intentional walk," Craig said. Beau pointed to first. *The Natural* flung his bat in disgust towards the Condo bench. Catcalls and boos came from the stands as *The Natural* trotted to first base. Their number five hitter came to the plate. On the third pitch he swatted a low line drive to right center. The runner on second took off, but so did Ralph. He got a good jump and was at full speed in the blink of an eye. He did a full extension dive and just caught the ball before it hit the ground, rolled once, and came up firing to Norm to double-off the runner at second. The entire infield waited until Ralph jogged in from the outfield and they clapped their gloves in appreciation as he ran by. Charley was beside himself. "Ralph, you're the man! You're the man!" Still five to two, Team Condo.

Tiny led off the seventh inning with another screamer down the third base line. The third baseman, totally gun-shy now of Tiny's grounders, let the ball play him. E5. Rusty followed Tiny. He hit it sharply up the middle. *The Natural* going to his left, scooped the ball just behind second, stepped on the bag, and fired to first. Smooth and easy: double play. Sammy followed with a single to left. Tony moved him to third with a seeing-eye grounder between first and second. Man on first and third with two outs. Norm was up. He worked the count full fouling off several pitches. It was a long at-bat. He fouled off a couple more before William threw low and outside. "Ball four!" Bases loaded. Two outs. Louie up.

Craig was ready to tear his hair out. Finally, our chance and who's up? Louie! Who could he sub in? One of the girls? No, no good. At least Louie's seen William's pitches twice now, he rationalized. But he knew that wouldn't make any difference. Louie hadn't come close to making any kind of contact! Called out on strikes both at bats. He's bailing out so much with his left foot, he looks like he's bunting…which, Craig suddenly thought, might not be a bad idea! "Louie, wait…Time!" he yelled to Beau. Beau put a hand in the air, and took off his mask. Craig drew Louie aside. "Bunt, Louie. Square around and just try to make contact. Then run like hell!" Louie nodded. Craig walked out to third base to Sammy. "Two outs, Sammy, with a force all the way around. Louie's going to try to bunt. You're off on contact!" Craig returned to the bench. Louie walked up to the plate. He didn't wait for the pitch. He squared around right away and waited for William to throw it.

William let it go and Louie jabbed at the pitch like a lion tamer poking a chair. "Strike one," Beau yelled. The next pitch was in the same place. "Strike two." Louie stepped out of the box. Try to bunt on the third strike? He looked over to Craig.

"Go for it!" Craig said.

"C'mon, Louie. Eye on the ball! You can do it," Charley yelled. He was not alone. Several people, including Virginia and Rebecca, were cheering him on.

William had his glove under his armpit and was rubbing the softball. He oozed confidence. Two strikes, no balls. Louie couldn't hit. He decided to brush him back before going for the kill. He threw inside. Louie ducked out of the way, but didn't let go of the bat which clipped the ball. It blooped maybe ten feet up the left field line. Craig bellowed, "Run, Louie! Run!" The catcher was the closest to the ball and went out for it. The softball had so much English on it that it would have made a cue ball proud. It also probably would have gone foul if left alone, but the catcher touched it in fair territory. It spun out of his hand and by the time he picked it up, there was no play at first, and he was too far away to tag the plate for the force on Sammy. His only play was tagging Sammy who was rumbling towards him like a freight train.

The catcher, who was a lawyer when he wasn't playing softball, weighed maybe one-fifty dripping wet; Sammy more like two-ninety. Who could blame him for not wanting to block the baseline to tag the black bearded Goliath bearing down on him? He reached out with the ball instead. Sammy struck it with his forearm as he barreled through. The ball flew out of the catcher's hand and rolled all the way to the backstop. William scampered after it. Sammy crossed the plate standing up. Tony was rounding third. He didn't slow down as he headed for home. William picked up the ball. The catcher rushed to cover home. William threw the ball as Tony began his slide. He slid into the glove and ball. The ball trickled out. "Safe!" Beau yelled. Louie ended up at second. The bench went wild, as did the fans in the stands. Charley started the chant, "LOO-EY, LOO-EY!" Ralph was next. He popped up to the first basemen. Five to four, Team Condo,

T was pitching great. She held Team Condo scoreless in the seventh, striking out two. She also led off the eighth. Hitless so far, she watched William take warm ups. She thought his velocity was down. She stepped into the box and hit the first pitch over *The Natural's* outstretched glove. Craig came to the plate. Trying to hit behind the runner, he lined sharply over the first baseman's head. T made it to third easily. Tiny hit a long high fly to center that most days would have gone out; but the wind had picked up considerably and kept it in. T tagged up and could have walked home. Craig also tagged and went to second. One out. Tie ballgame. Runner in scoring position. Rusty up.

"A hit's a run, Rusty! C'mon now, duck on a pond! Can of corn! You can do it!" Charley yelled. Louie smiled, wondering how in the heck Charley, who had never played the game, knew all the lingo. Crystal was cheering herself hoarse. So were Tony and Sammy. Craig clapped his hands on second: let's go! William wound up and fired it in.

"Ball one, outside," Beau said. Lots of infield chatter. Other than Charley, not much noise from the stands. No one was sitting on either bench.

"Ball two!"

"Good eye, Rusty. Just takes one!" Charley yelled.

Rusty pasted the next pitch, a gapper between left and center. It rolled all the way to the fence and Craig scored easily. Rusty ended up on second, holding his hands up in triumph. Charley almost fell out of the bleachers. Sammy and Tony made the final two outs. Six to five, Craig's team.

Team Condo didn't score in the bottom of the eighth, nor did Craig's team in the top of the ninth. Bottom nine: Team Condo was down to their last three outs. T struck out the first batter. Craig was talking into his mitt, telling himself to stay focused—only two more outs to go! His eyes darted all over the field, making sure everyone was positioned right. The next batter lined T's first pitch over Sammy's head, down the third base line. Man on first. The next guy up bunted. Sammy fielded it cleanly, but threw wildly to first. Rusty blocked the ball from going into right, but the runner was safe. Man on first and second, one away. Craig paced around like a caged lion. Charley didn't know if he could watch anymore. Beau swept the plate. "Batter up!" The next batter popped up to Rusty. The runners did not advance. Two outs. The first baseman was up, with *The Natural* on deck. He worked a three and two count. He fouled off a couple more pitches before T missed. "Ball four. Take your base!" Craig watched *The Natural* swagger to the plate. Oh Lord, Craig thought. He called time out and walked to the mound. The other infielders gathered around.

"Got to pitch to him, T. Don't see any other way. We can't walk in the tying run," Craig said.

"Make 'em earn it, T," Sammy said.

Beau came out to break up the conference. The players returned to their positions when they heard Louie yell for another time out. He ran up to Craig, out of breath. "Switch me and Tony! You know he's a much better fielder. It'd at least give us a chance if that guy smokes one."

Craig didn't argue. It made all the sense in the world. Why hadn't he thought of it? "Good call, Louie…Tony," Craig yelled out, "take right."

Beau put on his mask. The Natural rubbed some dirt on his hands and stepped in. T took a big breath. She windmilled, putting a little extra on it. The ball made a loud THWAP when it hit Tiny's glove. "Ball, low and inside." It was deathly quiet. Beau's was the only voice to be heard. Even Charley had shut up; he was too busy chomping on his fingernails. T windmilled again. The next pitch caught the outside corner. Beau's hand shot up. "Strike one!" *The Natural* backed out of the box, looking hard at Beau. T pitched another one to the same place. "Strike Two." T tried to remain calm. Only a strike away; careful, careful! She debated whether to try the outside corner again.

He's probably expecting that. She decided to go inside. Big mistake! *The Natural* turned on it, just like he had on his second homer. Although he hit a little under it, there was plenty of oomph for it to go out. Team Condo's players started jumping up and down, and the base runners began to slowly circle the diamond. The ball went up and up. A regular skyball. The higher it went, the more the wind caught it.

Tony backed up to the fence. A front was moving in and there were thirty-mile-an-hour gusts from the Gulf now. Instead of landing thirty or forty feet beyond the fence, the ball slowed, then seemed to stall high over his head. It was being blown back. Tony went to his left, then his right. He put his glove up, but the wind was so squirrely! His back was against the fence. No way, he thought, but then, at the last second, yes! He jumped as high as he could and snared the ball in the webbing of his glove, at least most of it. There was a lot of white showing. Ice cream cone catch! He bounced off the fence and fell to the ground, while covering the ball and glove with his other hand. It didn't fall out. Everyone looked at Beau who was three-quarters the way out to first base. He emphatically raised his arm. Ball-game over!

Everyone on Craig's team in the field threw their gloves in the air and raised their arms in triumph. To a player, they sprinted towards Tony. Laughing and whooping, they piled on top of him like they had just won the World Series. From the bench, Crystal, Linda, and the crabber's wife ran out, passing *The Natural* who had stopped in the baseline between first and second. In the stands, Charley was hugging anyone who would let him. Smiling, *The Natural* began slowly walking out to right field. Tony had been picked up by his teammates and was being thumped on the back when *The Natural* stopped in front of the throng. Everyone quieted. He extended his hand to Tony who took it. “Heck of a catch!” he said, still smiling. “Heck of a game!”

Chapter Thirty

Rusty was fileting some trout below his house when Tammy pulled up in her Volkswagon. She hadn't owned a car since her little pickup was totaled in the '93 Storm of the Century. There had been little need because she hardly went anywhere and there was always Norm's Subaru. After Biloxi, though, and moving out of Norm's, owning a car became imperative. She had bought a late model VW which enabled her to take care of any business she might have. It also made it possible to visit Bobby.

Tammy started up the stairs. "Down here, Tammy." Several pelicans were in the canal by the house. Rusty put the filets in a large baggie, and threw the rest of the fish into the water. Immediately a frenzied game of keep-away erupted. Rusty was rinsing his hands when Tammy walked up.

"Bobby called. He's heard that there'll be a delivery in a week or so."

Rusty had known that Tammy was going to return to Biloxi. He had asked her to tell Bobby not to call him directly; rather, he should call her at the Club, and she could deliver any message. Tammy had asked why, and Rusty said that he had promised Bobby that he wouldn't be implicated, and that he didn't trust the FBI: they might bug his phone to find out his source.

"Does he work Thursdays?" Rusty asked. Tammy nodded. "Then I'll check in with him later at poker." Tammy smiled.

"Can't wait to see the look on Beau's face tonight," she said. "Where is it now?"

"At Norm's. Rebecca's been taking care of it all week."

"Really sweet of Charley."

"Let's just hope Beau will accept it; although it wouldn't break Rebecca's heart if he didn't." Charley had secretly taken up donations for a new Labrador puppy for Beau and Virginia, and had driven to a breeder in Athens, Georgia, to pick it up.

"That seems to be working out well; Rebecca, I mean, moving into Norm's."

"She seems happy enough to get away from her mother...and I imagine it helps take Norm's mind off you a little." Tammy looked down at her sandals. "Tammy, no one's blaming you. A person's got to do what a person's got to do."

"Thanks, Rusty," she said, in a small voice.

"Ralph tells me you're going to try to lease the Club, too."

She sighed. "I'm tired, Rusty. I need a break."

"Apparently."

* * *

Beau looked up from his cards towards Crystal and Linda who entered the Club. They looked over to Beau, then quickly averted their eyes and sat at the bar where Tammy was drawing a pitcher of beer. Unusual for them to come in, let alone on a Thursday night, he thought briefly before turning back to his cards. Fifteen minutes later, T came through the door, holding it open for little Boda who was leading a shuffling Virginia by the hand. It wasn't one of Virginia's better days; why in hell was T bringing her here! He looked towards the bar again. Tammy, Crystal, and Linda were looking at him. He looked around the table. Charley and Sammy were smiling into their cards. The rest were stiffly poker-faced. Something's up!

He laid his cards face down and went to his wife while looking questioningly at T. “May I ask, T, why you brought my wife here?”

Before she could answer, Virginia said to no one in particular, “I have to use the little girls’ room.”

“Here, Virginia, I’ll take you,” T said, taking her hand. Beau watched them. Virginia’s shuffling was always a bad sign. Tiny came over and lifted his daughter onto his shoulders. Beau returned to the table, but didn’t sit.

“Okay, is something going on here that I should know about?”

Charley was all innocence. “Whacha talkin’ ‘bout, Beau? Sit down and play them cards. We been waitin’ on ya.” Beau started to sit, but everyone looked over to the door when Rebecca entered with a black Lab puppy in her arms. When she walked towards the poker table, the puppy saw people and began to squirm. She put it on the floor and it took off for the table, galomping over puppy-style. All eyes were on Beau.

Beau’s head snapped around from the puppy to Charley. “Charley, I told you I didn’t want a puppy! Virginia and I are too old! Nice gesture and all, but no way!”

“Aw, Beau, c’mon. You need…”

“Skillet!” Returning from the ladies room, Virginia let go of T’s hand and rushed up to the puppy. “Oh, Skillet, I’ve missed you!” she exclaimed, abruptly sitting down on the floor. The puppy jumped into her lap and tried to climb her front to lick her face. Virginia was bubbling with glee. Her hands were all over it. Beau glared at Charley. Besides believing that they were too old to have another dog, now Beau feared Virginia would withdraw more deeply into her shell once she realized the puppy wasn’t Skillet reincarnate. Every good day she had, she still struggled with guilt over Skillet’s death.

Tammy, Linda, and Crystal came over from the bar. Rebecca asked, "Miss Tammy, do you have a bowl for water?"

"In the kitchen, dear. Here, let me show you." They disappeared behind the swinging door. The puppy started visiting those who had crowded around. He was having a great time. Virginia, still sitting on the floor, continually giggled at his antics. Rebecca returned with the bowl full. When she placed it on the floor, the puppy rushed up to it. Inadvertently, the puppy stepped on the edge of the bowl when he started to lap the water. The bowl flipped up and soaked him. When he shook, he showered Virginia. Virginia laughed, and even Beau couldn't help smiling.

"That thar is the clumsiest puppy I ever did see," Charley said. "Maybe you should name it Clumsy, Clum for short."

"You can't do that, Mr. Charley. It might give him a complex! And it's not his fault; it's because of his paws. Look how big they are," Rebecca said, holding out the puppy's forelegs. "He just has to grow into them." It was true, the paws were gigantic for such a little puppy.

"Then you kin call him, Paws."

Virginia took the puppy from Rebecca. "Now why would you do that when he's already got a name? I gave it to him myself." Everyone was silent. Virginia began petting the puppy again. Her smile was ear to ear. Beau watched Virginia for a moment or two before going to her. "C'mon, Sugah, it's been a long day. Let's go home."

"Did you hear that, Skillet? Time to go." She clutched the puppy possessively to her chest, as if someone might take him away from her. Beau helped her up. They stood there long enough that Virginia looked from the puppy to Beau. "What's the matter, Dear?"

Resigned, Beau said, “Two weeks, Charley. If it doesn’t work out, I’m bringing him to your place. Understood?” Charley nodded. Rebecca looked hopeful.

“Who, Dear?”

“Charley, knows. Come now, Sugah.” Beau had his arm around Virginia as he escorted her to the door. He held it open. As she passed through, Beau turned. “Regardless how it works out, thank you, Charley. And I’m sure you weren’t alone in this.” His eyes swept all of them. “Thank you.” He shut the door behind him. It was so quiet, they could hear the couple make their way down the Club’s stairs.

Rusty broke the silence. “Reckon I have to make a couple of phone calls.” He walked over to the pay phone.

Linda approached Tammy. “Ralph says that you’re thinking of leasing the Club.”

“If I can find the right person.”

“I’d like to talk to you about that.”

Charley interrupted them. “Afore you sit down an’ jabber, Tammy, you got some mighty thirsty clients needs takin’ care of.”

In a loud voice, Tammy asked, “The usual for everybody?” Everyone nodded. Rusty covered the mouthpiece of the phone. “Me, too, Tammy…”

Tammy hustled over to the bar.

Chapter Thirty-One

"That's got to be the strangest looking aircraft I've ever seen," Rusty said.

"It's called a Sweitzer RU-38A Twin Condor," the Coast Guard pilot said. "It's used strictly for reconnaissance." The pilot, Rusty, and Special Agent Morales walked around the plane. The pilot pointed to the immense wings. "Even though it's only thirty-five feet long, it has an eighty-four foot wing-span—Sweitzer is mainly known for its gliders, so no surprise on the design. Twin-boom configuration with two Rolls Royce engines, one in the nose and one here in the rear." He pointed to the pods on the forward section of each boom. "This pod houses a multi-function X-band sea-search radar system with mapping capabilities. The other carries a F.L.I.R., Forward Looking Infrared system, along with a low-light TV system." They came to the nose of the plane. "Room for three: pilot, co-pilot, and the electronics operator behind them." He turned to Morales. "I understand that you know how to operate the electronics."

Morales nodded. "From cooperative missions with the D.E.A."

"Then Rusty will be up front with me." He continued talking about the plane. "And it is super quiet. It has an enhanced muffler system for the front engine. The exhaust is piped over the wings to further reduce any noise. The rear engine is used going to and from sensitive areas, but it is shut off during surveillance mode…What do you think?"

"Impressive," Rusty said.

"Only two of these babies ever made," the pilot said, leading them back to the Coast Guard Base's Information Center. They entered the building where Morales asked dispatch if he had heard anything. The seaman apprentice shook his head. "Okay," Morales said, "McMillan and I'll head to our hotel. Call us when you do."

* * *

Slater warmed up the engines of the *Pituca* after the septic truck pulled out of the Hamilton Harbor Yacht Club. He maneuvered the boat up to the fueling dock. Two docks over, dressed in shorts, a Hawaiian shirt, and flip-flops, a man sat on a bench reading the paper. Judging from his lack of tan, the man was probably a snowbird, Slater thought, or some white collar nerd who spent his pathetic life in an office somewhere. When the *Pituca's* tanks were full, Slater returned the boat to its berth. The man in the Hawaiian shirt folded his paper and walked to the marina store where he made a call from the payphone out front. When he finished, he strode up to a non-descript Ford and sat in the driver's seat. An hour later, a similar car pulled up and parked several spaces away. The *Pituca* could be seen from both vehicles. The man in the Hawaiian shirt started the Ford and left the marina.

At nine the next morning, the seaman apprentice received a call from the Hamilton Harbor Marina payphone. He relayed the message to Special Agent Morales. "The boat just shoved off. We'll have our search and rescue aircraft up in fifteen minutes to monitor their course and speed."

"We'll be there in a half hour."

"No need to hurry. It will most likely be hours before you'll go up. Just stay near your phone."

"That's a ten-four, Seaman."

Morales and Rusty were at the Coast Guard base six hours later when they received the news they were waiting for. The SAR aircraft's radar had picked up another craft coming from the direction of Mexico. At the present speed and course of both boats, it would intersect with Slater's craft in approximately four hours. There were no other crafts in the area. The agents monitoring Slater's movements over the last week knew that nothing had been brought aboard the *Pituca* which meant a transfer had to be made in transit. Heading due west out of Naples for hours instead of straight to Biloxi was another indication. It only made sense that the boat from Mexico must be carrying the cocaine. Two hours later, Morales and Rusty were in the air.

The pilot leveled off the Twin Condor at ten thousand feet and set cruising speed at a hundred and fifty miles per hour. Within a half hour, the radar picked up both boats. "Got them both," Morales said, "and they should intersect just about exactly as estimated."

"Being dark makes this a whole lot easier," the pilot said. "We'll bring her down to fifteen hundred feet for pictures when we're close. Rusty, night vision goggles are in the side pocket of your door."

An hour later, a mile still separated the two boats when the Twin Condor began to descend. The pilot turned off the rear engine. "You've got a half hour to take your videos before we have to return to base."

"Right. Let's do the Mexican boat first." Morales soon began filming. "Fishing boat's called the *Reina del Mar*, out of Cancún." He videoed the two boats tying up together. "Guy with a submachine gun over his shoulder on the cabin cruiser's taking the lines from the fishing boat. Looks Latino. Needs a shave: kick-ass camera you got here! No sign of Slater. Probably at the helm."

The pilot circled around. "That fishing boat is lit up like a damn circus! The diesels must be running; no way they can hear us."

"Bet they couldn't anyway; this plane's amazing! Makes me want to whisper," Rusty said.

"Looks like the Latino is opening the deck above the engines." Morales paused. "And here we go: payload time!" The Mexican crew had lined up on both boats. They began passing the cocaine bricks. "Still no sign of Slater. Wait!...Can just see the muzzle of another weapon sticking out from the helm. It seems to be pointed in the direction of the fishing boat captain on the bridge."

Slater was making sure that the Mexican captain behaved himself. José and Slater had traded positions, with José down in the hold this time, while Slater had the Heckler and Koch trained on the captain. José stuck his head up from the engine area. "Ready for the hose, *Jefe.*" Slater motioned for the captain to have his men bring over the septic hose. There were no jokes this time around. When the hose was set, Slater signaled the captain to turn it on. As the septic tank was filling, Slater raised his gun up a couple of inches until it was pointing at the captain's midriff. He had absolutely no compunctions about shooting the captain. "No funny tricks this time, *Capitán.* My boat took a lot of cleaning last trip. If you mess around, it'll be your boat that will need cleaning…and it won't be *mierda.* I'll give you a hint: it'll be something red and sticky!"

"All set," José yelled.

"Okay, Capitán, now!" The captain immediately signaled for the hose to be turned off.

It was all business, and quickly done. The hose was drawn in; the two boats separated and went their own way. The Twin Condor turned towards Tampa. The pilot engaged the rear engine and began to climb. "Did you get what you wanted?" he asked Morales.

"In spades! There was a hose brought on board and I'm not sure what that was all about, but the video will show the general area the coke was stashed. No pictures of Slater; not one; but I imagine that won't matter much once we get him with the dope in Biloxi.

"So you're headed there next?"

"Yeah. Your base has been very cooperative. McMillan and I are hitching a plane ride to New Orleans. We'll check in with the Coast Guard Air Station at Belle Chasse to coordinate the sting, then head up to Biloxi to wait for Slater's arrival. Should be fun."

"Not my kind of fun," the pilot said.

"Guess the FBI gets favored treatment. When I was with the State Police we never got such favors," Rusty said.

"That's because when it comes to law enforcement, stateys are about one step up from potbellied hick sheriffs."

Rusty didn't say anything. The pilot was suddenly busy checking his instruments. Finally, Rusty said, "You're a hard man to like, Morales."

"Doesn't make any difference to me, McMillan. What does make a difference is that you just stay out of my way for the next twenty-four to thirty-six hours."

Chapter Thirty-Two

The weather was turning ugly. The marine forecast had changed suddenly halfway to Biloxi. The wind picked up and the two-foot seas became four. Slater had known that there was a storm on the horizon, but it had been forecast to be a full day away—they should have had relatively calm seas for at least another twenty-four hours. The *Pituca* with her V-hull did admirably, but Slater had to cut back to thirteen knots. Even at thirteen knots, it was rough enough going and he needed the windshield wipers non-stop for all the spray. The *Pituca* would need a good hosing off in Biloxi, Slater thought; but that was a heck of a lot better than cleaning up Mexican sewage! He smiled. Ol' *Capitán* sure minded his P's and Q's this go-around: he knew I meant business. Slater's expression hardened. I would have shot him, too, if he had pulled anything like that again! Slater did some calculations. He knew they would now arrive in Biloxi much later than originally planned, probably around midnight. He sighed. Thirteen hours to go: one long-ass haul! Think about the bank account in the islands, he told himself. It began to rain.

* * *

In a light rain, Morales and Rusty strolled slowly by the Creole Seafood Company warehouse. It was their second walk-around. They stopped a few times so Morales, the tourist, could ostensibly take pictures of Rusty, but was in fact taking pictures of the building with its gate, doors, and windows. The guards weren't paying attention: they were in their little shelter by the gate, trying to keep dry. The pictures would be blown up on the computer and printed at the two room office complex the FBI had rented as command center. Because of the size of the shipment and not knowing if local law enforcement was being paid off, they couldn't take a chance: the sting would be conducted solely by the FBI with backup from the Coast Guard.

Morales and Rusty returned to the command center. The ten-member SWAT team from the New Orleans field office were lounging around the front office. All their field gear including firearms and bulletproof vests was stacked in the other office. Morales made his way to a large table in the center of the room. Two telephones, a fax machine, a computer, and a printer were on the table. Morales hooked his camera to the computer and soon had a dozen printouts of the pictures he took. He passed the pictures around to each man. In front of one of the walls was a very large whiteboard on a stand. Morales, with a photograph in one hand, sketched the Creole Seafood Company's layout with his other. When he finished, marker still in hand, he turned to face the men. "Your attention, please." It immediately became silent. Morales looked at his watch. "We have about five hours before Operation Stingray. This is the plan…"

* * *

Slater and José were about an hour out of Biloxi when they went through a severe squall. From the radar, Slater knew that they were passing between Ship and Cat Islands, but even with all but the running lights off, he couldn't see any lights from either one. In fact, he could barely see his hand in front of his face. At least the waves were not so large now, he thought. Still, he pulled back on the throttle. A half hour later, he and José could finally see some of the Biloxi lights. Slater took his hands from the wheel. He was surprised to find them sweaty. “Looks like we made it, José.”

“Si, *Jefe*! I theenk we get goood luck. The weather, eet get much worse.”

“You returning right away to Miami again?”

José smiled. “No, *Señor*! The *Don*, he tell me to enjoy myself for a few days. You theenk you can help me weeth that?”

Slater returned José’s smile. “*Seguro que si*,” he said, picking up the mike. He called the warehouse. “Coming in. About twenty or thirty minutes away. Over.”

“All clear here. How’s the weather out there? Over.”

“Shitty. Cats and dogs. Over.” Slater and José heard the man laugh.

“Not so bad here. We’ll keep a light on for you. Over.”

“Do that. Over and out.” Slater hung up the mike. “Better get ready to operate that spotlight, José. We don’t need to run aground or into some boat without running lights.” Once they were close to shore, José set the spotlight down. Even with the rain, the lights of the casinos lit up the water at least a hundred feet off shore.

Morales had a man stationed on the tip of the narrow isthmus only a hundred feet or so across from the Creole Seafood Company. He had a clear view of the big warehouse door the *Pituca* would pass through. He was to signal with one flash from a mega flashlight when he saw the boat approaching, then three flashes when the doors shut behind it. Morales had tried to delegate the job to Rusty, figuring it would keep him out of the way. While putting on their bulletproof vests, Morales had pulled Rusty aside.

"McMillan, I want you to be our signal man out on the point."

"Nope," Rusty said, cinching up the vest. "Not a chance."

"That's an order!"

"Tough shit! I'm not FBI, so you can't order me. And the deal all along was that I would take part in the action. I don't think that standing out on that point fits that bill. Excuse me…" Rusty walked over to where the weapons were stacked. He picked up a .40 Caliber Glock 20. Morales followed him to the table.

"You ever shoot one of those?" Morales asked.

Rusty nodded as he withdrew the magazine, then worked the slide. "Ten millimeter so it packs a wallop. Developed because of a problem you boys had in Miami in 1986. Got a fifteen round magazine, accurate, good sights, reliable. The grip angle isn't my favorite and it's a bit top heavy." He held it up and sighted along the barrel. "But, it'll do." He picked up a belt holster and clipped it on. He looked at Morales after he put the gun in the holster. "Yeah, Morales; I've shot one or two." Rusty picked up a pair of handcuffs.

"Alright, McMillan; you're in. Stick close to me when the action begins, but like I told you, stay out of my fucking way!" What a pain in the ass this guy is, Morales thought.

The man on the point saw the *Pituca's* running lights slowly approach. He flashed once. Morales picked up his handheld radio. Morales told the men to get ready. He turned to the two lead men. "Remember, first thing is to neutralize the guards. They probably have a radio in the guard shack. Imperative there's no warning to those inside. Let's make this simple, quick, and safe." The rain eased somewhat, and even from their vantage point, they could see the running lights pass the isthmus then disappear behind the front of the warehouse. "Okay, lock and load!" Morales and Rusty only had Glocks, but the others were heavily armed with pistols, shotguns, submachine guns. All wore heavy ballistic vests with FBI stenciled front and rear, night vision goggles were strapped to their brows. They heard two siren blasts. Less than two minutes later, there were three flashes from the point. Morales spoke into the radio. "Boat's inside." They heard the Coast Guard Dolphin helicopter approach. Morales flipped off the radio. "Okay men, let's go!"

The two security guards were in handcuffs within seconds. With Morales leading the way, followed by Rusty and eight agents, they entered the warehouse. They spread out as Morales stood by the door and shouted, "FBI. Drop to the floor, NOW!" A half dozen men were scattered around. Most were over by the bubbling holding tanks, but two were alongside the *Pituca.* They dropped the boat lines and ran. Morales fired a couple warning shots. They kept on running. Shots came from over by the bubbling holding tanks. The men there had crawled underneath the tanks had begun shooting at the agents. The agents returned fire as Morales turned off the light switches by the door. Immediately the entire warehouse was pitch black. "Goggles down!" Morales shouted, as he and Rusty headed towards the boat.

José was in the V-berth packing his bag when the action started. He pulled his submachine gun out from under the mattress, debating whether to go topside. Slater was in the aft master stateroom. No way did he want to shoot it out with the FBI. He wanted out of there. When the lights went out, he took off his slicker and removed his Top-Siders and tied them together. He put the shoes around his neck as he exited the stateroom to the rear deck. He quickly let himself down over the stern; muzzle flash was everywhere. The icy water took his breath away. He stayed as close as he could to the oyster-covered dock pilings and breaststroked his way towards the large overhead door. Bright light showed around the edges of the door. Even with the war going on inside, he could hear a helicopter's rotors outside: has to be Coast Guard or FBI watching the front, he thought. He shuddered, not from fear, but from the frigid water. Slater hesitated, trying to concentrate, trying to remember the wharf construction outside. He pictured the pilings and plank covered docks on either side of the narrow passageway leading into the warehouse. If he could just get under the dock! He dove down. The door was only three feet down in the water. Like the dock pilings, the bottom was oyster-covered. When he surfaced he breaststroked to the far right side of the door. He hyperventilated several times. He took the shoes from around his neck and held them in one hand while he took a deep breath and dove. He swam down several feet below the door and passed under. The water above him was bright with light. It was a short swim to where the water became black again under the dock. Still, he did not surface. He felt his way under the dock, cutting his hands on oysters that covered the pilings. But he wanted to get as far away from the light as possible before surfacing. He had no idea how long he held his breath, but it was a long time: the rest of his life. He gasped for air when he surfaced. He was almost at the far edge of the dock. He could see a few lights from the warehouses they had passed on the way in. They weren't much more than a hundred feet away. But it was open water. He looked back towards the light from the helicopter: it held steady on the building. The water in front of him was dark. As long as that 'copter stays put, I should be able to make it, he thought.

Morales and Rusty approached the boat. No movement, but Slater must be on board, Rusty thought. He also thought that with the advantage they had with the night vision goggles, the firefight wouldn't last long. He covered Morales as he climbed onto the boat and to the helm, then followed him down to the main stateroom. Morales eased carefully into the room with both hands on his gun extended in front of him. Nothing. The pocket door leading to the head and forward berths was recessed and wide open. The door of the head was halfway open. Morales saw a nearby light switch on the wall. He took a hand off his gun and, with his eyes glued on the forward berth area, felt along the wall for the switch, but his hand was too low and passed it. He briefly turned his head to locate and flip the switch. At the instant the lights came on, Rusty saw the end of a barrel stick out and around the bathroom door.

"Watch out," Rusty yelled, and threw himself at Morales, knocking him down. A burst from the bathroom caught Rusty square. Thirty rounds started low and raised up as the submachine gun spewed bullets. Rusty's thigh and hip were peppered as was the trunk of his body. The last two bullets pierced his neck. In all, twenty bullets made contact. Rusty fell to the floor, shielding Morales who returned fire. Ten quick rounds went into the bathroom door. There was the clatter of the submachine gun falling to the floor. Morales extricated himself from Rusty, and carefully approached the forward section. He could see that the V-berth was empty. He could also see blood seeping onto the bathroom floor. With a finger on the trigger, he slid open the pocket door with his other hand. José was sitting on the floor, his eyes distant, wood splinters in his face, and bullet holes in his head and chest. Morales recognized him immediately from the videos he had taken in the air. With his gun still trained on José, Morales kicked the submachine gun away. He checked for a pulse. There was none.

When Morales returned to the stateroom, Rusty was sitting, propped against the wall. He was dumbly looking at the fountain of blood spurting from his thigh. He slowly raised his head. His neck was a mess.

"Slater?" he croaked.

"No, the other guy," Morales said, as he whipped off his belt and tightened it above the spurting leg wound.

"Check the rest of the boat." Morales stayed put and pulled out his shirttail and ripped off a piece. He held it firmly against the wound. Rusty yanked Morales' hand away and replaced it with his own. "Go on!" Morales nodded. He climbed the stairs back to the helm. The lights were back on and he suddenly realized that there was no more gunfire. He looked around. Several men were lying handcuffed, face down on the floor. Four members of his team held guns on them, while others were heading towards the boat. Morales entered the cabin door of the master stateroom. He carefully descended. Nothing but an open, partially packed suitcase and a crumpled slicker on the floor. He checked the master bath. Nothing. The rear deck. Nothing. He looked out over the narrow waterway to the overhead door. Nothing. Slater was gone.

Morales put his gun away and took the stairs two at a time. Topside, he yelled to his men, "Officer down! Radio's by the door. Contact that chopper. Emergency evac! And I need two men here quick!" He went down to Rusty and knelt by his side in an ever growing circle of blood. Rusty's eyes were closed, his head slumped, and the hand and rag no longer covered the gushing wound. Morales knew that if a healthy man passed out from blood loss, it meant at least a thirty percent loss of his total supply. Morales hustled to the bathroom and, roughly shoving José aside, grabbed a *Pituca*-monogramed towel. He rushed back to Rusty and firmly applied the towel against the wound as he loosened the belt. The bleeding had slowed. Because of the tourniquet, or was he already bled out?

Two men came down into the cabin. They were both younger than Morales, taller, and much stockier. One was carrying a first aid kit. They did their best to bandage Rusty's neck and tended the other seeping holes in his thigh and hip. They could hear the chopper landing out in the parking area. Morales said, "Let's get him to that chopper!" As carefully as they could, the two men lifted Rusty. Morales kept the towel pressed hard against the thigh wound. They maneuvered Rusty up the stairs and off the boat. Two more men came up to assist. Morales constantly applied pressure as they walk-ran to the rear of the building.

One of the men carrying Rusty asked, "What happened? Rookie move?" They all knew that Rusty was not one of them.

Morales looked the man directly in the eye. "Not by a long shot! McMillan saved my life."

Chapter Thirty-Three

Slater started swimming across to the isthmus. Holding his shoes and with his extremities numb with cold, it was slow going. Halfway across he heard the pitch of the helicopter's rotors suddenly change. He turned to look. The helicopter rose straight up and over the warehouse and sunk down behind the building. Everywhere was steeped into darkness. Slater was heartened by the helicopter leaving; he might actually make it! But what was he going to do? He played different scenarios over and over in his mind. They all had weak points, but he knew he couldn't run and hide. How could he with no clothes, no money, no local contacts except the owner of the Paradise? The owner of the Paradise! He's played almost as big a role in all this as I have! He has to help; he can't risk not helping!

Slater arrived at the far shore with a plan. Luckily, with his stocking feet, the shallows were nothing but mud with no oysters or sharp rocks. His feet were so softened by the water that anything could have sliced him up, although he probably wouldn't have felt a thing. When he finally stepped onto dry land, terra firma never felt better. He hobbled stiffly up to the unlit corner of a warehouse where he squatted to put on his shoes. He was shivering mightily. He also couldn't make his fingers cooperate: they were clumsy with the laces. It took forever to untie them; he had to use his teeth. He put the shoes on, but quickly gave up on the laces because he'd just have to untie them again on the other side of the narrow peninsula. He stuck to the shadows as he crossed the isthmus. When he came to the water's edge, the narrow bay looked to be about as wide as what he had just crossed. The far shore was bright with lights and the Palace was close by. He kicked off his shoes, put one in each hand, and, shaking like a leaf, entered the water.

A half hour later, Slater stumbled into the hotel lobby, bedraggled and wet. Even at two-thirty in the morning there were plenty of people around. With the casino, the hotel never slept. Slater intentionally walked towards reception like a drunken man. Everyone stared at him as if he were dirt. The concierge was all concern. "Mr. Slater, what happened?"

Slater slurred, "Long story, Charles." Weaving, he hung on to the corner of the reception counter. "I'm not feeling too good and I'd like to go up to my suite, if you don't mind."

"Of course! We have your room all ready." Charles opened a drawer and pulled out a card key. He handed it to Slater. "If there's anything we can do, Mr. Slater, please let us know!" Charles looked around. "Your luggage?"

Slater gave him a drunken smile. "Part of the story, Charles."

"Jimmy," the concierge called to the bellboy by the front door, "come help Mr. Slater to his room." Jimmy hustled over, glad to be doing something, anything but standing by the door all night. Jimmy took Slater's arm and helped him to the elevator. There were two couples already there, waiting. They moved away from Slater when he drunkenly pushed the 'up' button. Slater's clothes were still dripping. A small pool formed at his feet; his shoelaces weren't tied. He looked like a bum. The elevator arrived. Jimmy escorted Slater in and pushed the button for his floor. The others reached around Slater to punch theirs. With Jimmy holding him, Slater stood swaying in the center of the elevator while the others hugged the walls. Slater wondered if they were surprised that he was going to the top floor where only the most expensive suites were located. Jimmy helped Slater to his door. Slater drunkenly searched his pockets. "Seems I don't have any money. I'll catch up with you tomorrow," he slurred. The bellboy touched his hat and left. Once the door was shut behind him, Slater, without a trace of a stumble, made a beeline to the phone.

He dialed one-one-one. A man with a gruff voice picked it up, first ring. "Yeah?"

"This Bruno?" Slater asked.

"Yeah."

"Slater, here."

"Yeah?"

"Let me talk to your boss."

"He's asleep."

"Wake him!"

"Your funeral." Slater heard the phone clunk down. He waited a good ten minutes, pacing back and forth, holding the phone to his ear. He thought about the raid. He had heard Morales yell FBI. The FBI didn't do a sting unless it had good information, and that meant they probably knew his name. If not, it wouldn't take them long to find out the name of *Pituca's* owner, and he was registered in the hotel under his real name. No, it wouldn't be long before the FBI came knocking.

"This better be good, Slater!"

"It is." Slater told the casino and hotel owner all about the evening's particulars. He also asked if the hotel's doctor could be discreet. He was assured this was indeed the case; that the good doctor received a very nice annual stipend. "Tell him, I need him here yesterday!"

"Hang on a second..." Slater heard him dial on another phone and speak to the doctor. He came back on the phone with Slater. "Doctor's on his way."

"Good," Slater said. He explained the rest of his plan and hung up. He paced around for a second or two before picking up the phone again. He called the concierge. "An' I don' wanna be disturbed under any circumstances," he slurred. "Not any!"

"Yes, sir, Mr. Slater. Don't worry... Sleep well, now. Goodnight."

Slater ruled out taking a shower. Better if they find him in these sorry duds! Soon there was a knock on the door. Slater's stomach tightened.

"Yes, who is it?" he slurred.

"Hotel Doctor."

Slater hurried over to let him in. "No time to lose, Doc." The doctor was carrying the proverbial black bag. "Did the bossman explain what I want done?"

"He did, but it's dangerous."

"Life's all about living dangerously."

"For you maybe. Go sit down on that chair." The doctor pulled out a little bottle and a syringe. "How much do you weigh?"

"About one-eighty." The doctor nodded and started filling the syringe, eyeing the level-marks closely. "What are you giving me?"

"Phenobarbital."

"That's not so bad; just a barbiturate."

"More dangerous than you might think. Ten percent of barbiturate overdoses result in death. Marilyn Monroe and Judy Garland for example. Ever heard of *therapeutic index*?" Slater shook his head. "Expect not," the doctor said, returning the bottle to his black bag. "Besides abusers craving intoxication or for help to come down from drugs like speed, barbiturates were traditionally used to treat anxiety, insomnia, and seizure disorders like epilepsy. However there's a fine line between those symptoms of intoxication and much more serious ones like falling into a coma, ceasing to breathe, death. The dosage is critical. That fine line is called the *therapeutic index.*"

"So, you're telling me this might kill me?"

The doctor shrugged. "With what I'm giving you, I don't think so, but it would be much safer if injected very slowly with an IV. Apparently, though, we don't have time for that."

"No, we don't. Shoot me up where I couldn't have done it myself. And make it look like a pincushion."

"Back of the neck should do it. Be prepared to be uncomfortable."

The doctor poked him several times before slowly injecting the drug. It took several minutes. "Probably won't come on full for a bit. Good luck," he said, closing up his bag.

"Thanks, Doc." Slater lay down on the bed, thinking that, regardless of the shot, he would conk out quickly. The trip over had been exhausting and then the sting and then the…the…" Slater fell into a deep sleep. He didn't see the doctor open the door and look carefully up and down the corridor, or his wiping the knob clean with a handkerchief before closing the door behind him.

Morales paced back and forth outside the operating room of the Merit Health Biloxi Hospital. McMillan had been in there for almost two hours. It wasn't looking good: he had lost too much blood, plus a bullet had fractured his pelvis. But it was the loss of blood that concerned the doctors. Luckily, though, the bulletproof vest had taken the majority of the bullets, and the neck shots had somehow passed through the fleshy portion without hitting anything vital. If McMillan survives, he'll probably have a hell of a scar on his neck, Morales thought. That wasn't all he thought about as he played the scene over and over in his mind. The rookie move hadn't been on McMillan's part, but his! Taking his eyes off the forward berth even just for that split second was inexcusable! What the fuck was he thinking! They had the night vision goggles, not the perpetrator. He should have made sure it was all clear before evening the odds by turning on those lights! Disgusted with himself, he walked to the critical care waiting room for some coffee.

Morales had gotten word that Slater had been located. He still didn't know how Slater had slipped through their fingers. Maybe he had never been there. Maybe he had been dropped off before the warehouse and the Latino had brought the boat in alone. He threw away the god-awful Styrofoam cup of coffee into a corner wastebasket. He didn't want to leave McMillan, but there was a car and two agents waiting for him at the hospital door. Morales checked his watch as he got in the car. Four-thirty. A decent cup of coffee would be nice, he thought as they drove to the hotel. The same concierge was on duty. "FBI," Morales said, showing him his badge and identification.

"Yes, Sir. How can I help?"

"You have a Joe Slater registered here. Do you know if he's in?"

"Yes, Sir; he is."

"How do you know? You didn't even look to see if his key was on the rack."

"Because I was at the desk here a couple hours ago when he came in, and I don't believe he has left." He smiled conspiratorially. "Even if he wanted to."

"What does that mean?"

"Well, Sir, he certainly seemed 'under the weather,' so to speak. I think he was pretty liquored up."

"What room is he in?"

"He's in a suite, Sir; but he gave me instructions that he not be disturbed under any circumstances."

Morales looked at the concierge for a full fifteen seconds without saying anything. The little man was nattily dressed in a charcoal-gray suit with a red bowtie and a matching red rose pinned to the lapel. His pants were pulled up extra high to cinch around a budding potbelly. He was going bald and had a comb-over.

"Perhaps you didn't hear me. I said we were from the FBI, as in Federal Bureau of Investigation. I think it would be wise for you to tell me what room."

The concierge fidgeted. "I should call my boss…You see, Mr. Slater is a great friend of my boss and I don't want to make my boss mad."

"That a fact? Interesting," said agent number one.

"Call your boss," Morales said.

"But, it's not even five o'clock in the morning!" the concierge said, looking at the clock on the wall behind the desk.

"Just call your boss, Dimwit!" agent number two said.

The concierge looked at the three agents. He picked up the phone and dialed. "Bruno, front desk. There are three gentlemen from the FBI who are demanding to see Mr. Slater, but Mr. Slater gave me explicit instructions not to be disturbed. I don't know what to do. Is the boss up by any chance?...Yes, believe me I know it's not even five, yet!...Yes, I'll hang on." The concierge put the phone into his shoulder and smiled nervously at the agents. "He's going to go ask." He put the phone back up to his ear. Morales fingers began to drum on the reception counter. "Okay, thanks, Bruno," the concierge said. He hung up the phone. "My boss says to assist you in any way I can. He said for me to personally escort you to Mr. Slater's room."

"Let's go," Morales said. The concierge called over to a bored Jimmy standing by the entrance and told him to watch the front desk.

In the elevator, agent number one said, "So, Slater's a 'great friend' of your boss…"

"Oh, yes! He comps Mr. Slater for most everything—his suite, meals, and bar bill."

Agent number one looked at Morales. "Doubly interesting."

The concierge knocked on Slater's door. There was no answer. He knocked again, harder. Still no answer. "Mr. Slater, please open up. The FBI would like to speak with you." There was no movement, they heard nothing.

Agent number one stepped in front of the concierge. He banged on the door. "FBI! Slater, open up!" Silence.

"I told you he was under the weather. He's probably sleeping it off," the concierge said. A door opened up two doors down. A sleepy man in pajamas stuck his head out.

"What the hell is going on? Keep it down!"

"Official government business. Go back to bed, Sir," Morales said. The man glared at them for a second or two before ducking back into his room. Morales turned to the concierge. "Can you open this for us or do we have to break the door down?"

"Yes. Please don't break the door, gentlemen! Just give me five minutes to go to the front desk."

"Make it four!" agent number one said.

"Yes, sir!" The concierge trotted back to the elevator. It opened immediately when he pushed the button. The agents waited impatiently. When the concierge returned, agent number one looked at his watch.

"Nine minutes."

The concierge was out of breath. "Elevator only goes so fast, sir."

Morales took the cardkey out of the concierge's hand. Agent number two took the concierge by the shoulders and moved him safely off to the side, saying, "Stay put until we give you the okay." The concierge nodded. The agents pulled out guns. The concierge's eyes widened.

One agent stood on either side of the door with guns at the ready. Morales, gun in one hand and the cardkey in the other, unlocked the door, shoved it open, and crouched in one motion. No movement. The lights were on. He pointed the gun this way and that. The suite had a lot of glass with a terrific view out over the water. The sun was just beginning to peek above the horizon They fanned out and carefully approached the wide open bedroom door. They could see the end of a king size bed. They also could see a pair of legs. They entered like they had from the corridor. Slater was sprawled out on the bed, dead to the world, his clothes disheveled and damp. His shoes muddy. Morales motioned the agents to check the bathroom.

The two agents gave Morales the okay sign and holstered their firearms. Morales holstered his gun and bent down to frisk Slater. He wasn't armed. Morales shook him. He barely got an incoherent mumble. He shook him again. Slater was dead to the world. Morales checked his pulse: steady but very slow. He pushed back an eyelid. Slater's pupil looked like a saucer. Morales turned and hurried to the front door of the suite.

"Does the hotel have a doctor?" he asked the concierge who was glued to the wall.

"Yes, sir."

"Get him up here immediately."

"Yes, sir." He took a step towards the elevator, but stopped and turned around. "Would it be alright to use the phone here?" Morales nodded. The concierge rushed in and made the call.

With his badge and ID in hand, Morales met the doctor at the door. "What seems to be the problem?" the doctor asked.

"Not sure. Possible drug overdose. Follow me." Morales led him into the bedroom. When the doctor saw Slater, he rushed up to the bed and immediately took his pulse. Satisfied, he brought a penlight from his breast pocket and checked both eyes. He bent down to listen closely to Slater's breathing. He shook Slater. Slater mumbled something, but didn't wake up. The doctor stood and walked quickly into the other room. Morales followed. The doctor picked up the phone and dialed 911.

"This is the Paradise Hotel doctor. We have a probable drug overdose. Possibly barbiturates. Eighth floor, Suite 809…I don't know. We'll look…Yes, thank you." He hung up the phone. "I believe you were right," he said, to Morales. "I don't think it's life threatening but I can't be sure. Better to err on the side of caution. Did you find any prescription bottles?"

"Didn't look."

The two men returned to the bedroom. Morales directed one of the agents to stand by the front door for the EMTs. The doctor stayed by Slater while Morales and the other agent searched for empty pill containers in both the bedroom and bathroom, and also Slater's clothes. They found none. "Damn," said the doctor. "Be nice to know what he took. They'll have to take a blood sample, or, if he comes to, a urinalysis." He started to roll up Slater's sleeves.

"What are you doing," Morales asked.

"Looking for needle tracks. He could have shot up." He examined both arms. "Clean." He took off Slater's shoes and socks and pulled off his pants. He examined his thighs, calves, and feet, before turning him over to look at his backside. No marks. He was pulling Slater's underwear back up when he said, "Hello…" He pulled the collar of Slater's shirt away a little to better look at his neck.

"What?" Morales asked, stepping closer.

"Take a gander," the doctor said.

Morales bent down. There was a cluster of what looked like needle marks. "How the hell did he get those there?" he asked.

"Got me. Clearly couldn't have done it himself."

The EMTs entered with a mobile stretcher. They checked the vital signs while the doctor told them that there were no pill bottles anywhere, but there seemed to be needle marks on the back of his neck. They covered Slater with a light blanket before strapping him to the stretcher. They started to leave. Morales stopped them and showed them his badge, saying that he wanted to accompany Slater in the ambulance. "Then let's go!" one of the EMTs said. Everyone, including the concierge and doctor, exited the suite. The two agents followed the ambulance. Morales puzzled over the location of the needle marks all the way to the hospital. As Slater was being wheeled into the emergency room, Morales walked up to the admitting personnel and asked about McMillan. He was referred to an emergency nurse. She told him Rusty was in a coma.

Chapter Thirty-Four

"The blood test indicates phenobarbital," the doctor said, "but not a lethal amount. As a precaution we'll keep him in the ICU on a respirator for a couple more hours. If he had ingested the drug, we could have given him activated charcoal to absorb the toxins and he'd have been out of danger much more quickly. But, unfortunately, that was not the case."

"So it was injected," Morales said.

"Yes, more than once, by the looks of it."

"Could it have been self-administered?"

"Not a chance."

"Doctor, I'd like to post one of my men outside."

The doctor's eyebrows raised. "If you feel that's necessary."

"I do."

Morales left agent number one by the door and proceeded down to the ICU nurses' station where a nurse was writing something on a clipboard. "Any news on McMillan?"

"Who?"

"The frigging man who was all shot up and has been in the ER for the past four frigging hours!" The nurse raised her hackles.

"And who might you be?"

Morales flipped open his badge. He felt like throwing it at her. "FBI, Madam. Now can you tell me how McMillan's doing?" The nurse gave him a look before she picked up the phone and dialed the ER. Morales ran a hand over his face. He was jittery from too many cups of bad coffee. He needed sleep. He was pissed off. "I'm sorry, Ma'am. It's been a very long night…and morning." The nurse's expression softened.

"I understand…" She turned back to the phone. After a few seconds, she said, "Thank you," and hung up. "Good news and bad news. The good is that, although they're still working on the hip, things have stabilized and they don't need to give him any more blood. He may have set a record in that department. The bad news is that he's still in a coma."

"Right. Thank you…and, again, I apologize." Morales turned and began walking down the corridor while pulling out his cellphone and quickly dialing. "Hey, Morales here. Do you have the personal file on McMillan?...Good. Look up who he put down to contact in an emergency…Wait a second…" Morales pulled out a pen and small notebook. "Shoot…Right, thanks…Not good. Stopped the bleeding and blood transfusion, but in a coma and still working on the hip…Yeah, I will, too." He signed off and dialed again. "Hello, is this Crystal Talbot? This is Special Agent Morales of the FBI. I'm afraid I've got some bad news…" Morales told Crystal what had happened, how severe, and where Rusty was. Crystal said she'd come to Biloxi as soon as she possibly could. Morales put the phone away and returned to agent number one outside Slater's room. The agent was speaking with a tall, distinguished looking man in an expensive suit.

When the agent saw Morales, he said, "This fella says he's Slater's lawyer and that he wants to know why I'm here."

Morales looked at the lawyer. "Because Slater's involved in some big time drug trafficking."

The lawyer smiled. "I seriously doubt that."

"Why do *you* happen to be here? Who contacted you?"

"That, sir, is of no consequence. Let's just say a good friend of Mr. Slater advised me of the situation."

"I see," said agent number one. "I think we know who that is."

The lawyer ignored agent number one. To Morales, he said, "I understand you have questions for my client. I would like to be present when you ask them."

"If you seriously doubt that Slater has anything to do with drug smuggling, then why, pray tell, do you want to be present?"

"Because officer, I have spoken with Mr. Slater's doctor. He explained that someone injected him with Phenobarbital and he will most likely be confused and his memory fuzzy until the drug completely wears off. I don't think it is timely or proper to be questioned by officers of the law who may intentionally try to further confuse or entrap him."

"Alright, suit yourself. We are waiting until the doctor takes him off the respirator. Might be a couple hours."

"Not a problem." The lawyer smiled. "It's all by the hour."

* * *

The nearest airport with direct flights to New Orleans was Tampa, four hours away. Crystal did some calculations. Four hours to Tampa, had to be there an hour and a half before the flight, just over an hour flight to New Orleans, then rent a car and drive another hour and a half: eight hours, the same as driving from Crescent Beach. She got on the phone. "Tammy, it's Crystal. Rusty's been hurt real bad in Biloxi, and I'm leaving here in fifteen minutes. Want to come with me?"

Crystal and Tammy passed through Perry about the time that an agent came in to wake Morales who had nodded off in the waiting room. "What's up?" Morales asked.

"Got an ID on the man you wasted. One José Ramirez. Occupation: gardener… for guess who?"

"The *Don* in Miami?"

"Bingo! Also, a messy job, but we found the coke. A pant-load, so to speak, in the holding tank. And get this. Slater had a gun safe aboard with a false bottom. Just so happens there was a Heckler & Koch submachine gun which is the same model ballistics said killed the judge and fishing guide two years ago. It's in transit now to our lab. And the last thing is that the sting went well at the fish camp outside Tampa. Got the owner and a half dozen bikers in custody along with a pound of cocaine."

For the first time in twenty-four hours, Morales smiled. "Great work!"

Agent number one walked into the waiting room. "Doctor says it's okay to question Slater now." Morales quickly got to his feet. The good news was like a shot in the arm and he almost bounced on his feet as the trio walked towards Slater's room. At the doorway the third agent left them, saying he'd be in touch as soon as he had more info on the submachine gun. Morales entered the room and walked up to the end of Slater's bed. The lawyer was already standing next to Slater who looked groggy.

"My lawyer says you have some questions for me."

"That's right, lots of them. Let's start with how three hundred kilos of cocaine happened to be on your boat."

"Three hundred kilos of cocaine!" Slater looked from Morales to the lawyer and back to Morales. "You're kidding!" Morales didn't say anything. "If that's true, I have no idea. In fact I don't really know how I got here…I mean, I was coming here to have some fun at the casinos alright, but I really don't remember much after about six hours out of Naples."

"You were going to make the trip solo?"

"Nope. There was a Mexican guy I hired to help me run the boat. It's a long haul from Naples. Where is my boat, by the way?"

"Don't worry. It's safe and sound. What is the guy's name you hired."

"Juan…Juan Montoya."

"Sure he wasn't a Colombian named José Rodriguez who worked for the *Don* of a Colombian cartel?"

"Juan, he said his name was. I don't know anything about any José or any Don."

"Alright, what do you remember?"

"I remember leaving Naples. The weather was good, although a little choppy…"

"You headed due west. Biloxi is northeast from Naples."

"Wind was out of the northwest, which meant taking the waves head on. We could go faster and have a smoother ride heading due west. We were going to do that until about sunset when the wind was supposed to change and come from the south. Again, it would be better and faster going."

"Makes sense to me," the lawyer interjected.

"About six hours out I went below to my cabin for some shuteye. That was the schedule Juan and I agreed on: six hours on, six hours off. I went to sleep…and that's really about the last thing I remember clearly."

"How did you happen to walk into the Paradise soaking wet?"

Slater looked confused. "I'm not really sure…"

"You don't have to answer him right now, Mr. Slater."

"No, no, it's alright" He looked at Morales. "I really don't. Just foggy, everything's foggy. But I do remember that every so often things around me in the cabin would start to come into a blurry focus, then all of a sudden, poof, it was black again. It seemed to happen several times."

"That would explain the needle marks the doctor told me about. That Mexican, or Colombian, or whoever he was, obviously kept shooting him up," the lawyer said.

"Juan? I don't believe it!...But I guess it does explain it."

"The question was how did you happen to walk into the Paradise?"

"Right. Sorry. I sort of remember going through one of those beginning-to-focus periods that was a little clearer than the others. I got up off my berth and somehow made it out the cabin door to the rear deck. I mean I could barely walk. I was like a drunk, tipsy as hell. I remember it was raining and it felt good. The boat wasn't going much more than an idle, and I remember being surprised that there were lights everywhere, close by. They were real foggy, a weird mix of different colors all running together; it was like looking through a rainy window. They had to be close because the reflections in the water came right up to the boat. I remember hanging on to the side of the cabin as I made my way to the side of the boat to get a better look. Next thing I knew, I don't know how, but I was in the water and the *Pituca* kept right on going. Maybe I stumbled. I…just don't know," Slater said, disarmingly. "That water was cold, I can tell you that! I guess it revived me or something because I knew it was sink or swim and I somehow made it to shore. The Paradise was almost right in front of me. I guess you know the rest. A bellboy helped me to my room, then I crashed on the bed. Guess I passed out again because the next thing I know, I'm here."

"How come you could function well enough in the water and walk to the hotel, then you're totally out of it when we find you?"

Slater held his hands up. "You got me! I've got no idea."

"My guess is," the lawyer said, "that Juan gave you an injection just before you went out to the stern. The doctor says phenobarbital takes awhile to knock a person out."

Morales turned to the lawyer. "Like you say, it's a guess." He turned back to Slater. "Doctor says you'll be staying overnight. I'm leaving a man here in case you get any ideas of disappearing." Slater was the picture of innocence. "I'll have more questions tomorrow."

"What time, Morales?" the lawyer asked. "No questioning without me here. Understood?"

"Alright, let's say eight o'clock."

Slater gave his best Robert Redford smile. "And I'll be happy to answer any questions you might have...hopefully a little clearer than I just did."

Morales left the lawyer and Slater. He was going to check on McMillan one last time, then get some well deserved sleep. Slater, he knew, was guilty as hell; but how the hell did he come up with this? It was all plausible; a judge or jury could easily be sucked in to the idea his boat was hijacked and he was the victim, not the villain. He shook his head in frustration. As he waited for the elevator, he saw Slater's doctor. He pulled him aside. "Doctor, I have one last question."

"Shoot."

"I was told that phenobarbital takes a little while to kick in. Is that true?"

"Yes. Unlike other short-acting barbiturates, its spreading across the blood-brain barrier and its penetration into other tissues can take twenty minutes, a half hour, maybe even longer, depending on the person's constitution and metabolism."

"Right, thank you, Doctor." The elevator arrived. From the boat to Slater's room could have taken easily less than a half hour. What the lawyer said was possible. Shit! Morales got out at the bottom floor and headed towards the emergency room.

Chapter Thirty-Five

Crystal and Tammy arrived at the hospital at five in the afternoon and were told Rusty had been moved from the ER to the ICU. After speaking with his doctor, the pair entered his room. He was still in a coma and was heavily bandaged: his neck, the top of his right shoulder, and especially his right leg from calf to past hip. There was a drain coming out of his thigh. His stomach and chest were massively black and blue. Two IVs were hooked up along with other wires running to space age machines. His heart was being monitored as well as his respiration. He was pale as a ghost. Crystal pulled the only chair in the room up to the bed. "Tammy, no need for you to stay. Who knows when," or if, she thought, "he'll come to. You should go check in, then see Bobby. He knows we should be getting in about now."

Tammy nodded and gave Crystal a hug. "I'll see you later. I'll be either at the bar or in the room."

Crystal smiled and said, "I'll be sure to knock."

Tammy raised her eyes to the ceiling and flipped her head; but the truth was she was eager to see Bobby again. She turned in the doorway and held up both hands with fingers crossed. After she left, Crystal sat in the chair. Damn you, Rusty McMillan, damn you all to hell! Crystal thought. Didn't I tell you not to get involved! That it was dangerous! That it was the FBI's job, not yours! Such a hunk of a man, so strong, and look at him! That beautiful body, an absolute disaster! And it must be screaming pain. No wonder he's in a coma! No, that's not right. The doctor said that the coma was not pain induced: it was because he had lost so much blood. They gave him blood for over four hours! Oh Lord, why didn't he listen to me! Crystal couldn't help it; she began to cry.

Compose yourself, girl! That's not what Rusty needs—a crybaby! What did the doctor say? Speak to him, he said. Let him know you're here. He might be able to hear you. It might help bring him back to the surface. It's happened before, he said. Crystal wiped away the tears. She took a deep breath. "Rusty, sweetheart, it's Crystal. I'm here. You are in a hospital in Biloxi, darling. Tammy and I drove over today from home. I love you so much. Please, please come back to me." She almost broke down again, but willed herself. She repeated how much she loved him, over and over again.

Crystal had dozed off. She woke and looked at her watch. Almost nine! She was starved. She had been told that the cafeteria was in the basement and, for a cafeteria, had really good food. Her stomach growled as she thought about it. "I'll be back soon, darling. I'm just going to go down and get a bite to eat." She took the elevator down to the cafeteria where she ordered a cheeseburger and a Coke. It was cheap. She devoured the cheeseburger while watching hospital staff come and go in their white coats. She soon returned to the ICU. When she stepped out of the elevator, not six feet away was Slater in hospital pajamas walking down the corridor. A man in suit and tie was right behind him.

Crystal froze. Slater! Jimmy's killer! Heading towards Rusty's room! Slater looked over at her. His confident, smug face triggered her response: she launched herself at him. She swung her fists like a man, screaming, "Killer, killer, killer!" Slater put his hands up, fending off the blows. His face was one of total surprise. Then anger. He slapped Crystal hard, stunning her, but only for a second. She redoubled her attack. She kept swinging and yelling, spit flew from the corners of her mouth. She tried to kick him in the nuts, but the man in the suit intervened at that precise moment. He took it in the shin. He swore. Wearing only sneakers, it hurt her as much as him. The man in the suit grabbed hold of her arms. She kept trying to kick Slater. A nurse and an orderly came running down the hall. She couldn't take her eyes off Slater. They were full of hate.

"What's your fucking problem!" Slater spat.

"YOU, YOU are the fucking problem! You murdered my husband! Two years ago, Slater. Jimmy Talbot! You gunned him and a client down in his boat. Remember, you SCUM!" She tried to lash out again, but the man in the suit, with the orderly helping, held her firm.

"You're nuts, lady, nuts!" Slater looked at the young nurse and orderly. "Put her in the psycho ward!" he said, backing away and turning around. He walked back to his room. Crystal stopped struggling. She watched him go down the corridor. At least he wasn't headed toward Rusty's room. The young nurse followed him.

The man in the suit felt her muscles relax. "You okay, now?" he asked. Crystal nodded meekly. He released her. So, did the orderly. The man in the suit watched Slater enter his room. It was four rooms down from Rusty. He said, "Believe me, Lady, I'm on your side here. I'm FBI and here to make sure Slater doesn't disappear. Why are you here?"

"My boyfriend was shot up bad. Maybe Slater did that, too."

"McMillan?"

"Yes."

"I'm truly sorry about that. How's he doing? Any change?" he asked, continuing to watch Slater's door.

"Still in a coma. I just grabbed something to eat and was returning when I saw that…that killer. Couldn't help myself. Guess it wasn't very ladylike."

The agent laughed. "I have to go along with you there."

"Excuse me, but I got to go to Rusty."

"We've all got our fingers crossed, Ma'am. McMillan's a good man."

Crystal nodded and returned to Rusty. She sat down and looked at him closely. Still no change. At least he looked peaceful enough. She thought about Slater. With him just down the hall, no way was she going to leave tonight. She decided to go down to the nurse's station to use the phone. She called the hotel and had them ring her and Tammy's room. No answer. She called the Paradise bar. Bobby picked up.

"Bobby, this is Crystal. Can you give Tammy a message for me?"

"Sure thing; but first, how's Rusty?"

"No change. Still in a coma. He's about bandaged head to toe."

"Bummer. What can I do?"

"Not a thing…except tell Tammy I'm staying here with Rusty tonight. Slater's in a room on the same floor; why, I don't know. But I'm not leaving Rusty alone with that son-of-a-bitch just down the hall."

"You got it. And good luck."

Crystal returned to Rusty's side. An hour later she was still cooing to him when Morales entered the room. He had come to relay some information to the man by Slater's door and to see how Rusty was. Crystal looked up. "Ma'am," he said, "I'm Special Agent Morales. We spoke this morning on the phone. I just heard about your run-in with Slater. I didn't know you were Talbot's widow; I assumed you were married to McMillan..."

"Not yet she isn't..." It was no more than a whisper, but it was enough to snap Crystal's and Morales' head around."

"Rusty! Oh God, thank you, thank you!" She started to cry. Morales felt a huge relief. He swallowed several times as he watched Crystal lean in to lightly kiss Rusty on the lips.

"You're getting my face all wet," Rusty whispered. Crystal laughed as she wiped her tears.

"How do you feel, McMillan?

Rusty continued to speak in a whisper. "Confused."

Morales said, to Crystal, "I'll go inform the doctor." He almost ran from the room.

Minutes later Morales and the night duty doctor with clip-board in hand returned. The young nurse followed the pair in the room. The doctor glanced at several of the machines before pulling the stethoscope from around his neck and listening to Rusty's heart and lungs. He shined a penlight into his eyes. "Follow the light with your eyes, please." Rusty did as the doctor said. The doctor looked again at the machines. He smiled at Rusty. "Welcome back. You're one tough cookie, Mr. McMillan; I think you're going to make it. How do you feel?"

"Happy to be alive...although I hurt pretty good."

The doctor checked one of the IVs. He increased the dosage of morphine. "You've about set two hospital records: longest blood transfusion and living to hear about it, and one of the shortest comas ever—about eleven hours."

"Eleven hours! Seems like just..." He turned to Morales, "What happened?" Rusty whispered. "Did you get him?"

The doctor interrupted. "No chitchat." To Morales, "Come back in the morning." He laid the buzzer by Rusty's hand. "Just push this if you need something."

Crystal reached for Rusty's hand. "Doctor, I was hoping to stay here tonight with Rusty? I promise not to keep him awake."

The doctor looked at them. He smiled. "Probably a good tonic." To the nurse, he said, "I still want you to check on him every half hour."

"Will it be okay to talk in the morning, Doctor?" Morales asked.

"We'll see. Okay, everybody, let's let Mr. McMillan rest." Crystal was left alone with Rusty. He soon felt warm and cozy from the morphine. His eyes began to flutter and his grip relaxed.

Crystal whispered into his ear, "What did you mean by 'not yet she isn't?'"

Eyes closed, smiling, he whispered back, "Did I say that?" He was asleep seconds later.

Four doors down, Slater wasn't sleeping; he was pacing the floor. What in God's name was that woman doing here! How did she know that he offed the fishing guide! Her husband, no less. And she looks familiar. I'm sure I've seen her before…not long ago, too. But where? She's a pretty good looker, but sure doesn't look or dress south Florida. No way I saw her around Naples. What was the name of that Podunk town they lived in? Crescent Beach, that's it. But I only drove around that dump once, to see where Talbot lived and what his boat looked like. I didn't see her there. The only woman I remember from that area was that pregnant Mexican waitress…Wait a minute! That license plate number Jack gave me, the friend-of-a-friend who told him about the waitress, the John Doe who stayed at the fish camp and busted Jack's balls. The guy told Jack I'd offed his best friend. The *Don* got his name and address for me, but said not to do anything until after the delivery, that the coke deal was more important. The guy was from the same town, but what was his name? He couldn't remember.

The young nurse came in. "You should be getting your rest, Mr. Slater." He glanced at her hand—no ring. He gave her his best Robert Redford smile.

"Call me Joe." He looked at her name tag. "Not tired, Joan; that crazy woman upset me," he said, disarmingly. "It's not every day someone gets accused of being a murderer. She's crazy. Did you put her in the psycho ward?" The nurse laughed and shook her head. She walked over to straighten the bed. "What was she doing here, anyway?"

"Visiting her boyfriend. He's hurt real bad…all shot up."

"Really! Here in Biloxi? Poor guy. Guess that woman had a right to be upset. How did it happen?"

"No idea."

"Do you know his name?"

"Mr. McMillan." That's it! Slater thought.

"I know a McMillan from Biloxi. Really nice guy. About five-nine, black hair. He's a barber at the Paradise. Sure hope it wasn't him."

"It's not. This guy's got to be about your height, and real stocky like a football player. And rusty red hair, not black…There, all set Mr. Slater."

Slater gave her another one of his special smiles. "Thank you, Joan. You spoil me!" Joan left. Slater began to pace again, back and forth, back and forth, back and...Suddenly he snapped his fingers. He had it! That guy in the Paradise bar who kept staring at me! He was stocky as hell, had red hair. And the woman. She was at the bar, too! That's where I saw her! Kept glancing over. Son-of-a-bitch! The friend-of-a-friend!"

Chapter Thirty-Six

Slater was chomping at the bit to get out of the hospital. The lawyer brought him street clothes at seven-thirty. Morales arrived at eight.

"I hope this won't take too long; the doctor has given me the okay to leave," Slater said.

"Sorry to disappoint you, Slater, but you're going downtown from here. You're under arrest."

"What for!" Slater exclaimed.

"Smuggling three hundred kilos of cocaine, for starters."

"Don't worry," the lawyer said, "I'll have you back on the street in a half hour. You're way off base, Morales! Mr. Slater's boat was commandeered, for Pete's sake; my client was kidnapped and drugged. He had absolutely nothing to do with it. You should be arresting that José fellow, not Mr. Slater."

"Pretty hard to do; he was killed during the sting. Believe me I wish we could talk to that pal of yours, Slater, because we believe that he injected you right before the sting and left you off somewhere."

"Why in hell would I do that? I wouldn't have known anything about your bust." Slater was relieved that José had been killed: dead men tell no tales.

"You're a smart guy, Slater. Maybe you were just being cautious."

Slater snorted. The lawyer said, "Ridiculous!"

"What about my boat?"

"Confiscated."

"I get kidnapped, have nothing to do with the cocaine, and my boat gets confiscated?"

"We've got aerial pictures of the Mexican fishing boat being off-loaded: the *Reina del Mar*. The transfer was smooth, no hesitation. The Mexicans knew exactly where to hide the contraband...Why did you have your holding tank cleaned out right before you left Naples if it wasn't in preparation for the cocaine bricks?"

"I had it cleaned out because it was full of shit!"

"According to the septic people, it was barely a quarter full..."

"This whole thing is ridiculous. The sooner we go downtown, the sooner you'll walk. Let's go," the lawyer said.

Morales opened the door for his two agents outside. "Book him. I'll be there shortly." Slater left with an agent on either side. The lawyer followed. Morales watched them enter the elevator before walking down to see Rusty. He stuck his head into the room. Crystal and Rusty had breakfast trays on their laps. Rusty was looking a lot better. "Knock, knock." Rusty motioned with his left arm for him to come in.

"Wish I could offer you a chair," Rusty said.

"No problem." Morales stood at the head of the bed.

"So, did you get Slater?"

"Sorta. He wasn't on the boat."

"What! Then who the hell shot me?"

"The Latino...What do you remember?"

"Covering you when you boarded. Then...nothing."

Morales looked at Rusty for a long time without saying anything. "You saved my life, McMillan." To Crystal, "McMillan here is one brave man."

No smile from Crystal. "Or one brave fool! He shouldn't have been involved in the first place, Mr. Morales. This whole thing was your job, not his!"

"Believe me, I fought his taking part, but I got outvoted." Morales turned back to Rusty. "And I'm fortunate I was. Thank you, McMillan, from me and my family."

Rusty looked at Crystal and shrugged. "All news to me." After a moment, he turned back to Morales and smiled. "If that's true, then maybe I can ask a favor?"

"Name it."

"Call me Rusty?"

Morales returned the smile. "You got it…and you call me Pete."

"Deal. Now tell me what's going on, and how you 'sorta' got Slater."

Morales brought him up through Slater's arrest. "His lawyer's right, though, he'll have Slater out in no time. It's a damn shame we didn't get a clear picture of Slater helping off-load the coke, but we didn't. But I got some good news. Hidden on the boat was the same model submachine gun that was used on Mrs. Talbot's husband and the judge. It was sent to our Lab and, guess what, ballistics matched the bullets we fired with the bullets embedded in Talbot's boat. That's why we arrested Slater, we knew we couldn't hold him, but at least we could have him fingerprinted. Within an hour or two we should see if those prints match those on the gun. We also busted the owner, Jack, at his fish camp. He was caught red-handed with plenty of goods and he's agreed to a plea bargain and reduced sentence in exchange for ratting on Slater. So, no more alibi. Two agents are presently on their way to talk with the Mexican waitress to tell her all the news. We're hoping that she'll decide to cooperate again." He looked at Crystal. "I think we've got more than a decent shot of getting Slater for your husband's murder."

"You've been busy," Rusty said, simply. "All good news. And I'll bet the boss of the cartel will be shitting bricks when you bring Slater in for murder, wondering if he'll negotiate a deal in exchange for information on him. I imagine Slater knows one heck of a lot." Morales didn't say anything. A pregnant pause. "Will he be offered a deal, too?"

Morales looked away, then back again. "I can't say. But I will say that the *Don* is a much, much bigger fish, and the Bureau would be very excited if they could get the goods on him."

"You know, all this," Rusty said, looking down at his hip and bandaged leg, "was worth it if we get Slater." He looked over to Crystal, then back up at Morales. "But, Crystal and I don't give a rat's ass about some *Don* in Miami. We want Slater."

* * *

The *Don* was a powerful and exceedingly wealthy man. He had moles wherever he conducted business. He also had very well paid informants in the government agencies that counted; the FBI being no exception. In relation to the cartel's business, he was kept very well informed. Consequently, he was extremely concerned about Slater's situation. Through an intermediary, the *Don* had instructions delivered to the owner of the Paradise hotel. The hotel owner passed the instructions on to Slater.

"You're too hot, Slater! The *Don* says he wants you to disappear to Colombia. He's got it all set for you down there. But you're being watched here. Bruno says there's an agent by the elevators, so we're going to have to sneak you out and get you to Gulfport where a boat will be waiting to take you to Colombia."

"Boat! Why not in one of his planes?"

The hotel owner shrugged. "Don't know. But those are the instructions."

Slater thought, *mierda*! Goodbye to the *Pituca*, the Porsche, my shotguns, life in Naples! But, what the hell? Got to be able to roll with the punches. And I got the dough in the Caymans to live like a king down in Colombia, or most anywhere else. Hell, the *Don* will set me up good, anyway. Plus he's got plenty of business down in S.A. And there are plenty of beautiful women in Colombia, especially Cali! And what about the girls on Copacabana in Rio! *Muy calientes*! Or those classic Latin beauties at Viña del Mar in Chile!...I can't believe how this trip turned into such a rat's nest. I wonder if it was because of that redheaded guy? Maybe some day if I make it back to the States, I can pay him a little visit…But, it doesn't matter, now. Hell, the change of scenery will do me good.

The laundry was hauled from the hotel to the cleaners every afternoon and returned early the next morning. Bruno escorted Slater down the service elevator to the basement where a cargo van was waiting. He handed Slater a small bag. Slater looked inside. There were a couple changes of clothes, toiletries, false passport, and a stack of ten one-hundred dollar bills. Slater climbed into the back. He sat on a pile of sheets as he continued to contemplate this turn-around in his life: from boating in the *Pituca* to riding in the back of a windowless van full of dirty pillowcases with lipstick smears and stained sheets. Less than a half hour later he was at the docks in Gulfport. A Latino met the van and escorted Slater to a shrimp trawler with idling twin diesels. A mate escorted him below to his cabin. The boat shoved off while Slater was still below.

When Slater came topside, the captain was at the helm. He smiled at Slater. "*Hola, Gringo*. We meet again, eh?" It was the *capitán* of the *Reina del Mar*.

"What are you doing here! Where's your boat?"

"Cancún. Your lucky day, *Gringo*. You get me as *capitán* all the way to Colombia."

"But why you?"

The Mexican shrugged his shoulders. "*Quien sabe*? Who knows? But I was chosen…Things did not go so well, eh, with the *drogas?*"

"No, José is dead. And they took pictures, too, when we were off-loading your boat. They have pictures of the *Reina del Mar*…maybe of you, too."

"Aay, that ees bad, eh? I theenk you screw up big time, *Gringo*."

"I didn't screw up, *Capitán*!"

The Mexican shrugged his shoulders. "Someone deed." Slater looked behind him. The sun was setting. He went below. They were forty miles out in the Gulf when Slater returned top-side. The mate was at the helm.

"When are we going to eat," Slater asked.

The mate held his hands up. "*No comprendo. No hablo Inglés*."

"*Cuando vamos a comer?*"

"*Luego*."

Slater sat on the raised co-pilot's chair. He wondered what 'in a while' meant; he was hungry. They still hadn't eaten when darkness fell and the captain came up from his cabin. He stood behind the two men, scanning the Gulf. Not a light anywhere. Slater was staring straight ahead through the boat's windshield when he asked, "The one thing I can't understand, *Capitán*, is why the Don wanted me to go by boat when he's got a half dozen planes going back and forth to Colombia.

The *Capitán* reached to the small of his back and pulled out a pistol. He put it up to the back of Slater's head and fired. "Because, *Gringo*, you know too much." The mate pulled back on the throttle, and together with the *capitán* threw Slater overboard after going through his pockets. While the mate was cleaning up the tracks of blood, the *capitán* went below to Slater's quarters. He open the bag and pulled out the thousand dollars and put it in his pocket. He picked up the bag and returned topside to throw it overboard.

* * *

Two weeks later, Special Agent Morales returned to the Biloxi hospital. He found Crystal and Rusty in the rehab center where Rusty, sweat covering his face and holding on to the parallel bars, was struggling to walk with the assistance of a physical therapist. Rusty looked like he had lost thirty pounds. Morales didn't interrupt the session; he remained standing at the doorway until Rusty was back in his wheelchair. Rusty waved and Crystal wheeled him up. They shook hands.

"What's up, Pete? Shouldn't you be in Atlanta?" Rusty asked.

"Got some news."

"Locate Slater?"

"Sorta…"

"What's that mean?"

"Shrimpers found the body, or what was left of it, floating in the Gulf ten miles off shore. Single bullet through the rear of the head, small caliber, hollow point."

"Sure it's Slater?"

"Teeth. Positive ID."

Neither Rusty or Crystal said anything. Rusty turned in his chair to look at her. She put a hand on his shoulder. Rusty turned back to Morales. "Execution?"

"That's our take."

"Makes sense…Guess that's it, then. Not the scenario I imagined, but it'll have to do… It's finally over…Funny, though, I don't really feel anything, no great satisfaction…no, that's not true. I feel relieved, lighter, like a weight's been taken off…" He squeezed Crystal's hand.

"But that's not quite all, Rusty. Soon as you're back on your feet, the Bureau wants you to come to Atlanta to receive a well deserved medal. Going to be a big deal. Even Smathers and some of your other statey buddies will be invited."

Rusty didn't say anything. Crystal squeezed his shoulder again. "Tell you what," Rusty said. "I'd trade that medal for something else in a heartbeat."

"A new hip?"

Rusty laughed. "No, for the Heckler & Koch you found on the boat."

"Why that, for God's sake?"

"To throw in the Gulf where we scattered Jimmy's ashes. I want him to know."

"I think maybe that could be arranged, but we'd have to bend the barrel or something to make sure it can't be used again."

Rusty smiled. "I don't think Jimmy'd care."

Chapter Thirty-Seven

Amazing the contrast between early spring and mid-summer, Rusty thought, gazing over the marsh: golden brown to deep green in the span of three months. Been away far too long, that's for sure! It was low tide and he turned his attention to the army of fiddler crabs slowly moving as one on the far bank of the canal. A little blue heron landed nearby and immediately the crabs headed for cover in the marsh. Mud-eaters, that's what Charley calls them—says the fiddlers get their nutrients by shoveling mud into their mouths. That must be tasty! And he says the she-crabs got the advantage there because they got two little claws to stuff their faces while the guys got that big claw that just gets in the way. According to Charley, about the only thing the big claw is used for is to wave back and forth in front of their burrows during mating season. It attracts a female who goes down the hole, and the guy follows, plugging the hole behind him with a dab of mud. Some honeymoon!

Rusty heard an airboat start up. Must have launched over at City Park. Please head north, he thought; don't come this way. No such luck, within minutes it came around the bend. Shorebirds and waders fled before it, and there was no escaping the painful throb that permeated his whole being as well as the whole town. It was a blasphemy on this beautiful late afternoon! Like the birds, Rusty fled the noise. He reached for his cane and limped inside. He was wearing shorts, revealing the raw, red souvenirs from the sting in Biloxi. It had taken two subsequent operations on his hip and three months to heal, progressing from wheelchair to crutches to a cane. The good news was that the doctors were confident that he would be close to a hundred percent in another month or so as long as he kept up with his therapy.

The noise from the airboat was almost as bad inside. Rusty switched on the TV and turned up the volume. He flipped through the channels, stopping at a local Gainesville station when he saw himself on the screen. Old footage was shown of the warehouse in Biloxi and the *Pituca* while the news correspondent described the cocaine bust as the largest in the history of the FBI, and that it had been made possible by one Rusty McMillan who yesterday was awarded a medal for conspicuous bravery in the line of duty. He thought of the offer from Captain Smathers who had attended the ceremony. Smathers wanted him, when he was totally recovered, to return to the State Police as a sort of special detective: no uniform, strictly part time, on an as-needed basis. Rusty could refuse any mission he wanted. Smathers said he was too talented and valuable to go out to pasture at such an early age. It was quite an offer, but Rusty didn't tell Crystal because she would think him totally nuts for even considering it…which he was. The telephone rang.

"Did you happen to see the five o'clock news?" Crystal asked.

"Just so happens I did."

"You're a hero!"

"Aw, shucks."

"You going to poker tonight?"

"Yup, though I'm going to be a little 'rusty,' so to speak.

"Ha, ha."

"Going to change and cook up a burger first."

"How 'bout I come over and cook it."

"Good idea. I might be in the shower when you get here."

"Then I'll come over a little early. Make sure you got an extra towel." Rusty smiled…

After dinner, Crystal returned to her house in Jimmy's old truck. Rusty filled his pockets with quarters and climbed into her car that she'd loaned him because it was a heck of a lot easier to get in and out of than his truck. As he pulled up to the Club, he was surprised by the number of pickups in the parking lot on a Thursday night. He slowly climbed the stairs and entered. Most of the poker players were already there. As he hobbled over, they, along with everyone else in the Club, stood and applauded. Apparently everyone had heard about the medal. With his fair complexion, Rusty turned bright pink and it took forever to walk to the poker table. People applauded until he sat. "Okay, okay," he said, to the poker players, "What say we get down to business…"

Beau, smiling broadly, said, "Your deal."

Rusty shuffled the cards. "Five card draw, nothing wild." As he dealt, he asked Charley, "Where's Louie?"

"Ain't came yet—been workin' almighty hard on his booth for Saturday. Been mighty secret 'bout it, too. Made hisself a tent o' tarps so no one sees 'im a-workin' on it."

"An' what 'bout you, Charley?" Sammy asked. "You got yur Mustang out in the weather and yur carport tarped, too. You ain't let nobody seen nuthin' neithers."

"My progative, Sammy!"

"Prerogative, Charley," Norm said.

"Whatever."

"I should be chargin' you two fer usin' my truck. 'Tween the pair o' you, musta made twenty trips goin' to the dump," Tiny said.

"You don' 'go to the dump,' Tiny; you 'come from the dump.'"

Norm laughed. "True enough, Charley. I'll take three, Rusty."

"People complain how's we don' recycle none here. That ain't true, not by a long shot." Louie entered and walked over. "Jest look at Louie and me, fer example. Ain't that right, Louie?"

"What's that?" Louie said, sitting.

"That we been a-recycling a storm these las' few days."

"True enough. And Lucifer's been a Godsend! I swear that man knows where every stick of wood, piece of metal, and tire is located. He's got a pretty good handle on the dumpsters, too. One thing, though: you about need an interpreter to understand him."

Lucifer was the caretaker of the dump who lived in a little shack on the outskirts of town. At the dump, he had built a ten foot tall chair out of scraps that resembled a lifeguard's chair, complete with cushions and a big Cinzano umbrella. He climbed up by means of a bent aluminum ladder he cut to fit and lashed to the side. All day, six days a week, he'd be in that chair listening to country western on his transistor radio and watching his domain like a hawk.

"That's because he ain't never had no schoolin', Louie. Don' know how to read and write," Charley said. "He lived in the marsh his whole life 'til his maw died. Might say they was a close-knit family: 'magine his family tree 'bout looks like a stick."

"How many, Charley?" Rusty asked.

"Three."

"Two fer me," Tiny said. As he rearranged his cards, Tiny asked, "So neither one of you two are goin' to tell us what you got cookin' for the festival Saturday?"

"Nope," Louie and Charley said, in unison.

The others took their cards. Beau kept betting until everyone but Sammy backed out. "I'll call, Beau."

"Jack high straight," Beau said.

Sammy slowly and dramatically laid down his cards one by one. "Flush!"

"Damn," Beau said. Sammy began to rake in the quarters.

"How are the girls doing, Sammy?" Norm asked.

"Right good, an' I think they be enjoyin' themselves now, too; 'though, if'n it was jest Rebecca an' me an' them clams, might be somethin' else. Was a bit tough at first fer T.L., that stands fer Tallahassee Lassie which is what I call O.C.'s daughter, but them two gurls work good together. Them baskets with the clams and mud is heavy, an' takes both of 'em to dump one in the tumblers, but they manage. T.L. don' much like a-pickin' out them critters that's get in with them clams—like slimy dog fish, pistol shrimp, brittle stars, an' sech, but when she seen Rebecca do it, she hunkered down… Real nice o' you, Norm, to let T.L. bunk with Rebecca during the weekdays when O.C. and his wife is in Tallahassee."

"That girl's done wonders for Rebecca! And Rebecca's hoping to bunk with her in the fall so she can attend high school in Tallahassee. She's been saving every penny so she can pay her own way," Norm said.

"Don' know how Katharine will feel 'bout that, but I think it'd do Rebecca a whale o' good," Sammy said.

"I hired both of 'em to help me in my booth Saturday," Charley said. "You got anybody helpin', Louie?"

"Linda," he said, nodding towards her behind the bar.

"She really going to take the Club on?" Tiny asked.

"Signed an agreement yesterday," Ralph said, not looking at Norm. "She'll get paid for working with Tammy until September; then Tammy's out of here and she'll be on her own."

"I'll be helping her with the books," Louie said.

One look at Norm's face made Craig quickly change the subject. "William and I are going to march in the parade with a banner for the Crescent Beach Bashers."

"Can't hardly believe you two is buddies," Sammy said.

"I wouldn't say buddies, exactly, Sammy, but he's not that bad of a guy, and he's a damn good softball player. It was his idea to combine players from both teams to form the Bashers for the slowpitch league. We're undefeated so far, and I figure we got more than a good chance to win the tournament at the end of the season."

"We're here to play poker, ladies, not chitchat all night. Louie, I believe it's your deal," Beau said.

Louie shuffled the cards. "Five card stud, deuces wild…"

* * *

The town lucked out for the Scallop Festival; the day was cloudy and cool, but with no rain in the forecast. The field next to the library was full of vendors selling anything from generous plates of swamp cabbage to whacky metal sculptures made from old tools and car parts. A string of brightly painted mini-cars pulled by an old Farmall Cub tractor provided rides for the kiddies. Both sides of Main Street were lined with spectators for the entire parade route. The parade lineup began at ten-thirty and was organized by Norm near the cattle gap. At eleven sharp the fire engine's siren sounded and the parade was on. The Color Guard led the way followed by the festival queen. The queen was determined each year by a scallop shucking contest held on the slab below the Crescent Beach Club. This year Katharine, Rebecca's mother, had won easily. The only possible challenge to her would have been T who had beaten Katharine three years ago. However, the rules stipulated 'one and done:' past champions were not allowed to compete.

The festival queen was followed by Beau wearing his mayoral sash and driven by Rebecca and T.L. in his golf cart. Homemade floats and decorated golf carts followed them. An old skidder driven by Tiny pulled a hay wagon that had been doctored to look like a shrimp boat complete with netting hanging from outriggers. It advertised the T&T Shrimp Company. T sat on a hay bale in the center of the boat hanging on to a giggling Boda who was dressed up as a shrimp and waving to bystanders. Craig and William walked down the center of the street carrying their banner, a sheet stapled to a long stick that said,

SUPPORT YOUR LOCAL SOFTBALL TEAM
CRESCENT BEACH BASHERS
6 WINS—0 LOSSES
NEXT GAME VS. STEINHATCHEE
JULY 9—3 P.M.—AT HOME

The Marina's float advertised Mercury motors, boat storage, and boat lift service. Tammy had her usual golf cart that advertised the Club. She and Linda sat side by side, waving to the crowd. A bevy of assorted participants were in the parade, mostly decorated golf carts, but also bicycles, four-wheelers, even people walking a dog or two wrapped in red, white, and blue bunting. The final golf cart before the fire engine brought up the rear was decorated by the library with large, painted cardboard books attached to the sides and rear. On the front was a sign that said,

SCALLOP FESTIVAL
SPONSORED BY
THE CRESCENT BEACH LIBRARY

Sticking up from the roof was another large cardboard sign that said,

READ A BOOK
IT MIGHT MAKE YOU SMIEL!

When the parade was over and everyone had returned to their booths, Rusty and Crystal walked over to the field full of vendors. So did everyone else; it was a zoo. In the center of the field, opposite each other, were Louie's and Charley's booths. It was like a face-off: both had more customers and spectators than any of the other vendors by far. Rusty and Crystal walked up to Charley's booth and immediately broke into laughter. Charley, dressed in a tuxedo too large for him and soaking wet, was sitting up on a hinged perch suspended over a round stock tank, five foot in diameter and filled with water. Sticking out from the perch was a two-by-six with a round metal bull's-eye attached at the end. The other end had a piece of metal that slipped between two cogs attached to the supports of the perch. Push on the bull's-eye and the piece of metal would pop out away from the cog, and the perch would collapse. At the front of the booth was Rebecca, taking in the money and saying in a loud voice, "Hit the bull's-eye and knock Charley in the water! Three throws only two dollars!" Standing next to Rebecca was T.L. who was handing Craig three softballs.

"Whooee! Lookee who we got here! Craig, you couldn't hit that ol' bull's-eye if'n you were at it all day. You jest be throwin' yur money away, so to speak, but that's alright—goin' to a good cause…namely ME!" Charley said.

Craig hefted one of the balls. He stepped a little away from the counter so he could step into his throw. He fired a bullet. Dead center! The bull's-eye clanged, down went Charley into the water, and the crowd around the booth roared. Charley came up sputtering and wiping the water out of his eyes. He looked totally bedraggled. Rusty and Crystal laughed along with everyone else.

Charley re-cocked the two-by-six, saying, "So you was lucky, Craig! That be called 'beginners' luck.' Might as well give them softballs back to them two purty gals 'cuz you ain't a-never goin' hit that thar bull's-eye agin!" Charley climbed back up. Craig stepped back and let go. Clang! Another hit, and another dunk. The crowd roared again; even the two girls giggled. Charley slowly climbed up. This time he kept his mouth shut. Craig threw, but the sight of the sopping wet Charley anticipating another throw of doom had Craig laughing so hard he wasn't even close.

Rusty said, "Even with this bum leg, Crystal, I got to try." He caned over to the end of the line. Crystal went over to Louie's booth.

"Step right up, Ladies and Gentlemen! Pick yourself a winner! Pick your thoroughbred and get a chance to win this beautiful trophy and a hundred dollars in the grand championship race at the end of the day! Just win one race and your stallion will automatically be entered in the finals that will be run right before the raffle in City Hall. Only three dollars with a chance to win a hundred! Step right up!" Wearing a pouch around her waist, Linda was taking money in hand over fist while Louie helped kids and adults alike select their entries from two old sheetrock buckets full of fiddler crabs. Each crab chosen was placed in a red plastic cup until race time.

Louie continued, "Alrighty, we have enough contestants to run the next race. All entries must go to the starting gate immediately."

Louie had built a five foot by eight foot table out of wood scraps from the dump. The table's front legs were shorter than the rear, so it was tilted downhill. Screwed down to the top of the table were ten PVC gutters, each painted a different color and numbered one through ten. At the high end of the table, slots were cut almost all the way through the gutters so that a single board that spanned all ten gutters could be dropped in edgeways and taken out easily. Another board capped the end of the gutters four inches beyond the slots so that each gutter had a little sealed compartment until the slot board was pulled up. Behind the gutter, on a stand was a large grease board with the names of the winners of the races.

"Alright, place your fiddler crab in one of the spaces behind the starting gate." Soon ten little crabs were each in a compartment. "Now take your cup down to the end of the racetrack and hold it under your crab's lane. First crab to fall in the cup is the winner." When everybody was ready, Linda rang a cowbell and Louie lifted the starting gate. Louie was also the race commentator. "They're off! Number three is first out of the gate with seven, nine, and six right on his tail! Numbers ten, four, and five haven't figured out there is a race on. Number one is a slow starter but seems to be catching on. Keep your eyes on number one, ladies and gentlemen; might be a dark horse. It's number nine and six in the homestretch! Number one is coming up fast! It's number nine and number one down to the wire! It's number nine by a claw's length! Congratulations number nine!

"Number nine, let me get your name so I can write it on the board back there. You others kindly put your crab back in the bucket and return the cups to Linda." Number nine was a six-year-old girl named Kelly. "Now, Miss Kelly, you have the choice of using the same crab for the finals, or choosing a new one." The girl's parents explained the procedure. She chose to stick with her crab. Louie wrote the girl's name on her cup and placed it in one of the holes he had routered into a board suspended between two sawhorses. "Now remember, Miss Kelly, you should be back here by four o'clock." Kelly didn't want to leave her crab—she had to be dragged away by her parents.

Louie turned to the crowd at the front of the booth. "Ladies and gentlemen, will our next race participants please step forward." Crystal approached Louie holding her red plastic cup. It turned out Crystal's entry was an explorer, but he never found the finish line. She had to pick it up out of the gutter to return it to the bucket. Linda conveyed her condolences with a smile when she took Crystal's cup. Crystal looked over toward Charley's booth; Rusty was next in line. She hurried over.

Tammy was at the first booth along Main Street looking at the whacky metal sculptures when Norm walked up. "I think you should buy the buzzard," he said.

She turned and smiled. "Nope, already got too much stuff. Clever, though." They went from sculpture to sculpture which, because Crescent Beach was such a sports fisherman's haven, were mostly of a fish-sea theme. But there was the occasional gargoyle, or bric-a-brac like horseshoes welded together to spell 'welcome.'

"How about I buy you a bowl of gumbo and we talk?" Norm asked.

"I'd like that."

They took two bowls of gumbo over to one of the picnic tables in the library parking lot. A small group playing country western was by the library door, surrounded by spectators seated on bales of hay.

"So you're really going to lease the Club to Linda."

Tammy nodded. "She takes over September one, but I'll be helping her through Labor Day weekend." Norm took a plastic spoonful of gumbo.

"Then what are your plans?"

"Head to Biloxi as soon as I get packed up." Norm took another spoonful.

"Then what?"

"Head out west in Bobby's camper." Tammy's gumbo was untouched.

"Better eat or it'll get cold."

"Norm, any chance you would take Huey? Two birds in a camper's asking a lot. And I know you'll take good care of him."

"My little feathered buddy? Of course. I've missed him."

"Thanks." She began eating her gumbo.

"Send me a postcard or two and let me know how you are."

"Alright."

"And Tammy…" Tammy looked up from her gumbo. "If Bobby ever starts beating on you, let me know and I'll come running."

Tammy squeezed his hand. "He's not drinking alcohol anymore. His beverage of choice these days is carrot juice."

"'These days.' Just remember what I said."

"Norm, you're such a good person."

"Yeah? Ever heard 'nice guys finish last?'"

"You deserve better than me. Someone more educated, with more of your background. And someone who's not stir crazy and knows what the hell she wants out of life! Don't worry, you'll find yourself another woman soon…and better suited than I ever was."

"Thanks, but that's bullshit! Here's another cliché for you: 'Three strikes and you're out.' Think I'll just stay with two strikes on me…Anyway, I hope you'll be happy. Are you going to the raffle?"

"You bet. I bought forty tickets…trying to support our local library and all. Why?" Norm reached into his pocket and pulled out a strip of tickets.

"I wondered if you'll collect for me if I win anything. Louie will be closing up his booth about then and I want to make sure that pile of fiddler crabs get back to their colony in the marsh a.s.a.p. He got them way out near the landing strip so it'll take a while."

Tammy smiled. "You're too much."

Norm stood and handed her the tickets. "Good luck at the raffle." He picked up the styrofoam bowls and threw them into a trash bin as he walked away.

Charley and Louie were at it all day. Both were worn out by the time the final race was run, just before four-thirty. The little six-year-old girl ended up winning it all: she was wide-eyed when Louie presented her with the trophy and counted ten ten-dollar bills into the palm of her little hand. By then most of the people had left for City Hall, and most of the vendors had begun to pack up. Linda left the pouch with Louie and had gone to City Hall, too. Charley, in dry shorts and tee shirt, came over with the pouch Rebecca had been wearing and a cold six-pack of beer.

"Time o' reckonin's at hand," Charley said, pulling up two chairs to Louie's booth and popping two beers. They pulled out the bills, dumped the coins on top of the ticket table, and began counting.

Louie was first. " Three hundred and sixty-six, including the hundred dollars for the winner."

A couple minutes later, Charley was smiling ear to ear. "Three hundred and ninety-eight! Hot dang! Guess that makes it three hundred and forty-six fer you, Louie."

"How do you figure?" Charley stuck out his hand.

"'Cuz you owe me twenty bucks." Louie handed him twenty ones which Charley added to his tall stack. "No hard feelin's," Charley said, popping another beer for Louie.

Louie took a swig. "None taken." He shook his head side to side. "I just can't believe it."

"What?"

"That a hundred and ninety-nine people paid money to dunk you."

"'Twere'nt quite that many. Plenty missed first time aroun' and kep' payin' until they didn'. If you wasn' a-tendin' yur booth, would you have paid two bucks to dunk me?"

"In a heartbeat!"

Charley smiled. "Thar you go then."

Norm walked up. Charley's grin was tattooed. "Pretty obvious who won the wager. Congrats, Charley," Norm said, picking up both sheetrock buckets of fiddler crabs.

"Norm here is one o' them who missed and kep' payin', Louie. Sixth throw if I ain't mistakin'."

"That's right, and worth every penny. Where'd you get that tux, Charley?"

"Salvation Army. Had some stains on it so 'twere cheap—five bucks. The tank I borrowed from Ol' Man Butler outside o' town. Speakin' of," Charley said, standing, "best be skedaddlin'. Goin' take a while to drain them two hundred and eighty gallons o' water, an' Ol' Man Butler wants it back afore sundown."

Epilogue

Beau and Virginia were walking arm in arm, watching their young Lab dutifully check the smells of every bush and tree on the condo grounds. Over the last six months the dog had grown from a clumsy puppy into a tall adolescent. Beau was thinking of Rebecca as he gazed towards the trailered boats lined up under the condo. Rebecca had told Norm that she had taken part in the heist the night of Norm and Tammy's party. In turn, Norm had discussed with Beau what to do about it. Even though Rebecca had wanted to pay the condo people back over time, Beau and Norm convinced her to let it be. They felt that she had taken part only because of Billy, that making her drug addiction and theft public would certainly damage her and her family, and that it could possibly trigger a relapse for her. She had suffered enough, plus Rebecca had paid back every cent of Tiny and T's shrimp money, and then volunteered to babysit Boda for free. Miraculously, the theft had been kept hush-hush—something quite rare in Crescent Beach. And now Rebecca was living with O.C. and his family, and enrolled in a Tallahassee high school. She had an excellent chance to do something with her life. No, they felt, no way should she open that can of worms! As it is, Beau thought looking around, it appeared that everything had been replaced in spades. And more than likely insurance had covered most, if not all, of it.

Beau whistled and called out. "Paws, let's go." The Lab bounded over and rubbed up against Virginia who laughed delightedly and pet him. It hadn't taken more than a few days before Beau decided to keep the puppy. It had been such a salve for Virginia: the puppy could soften even her most anxious moments. She would giggle delightedly at the puppy's antics, and housetraining the puppy made her feel useful again. In her clearer moments, together they had decided to keep Charley's suggested name for the puppy, although occasionally she would have a relapse and call him Skillet. But, for the most part, it was Paws.

Beau and Virginia always turned right these days after passing the ballfield, rather than walk out towards the pond and the Big Bend Wildlife Area. He thought Virginia might be reminded of her and Skillet's ordeal which could send her in a downward spiral for days. They stopped to watch the progress of the new tennis courts. Through William's diligent research and diplomacy, he had talked the owners of the land between the marsh and the ballfield into selling to the town. The necessary funds had been provided by William and the condo people plus a few others, and the price was more than reasonable because the land was too low and close to the marsh for any legal house construction. Once the property had been turned over to the town, the state grant kicked into action. Fill had been brought in which was packed and leveled by Tony who won the bid for both the site preparation and cement work. Tennis court construction experts would be brought in to properly finish off the surface when all the concrete was in the ground. They watched Tony and a couple others stake the corners and run string all the way around for one of the courts. His crew began carrying over the forms while Tony set up his transit. Paws ran up to Tony who petted him. Paws bounded off seconds later, crossing the leveled area to pee on one of Tony's tires. Beau whistled shrilly for the dog to return.

"Sorry about that, Tony," Beau yelled over.

Tony laughed. "No problem, but might be good to keep him at home when we pour."

"Just let me know when."

Tony waved and went back to leveling the transit.

This was the third time that Beau and Virginia had walked by Tony and his crew. It was also the third time that Virginia asked, "Who's that, Beau?"

"Tony, dear—the concrete guy who lives near Rusty."

"Oh. What's he doing?"

"Building two tennis courts."

"That's nice."

When they arrived at Main Street, Beau hooked the leash to Paws. They walked down the street then turned left to cross Humpback Bridge. They took the roundabout way to Rich Man's Row, passing Crystal's house. Rusty's boat wasn't there. "Rusty must be out fishing," he said, to Virginia. "I've heard the trout have started coming in."

"That's nice, Dear."

Beau looked out towards where the main channel led into the Gulf. He pointed. "There he is, Sugah. Looks like Crystal's with him."

Crystal was indeed with Rusty. And so was Slater's Heckler & Koch submachine gun with a bent barrel. They had waited until Rusty's hip and leg were pretty much a hundred percent before going out to where Jimmy's ashes had been scattered. Last week the weather had been iffy because of Tropical Storm Gordon that had formed off Guatemala and come across from the Yucatan. But today was a beautiful late September afternoon in the high seventies with a slight breeze. Rusty and Crystal were in no hurry: they didn't have to go far. Jimmy's ashes had been spread a quarter-mile off the point where both the marsh and town were visible. Crystal had picked this spot because Jimmy had told her time and again that he never tired of seeing "that big ol' orange sun" come up over the marsh. The area had been crowded at sunrise for his service, peppered with boats full of people paying their last respects. This afternoon, though, almost exactly three years later, Rusty and Crystal would perform their own private ceremony.

"Right here, Rusty," Crystal said. "It's as close as I can tell." Rusty turned off the motor and stuck his Power Pole anchor in the mud. They sat in silence for awhile. Finally, Rusty stood.

"Let's do her," he said. Crystal nodded and joined him. Rusty picked up the gun. "Together..." Crystal nodded again. "You take hold of the barrel, we start swinging it at 'one,' and at 'three,' we pitch it." Crystal grabbed hold. "First, though, I want to say something…" Rusty turned so he was facing the marsh. "Jimmy, Rusty here. I know you probably can't hear me and this might seem kind of crazy, but I've wanted to tell you that I felt all this time like I let you down. I've felt guilty as hell ever since your death and I swore to myself I'd get your killer and he'd pay. It didn't work out the way I figured, but it'll do. He's dead. His name was Slater and you were right—he was part of the Colombian cartel from Miami; it's just that he wasn't a Latino—he looked like the all American boy which I expect I don't have to tell you now. Crystal and I got his gun here, the one that killed you and the judge. I thought you should have it. We're going to throw it out to you, and then I figure I can finally put all this behind me. And maybe it'll help you rest in peace, too. I hope so. One last thing. I'm taking care of Crystal, like I said I would. Crazy thing is, she's taking care of me, too; but maybe you had that figured all along. Anyway, just thought you should know. And here comes the gun." Rusty looked at

Crystal. "One, two, THREE!" They launched the gun in a lazy arc and watched it flip a couple of times before it splashed into the water.

On the way back in, Rusty finally told Crystal about the job proposal Captain Smathers made when he had received the F.B.I. medal.

"You're kidding! That's the craziest thing I've ever heard! You told him no, I hope."

"Not exactly…"

"Rusty!" she almost shouted. "You just healed up from umpteen bullet holes and a fractured hip joint! Three months of pain for what? A little gold medal and an offer to do it all over again?"

"I've discovered I like catching the bad guys. Beats the hell out of cleaning up bodies strewn all over the highway after a head-on which is what I used to do."

Crystal looked at him in disbelief. "What if the bad guys aren't bad guys?"

"What do you mean?"

"Where are we coming from right now, for Pete's sake! You were sent to bust Jimmy because he was a so-called 'bad guy.' Are you telling me Jimmy was one of your 'bad guys?'"

"No, of course not…and I didn't bust him!"

"You could have. How long do you think you'd keep your job if you made your own assessments on who to bust and who not. You'd be going against your superiors, and probably be an accomplice to boot! But that's beside the fact that it's dangerous as hell! What did you tell Smathers?"

Rusty shrugged. "Maybe." Crystal turned away from him, shaking her head.

They were silent the rest of the way in. Rusty tied the boat and began to rinse it off while Crystal stormed up the stairs to the house. He was about done when she came down and handed him a beer. “Thanks,” he said. “Are we still on for dinner at my place?” She came up close to him.

“Of course…Rusty, listen to me. I love you and I just don’t want you to get hurt. I’ve lost one terrific guy, and I couldn’t stand to lose you, too.”

“Understood.” They embraced. Rusty looked at his watch. “If I put the steak on at six-thirty, does that work?”

“Yup.”

Timing is everything, he thought on the way to his house. He had thought tonight should be the night, but now after the Smathers thing he wasn’t so sure. He debated with himself right through dinner. He had a hard time making conversation he was so preoccupied. Crystal didn’t ask him what was up even though she picked up on it right away. And the candlelight steak dinner with expensive red wine? What was that all about? Rusty cleared the plates and returned with a cordial for each of them.

“Here’s to Jimmy!” Rusty said, holding his glass up. They clinked and sipped.

“And here’s to us!” Crystal said.

“I’ll drink to that!” Rusty said, smiling. His face suddenly turned serious. He put his glass down and took her hand in both of his. Crystal looked at him curiously. “Crystal…I…er…”

“What?”

Rusty took a deep breath. “I’ve wanted to do this for a long time now, but I couldn’t until I had things square in my head with Jimmy…Well, they’re square now, so…” He took another deep breath before blurting out, “Will you marry me?” Crystal was taken totally by surprise. Shocked. But of course she’d marry him, she thought. Who could ask for a better man? She loved him to death! Rusty felt a huge relief that he had finally gotten it out. "Maybe I should go down on one knee," he said, smiling. He started to kneel but the muscles in his wounded thigh wouldn't cooperate and he pitched to the side; he just grabbed onto his chair to keep from falling over.

Crystal bolted to him and grabbed onto his shoulders. "Are you okay?"

"Damn leg charley horsed or something. Guess that was a bad idea." He grimaced as he struggled up to his chair, massaging his thigh. Rusty's leg giving out was like a slap to her face. Marry a man who might take that job Smathers offered? He comes home one night all shot up?…Or maybe doesn't come home at all? These thoughts and others passed through her mind. Rusty waited. Finally he said, softly, "You haven't answered me, Crystal."

"Before I answer, I've got a question for you."

"Shoot."

"Are you going to take Smathers' job or not?"

"Like I said in the boat, maybe."

"Then my answer to you is the same: maybe. Rusty, I love you more than anything, but I couldn't bear it if you were to get hurt again, or worse. I just couldn't…" She stood and took the cordial glasses to the sink. "Thank you for a wonderful dinner, but I think I should go now." Without another word, she left.

* * *

Norm was approaching downtown Perry. He was on a mission. When Rebecca had told him all about Virgil, he was furious and wanted to turn him in. Rebecca begged him not to for two reasons. The first was that she would be brought in as a witness if Virgil were prosecuted and everyone would not only learn of her addiction, but also that she had sold her body to a *black* man for drugs. She would never live it down. Her life in Crescent Beach, if not north Florida, would be over—it was no coincidence that not a single black person lived in Crescent Beach, that many of the houses flew Confederate flags, and that the N-word came up in conversation. The second reason was simply that Rebecca did not want to be the snitch. Whether it was some intrinsic code of perverted honor among young people or if it was because Virgil had at least always been straight with her, she just did not want to be the rat. After much discussion, Norm agreed not to go to the police; at the same time, he could not tolerate the idea that this depraved soul could continue to corrupt Perry's youth. "Rebecca," he had said, "Billy died because of drugs. You almost did. It's scum like this that's responsible. If we don't put him in prison, then we've got to at least get him out of Perry."

Norm waited until Rebecca was comfortably situated in Tallahassee before making the trip into Perry to confront Virgil. No one knew a thing about it: he had told no one, not even Beau. Dressed in a beige linen suit complete with necktie, he parked his Subaru near the ancient pharmacy with the brick façade on Jefferson Street. He walked down to the boarded building that Rebecca had described. When he was halfway down the alley, he could see the hood of the shiny black Chevy Malibu parked behind the building. Virgil heard him approach and looked up from his newspaper. Norm didn't waste any time.

"Virgil, I think it's about time you left Perry…for good." Virgil's eyes lazily looked Norm over, then down the alley towards Jefferson Street, and slowly scanned the fenced in area and buildings surrounding his car before turning back to Norm. No cops.

"An' just who the fuck you be, Suh?"

"I represent three of your customers who are minors," Norm lied. "In consideration of their future and to avoid adverse publicity, their parents will not go to the police if you leave Perry, never to return, within forty-eight hours. If you do not, then Virgil, they and their offspring will press charges—lots of them. I assure you that the minors will testify in great detail, including the whereabouts of your woodlot where you hide drugs.

"Aah, you be an attorney-at-law, then…" Norm said nothing. "Well, Suh, I don' know nuthin' that you be talkin' 'bout."

"That's too bad. It's a lose-lose, Virgil: three young people's lives will be marred and you'll go to prison for at least twenty. Hope you like Raiford, Virgil, and sure hope you like it up the ass." Norm turned on his heels and walked away. He didn't get far.

"You say 'forty-eight hours,' Suh?" Norm stopped, but didn't turn around.

"That's right."

"Maybe I think 'bout it."

"I wouldn't take too long." Norm continued walking and returned to his Subaru.

Whoa, where'd that dude come from! An' what three customers? Virgil pictured his customer list. He also calculated his woodlot inventory. How'd the dude know about that? It didn't take long before he started nodding his head. Missy! She be the only one who knew. Shee-it! That girl done turn on me! Damn shame: good poontang. But who be the others? He wasn't sure. Lots of them, but only a few whose parents could afford a lawyer.

Don' matter none; gotta split. Ain't got no choice. An' business been bad anyways; none o' these kids got any bread. Penny ante. But where to? Crystal River? Not much competition there. Got Crystal River High…But that be same old: no bucks, no business. Need bigger, where there be a couple high schools, maybe a university with them rich kids. Yeah, university. Gainesville. Naw…too many brothers be operatin' there. That be dangerous territory. Tallahassee? Ain't heard nuthin' much goin'on there. Be worth checkin' out. Sooner the better. First, gotta check out the woods when it be dark. Make sure no one watchin' and move the stash. Take me ten minutes to pack. Guess I be goin' to the state capital with all them crooked politicians! Virgil smiled. Always be room for one more crook.

Norm took off his tie and coat and threw them in the back seat. He bought some groceries before returning to Crescent Beach. He stopped to pick up his mail. He hadn't gotten it in a while and he had a pile. When he returned home, he threw the mail onto the dining room table. Huey chattered excitedly at his arrival. Norm took him out of his cage and put him on his shoulder. He sat down to go through the mail: *The American Journal of Medicine, The New Yorker,* electric and water bills, credit card bills, flyers, and an oversize postcard with a picture of glorious mountains on either side of a picturesque valley. The sky was cobalt blue, the mountains were rugged and bare on top, and below the tree line scattered dark spruce contrasted sharply with the autumnal yellow of blankets of aspen. The valley was green and bisected by the silver serpentine thread of a river. On the bottom of the card it said, Independence Pass, Colorado. Norm's stomach did a flip-flop. He quickly turned it over and began reading.

Dear Norm, here's your postcard, but you will need to put on your reading glasses because I'm going to write tiny to fit it all in. A heck of a lot of driving but I've seen so much in such a short time! First was the Grand Canyon. The pictures don't do it justice! The size, the colors, everything! One thing though and that is I felt like a foreigner. Almost everybody was speaking some other language. Next was Canyon de Chelly which is pronounced de Shay. That's in northwest Arizona. I think it was my favorite of all. It's sacred Navajo land and has neat sandstone spires and you're allowed to walk down in on only one trail, the White House trail, I think. It's beautiful and mysterious. We also saw Mesa Verde and all the cliff dwellings, but it was crowded like the Grand Canyon with tourists. Next was the Great Sand Dunes. You had to wade across a river to get to them. It was amazing, like having the Sahara Desert in your backyard! It was tough climbing the dunes. I didn't get far, but Bobby climbed to where he was only a speck in the distance. He said it was a good workout. I believe him! Now, we're in Colorado on our way to Aspen. Bobby met a fella some time ago in the Paradise bar who owns some land near there. He said Bobby could camp on it and that's where we're headed. Norm, Bobby is treating me very well and we're having fun and I'm learning and seeing so many new things. It's just what I needed and I have to say I'm not missing the Club a bit, although I do hope that Linda is coping okay. And I DO miss all my friends. Please say hi to them for me. When it gets too cold here, we're going to head to the canyons of southern Utah. I'll send you another postcard then. Love always, Tammy

Norm set the card down. Huey flew down and started chewing on the edges. Norm shooed him away, and re-read the card. Again he returned it to the table, and again Huey came over to nibble on it. He stuck his finger in front of Huey's chest and he hopped on. Norm put Huey on his shoulder and walked over to the large window facing the Gulf. Rusty and Crystal were a stone's throw away, coming in at an idle. He didn't see them. Huey chattered excitedly into his ear. He didn't hear Huey either.

* * *

"This is it!"

"This is what, Bobby?" Tammy asked, looking up from studying a roadmap of Colorado.

"Where I'm going to spread Whacko's ashes," he said, quickly pulling over to a graveled vantage point. "Whacko said he wanted to be up high with a pretty view. Doesn't get much prettier than this. It looks like one of those calendar pictures he was always putting on our cell wall!" Tammy looked out. Bobby was right, Tammy thought, doesn't get any prettier. And it looked exactly like the postcard she had just sent Norm—same valley, mountains, river, and those yellow aspen!

They got out of the truck. Bobby went into the trailer, returning with the walnut urn that contained Whacko's remains. He carefully set it on the ground, then opened the tailgate and camper cap to pull out a shovel.

"I thought you were going to scatter his ashes," Tammy said.

"I am; but I don't think Whacko wants critters chewing on what's left of his bones." Bobby looked around. There was a path on the other side of the road leading to higher ground. He crossed over and began hiking up the trail. Tammy followed.

Whacko had been Bobby's cellmate at Raiford Prison for a good portion of the seventeen years Bobby was there. Bobby had been drunk in a bar when some stud dressed in western duds had hit on Tammy. Bobby went ballistic when Tammy flirted back, and he beat the crap out of the guy. Unfortunately a statey was called in and Bobby beat the crap out of him, too, and Bobby had been sent up. Whacko was in prison for cooking and dealing meth, and supposedly involved in a shootout between two drug dealers at his meth lab that resulted in a death. However, Whacko's only involvement was trying to comfort his dying wife who had been struck by a stray bullet. A University of Florida law professor, working *pro bono,* got him out early.

Bobby served his full sentence. Whacko met him at the prison gate the day he was released. Months earlier, at Bobby's request, he had located Tammy, even though they had divorced right after Bobby was sentenced. Whacko rented a rundown trailer in Crescent Beach. There he and Whacko moved in together, and Whacko even got Bobby a job at the local marina. Whacko continued to cook meth, and when he died from sampling too much of his own product, Bobby discovered a note addressed to him in a shoebox in Whacko's closet. The note was from Whacko and the box also contained a key. Whacko wrote that the key was to a safety deposit box and that he wanted Bobby to have the contents. He only requested that Bobby have him cremated and to scatter his remains in a 'purty spot way up high someplace.' Bobby found a hundred thousand dollars in cash in the box. Bobby was blown away and, considering their history and now the money, there was no way in hell that he wouldn't honor Whacko's request.

Bobby and Tammy zigzagged their way up the mountain. They came to an alpine meadow. Bobby turned around and looked out over the valley. He smiled. "Whacko's going to love this." He took the lid off the urn. "Want to spread some?"

"No. I think he'd just want you to."

"Probably, but you got a connection, too. I talked to him about you for years." He handed her the urn and had her fill his hands. He scattered the ashes all around. When they were gone, he buried the urn in the middle of the meadow. "There," he said, and sat down by the fresh grave. Tammy sat next to him. He gently patted the fresh dirt. After awhile, he said, "It's probably hard for you to understand the bond we had. Whacko was my cellie. With all the things you go through in a place like Raiford, a cellie can become more important than a brother. Prison is full of varmints scurrying around, sticking to the shadows, trying not to draw attention. Then there are the raptors. The raptors are made up of violent prisoner gangs and corrupt guards. They can attack you for most any reason at any time. Whacko and I were two little varmints. We had to stick together. It was like we were two swimmers with spears, back to back, surrounded by sharks. Together we had a better chance for survival…Rest in piece Whacko." Bobby stood and extended a hand to Tammy. He pulled her up. "C'mon, Babe. Let's get on down to Aspen, buy some groceries, and see what that guy's land looks like."

Two hours later they were on a well maintained gravel road heading up a mountain. "We've come eight and a quarter miles since the turn," Bobby said.

"We're close, then. Directions say you should be coming to a barb wired fence soon. There's a gate only a couple hundred yards from the beginning of the fence." True enough, less than a minute later there was a fenced in meadow to their left. And then the gate. Tammy hopped out and let them in. They followed a road of sorts with grass running down the middle. "We're supposed to follow this to the end," Tammy said. It went downhill, then through some spruce, and finally curved to the right where it leveled out and ended. There was a campfire ring, an old fashioned pitcher pump, and an outhouse. The site looked out over a teardrop shaped lake, surrounded by mountains on three sides. It was a magnificent, magical spot. Bobby and Tammy looked at each other and smiled.

By the time they unhitched and had the camper leveled, the sun was sinking fast. “I’ll hustle up some cheese and crackers, and we can toast the view,” Tammy said.

“I’ll get the chairs and table from the truck.” Bobby pulled the table out first. By the time he dug out the chairs, Tammy had the cheese and crackers, a glass of wine, and a glass of carrot juice on the table. Bobby set the chairs down. When Tammy began to sit, he rushed behind her to push her chair in.

“Why thank you, Bobby. That’s a first.”

“So is this,” he said, sweeping a hand across the horizon. “It just doesn’t get any better!”

“I’ll drink to that,” Tammy said, raising her glass of wine. Bobby reached for his carrot juice, then stopped.

“This calls for a real celebration,” he said, and rushed into the camper. He returned with two large plastic cups and a bottle of champagne. He popped the cork and the champagne bubbled over. He filled both cups to the brim, and handed Tammy hers. “Here’s to this…and to us.” He started to tap her cup. Tammy’s face was transparent. “What’s wrong, Babe?”

“Bobby, this is real champagne, isn’t it?”

“Of course.”

“But it’s alcohol!”

“Yeah, but just champagne; it’s not like booze or anything.”

“But…”

“C’mon, Babe, live a little!” Bobby drained his cup in three swigs, and reached for more.

Made in the USA
Columbia, SC
06 January 2025

48863647R10211